THE SURVIVOR

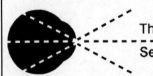

This Large Print Book carries the
Seal of Approval of N.A.V.H.

CRIME SCENE: HOUSTON

THE SURVIVOR

DIANN MILLS

THORNDIKE PRESS
A part of Gale, Cengage Learning

GALE
CENGAGE Learning·

Detroit • New York • San Francisco • New Haven, Conn • Waterville, Maine • London

LIBRARY OF CONGRESS CATALOGING-IN-PUBLICATION DATA

Mills, DiAnn.
  The survivor / by DiAnn Mills.
    pages ; cm. — (Crime scene: Houston series ; #2) (Thorndike Press large print Christian mystery)
  ISBN-13: 978-1-4104-5919-0 (hardcover)
  ISBN-10: 1-4104-5919-5 (hardcover)
  1. Houston (Tex.)—Fiction. 2. Large type books. I. Title.
PS3613.I567S87 2013
813'.6—dc23   2013009381

Published in 2013 by arrangement with The Zondervan Corporation LLC

Printed in Mexico
1 2 3 4 5 6 7 17 16 15 14 13

To my Story Sisters:
Debbie Macomber, Karen Young,
and Rachel Hauck

NOTE TO READER: SOME DRAMATIC LICENSE HAS BEEN TAKEN REGARDING FBI PROCEDURES. ANY ERRORS IN ACCURACY ARE THE AUTHOR'S.

CHAPTER 1

HOUSTON, TEXAS
JANUARY 16
10:00 A.M. WEDNESDAY

Miss Walker,

Twenty-three years ago, I survived a killer's brutal attempt on my life. My story must be told. Can you help me?

Amy Garrett, PhD
Freedom's Way Counseling
(832)555-0189

Finding suspense story ideas could be grueling, but the concept that just landed in Kariss's in-box could be her next bestseller. She'd been approached by enough eccentrics to recognize someone looking for big bucks and a sensational slice of life. She felt sorry for most of them but always wanted to help, no matter how ludicrous their stories. Still, none of those people had ever had PhD after their name or a business phone number listed with their signature.

The email lured Kariss to the place where words and emotion blended in a feverish dance. Kariss herself had survived an attempt on her life the previous summer and knew the courage it took to tell anyone about the horror. She reread the message. Why would this woman seek her out? Why would she choose to tell her true story in a novel? Only one way to find out.

Kariss pressed the number into her phone.

"Freedom's Way Counseling. How may I direct your call?"

Hurdle number one — this was a legitimate business. And Dr. Garrett's name did seem vaguely familiar. Then again, as a former Channel 5 news anchor, Kariss knew quite a few names and faces.

"I'd like to speak to Dr. Amy Garrett. This is Kariss Walker." She waited while the call was being transferred.

"Dr. Garrett here. Kariss Walker?"

"Yes. I just received your email. Curiosity got the best of me."

"Thanks for responding so quickly. Are you currently online?"

"I am."

"Would you like to go to the website hyperlinked in my email? That will tell you a little about me."

Kariss clicked as instructed. Amy Garrett, founder of Freedom's Way, specialized in counseling women who'd been victims of violent crimes. She held doctorates in psychology and social science.

"Click on 'About Freedom's Way.' That says it best," Amy said.

The powerful words of the biography drew Kariss into Amy's world.

At the age of nine, I survived a brutal attempt on my life. I understand your pain and confusion, and I have felt the despair. Through caring counselors, I found healing. Now I want to offer you the same pathway to life.

Freedom's Way cares about you. We are committed to helping every woman who has ever been traumatized by a vicious crime. Your first step to healing is only a phone call away.

Don't let finances stop you from overcoming emotional pain, a sliding fee scale is available.

"Come to me, all you who are weary and burdened, and I will give you rest."

— Matthew 11:28

Freedom's Way was a Christian counseling service.

"Why fiction?" Kariss said.

"Can we meet to discuss this? I'm booked until three thirty this afternoon, but I have an hour window then. Are you available at three thirty?"

Kariss's mind spun in a flurry as she considered whether she wanted to get involved. The woman seemed overly aggressive, but intrigue won out. "I'd be happy to talk to you — to gather more information. I see your office isn't far from my home."

"I'd rather meet outside of my practice. How about the Starbucks across from Crystal Point Mall?"

"Perfect."

"Miss Walker, it's important we keep our discussion confidential."

"I plan to come alone."

"Good. But please don't tell anyone about this. I'll explain later."

Strange request, but maybe Dr. Garrett had approached other writers as well as Kariss. "Okay. See you then."

Kariss stared at the phone before placing it on her desk, and then she reread the doctor's email. Why had the woman contacted her? The answer would have to wait until three thirty. If Kariss could keep her inquisitive impulses at a manageable level until then.

She continued reading her other emails.

A writers' group wanted her to give a workshop on character and plot. They had no budget to pay a speaker, but she could bring books to sell. Kariss sighed and agreed.

Her nephew had sent his latest poem. At age ten, he was in love with a redheaded little girl who ignored him. Kariss took a peek at the poem and laughed.

Mom confirmed Sunday dinner after church.

Two spam messages. No one could use that much Viagra. She moved them to her Junk folder.

Kariss studied Dr. Garrett's words again. When she googled the woman's name, several sites popped up. Many churches and community organizations had hosted her as a keynote speaker. Kariss returned to Freedom's Way's website and continued reading.

There were testimonies from women who'd been given the tools to live again after being shaken by violence. Survivors. Warriors in their own right. By the third testimonial, Kariss had to reach for a tissue.

She moved on to Facebook. Amy Garrett's posts were faith based and compassionate.

She recommended books and websites to help women achieve good emotional health. An upcoming Gulf Coast Christian Women's Conference, to be held at a large church in downtown Houston, featured Amy as the keynote speaker.

Dr. Amy Garrett was not only a survivor but a haven for abused women as well.

Unbidden memories about what had happened to Kariss while researching her previous novel surfaced in her mind. She'd made a few stupid decisions and nearly botched an FBI investigation. If not for her loving family, a good counselor, and her renewed faith, she'd probably be in need of Freedom's Way herself to work through her own nightmare of being a crime victim.

She'd meet with Dr. Garrett . . . hear her story and ask questions.

11:00 A.M. WEDNESDAY
FBI Special Agent Santiago Harris, known as Tigo, realized he smelled like the thirteen-hour stakeout he was on. The pizza he'd eaten before dawn still lay sizzling in his stomach. But he was determined to help bring in the new self-proclaimed leader of the Houston gang called the Skulls, which had ties to a Mexican cartel.

Pablo Martinez had entered an apartment

14

on the southeast side of town shortly after ten o'clock the night before with his girl-friend and another gang member. An informant had said that Martinez had stashed stolen assault rifles, handguns, and explosives at the apartment and would be using them on a rival gang. Although Martinez had slipped by the authorities in the past by way of the legal system, that was about to end. So Tigo and his team waited. All the FBI needed to make the arrest was for Martinez to set foot outside the apartment with the stolen arms. Of course, if they'd known how long this would take, they could have obtained a search warrant.

"Something about this bothers me." Tigo lifted his binoculars to the curtain-covered windows. "Are we the ones being set up?"

Ryan Steadman, his partner, yawned. "If I didn't know better, I'd swear they'd already left."

Tigo handed him the binoculars. "You have tomato sauce on your pasty-white cheek."

Ryan frowned and brushed his face.

"Makes me wonder what they're doing in there," Tigo said. "Building a compound? I'm going in."

"Are you crazy?"

"Do you have a better idea?"

"What are you going to do, deliver a pizza?"

Tigo reached for the empty box that lay on the truck floor by Ryan's feet. "Who can refuse pepperoni and extra cheese?"

"You're sure?"

"I've got things to do, and nailing Martinez is in my way." Tigo picked up his radio.

"A shower is at the top of my list," Ryan said.

"Mine too. Along with arresting anyone I can find who's involved with gangs. You know my personal war." Tigo smoothed out the dent in the empty pizza box caused by Ryan's size 11 foot. "This gang business has me in a bad mood."

"Or maybe it's because Kariss hasn't returned your phone calls."

Tigo scowled. "She has her life, and I have mine. We're over. And that's not what I'm talking about. I have an arrest to make."

"Then explain why you can't say her name."

"Cover me. Martinez is mine."

"I'll be sure to write that on your epitaph." Ryan gestured toward the second-story apartment. "Nothing is stirring. Maybe they got high and are sleeping it off."

Tigo chuckled. "That would make our job easier." He opened the door to his pickup and radioed backup of his intent.

"Hold on." Ryan pointed to three small children who were playing at the other end of the walkway near Martinez's apartment. "Let's get those kids out of there." He spoke into his own radio, and seconds later, the kids disappeared.

Stealing up the exterior metal steps to the apartment gave Tigo a few moments to scan the area. Martinez could have men posted inside another apartment. His fingers rested on his Glock, which was positioned under the pizza box. Uneasiness dripped into his brain. Thirteen hours in a one-bedroom apartment didn't make sense. No one in or out. No gunfire. No visitors. Only quiet.

Ryan covered Tigo from the bottom of the steps, and two other agents stood on opposite ends of the building.

Tigo knocked on the door. "Pizza delivery." He counted to ten and repeated the knock and announcement. He dropped the pizza box on the landing.

Ryan joined him, and they nodded the go-ahead to each other.

"FBI! Open up!" Tigo turned the doorknob. Unlocked. A chill swept up his arms. Glock raised, he swung open the door. Three mutilated bodies lay across a sofa and chair. Their throats slit.

CHAPTER 2

3:25 P.M. WEDNESDAY

Kariss scanned the coffee shop for a woman who resembled the photo of Dr. Amy Garrett she'd seen on the website. This first meeting would help Kariss decide if the writing project was a good fit and if the two women could work together. Skepticism had wiggled into her thoughts since the call. The more she researched the story online, the more the project looked like a nonfiction book. And Kariss was a novelist.

"Ms. Walker?"

At the sound of her name, Kariss turned toward a corner café table, where the owner of Freedom's Way waved. She was an attractive blonde and wore a gray suit with a vivid green scarf. Excitement bubbled through Kariss at the thought of writing another suspense novel, but it warred with her feelings about working with a psychologist. What if the famed doctor saw a crack in Kariss's character? Or pointed out some weird aspect of Kariss's personality that indicated she needed to be on medication or hospitalized? As if Kariss didn't already recognize a few quirks. Creative people always had them.

Amy rose from her chair and shook Kariss's hand. She was a good six inches shorter than Kariss. The petite woman's wide-set blue eyes brimmed with intelligence and something else, possibly curiosity. Good, they were on even ground.

"Shall we order and then chat?" Dr. Garrett said. "I'll buy since I suggested the meeting."

A take-charge woman. Kariss relaxed just enough to smile and agree — this one time at least. As long as a latte didn't obligate her to spend four hundred pages with a story that didn't work.

"Dr. Garrett, I've looked forward to meeting you all day. I'm flattered to be in the company of a woman who has helped so many other women achieve emotional independence."

Amy shrugged. "It's who I am, but thank you. I've been excited too. Please, call me Amy."

"And I'm Kariss."

"I hope this is the beginning of something

grand. This project is special, actually a dream. I wish we had more than an hour to talk, but I have a heavy client load today." She glanced around. "Is this table okay? I prefer facing the door."

"Sure. It's fine." Odd that Amy appeared to be nervous.

"Do you have a watch so we can keep track of the time?" Amy said. "Oh, you're not wearing one. And I left mine on my desk."

Kariss shook her head. "I can't wear one. Too much electricity in me. The watch always goes wild." She pulled out her iPhone and set it on the table between them. "I'll keep track."

"Thanks," Amy said. "I've never met a real author."

Kariss laughed. "I've never had coffee with a woman who held two doctorates."

Amy used organic sugar in her soy latte, while Kariss sipped on a mocha latte with no whipped cream.

"I'd love an oatmeal-raisin cookie," Amy said after taking a drink.

"Yum. That sounds good. A warm oatmeal cookie. But they're huge."

"We could split it."

Kariss agreed. After purchasing the cookie, she bit into a juicy raisin while Amy reached for a small bottle of hand sanitizer and used it, twice. Time to get the show on the road. "I'm —"

Amy raised her hand. "First of all, let me tell you I read lips. I'm going deaf. Not there yet, but it's inevitable."

Counseling, speaking events, conferences, and media appearances had to be difficult with a hearing impairment. Kariss's admiration for Amy grew. "How do you manage communication in so many different settings?"

"It's not a problem unless I can't see the person I'm talking to. For phone calls, I have a special tool that writes out the words for me, so that works pretty well. However, I prefer text or email rather than voice messages. Faster." She laughed. "So no clandestine meetings in the dead of night, okay? Seriously, I do appreciate your willingness to discuss a potential novel."

"I'm intrigued with your story, what little I know of it," Kariss said. "I have a number of questions. The first that springs to mind is why me for this project?"

"You're a bestselling author."

"I'm not the only one."

"But you're a bestselling author who's become a Christian. Nearly shipwrecked your career with that announcement last year."

Although Amy received a gold star for doing her homework, Kariss was a long way from accepting the task of writing the story or allowing accolades to affect her judgment. "I also changed genres from women's fiction to suspense. Have you talked to other writers?" Kariss said, turning the focus away from herself.

"Not yet. I very much admire how your research for your latest book eventually led to solving the child's murder."

"My impulsive nature nearly got me killed." Kariss's pulse raced as she was hit by a barrage of memories — always the blood. "I intend to never risk my life gathering research again."

"Are you doing okay with the trauma?"

Kariss felt the psychoanalysis to the tips of her hot-pink toes. The nightmares had lessened but were still there. "I'm good. Just wiser. Took a self-defense course. So tell me why your story should be told in a novel, using a character to experience your tragedy. In my opinion, nonfiction has the potential to help many suffering women take a positive step toward healing. They'd be impressed by knowing your full story."

"To inspire them." Amy leaned closer. "To

show my clients they can be survivors. Fiction reaches a wider, even different, audience."

"I understand," Kariss said. Amy had put some thought into this project.

"And a novel is a nonthreatening environment," she said. "An abused woman would feel safe within the confines of a fictional story and hopefully feel inspired to change her current situation. But she may not read a nonfiction book for fear the wrong people would find out."

Kariss nodded. Point taken. "Biographies are fact, and novels are filled with emotion. That's why readers keep turning pages. They're involved with the characters. In your case, many could identify with the story line."

"Another reason for my story to be fiction. You and I have fought the demons of terror. We also care about those who've been victims of violent crimes." Amy smiled. "I researched you before I wrote the email."

"I guess you did."

"Your days of TV reporting proved your passion for helping others. And it shows in your novels as well." Amy appeared to study her. "Too many of my clients don't know how to escape their abuse or roll up their sleeves and get to work."

To Kariss, Amy's words sounded artificially noble, even rehearsed, but why? What motivated the woman? Kariss sat back in her chair and nibbled on her portion of the cookie.

"So you think a novel is a better choice to accomplish this?"

"I do." Amy's confident tone and subject change indicated the matter was settled. She took a bite of her cookie and smiled. "This is so much better warmed."

"It's been twenty-three years since your attack. How long have you been considering having your experience written into a novel?"

Amy took a sip of her latte, her fingers circling around the cup. "A few years."

"Why tell your story now?"

For a moment, pain flickered in the woman's face. "It's the only way."

"Only way for what?" It had to be more than a means to help her clients. "Is your assailant still in prison?"

Amy didn't even blink. "He wasn't apprehended. Understand that my attack occurred before it was popular to use DNA in investigations. In short, he got away with it. Kariss, I want my story written as a suspense novel."

"If a fictional book of your story is released, he could see similarities."

"I doubt he'd read it."

"But what if he does?"

"If he happens to pick it up, I'll be okay, because I don't want my name on it."

Did she not want her name on the project because she was afraid he'd see it? "You don't worry that he's been following your life?"

"Not in the least."

"Did your attack occur in the Houston area?"

"Yes. Montgomery County." Amy moistened her lips. "It was during the spring of my third-grade year. We lived on a small farm. It's built up into a subdivision now."

"Why tell your story at all? Just the thought has to be frightening for you."

"As I said, this is for all the women who live in paralyzing fear." Amy tilted her head, her emotions appearing distant.

She was hiding something. "Tell me briefly what happened when you were nine."

Amy took a deep breath, one that filled her face with darkness. "I was abducted from my bedroom while my family slept. Then I was assaulted, had my throat cut, and was abandoned in a field. A couple of boys found me the following morning."

Whoa. Kariss could only imagine the

nightmares. "I'm sorry." Now she understood why Amy wore scarves and turtlenecks in all her pictures.

"Thanks. I dealt with it a long time ago."

Really? Kariss doubted it, especially since the assailant was still running loose. "I can't imagine the horror."

"Made me a little fearful."

Kariss would keep this conversation stored in her memory bank. "If we move forward with this project, how do you envision the financial aspect?"

Amy shook her head. "I don't want any monetary compensation, and I'll have my attorney draw up the papers indicating so."

The response made little sense. "Why? What about your practice? Couldn't your scholarship fund benefit from a cushion?"

"My reasons for having my story written have nothing to do with money. I'll share more of my thoughts about that at another time."

Kariss needed more information before she committed to writing the book. "How much of your story do you want included in the novel?"

"Every detail exactly as it happened."

"The art of fiction means including elements that might not be factual. Nonfiction would be a better venue for you."

Amy shook her head. "I disagree."

"Surely you know the danger in pursuing this."

Amy smiled. "It's only fiction."

CHAPTER 3

Tigo sat across the desk from Special Agent in Charge Linc Abrams, known as the SAC. The two had been friends since college days, and now they were on the backside of thirty. His old friend frowned at the computer screen. His shoulders lifted and fell. This morning's findings were a setback, but they'd hit speed bumps before. Something else must be troubling Linc.

Tigo had showered at the FBI complex, but he hadn't shaved. The scruffy growth itched, fueling his frustration of not knowing who'd killed Pablo Martinez, his girlfriend, and the other gang member, who happened to be Martinez's bodyguard.

"So we have three murders and no assault rifles?" The lines across Linc's dark forehead deepened. "All those hours watching that apartment, and the guns are gone."

"The killer had to have been waiting for

28

Martinez. Must've passed the weapons through a back window to avoid being seen."

"We'll have to see what the fingerprint sweep finds. Plenty of men wanted Martinez dead, but who would slit his throat and take the time to mutilate the bodies before confiscating the weapons?"

"His girlfriend's sister has ties to the Skulls," Tigo said. "She could have set up her sister. Both women grew up with the same values. It's all blood-in, blood-out."

Linc eyed him. "Cynicism is in full force."

"I'm tired." Tigo knew that more than disillusionment weighed on him. No sleep in over thirty hours was only part of the problem.

"How long has it been since you saw Kariss?"

If Linc hadn't been the SAC and his friend, Tigo would have told him to lay off. The situation with Kariss had nothing to do with his job performance. "What does she have to do with the case?"

"Your attitude. How long have we known each other?" Linc steepled his fingers.

Tigo knew where this was going, but the net had been tossed. "Sixteen years."

"How long since you were serious about a woman?"

"Don't have time for relationships." They never worked anyway.

"Right. Call her and patch it up. Suck up that Argentinean pride and take responsibility for what separated you two." Linc smiled with his matter-of-fact advice. "Fix it."

"It's not that easy."

"What's the problem?"

Spilling his guts wouldn't fix a thing. "Linc, it doesn't matter. It's over. I'm done with women."

Linc stood and leaned over the desk, his six-foot frame tense. "All right. But sometimes your stubbornness isn't your best attribute."

"I'm tired and my game's off. I don't appreciate being made a fool of, especially in gang warfare."

"None of us do." Linc's frown returned. "I have another situation to discuss. At ten thirty this morning, Joanna Yeat and her daughter were killed in a car explosion triggered by a cell phone. Forensics is on top of it." He pressed his lips together. "HPD has asked us to assist. So I'm taking you and Ryan off the current case to find out who killed Jonathan's wife and daughter."

Tigo detested unfinished business. The Houston Police Department's investigators were good enough. But Jonathan Yeat and

Linc were friends. "Linc, I know this is tough. I remember Jonathan from our college days, and we talked here in your office a few years ago. But I hate to have Martinez's murder get by us. Can't you put our bomb techs on it?"

"Ryan used to be a bomb tech. You don't understand, Tigo. Jonathan is like a brother to me." Linc paused. "Once the Yeat case is finished, then you're back on gang business."

Tigo got the picture. No choice in the matter. "Okay. We'll get on it."

"Jonathan's in bad shape, and he's worried about his sons."

"Any suspects?"

"Not yet." The bitterness in Linc's voice was a rarity. "That bombing was meant for him, not his wife and daughter. They traded cars for the day."

Tigo recalled a news release earlier that week. "Monday Jonathan laid off two hundred employees. There's your bomber. His labor pool is infested with piranhas."

"We're researching the threats, but nothing concrete. Some of the past employees have alibis and some don't."

Tigo thought about the reports that had come through after the layoffs. Jonathan Yeat's commercial construction business had been hit hard by the recession. "The media claim he turned on his own employees. To me, that's a possible motive for murder. With his policy of hiring ex-cons, he walked a tightrope."

Linc walked to the window, where traffic sped by on US 290. "Jonathan and I grew up in a neighborhood where the life expectancy of an African-American male was twenty-eight. We wanted to make a difference. We thought getting an education would keep our families safe."

"There aren't any guarantees."

"I know. Such a waste. Yvonne and I worked alongside Joanna and Jonathan building a church in San Paulo. Camping trips, football and basketball games. Plenty of good times." Linc drew in a sharp breath. "You're right. Jonathan's ministry of giving ex-cons a second chance might have killed his wife and daughter. Most of his employees are young African-American and Hispanic males with a history of violence."

Tigo admired Yeat's dedication to helping others better themselves, but maybe he'd been too trusting. "Please give my regrets to Yvonne."

Linc shuffled papers on his desk. "Thanks. She's in shock right now. Hard to work alongside a man in church, know his heart, and have him face a tragedy. I know I can depend on you and Ryan." He picked up his Blackberry. "Sending the information now. I haven't briefed Ryan."

"He had a situation at home but should be here within the hour."

Linc nodded as though he knew about the decision Ryan and Cindy had to make about her bedridden mother. "Didn't mean to pry about Kariss. You've also been a brother to me, and I want to see you happy."

Just the mention of her name bothered Tigo. "You have too many other things to worry about without tossing my problems into the mix. We'll find this bomber."

"Jonathan and his sons have 24/7 protection until an arrest is made. I talked to him briefly around noon, and Yvonne and I will see him later this evening. I'll send you an update."

"Has anyone questioned his sons? Teen boys have ways of making enemies."

"Jonathan indicated they've kept their noses clean, and I've seen nothing to indicate otherwise — both in church and youth group. But let's look at every angle." He studied Tigo. "I know you and Ryan are exhausted, but if you could spend a few minutes talking to those boys before heading home, I'd appreciate it."

"I'm willing. I imagine Ryan is too."

"Then go on. The file sent to your and Ryan's Blackberrys includes Jonathan's interview with HPD right after the bombing. I'll let Jonathan know you're coming."

Tigo longed for a bed — and an antacid, since the pizza kept resurfacing. But Ryan had the same sleep deficit. Neither of them would put their own needs ahead of Linc's request — he was more than a friend. More than their SAC. Something about him ordered the lives around him. Ryan said the power rested in Linc's faith, but Tigo was still exploring that aspect.

In the hallway outside Linc's office, Tigo read the initial report about the car bombing. Insane situation. Joanna was taking their daughter to an orthodontist appointment when the Lexus exploded in the driveway and killed them both. The explosion occurred outside the front gate of the Yeats' massive home, destroying the car, a section of the iron gate, and the right side of a stone wall that bordered the property. The bad guy had probably wanted to see the explosion and had most likely watched from close by.

Everything pointed to Monday's layoffs. A wife and mother as well as an eleven-year-old little girl had been killed because of some idiot's vendetta.

Tigo stepped into an empty elevator, resolved to find the car bomber — beginning with interviewing the two sons. Maybe they'd seen someone loitering near their home.

Tigo would commit his best to the case, not only because of the violent nature of the crime and his friendship with Linc, but also to keep his mind off Kariss. He'd decided to shake off her rejection and go on with his life. Hadn't worked yet, and the memories drove him nuts. Tanned skin. Dark, shoulder-length hair that always had a wind-blown look. A smile that made his knees buckle.

There he went again, remembering instead of forgetting. Tigo had ruined the relationship simply by definition of who he was. Their problems went far deeper than a mere apology or two dozen red roses would ever fix.

The elevator door chimed and opened. He could call her. Check on her. Make sure she was okay and listen to her voice. He checked his Buzz Lightyear watch and saw he had time to call. Her sister's baby had been born in November. That would help carry the conversation for longer than ten seconds. He pressed a number on his phone

— Kariss's number still on speed dial. Her brown eyes danced in his mind. But they didn't dance for him.

She answered on the third ring.

"Hey, this is Tigo. How you doing?"

"I'm good. How's work?"

Her words were cool, polite. "One case after another. How about you?"

"Busy."

She sounded distracted. He heard music in the background. Was she with another guy? "Did I call at a bad time?"

"I'm meeting with someone."

His ego hit ground zero. "And I'm late for an interview."

"I'll call you later. Take care."

The call disconnected. What made him think she would return his call? Time to focus on finding whoever had inflicted tragedy on Jonathan Yeat's life.

CHAPTER 4

Kariss left the coffee shop after agreeing to contact Amy in a few days. The novel idea fascinated her, but unanswered questions prevented her from moving forward. The writer in her needed to think about Amy's insistence that the book include every detail of her traumatic experience. The world of story didn't always mesh with fact. Some of the details might not be necessary and could drag the plot.

Unless a person was a prominent figure, most people who wanted their life story told usually had only one incident of reader interest. Amy had many accomplishments and women who valued her counseling, but the FOX News camera and local TV channels weren't focused on her office door. Kariss hadn't explained the raw truth to Amy about what she wanted, but at their next meeting, she had to be honest about the writing project.

Amy wanted none of the proceeds. Why?

Kariss liked Amy. That wasn't a problem. And the woman's dedication to counseling victimized women added stars in her eternal crown. But until they agreed on the novel contents and characters who responded to life according to their values, Kariss wouldn't accept the project.

Since she had ended her relationship with Tigo at Thanksgiving, all Kariss did was write. Supposedly her workaholic nature would help her forget him. But it hadn't helped at all. Book two in her suspense series was in the final draft stage, meaning it would release six months after the first. And she'd outlined an idea for a third book using the same characters, the ones she'd developed when Tigo helped her with FBI research. But despite her writing, all she could see was Tigo's face, and all she could hear was his voice and his incredible deep-throated chuckle.

His earlier call had sent her emotions into a whirlwind of heartache and what-ifs. His image had stepped unbidden into her mind — gorgeous olive skin, deep brown eyes veiled by long lashes, and thick, dark hair. The looks of a perfect hero. No words could describe her distress, but Kariss refused to succumb to tears and regret. A survivor moved forward and learned from the past.

A writer's best work was supposed to come from personal pain, but Kariss hadn't expected this torment. The idea of putting her scattered emotions about Tigo into a character's life seemed to cheapen what they'd gone through together. The weeks since their parting had only increased how much she missed him.

Dating an unbeliever had been wrong, but the attraction had been stronger than her values. They'd tasted death together and survived. That meant something, to her at least. Still, Tigo had betrayed her trust.

She was better off.

Kariss possessed the trophy for being stubborn, and one day she promised herself she'd waken and find that her infatuation for Tigo had vanished.

She should call him back. Not returning his previous calls was one matter. Lying to him jumped the fence of integrity. How could she manage a conversation without asking to see him? Without compromising her stand?

At a stoplight, she fished her phone from her purse. He'd called from his Blackberry, not his personal iPhone, so she'd call his business line. Maybe he'd be unable to talk.

With a prayer for wisdom, she punched his speed-dial number. Odd . . . having him listed there gave her hope.

"Kariss?"

The driver behind her blared his horn. She pulled through the green light and turned into a Walmart parking lot. With her emotions fluttering like this, she'd probably cause an accident. "Hey, I'm calling you back."

"Thanks." He sounded distant. "How are you doing? I . . ." He paused. "I guess Vicki's little girl is almost two months old now."

"She's growing much too fast. So sweet and good."

"And Vicki?"

"Adjusting to life as a new mother."

"Give her my best. The baby's name is Rose . . ."

"Rose Elizabeth."

"Middle name the same as her Aunt Kariss's."

He remembered. She couldn't help but wonder if other things about her . . . about them . . . still existed in his memories. "Yes. I'm hoping she'll not go the path of a writer. You know, the drama queen and all."

They both laughed.

"I'm looking forward to seeing our book

in print."

Did he have to say "our"? She nearly cratered. "I'll make sure you have one of the first copies."

"Great. What are you writing now?"

"Finishing up the second book in the series."

"Had to have round two with the FBI agent?"

"The editor thought he was a hunk." Why did she say that?

"Didn't you model him after me?"

"Very funny. I have a whole dossier of heroes."

"Are you seeing someone?"

Her stomach fluttered. Oh, Tigo . . . How could she when no man measured up?

"Guess that's none of my business," Tigo added before she had a chance to respond.

"It's okay." Best she not state the truth.

"I've been going to church with Ryan. Thought you'd want to know."

Her mouth went dry. "I'm glad, Tigo."

"Hey, I've got to go. Duty calls."

"Sure." Kariss felt relief and disappointment at the same time. "Be careful." The tremor in her voice nearly gave her away.

"Always. Thanks for returning my call."

The phone shut off, just like the end of their relationship. She wanted to dwell on the sound of his voice. Bigger than life. Her hero, her . . .

Kariss pressed in Vicki's cell number. "Hey, sis. I'm at Walmart. Do you need diapers?"

"You don't need to get them."

"But I'm here. Need anything else?"

"Kariss, you haven't been to Walmart since you and Tigo broke up. Remember when you bought three hundred dollars' worth of things you didn't need?"

And returned them all a week later. Kariss shook her head. Why did her sister, who already shared Kariss's shoulder-length, dark brown hair and similar looks, also have to read her so well? "We need paper towels and toilet paper. And I'll grab a box of baby wipes with the diapers." Forcing a laugh, she glanced around to see if an onlooker could see she was struggling for composure.

"Did you see Tigo? Was that your three-thirty appointment?"

"No. I met a woman who has a potential story idea. But he called during that time, and I called him back."

"Now you're a mess. Finish up your shopping and hurry home. While Rose slept, I made Stroganoff. She'll be out until after six, so we can eat and talk. I'll put a box of tissues on the table as a centerpiece."

"I'm over the relationship. Remember? Besides, you're bossy."

"I'm older. It's my job. And since I'm living with you until I can provide a home for myself and Rose, I have to take responsibility for something."

Kariss hadn't told anyone the truth about her and Tigo. Maybe it was time to face the problem head-on.

CHAPTER 5

4:45 P.M. WEDNESDAY

Tigo dropped his phone into his truck console, not really ready to talk to Ryan. Regret pelted him. He'd rather face a dozen bad guys with machine guns than the reasons he and Kariss weren't together anymore. The six-lane expressway and bumper-to-bumper rush-hour traffic fueled his contempt — for himself. He drove US 290 south to the 610 Loop, passing the sky-high buildings of the prestigious Galleria area before jumping onto the Southwest Freeway and then driving to the exclusive neighborhood where the Yeat family lived . . . what was left of them.

"You did just fine," Ryan said, as though reading his thoughts. "But from the look on your face, your blood pressure's up."

Tigo forced a chuckle. "I'm not on medication yet." He rubbed the back of his neck. "I sounded like a wuss."

"You sounded like a man who wishes things were different."

"That too."

"How is she?"

"Good, I guess. She's probably seeing someone." The sadness he wanted to hide was evident to his own ears. Buzz Lightyear would be embarrassed.

"I doubt it."

"She evaded the question."

"Tigo, it's been almost two months. Both of you have had time to think about what happened. Any chance of getting back together?"

"The problem is me. My fault."

"I'm sorry. I hate what it's doing to you. If you want to talk, I have a good ear."

"And ruin my macho image?"

"Are you praying?"

Praying meant Tigo had a relationship with God, understood who He was and acknowledged He created the universe. Hadn't happened. "It's tough. Real tough. How are you and Cindy doing?"

"Trying to figure out how to handle her mother's condition," Ryan said, sounding as frustrated with that situation as Tigo felt about his. "When I went home, Cindy was crying. She and her mother never got along, and now with the dementia and stroke, a good relationship isn't in the future. We don't have room for her mom unless the kids double up, so I suggested a nursing home. We argued."

"Ouch. We're batting zero in the personal relationship department. Let's talk about Jonathan Yeat so we can get this interview with his kids out of the way."

"Sure. I'm beat, which I'm sure has a lot to do with my outlook on the home front." Ryan reached for a bottle of water. "I haven't met Yeat, but his reputation's out-standing."

Tigo's mind swung into case-detail mode, pushing aside anything that distracted him. "Linc's torn up, but he's approaching the investigation logically. Thinks you and I can solve it. Values your bomb-tech days."

"Can't solve it without sleep. Hope I have enough sense to ask the right questions." Ryan pulled out his iPad. "Yeat received four threats after the layoff. One of the suspects has an alibi. One we need to question. And a third person is missing — a woman."

"That's only three threats, dude. You really need to get some sleep. All have records?"

Ryan groaned. "Yes."

"I know the answer's in the layoffs, but Linc wants to turn over every rock. Tell me what you know about his sons." Tigo blinked, his eyes stinging as though grit was all that was forcing them to stay open. If the dark circles under Ryan's eyes were any indication of how Tigo's looked, they'd be better off handing this interview to a couple of other agents. But he'd given his word to Linc.

"They're ages sixteen and seventeen. Good grades. The older boy's a junior, and the younger boy's a sophomore. Both play basketball. The older one is on the varsity team and has scouts all over him. The younger is on the JV team and isn't as talented."

"You must be into high school sports."

"Always. My son will be there one day. Basketball. You've seen him play."

Tigo laughed. "Yes, and he's beaten both of us."

"Sports don't mean those boys are immune to threats or drugs. Look at the big leaguers. Sometimes the temptation is worse, especially with money — and the Yeat boys have plenty of that at their disposal."

"I agree. What about Jonathan and his wife? Any marital problems?"

"None that we know of. Media reports show his grief, and he's pressing us and HPD to find those involved."

"I want to know everything about their relationship. Could be he didn't know about a problem."

"The little girl's the most innocent victim here. She wasn't old enough to make a bomber mad." Ryan blew out a breath. "I'd tear apart someone who tried to hurt my family."

Tigo didn't have a family, but he understood every adult's responsibility to nurture children. He had a picture of a little girl, named Cherished Doe, in his desk drawer. She'd been a cold case for five years until her death was recently solved. It served as a reminder of what happened when deranged people weren't brought to justice.

Jonathan Yeat and his family lived in a gated community with every amenity imaginable. Through the Yeat Foundation, he gave back to those less fortunate in the way of college scholarships, funding after-school programs in poverty-stricken areas, sponsoring sports teams, and — his number one project — providing jobs and guidance for former inmates.

Ten minutes later, Tigo parked outside the community entrance, sliding in behind the car of a bomb tech assigned to investigate and gather materials around the scene of the explosion. Three police cars were sandwiched between media vans near the entrance of the community, outside the yellow crime-scene tape.

"Once we get caught up on sleep, we can look at this more objectively," Tigo said. "I think it's a cut-and-dried case of an ex-employee seeking revenge, but maybe not. I'll need time to examine the reports."

"I'll review them tomorrow before the drive into work."

"What do you say we conduct our own interview with Jonathan in the morning?"

Ryan set his bottle of water in the cup holder. "Sure thing. Questions were racing through my mind when I skimmed Linc's report." He peered toward the gates. "Isn't that your old friend Mike McDougal pushing his luck at the crime scene? I'm surprised Channel 5 still has him employed."

"He walks a fine line between criminal and reporter." Tigo recalled Kariss's claim that she'd dated him at a low point in her life.

The agents made their way to the gate, where McDougal argued with an HPD officer.

"Sir, you know the law. Back off," the officer said.

"The folks of Houston have a right to see what's going on," McDougal said.

Tigo sidled up to the blond-haired man. "Haven't we been down this road before? Or have you forgotten that media types don't cross the yellow tape that ropes off crime scenes?"

McDougal gave his typical sneer. "My old friend Agent Tigo Harris. Excuse me, Special Agent Santiago Harris. How's Kariss these days?"

"She's fine."

"Saw her at an authors' dinner at Christmas. She flirted with every man there. Thought you two might have split after she wrote her novel. She has a tendency to use people."

That wasn't Kariss, but he wasn't going to let McDougal get under his skin. "The fact is, you're attempting to break through crime-scene tape. Again. Are you going to obey the law, or do you want to cool your enthusiasm in jail?"

McDougal raised his hands, including the one holding his camera. "The public wants to know what's happening."

"And they'll be informed. Just remember your boundaries."

"That's the way it is with law-enforcement types," McDougal said. "Give them a badge, and they think they have power over the rest of us. Ever read my blog?"

McDougal's blog fell under the categories of gossip and lies. A joke to anyone with intelligence. Tigo and Ryan left the man rambling to the police officer about his infamous blog and walked toward the Yeat property, which was adjacent to the community entrance.

Police and FBI agents swarmed all over the grounds. Tigo approached the FBI team that was combing the crime scene and requested a full report of their findings be sent to his Blackberry. A section of the front iron gate and the right side of the stone wall had been destroyed. Later Tigo would study the photos being taken to see if any faces in the crowd stood out. Bad guys often returned to their own crime scenes as bystanders.

"Tigo."

Tigo turned to see HPD Detective Ricardo Montoya walking their way.

"We're working together again," the detective said.

"Only the best, right?" Tigo grinned. "Hope we can get this wrapped up soon. What have you got?"

"All evidence points to a disgruntled employee." Ric gestured toward the crime scene. "We'll know more when the reports are in."

"What can you tell us about the bomb?" Ryan said.

"Sophisticated. Not much else yet. We're still gathering forensics. At this point we don't detect aluminum nitrate or know the fuel."

Tigo didn't voice his thoughts. He'd wait until he saw a report. "Keep in touch. The media's all over this."

Ric nodded. He started to say something, but his phone rang and he answered it instead.

Tigo and Ryan made their way to the carved double doors of the home and greeted two police officers. Ric called for the officers to admit them. Once Tigo and Ryan stepped inside the marble foyer, an officer stood sentry.

"FBI Special Agents Ryan Steadman and Santiago Harris to speak to Mr. Yeat," Tigo said. They flashed their IDs, and the officer examined them.

"I'll see if he's available."

"Tell him FBI Special Agent in Charge Linc Abrams sent us."

The officer spoke into a radio.

Tigo's gaze swept to a staircase that wound to the top floor. A three-tiered chandelier glittered, just as he would have expected in a home of this size. No sounds.

Little smell, except for the rich scent of wood and a faint floral sweetness. What seized his attention was a wall-sized family portrait of the Yeat family. Tigo focused on Joanna, a striking African-American woman with wide-set, honey-colored eyes that peered into the camera with a sparkle. The boys resembled their father with darker skin and features, but the daughter, Alexia, had lighter brown skin, like her mother, and the same captivating eyes. She would have been a beauty. If she'd lived.

Viewing the portrait of the once-complete family deepened Tigo's determination to find the person who was responsible. Conscious of Ryan standing beside him, he felt compelled to comment. "Senseless," he said. "All we can do is stop someone from ever committing such a crime again."

Jonathan Yeat stepped into the foyer dressed in dark slacks and a pale-blue dress shirt. Body erect, he looked like a man who was accustomed to a professional world. But solemn eyes gave away his sorrow. He shook each man's hand. "Linc said to expect you. Tigo, I'm glad you and I know each other. I've talked to enough strangers today."

"We understand this is difficult," Tigo said.

"Keep expecting to wake up from this

horrible nightmare." Jonathan swallowed hard. "I'm here to do whatever it takes to find my wife's and daughter's killer. I speak for my sons too. They're aware you have a few questions." He took a deep breath, no doubt to steady himself. "Nothing in life ever prepares you for such loss. I . . . I gave my statement to the police and to Linc. I'm sure you have it, but I'm available anytime."

"Thank you, sir," Tigo said. "We can talk to you in the morning. Right now we'll make this interview with your sons brief."

"I understand you two came straight from a stakeout. I appreciate this."

Tigo nodded. "I imagine we look worse than we feel."

Ryan pulled out his iPad. "We're here to expedite the investigation and give you some peace about what's being done."

"Linc said you two are the best. I'm afraid my sons may be the next target of this crazed killer. I'm not letting them go anywhere until he's found."

"We understand, sir," Ryan said. "We all hope an arrest can be made soon."

"I've given the authorities the names and contact information for my employees, past and present, and those persons who have access to my home, which includes the pool service, the maid, pet groomers, yard men, and pizza delivery. That's all I could think of."

"No problem. We'll be researching every name on the list and working with HPD," Tigo said. "Any projects here at the home in the last six months?"

Jonathan glanced away. "Four months ago I had the pool plastered. Before that Joanna had the flooring and countertops in the kitchen replaced. I'll locate the companies used and get the information to you." He startled. "I forgot about the woman who designs Joanna's clothes. Didn't think about her. I'm sorry."

"No problem. Just add her contact information." Tigo nodded toward Ryan, who was taking notes. "Sir, do you have any questions for us?"

"Not at the moment. When I think how happy we all were this time yesterday . . ." Jonathan gestured toward a doorway. "Right this way, gentlemen. We're in the kitchen where it's easier to talk. You know teenagers."

Tigo expected to see family and church members seated at the kitchen table with Jonathan's sons. But he didn't see anyone gathered to comfort the grieving family except one man, who leaned against the kitchen counter. The clerical collar gave away his profession, but the man resembled Jonathan. Ah, yes, Linc had said Jonathan's brother was their pastor as well.

Viewing the intense emotions of those present, Tigo pushed aside his exhaustion to focus on the sons. The morning's tragedy and the impact of reality were unfair to kids, yet they might know something that would lead to an arrest.

The pastor extended his hand. "I'm Pastor Taylor Yeat. Anything I can do to help, just let me know."

Jonathan turned to Tigo and Ryan. "Do you have a problem with my brother being present during the interview?"

Tigo offered a thin smile. "Questions and answers are confidential."

"That's my line of work," the pastor said. "I'm a shoulder to my family."

"I understand." Tigo questioned this logic of the family dynamics, but he'd play it out. "We'll be brief."

The older son was slumped over the table. He straightened, his eyes red and swollen. The younger folded his arms across his chest, hostility showing in his eyes. Both boys' attention was riveted on their father.

"Curt, Ian, these men need to talk to us. That's why I sent the others home. No one needs to witness any of this." Jonathan nodded at the agents. "Please, sit down."

The sooner Tigo and Ryan interviewed the boys, the sooner they'd be able to get some rest and then find the bomber. Tigo studied the grieving boys. The older seemed to be suffering the most. "Linc Abrams is our boss, and we understand you know him well. We promise we'll do all we can to find who did this to your mother and sister."

"We need your help," Ryan said. "I'm mostly the note taker, and Tigo asks the questions. We're a team."

The younger boy stiffened. "We've already talked to the FBI and the cops."

Ryan nodded. "Repetition helps us see things we didn't before, and sometimes it jars details from our minds."

"I'm all over it." Curt gave Ryan good eye contact. "But my brother needs to find his manners."

"Get off my —"

"Mom would want us to cooperate," Curt said. "What if the guy who did this comes back for Dad or one of us?"

"Yeah, yeah. That's why we can't take a crap today without someone following us around."

"Calm down, son. I know this is hard." Jonathan's jaw tightened. "You think my sons might know something about the bombing?" he said to the agents.

"We have to look at every possibility, every contact Curt and Ian have made," Ryan said. "If any of the kids at school have made threats, then we need to know about it. That means individuals and groups."

"It's cool, Dad," Curt said. "I want to help."

"You think because we're black, we belong to a gang?" Ian pushed back from the table and stood. "Mom and Alexia are dead, and these two are wasting time talking to us when they could be looking for the killer. I don't appreciate scum throwing the race card." The bitterness in Ian's words and his rigid body revealed the extent of his misery. "One of your projects did this, Dad. It's your fault."

"Ian" — his father's tone was gentle — "we're all hurting here. No one's tossing a race card, and we know the likely suspect is one of the people who was laid off. These agents are friends of Linc's, and they're professionals. They want the killer found too."

Tigo had been an angry teen and knew the meaning of the word *rebellious.* "All of us want the same thing," he said. "This guy found and justice served."

"Well, I don't have anything to tell you."

Ian shoved his chair under the kitchen table and stomped out of the kitchen.

"I'll talk to him," Pastor Yeat said. "Agent Harris, I hope you find who did this despicable thing soon." He handed Tigo a business card. "My office, cell, and home numbers are there. My wife's the church secretary, and she can always find me."

"Thanks." The card might come in handy, especially if any of Jonathan's employees were also church members.

Jonathan glanced at Curt and then trailed after Ian and Pastor Yeat, leaving Curt alone with the agents. Tigo made another mental note. Possible favoritism?

The teen clenched his hands, his pain evident in tear-filled eyes. "My brother's hurting," he said.

"So are you," Tigo said.

"It's different with me. I'm the oldest. Supposed to be the strong one."

"My mother died several months ago." The moment Tigo spoke the words, grief punched him in the gut. "I miss her every day."

"Don't start with the God stuff. I've heard so much today that I can't stomach another round. So don't go there."

"I understand. But you and I have a connection."

Curt swiped at his eyes. "Mom was the best. Always had time for us. Listened. Got in our faces when we needed it. Praised us. Didn't compare us."

The latter comment piqued Tigo's attention, the note of sarcasm within, but he'd think through that later. "You mean your mom didn't have the same expectations in the way of interests and grades?"

"Yeah. We're all different. I'm the responsible one. Ian's more sensitive. Alexia was our princess."

"Everyone like your mom?"

Ryan continued typing on his iPad.

"Who wouldn't? She always made me proud. One look at her, and the guys at school wanted to be at our house." He smiled. "And my baby sister would have grown up to look just like her."

"Who was here with you before we arrived?"

"Aunt Wanda — that's Uncle Taylor's wife — and my mom's sister, Aunt Angela. Aunt Darena's working. Some of the church people, but Dad sent them home before you guys showed."

That made sense. "Did you ever hear your parents argue?"

"No. They got along fine. What's that supposed to mean anyway?"

"Just a routine question, Curt." Tigo reached for a little tact. Ryan should have conducted the interview. "Ever hear your mom have a disagreement with anyone?"

"Not often. Are you thinking it's someone she knows?"

"What about someone who might have been jealous?"

Curt stiffened.

"Anyone is capable of taking another person's life," Tigo said. "If you give us a name, we'll simply look into that person's life to see if there's a motive."

"Then you'd have to talk to her sisters. They don't have what we have. But . . ."

"What, Curt?" Tigo kept his tone even, calm.

"I think the bomber was one of the people who was laid off. Threats were made, and most of those guys think with their fists."

Tigo wanted to explore the jealousy aspect. "Do your aunts live in Houston?"

"Forget I said that. I'm not thinking straight. Just trying to find a reason."

Twenty minutes later, Tigo and Ryan thanked the teen. They spoke briefly to Jonathan but tabled any more questioning. They needed time to catch up on sleep and analyze Curt's and Ian's reactions along with the various reports and interviews the other agents had collected.

Once in the car, they felt exhaustion settling in. The lines drawn on Ryan's face said he felt the same as Tigo. "What do you think?" Tigo said.

"Curt's a smart kid. Do you think he knows more than he's letting on?"

"Possibly. He hesitated in responding, but I imagine he's fishing for someone to blame. Joanna's sisters might offer a clue. I want a list of both boys' friends, grades, and ambitions, and their teachers' perspectives." Tigo's thoughts raced on, consuming him. "Why didn't we see a woman's touch in the kitchen? No baked items or casseroles. Is it too soon for church ladies to bring in food?"

"Not sure. Maybe there hasn't been time. Especially if they came as soon as they got the news."

"One thing is certain . . . Curt's hiding something."

"Or thinks he is. Ian's a lit fuse."

"Jonathan and Pastor Yeat took after him without one thought for Curt. Wonder how the kid feels about that."

CHAPTER 6

In the damp warehouse, Kariss struggled against the duct tape sealing her mouth. The ropes that bound her hands were slicing into her wrists. The stench of filth curdled her stomach, increasing her urge to vomit. Twenty feet away, three Hispanic gang members drank beer and played cards. They spoke in Spanish about what they planned to do to her, no doubt waiting for the call telling them to finish the kill. Raw fear twisted her heart while white-hot pain spread through her rib cage when she breathed. Their beating had left her in excruciating pain, and she could barely see through her swollen eye.

Death would be a welcome guest.

The door to the warehouse squeaked open, and the sound of men's voices filled Kariss with terror. She recognized Wyatt —

Vicki's ex-husband, the man who'd sold out Kariss to the gang. The other man was one she'd met before, a man involved in white-collar crime. They walked closer. Wyatt ripped off the duct tape, causing blood to seep into Kariss's mouth.

"The FBI is onto you," she said. "You won't get away with a thing."

"Big talk, considering."

"These guys used you." It hurt Kariss to talk, to breathe. "They'll kill you for sure."

"Don't think so," Wyatt said. "I've earned my rights."

The second man lifted his pistol. Then Wyatt lay at Kariss's feet in a pool of thick red blood, a bullet in his forehead. Kariss hated what he'd done to her sister, but she hadn't wanted him dead.

The door squeaked again. This time gang members dragged in Tigo. They pounded his body until he collapsed. Blood flowed from his nose and mouth. The gang members were going to kill both Kariss and Tigo. Where was the FBI?

Somehow her wrists were free . . . but Tigo wasn't moving. A gun was kicked across the room. Kariss grabbed it and shot the man poised to kill Tigo. The blood . . . always the blood.

Kariss woke with sweat dripping from

every inch of her body. When would the nightmares end? The facts were distorted in her nightmares, but they always ended the same. Kariss tried to hit Delete on every black detail in her memory bank, but the flashbacks always crept unbidden into her nighttime hours. What would make them end?

7:15 A.M. THURSDAY

Kariss attempted to concentrate on the line-by-line edit of her novel instead of Amy Garrett's proposal. Habitually, Kariss sailed ahead of deadline, and her practice of turning in manuscripts early gave her favor with the publishing house. Having had several books on the *New York Times* Bestseller List helped too. She loved being a writer, weaving romance with a suspenseful plot, but the tedious process was like giving birth to barbed wire. The latter wasn't a Kariss Walker quote, but it sure fit when frustration and stubborn characters took control. Or when she couldn't wrap her brain around edits because something else was occupying her mind.

Kariss reached for her coffee cup and pushed aside yesterday's stale chocolate-chip bagel. Closing her eyes, she willed the words to flow from her fingertips. Maybe that was the trick. She should stop staring at her favorite cup with the words "Inspire Creativity" written across the side and concentrate on the canvas of her mind.

That didn't work either.

Sleep had evaded her the previous night. At first her thoughts had been consumed by Amy and admiration for the woman who'd survived a vicious attack. Kariss felt a kinship with her, a need to befriend her.

Questions about the book idea had flitted through her mind as though butterflies had taken residence, lighting on one petal of an elusive flower and then another. Odd how her brain worked, speaking to her in literary form while the words on paper were orchestrated to create mood and emotion.

Then the nightmare had taken over.

The picture of a kaleidoscope on Kariss's office wall was a reminder of the many colors and shapes of her characters, images of people who'd touched her life. Some of whom she'd like to forget. Kariss picked up a kaleidoscope on her desk, one of many in her collection, and peered through it while looking out the window. The light gave distinction. My, how her philosophical side had taken over that morning. Kariss replaced the kaleidoscope and positioned her fingers on the computer keyboard.

Kariss wanted to embrace Amy's story. After the previous night's reminders of how violent crimes affected the innocent, Kariss realized Amy's story had to be written. Amy would need to be convinced that she might need to compromise on some of the factual details to craft an inspiring novel.

She brought up a new document and titled it "Amy Garrett Questions."

1. What were you doing before you went to bed the night of your abduction?
2. How were you woken from your sleep?
3. Did the assailant give you a reason why you were his target?
4. What do you remember about him?
5. Were you conscious in the field where he left you?
6. What thoughts went through your mind while you waited for death?
7. What kept you struggling to hold on to life?
8. Were you conscious when the boys found you?
9. What would you do if you came face-to-face with the man who thought he'd killed you?

Kariss would have to pose those questions, along with many more, and Amy would need to reach deep inside to answer them. Could the woman invade her past to repeat what her mind had possibly hidden or denied?

Why did she want to go through this after twenty-three years? Kariss didn't believe that it was all for the good of women who'd been victimized. Too much time had elapsed. That might be part of Amy's reasoning, but not all of it.

Too antsy to stay inside her condo another moment, Kariss packed up her laptop and prepared to drive to Montgomery County. She'd visit the sheriff's department in Conroe, where records were kept, and hope the officer who'd worked Amy's case was still there. If he had any of Tigo's and Ryan's tenacity, the reality of an unsolved crime against a child would still haunt him.

Linc probably had the whole file. But Kariss refused to bother him or anyone at the FBI. Not after what happened with Tigo. Not since her heart decided to take a nosedive every time she thought of him.

CHAPTER 7

8:00 A.M. THURSDAY

After sleeping ten hours, Tigo drove to the office with his triple espresso beside him. It was guaranteed to shift him into high gear. He needed time to study the reports from the Yeat case and learn more about the bomb. The types of components used often led to where the items had been obtained and who had access to them. So far, investigators had been able to gather enough bomb fragments to determine that the device had been triggered by a cell phone. Efforts were also under way to determine whether a phone discovered in a Dumpster near the crime scene had been the triggering device. No fingerprints had been found on the phone, so whoever threw it away had covered his tracks.

Linc had phoned him before he'd left for work, asking what Tigo and Ryan had learned yesterday afternoon. Tigo had already sent their report via the phone, but after Linc's visit with the Yeats last night, Linc wanted to offer them closure. An impossibility at this point. Solving the case wasn't going to happen today or tomorrow, no matter how close Linc and Jonathan were or how many FBI agents and HPD personnel worked the case. Tigo was cynical, as Linc stated yesterday, and he had a gut feeling this case wouldn't be easy to solve. The interview with Curt and Ian confirmed his suspicions that this family had its share of problems.

Law-enforcement officials needed more than twenty-four hours to conduct a thorough investigation, but Tigo understood the pressure Linc was under. Media couldn't get enough of the crime. Many people had loved the entrepreneur Jonathan Yeat and his wife for their countless charitable acts. Could someone have wanted to end their goodwill efforts?

Tigo parked his F-250 Lariat and hurried inside the FBI building, the espresso acting as an engine additive to his veins. In his cubicle, Tigo scanned the list of suspects, and two people grabbed his attention — Roger Collins and Carolyn Hopkins. Both had done time, and both had threatened Jonathan. Roger didn't have an alibi, and the woman hadn't been located. Tigo called the FIG, Field Intelligence Group, for a comprehensive report. All he had at this point was a possible motive and two hundred laid-off employees as suspects.

He'd talked to Ryan about postponing Jonathan's interview until this afternoon. Yesterday's meeting with Curt and Ian had left a few blank spaces, but it had opened some new possibilities as well. Tigo and Ryan wanted to check out the boys' high school, an upscale public institution that drew its students from wealthy neighborhoods.

Teens were either brutally honest or said nothing. Rarely in between. In Tigo's experience, teachers saw a partial picture of their students' personalities. Coaches, however, were usually able to zero in on the phonies and the bullies, often before parents realized the truth. Curt's coach might have insight on the Yeats' home life that would assist the investigation.

Conscious of Ryan standing in the doorway of his cubicle, Tigo tossed him a greeting.

"I'm a new man," Ryan said. "I'm getting too old for this. Next time, you can ask one of the younger guys to do a stakeout."

Tigo grinned. "What happened to the

male-bonding thing?"

Ryan shook his head. "We'll go fishing, and the food won't give me heartburn."

"Were you and Cindy able to talk?"

"A little this morning. I still hate the thought of our kids being shoved into one bedroom, splitting the area between American Girl dolls and Spider-Man. But Cindy thinks the sacrifice would be good for them. The verdict's still out." He sighed. "Have you checked the newest developments in the Yeat case?"

"What's that?"

Ryan's grim look said the situation had grown worse. "New updates. Joanna Yeat filed for divorce on Tuesday, the day before the bombing. Claimed insupportability."

Tigo frowned. "Which means she no longer wanted to be married to Jonathan. Which means they were not the perfect couple. Which also means he lied to us and the police. Insupportability? She wouldn't have had to prove a thing to get the divorce, and Jonathan couldn't stop her. I knew we were picking up on something from Curt and Ian." He drummed his pen on the desk.

"Yeah. Hard to believe Joanna would file for divorce without the kids knowing their parents had problems."

"Your kids hear you and Cindy argue?"

Ryan nodded. "We try to keep our disagreements private. But they aren't stupid. And ours are only in grade school."

Tigo thought about Curt. The boy wore the oldest-child, responsibility-ridden shield like a coat of arms. "So much for our plans to visit their school. I imagine those boys knew about the divorce. I have no problem interviewing them separately, although Jonathan might object."

"Good luck getting any information from either of those boys."

Tigo grimaced. "I only have myself to refer to, and trust me, I took 'bad boy' to a whole new level. My mother didn't let anything pass. She took consequences seriously."

"I remember when she let you sit in jail."

"Did community service picking up trash too."

"Was that before or after she found out you were thinking about joining a gang?"

"After. I felt like I was handcuffed to my mother."

Ryan chuckled. "That's why you have me. To keep you in line. Hey, been thinking . . . Yesterday we might have been conned."

Tigo had the same inkling. "I agree."

"We've been looking at a bombing supposedly done by a disgruntled ex-employee,

73

but the situation's changed. Check your phone. Media's all over this. The new angle is the grieving husband and father may be a killer. Or the grieving husband and father was unaware of his wife's marital unhappiness, and a jealous lover potentially bombed the car."

Tigo snatched up his iPhone. It had been alerting him to news releases, but he'd been ignoring it to focus on the work before him. Headlines swung him into analysis mode. News anchors were debating whether anyone really knew Jonathan Yeat.

"He could have planted a bomb in the car and waited for the right moment. But I can't imagine him killing his own daughter," Tigo said.

"I'm thinking more about a lover. A vindictive man who wanted to get rid of Jonathan or Joanna. And who wouldn't care about a child."

"Either way. You and I have been at this long enough to know anything's possible," Tigo said. He and Ryan needed to interview Jonathan and get the facts instead of deliberating media speculation. "I wonder what Linc's take is on this? Jonathan told him that Joanna asked to use his car at breakfast because the brakes were slipping on hers."

"But did anyone else know this?" Ryan said.

"Jonathan claims not. I wonder if the boys had already left for school." Tigo pondered what little he knew for sure. "I don't think Jonathan had a hand in this. That would mean he manipulated Joanna into taking his car. But we need to talk to him about Joanna filing for divorce. His grief appeared real yesterday, but was it for Joanna or Alexia?"

Ryan leaned against the doorway. "What about extended family? Curt hinted that his mother's sisters were jealous, and only one of them visited the Yeats yesterday. Makes me question whether they really were an idyllic family."

"Let's head over there and get some questions answered now." Tigo reached for his phones and keys, itching to make an arrest. "A woman killed by a bomber is tragic, but a little girl blown to pieces makes me furious. I want to talk to every member of the family until I'm satisfied."

"That's not all."

Tigo cocked a brow. "Bring it on."

"Ian slipped away last night. Climbed out of a second-story window in the back of the house. A police officer caught him coming in at two thirty this morning. Refused to state where he'd been."

The Yeat family was a train wreck.

CHAPTER 8

9:30 A.M. THURSDAY

Kariss exited I-45 and headed toward Montgomery County Law Enforcement Center, where the sheriff's department was housed. So many bail-bond establishments lined the road, she wondered how they all stayed in business. But for the incarcerated, these establishments provided a way for friends and family members to get them out of jail whether or not they deserved a get-out-of-jail-free card. The complex Kariss wanted was on the far side of the tree-lined railroad tracks that divided the city. She laughed. So who was on the wrong side of the tracks?

At the county sheriff's office, Kariss explained to one of the clerks that she was a writer and wanted to use, as the basis for a novel, a twenty-three-year-old cold case in which Amy Garrett had been the victim of a violent crime.

77

"Excuse me while I search for those records." The young Hispanic woman left the front desk.

Kariss reached into her purse for her Kindle, one of the toys she hadn't yet destroyed with her body's overload of electricity. But she had trouble concentrating because her attention remained fixed on the door the receptionist had disappeared through. Finally the young woman returned.

"The original officer assigned to the Garrett case is here and will speak to you."

What great luck. Kariss had feared the officer might have retired by now.

Kariss was shown back to an office, where a graying man stared at a computer screen. When she stepped into the room, he looked up, pushed back from his desk, and limped over to greet her. Now she understood why the officer was at the station.

He reached out to shake her hand. "Sergeant Bud Hanson."

"Kariss Walker. Thank you for agreeing to talk to me about Amy Garrett."

He sat and motioned for her to do the same. "Amy's case is one I've never forgotten." He reached inside a drawer and pulled out a small framed photograph of a smiling, freckle-faced little girl. "This is Amy at age ten, about a year after the assault." He pointed to the picture. "She's wearing a turtleneck to cover the scar on her neck, but she looks like a normal, happy kid."

Kariss stared at the younger version of the woman she'd met yesterday. The photograph reminded her of the one Tigo had in his desk drawer — a photo of Cherished Doe, the little girl who'd been killed and remained unidentified for years, until he and Ryan solved the case last year.

She returned the photo and thanked Sergeant Hanson. "I met Amy yesterday. She's a wonderful woman."

"I haven't given up on finding the man who assaulted her. And I'm not retiring until I see him cuffed." He studied her as if expecting a rebuttal. "So you're writing a book about her?"

"I'm exploring the possibility."

"Amy and I talk every few months. Is it a biography?"

"A novel."

He frowned. "She mentioned that a couple of months ago. Frankly, I don't recommend writing any kind of book, especially a novel. I've told her that."

"Why?"

"A novel needs an ending, and Amy's story doesn't have one. The assailant is still out there somewhere. Since we've never found him, I assume he left the state. But we don't know."

"So you think a novel might cause him to remember what he didn't finish?"

"You're right there, little lady. A psychopath can keep his instincts hidden for years until a trigger drives him to kill again. Being reminded of his failure could be the tipping point that draws him out of hiding." He leaned forward. "Twenty-three years ago, when I saw Amy in that field, I believed she was dead. Her little throat had been slit from ear to ear. Only by the grace of God did she survive the attack. Of course, you can read all the details in newspaper archives at the county library. The story's also online." He shook his head as though remembering. "If that happened today, we'd have DNA and advanced technology to nail the guy."

"Were there any clues?"

"None. We combed the area. Springtime. Tall grass. We were on our knees, praying and looking for anything to find Amy's attacker. I think all of us adopted her. We guarded her outside her hospital room. We returned countless times to the scene of the crime, and we beat ourselves up because we couldn't find him. All these years, and the memories still rush over me." He clenched his fist.

"I'm sorry."

"Talk her out of this," he said. "She's putting her life in jeopardy. Tell her to keep journaling. She doesn't need a book. Once a psychopath, always a psychopath."

Kariss considered what little she knew about Amy, and her admiration and intense respect for Amy grew. The little girl had fought to live, and her courage increased Kariss's desire to write the best possible novel, to be another cheerleader for the survivor. But Amy didn't believe she'd be exposed to danger. Could Sergeant Hanson be overreacting?

10:05 A.M. THURSDAY

"Where did you go last night?" Tigo repeated the question to Ian Yeat for the third time.

"I had things to do." No eye contact, only a belligerent attitude that seemed to seep from the pores of his skin.

Jonathan pounded the kitchen table. "What was so important that you had to sneak out of your home and away from those who were here to protect you? Whoever killed your mother and sister is still out there." The lines in his face looked like a war zone. "I don't need another family

81

member dead."

"Right, Dad. Don't play the hero for me or the FBI. It's lame. It sucks." Ian settled back in his chair and lifted a can of Dr Pepper to his lips.

Jonathan stood, his composure gone. "I'm trying to be understanding here, but what are you talking about?"

"When were you and Mom going to tell us about the divorce?"

Tigo watched a play of emotions scatter across Jonathan's face. Was the divorce a surprise to him? Tigo studied him . . . Jonathan had had no clue about Joanna's decision.

"I learned about it when you did."

"Liar. You —"

"Shut up, Ian." Curt, who'd been watching his dad and brother, jumped to his feet. "You aren't the only one grieving Mom and Alexia."

"Time out," Tigo said. "Sit down. I've heard enough." He shot his best intimidating glare at Ian. "I'm not your dad. I asked a question, and I want an answer now. You can cooperate, or we can take a drive to the FBI office."

Ian licked his lips and rubbed his face. "It's too complicated."

"I'm a smart guy."

"I can't. It's private."

Tigo counted to three and nodded at Ryan. "Let's go. Haven't formally interrogated a kid in a long time."

"Wait." Sweat beaded Ian's forehead. "Okay, I went to see a girl. She lives in our subdivision, about a ten-minute walk."

Tigo recognized a lie when he saw one, and Ian had the darting gaze to go with it. "Wrong. Start all over, and this time tell me the truth. My patience's worn thin." He jabbed his finger in Ian's face. "I know how to get the truth. A stint in the Middle East with the marines taught me how the other side extracts information."

"Do you need a lawyer?" Jonathan said to Ian, throwing a curveball. Did he think his younger son had information about the bombing?

"No. I . . ." Ian narrowed his eyes. "Do you think I killed Mom and Alexia?"

"I want the truth. We all do," Jonathan said. "You were up to no good last night. We all know that."

Something told Tigo this wasn't the first time the kid had broken a rule.

Ian stared at the can of Dr Pepper. "One of the guys from school texted me. I went to his house to talk to him. He said he heard his parents talking about Mom screwin' around, and he'd seen her at the mall with another man."

"Talk or fight?" Tigo's eyes locked onto Ian's.

"Does it matter?"

"Until two thirty?" Tigo said.

Ian drew in a breath. "I wasn't going to come back. Took him a while to talk me into going home."

Tigo believed he spoke the truth. "Why weren't you going to come home?"

"I . . . I'd seen Mom with that guy too. I didn't know him. Anyway, after I saw them together, I asked her about him."

Tigo leaned in closer. "When was this? I need the whole story."

Ian cast Jonathan a helpless glance. "I didn't know how to tell you."

"Now's the time, son," Jonathan said in a gentler tone.

Ian waited a few more seconds before beginning. "About two weeks ago, on a Saturday afternoon, I needed to ask Mom something, so I looked for her in her office. She was talking on the phone, and the conversation was loud, so I stood outside her door and listened." He took a deep breath. "She told someone, 'You won't get away with this' and 'You won't ruin my family.' Then she didn't say anything for a while. I started to knock, but then I heard her say, 'I'll meet you at the food court at the mall. Twenty minutes.' I backed away from the door and went to my room. When I saw her leave, I followed. Took your car, Dad . . ." Ian paused and looked at his dad.

Tigo glanced at Jonathan. At sixteen, Ian probably had a driver's license, but he couldn't legally operate a vehicle without adult supervision.

"Go on, son," Jonathan said, frowning. "You followed your mom . . ."

Ian nodded. "I watched her and this white man. She couldn't see me. She was upset and finally left. It took me a while to confront her, but when I did, she said it was none of my business. That was last Sunday. We had a big fight. I'd never seen her that . . . weird. Maybe scared. I thought she was afraid I'd tell you she was messin' around. I said some bad things. Never had a chance to apologize."

Tigo pieced the story together. Joanna had problems with a man who'd obviously threatened her. She'd met with him, and Ian witnessed it and then confronted her on Sunday. She filed for divorce on Tuesday and had been killed with his sister on Wednesday. "This kid you went to see last night . . . Did he say anything else?"

85

"He just wanted money not to tell anyone about seeing them together. I've been thinking. Maybe she thought going to a busy place would keep her safe?"

"Probably so," Tigo said. "Did you give this kid money to keep quiet? That's blackmail, Ian."

His gaze flew to Jonathan's face. "I took three hundred dollars from Dad's stash."

"Give me the kid's name, and we'll handle it," Tigo said. "We'll get your dad's money back. I need for you to come with me to the FBI office. Our artist there can make a sketch of the man you saw with your mother."

"Okay." Ian's eyes filled with tears. "Dad, I'm sorry. I was going to tell you. I'm sure that guy killed Mom and Alexia." He buried his face in his hands. "I never told her I was sorry."

CHAPTER 9

Tigo picked up his iPhone. He studied the Buzz Lightyear phone cover that showed his hero striking a pose. "To infinity and beyond." Right. His relationship with Kariss had taken him nowhere.

She'd given him the phone cover a week before Thanksgiving. The week before everything went wrong.

They'd spent Thanksgiving with her parents in Texas City. Wonderful family. Her mom was almost as good a cook as his own mother had been. They'd laughed. Teased. Played football in the backyard. Kariss had acted strangely from the time he'd picked her up that morning until he brought her home, but he figured she'd tell him when she was ready. Vicki had gone to bed, exhausted by new motherhood, and left the two of them alone. He suggested watching a movie, not wanting the day to end.

"Tigo, we need to talk," she'd said.

He'd been right. "Sure, babe. What's up?"

She walked into the living room and sat in a chair, not on the sofa where they normally planted themselves. No smile. What had he done?

"This must be serious," he said.

"It is."

"Tell me so I can fix it."

"I hope you can." She took a deep breath. "When were you going to tell me about your marriage?" Her gaze bored into his face, and he sensed her anger.

Heat rose from his neck. "When the time was right. Didn't think it was important."

"You and I were nearly killed. We're friends and we're in a relationship. That means honesty."

Hard to trust his own heart with another woman after Erin's betrayal . . . even a woman as good as Kariss.

"Tigo, I need an explanation." Her voice was flat, cold.

"Who told you? Ryan or Linc?"

"Does it matter?"

"Are you looking for a reason to stop seeing me other than the church thing?" He'd flung the last two words at her.

Kariss blinked back tears. "Is that the way

you see it? What else have you kept from me?"

"You're not my wife, Kariss. We're dating."

"Not anymore." She'd stiffened. "I'm finished."

She'd stuck by her word. If Tigo could shove aside his ego, he'd see that she'd been right. Yeah, they had a few things to work out as they got to know each other.

The Christian thing was an issue. Tigo remembered his mother's urging him to seek God. She'd married an unbeliever and ended up being left to raise Tigo alone. So much junk for Tigo to sort out . . . A future without Kariss meant diving into his work and abandoning those things he'd always wanted.

Solving crimes that centered on senseless murders only reminded him of the unfairness God allowed in the world. Tigo had become cynical, but he didn't want to be.

3:00 P.M. THURSDAY

Writing Amy's story consumed Kariss's thoughts. She'd returned from Conroe, plugged in her laptop, and then decided to go for a three–mile run in hopes of reducing the adrenaline that zipped through her veins. Between Sergeant Hanson's recollection of Amy's attack and a trip to the library, where she'd read the newspaper account-ings, Kariss was definitely into Amy's story.

Sitting at her computer now, she pushed aside the reality of a horrible cold case and focused on the craft of writing. She'd been in this place before when she fictionalized the story of Cherished Doe, the little girl found dead with no identity. The passion she had to defend abused children still stirred her heart. Always would. She under-stood why Sergeant Hanson couldn't forget Amy's case. She'd had her own experience with a child in danger.

While working at a day-care center during her college years, Kariss had tried to save a toddler who'd been trapped inside the building when it caught on fire. The little girl had died, and Kariss still bore the physi-cal and emotional scars. A few months ago, she'd recognized the need to unpack the guilt and accept forgiveness — mostly of herself. Although she hadn't been blamed for the child's death, the idea that she could have done something more had stalked her for years. And she'd deserted God in the aftermath.

Sometimes she believed her issues had dis-sipated. Other times, like today when read-ing about Amy's horrendous attack, the old memory tapes replayed. Perhaps Kariss hadn't fully embraced what it meant to forgive and forget. What she did know was children deserved a chance to live normal, happy lives. When that didn't happen, someone should be held responsible.

Shoving those thoughts aside, Kariss focused on Amy's story and allowed possibilities and plot twists to mingle with her creative juices. The idea took a bend in the road when Kariss thought about the man who'd tried to kill Amy. After twenty-three years, the assailant might no longer be alive or might be too old to care. Amy claimed to feel safe, but was she being naive? An icy chill swept over Kariss. The man could have gone on to kill other victims and might still regret Amy's survival. Kariss needed to have that discussion with her to make sure she understood the full picture. The assailant might never read the novel or connect it to Amy, but Kariss and Amy needed to be realistic about the risks if they were going to work together.

She checked her email and scrolled through the list of what she wanted to read. One subject line, "True Story Alert," caught her attention. Although she didn't recognize the sender, she read the contents.

"IF YOU PLACE YOUR HEAD IN A LION'S MOUTH, THEN YOU CANNOT COMPLAIN ONE DAY IF HE HAPPENS TO BITE IT OFF."

She recognized the Agatha Christie quote. It made no sense, so she pressed Delete.

Her iPhone alerted her to a low battery. She connected a cord from her laptop to the phone and allowed the devices to sync. As the process began, Kariss stared at the computer screen, as if daring herself to look at the pictures from the past twelve months. Her attention swung to the office door and hallway. Good thing Vicki was in Texas City for the day with Rose. If her sister discovered Kariss viewing photos, she'd ask about Tigo again.

Kariss could take a quick look before returning to work. A glimpse of the past would only take a moment. What would it hurt? She clicked on the file, and the screen came alive with memories she knew she should forget.

She was such a fool.

But there she was looking at the history of a relationship gone south. Special Agent Santiago Harris had touched her heart, and she was supposed to be snatching it back.

Kariss and Tigo's first photo together had

been taken at the Houston Zoo near the Africa exhibit. She smiled at the screen. When it had started to rain, they'd walked across the street to the Houston Museum of Natural Science to visit the butterfly center. When a blue morpho landed on Kariss's shoulder, Tigo had kissed her. His grin captured her as much now as it had then.

She studied another picture, snapped at Ryan's house with his family and Linc's. Tigo and Kariss had been invited to a barbecue there for a Labor Day celebration. They looked so happy together. Kariss believed in happily ever after — after all, she wrote suspense with a touch of romance — but it obviously wasn't meant for them.

She clicked on another photo and covered her mouth to stifle a laugh. They'd been at the mall near her house and had stopped at the Disney store, which was Tigo's favorite. He had picked up an obsession with Buzz Lightyear, as though his little-boy days hadn't stepped into adulthood. He wore a watch with Buzz on it, kept a box of Buzz Band-Aids in his truck, and quoted Buzz lines from *Toy Story* — but only when it was just the two of them. Kariss had snapped pics of him drooling over Buzz T-shirts, pajamas, stuffed toys, and a child's plastic plate and cup. He said he was practicing for when he had a son.

Sobering, the thought reminded Kariss of Tigo's child, who'd died. It had been a miscarriage . . . She doubted that Tigo even knew the baby's gender. But after his comment in the Disney store, Tigo'd had a good opportunity to tell Kariss about his past. Instead, she'd had to learn the truth from someone else.

Kariss sighed and clicked on another photo. Tigo had decided they needed a hobby, so he'd bought mountain bikes for them.

"Houston doesn't have mountains," she'd said. "Only anthills. Are you planning road trips too?"

"They're trail bikes. You're going to love this."

"What part? Pedaling in one-hundred-degree temps or the damp rain in winter?"

"Spoilsport. Where's your sense of adventure?"

"On my treadmill. It's called iFit, and it's powered by Google Maps."

He laughed. "We have helmets too."

She groaned. "I hate those things."

"Messes up your hair?"

He had her on that one. "What color is mine?"

"Metallic green. Mine's black."

"I'm surprised yours doesn't have a head shot of Buzz."

"Don't think I didn't try."

Staring at the computer screen, Kariss realized those moments were gone now. Just when they'd started to know each other, Kariss had learned the unthinkable.

Vicki had snapped a pic at their parents' home in Texas City on Thanksgiving Day. All of her siblings and nieces and nephews had been there. Mom had baked a carrot cake, and Tigo called it "crack cake." Mom had sent a huge piece home with him to satisfy his addiction. That evening is when it all ended.

Kariss knew she should get rid of the reminders forever, but the absence of smiling faces wouldn't erase how she felt about Tigo. The longing made her ache. And writing suspense novels was a poor substitute. It only put her mind in another place for a while. But she knew what God would say, and there she found the courage to stand her ground.

CHAPTER 10

In an interview room, Tigo and Ryan studied the bomb report. Outside, thunder rumbled.

Tigo fumed with irritation. "The weather fits our new information. Forensics found Semtex. That confirms our bomber is not an amateur."

"A pro who has ties to Eastern Europe, the Middle East, or Mexico," Ryan said.

"Let's run the reports through the system and see what we find. Does Jonathan deal with any overseas accounts?"

"One way to find out." Ryan pointed to Tigo's Blackberry.

"You let me have all the fun." He pressed in Jonathan's number.

"I need to check his employees' records again," Ryan said. "See if there's a link."

Tigo nodded. "Hi, Jonathan. Ryan and I are looking at the forensic report, and one of the bomb's components has raised a flag. I'm putting you on speakerphone. What do you know about Semtex?"

"What is it?"

"An explosive produced outside the U.S. It's a solid, odorless plastic. Real popular with terrorists. Do you do business in Eastern Europe, the Middle East, or Mexico?"

"I have few connections outside the U.S." Jonathan's curt response was understandable. Since the announcement of Joanna filing for divorce, the media had been making hourly reports, and most were not flattering. "I use American-made products and conduct business here."

"What about Mexico?"

"None." Jonathan's voice rose.

Tigo had no intention of feeding Jonathan's fury. "We need the names and contact information of those in your company who are of Middle-Eastern or Hispanic origin. We also want the names of any of your office staff who might have traveled to those areas recently."

"Joanna and I took a missions trip to Chile last summer. To the best of my knowledge, we didn't make any enemies. Neither did we smuggle in explosives." Sarcasm continued to creep into Jonathan's words.

No wonder.

"This is a new angle that allows us to focus on who planted the bomb. We now have a lead, and it's a good one."

"Obviously I was the target, as we originally thought."

"Possibly. We'll be in contact." Tigo disconnected the call. "This case has to be about more than a disgruntled employee."

"That bombing was planned far in advance," Ryan said. "No one could have obtained Semtex and devised a bomb between the time Jonathan announced layoffs and when it exploded."

"So someone wanted Jonathan dead bad enough to hire a bomber, or that person had the skills and means to build an intricate bomb himself." Tigo glanced at Ryan. "We had a motive when it first happened, but with the forensic report, that no longer has viability. Looks like the layoffs were a coincidence."

"Or the bomber used the timing to put his plan into action. Let's look into Jonathan's contractors and subcontractors and who they're connected to. And his competitors. Has Jonathan been awarded contracts and made a few enemies in the process?"

"Good point. I still wonder about the man

Ian saw with his mother." Tigo paced the floor. Ian's attitude had changed once they arrived at the FBI office. He'd cooperated more than Tigo had expected. But the facial-recognition software hadn't revealed anyone in the national database who resembled the man from the artist's sketch.

"I was hoping it would be an easy case," Ryan said.

"Then it wouldn't be fun." Tigo shoved his hands into his pants pockets. "We'll spread out the investigative reports and find the link that leads to the bad guy."

"Like Sherlock Holmes?" Ryan laughed. "Guess that makes me Dr. Watson."

"Elementary." Tigo grinned. "Remember the kid who blackmailed Ian? Let's have him come in and give us a description of what the man looked like."

"You think Ian's lying?"

"My gut tells me he's hiding something. All three of the Yeats are. Any ideas?"

"A threat to the family? Now that we know about the Semtex, that could be a strong possibility. But why hide it? Unless they've heard from the bomber since then and extortion is a factor."

"We'll ask. See if we can't get tuned in to their channel."

"Curt and Ian . . . Brothers are fiercely

loyal," Ryan said. "My brothers and I fought all the time, but we'd never rat on each other."

"Curt seems to have his act together. He's strong, but let's hope he's not so independent that he won't be forthcoming with information." Tigo understood the Yeats were hurting, but until they all came clean, nothing would be resolved. "I think it's time we visit their high school. I want to find out what the teachers, coaches, and other students have to say about them."

6:30 P.M. THURSDAY

Rose slept in Kariss's lap, and Vicki folded baby clothes. While Kariss had been in Conroe exploring Amy's story, the baby had been tossed around from adoring grandparents to an elderly aunt, but during the ride home from Texas City, exhaustion had overtaken her little body. Tomorrow morning, the three would be making an early trip to one of Vicki's friends in the Tomball area for breakfast.

"You don't have to hold her." Vicki bent over her daughter and brushed a kiss across her forehead.

"I'm good." Kariss admired Rose's little round face, dark curls, and pert nose. "She looks like you."

Vicki peered into her daughter's face, as if seeing her for the first time — a mix of adoration and awesome wonder. "I wanted her to have her daddy's eyes. But maybe it's better this way."

Kariss refused to go there. She'd not fully revealed everything Wyatt had done. Vicki and Rose were better off not knowing, and Kariss hoped her feelings toward Wyatt weren't too harsh. Forgiveness was one thing. Recognizing a dangerous situation was another.

"I need to go back to work." Vicki piled a stack of fresh-smelling sleepers on the coffee table. "I'm thinking in about six weeks."

"Need or want to go back to work?" Kariss would gladly help with any finances.

Vicki tilted her head. "I'm thinking a couple of shifts at the hospital will keep my skills sharp. Remember, my goal is to put aside enough money so Rose and I can have our own home."

"I love having you here. Don't rush things, sis."

Vicki smiled. "I can't mooch off you forever, and you didn't get your independence from strangers. Anyway, Mom said she'd drive here to watch the baby."

"I'm just wondering if it's a little soon for you and Rose."

Vicki eased onto a chair. "I have my tormenters too. Loving Wyatt was the biggest mistake of my life. What you haven't told me about the night of his murder and what the media reported implicate him worse than I ever imagined. By the way, I'm still waiting for your version."

"It's in the past, and your being Rose's mother is what matters."

"In many respects, I agree. But someday I want the truth." Vicki folded her hands, her unique way of passing time while she formed her words. "You haven't worked through every part of that experience either — the kidnapping or why you and Tigo aren't together anymore. You two were solid, inseparable, and then it was over. And, sis, you haven't begun to get over him."

"I'm dealing with it. God's faithful, and my Wednesday-morning Bible study has given me strength to forgive and move on."

"What about the nightmares?"

"Still there, but not as often."

"Not talking about Tigo doesn't do your heart a bit of good."

Vicki was right. Keeping her feelings bottled up meant that when Kariss finally did uncap them, the fizz would dribble for a long time. Kariss took a wistful look at the sleeping baby.

"Was it Conn on Thanksgiving Day?"

Kariss remembered what her brother had said. It hadn't helped what she'd learned. "His glossy statement about me dating an unbeliever?" She shook her head. "As if he had a clue. He goes to the church of Saturday night bar fights and Sundays in jail."

"He was really out of line. Dad did a good job of ending it. I mean Tigo was going to church, thanked Dad for the new Bible —"

"Sis, that wasn't it. Telling you isn't easy, but I'll try."

"You've always been there for me, and now it's my turn. Take a deep breath while I get a box of tissues. Something tells me we'll both need them before you're through."

When Vicki sat down with the tissues, Kariss began.

"On Thanksgiving evening, we came back here. After you went to bed, Tigo wanted to watch a movie, but I told him we needed to talk." Kariss picked up Rose's teddy bear, hoping it might offer a little comfort, though she knew her security was in God, not her niece's toy. "I needed to ask him about something he'd neglected to tell me."

The memory sliced deep . . . his words . . . her realization . . . the decision. Kariss's cell phone rang, and she grabbed it before it woke Rose. A quick glance told her it was

Amy Garrett, a call she needed to take. But she had no problem with Vicki hearing a one-sided conversation. Her sister's input was often a vital perspective. She answered.

"Hi, Kariss. I wanted to check back with you since we last spoke. Is this an okay time to talk?"

"Sure." Kariss welcomed the opportunity to put a pause on her discussion with Vicki.

"I've been praying about what I should do regarding my story — nonfiction or fiction. I want to continue with the idea of a novel. I appreciate your weighing in on the reality factor. Reliving the whole thing *will* be difficult, but I'm committed to the book."

"Amy, moving forward with this is exciting. I've decided I want to write this novel for you, as I believe your courage and survival will inspire every reader. But not at the expense of sinking you into depression. I have to know every painful moment. People read novels for the emotion, among other things. I don't know how much of your tragedy can be included in the story until I hear the entire thing. I'd like you to think about the treacherous waters ahead. And what it means if your assailant has a vendetta."

"I appreciate your concern. I won't leave anything out."

Amy's responses still sounded canned to Kariss, as they had at their first meeting. That would need to change if they worked together. "This project needs to be built on trust. I have questions, and I'll need to have honest answers."

"I think you're referring to being open about the man who assaulted me. I've lived with the threat of him for years. It hasn't stopped me from achieving any of my goals."

"But you haven't gone public with the story before, other than the newspaper reports."

"I'm not the least concerned," Amy said. "Shall we get together Saturday afternoon around two thirty? I want to get started answering your questions and filling in the details."

Kariss would question her again when they met in person. "Saturday afternoon should work fine. Is it okay if I record our conversations?"

"I expected it. Due to the topic, would you mind coming to my office? It's not far. I don't want what I have to say overheard in a public place until it's in book form."

"No problem. I know where your office is located."

"Good. And Kariss, please don't post this

on Facebook or Twitter." Amy's voice faltered. "My family doesn't support my decision, but I'm moving ahead regardless."

CHAPTER 11

Tigo's patience had been stretched to the max. Inside the high school boys' locker room, the head basketball coach, Frank Ofsteller, eyed him and Ryan as though they'd been caught smoking.

"Why do you want information about Curt and Ian Yeat?" Suspicion and a thick layer of distrust crusted his words. "Their mother and sister were blown to pieces in a car they weren't supposed to be driving. Looks cut and dried to me. The two are paying for an act of revenge. Those boys need time to grieve. To get past this."

"We're investigating every angle," Tigo said. "Did either of them have problems with the other players?"

"No."

"Did they run with a specific crowd?"

"You're wasting your time, 'cause you

haven't caught the jerk who killed Mrs. Yeat and her daughter. Are you saying that because Curt and Ian are black, they look for trouble? Run with a gang? 'Cause you're nuts. My boys are good kids."

Tigo glanced at Ryan in hopes his partner could defuse the coach's defensiveness.

"Race hasn't a thing to do with this," Ryan said. "We're only looking for those persons who might want to harm these boys. We want the killer found so the family can deal with life today and not fear for their future."

"It doesn't matter which one of you is asking the questions, because neither of you know what you're talking about."

"Sir, I'm sure your team has been affected by this too, which is why we need your help," Ryan said.

"Forget it."

Ryan chuckled, which meant he was ready for Tigo to tighten the noose.

"For the past fifteen minutes, you've avoided every question we've asked." Tigo stared into the coach's face. "You've looked for an excuse to toss us out of here like a pair of dirty socks. We can get a subpoena for school records, or you can answer our questions. Unless you want to drive to our office. Your choice."

The coach stepped into Tigo's personal

space, nose to nose. He looked to be in his early sixties and was definitely in shape.

"You have something to say?" Tigo smiled into the coach's smirk.

"I don't appreciate your method of investigation, marching in here with your fancy FBI credentials. You don't own me or this school. All I ask is that my boys work hard, make decent grades, and keep their noses clean. Period."

"I think you have something to hide."

The coach pursed his lips. "My boys' personal lives are just that. If they need to talk, I'm here to listen. Curt and Ian live by my rules."

"At the beginning of our interview, I asked if they were well liked by their peers," Tigo said. "I'm still waiting for an answer."

"Of course. Lots of friends." The coach took a step back. "Curt has outstanding skills, and he's a highly respected team player. Scouts have been looking at him since he was a freshman. Ian's working on his game."

"Any fights?"

"I'm their coach, remember? If there's ever a problem, I take care of it. Look, I have things to do. Talk to the counselor. I have a class to prepare for and a team that's not ready for tonight's game."

Tigo's patience had worn thinner than a piece of paper. "When's practice?"

The coach raised a brow. "After school. But we have a crucial game. You're not —"

"We'll be here at two forty-five to talk to the team and their parents. Make sure you phone them, Coach Ofsteller. That still gives you plenty of time to practice."

Once they left the coach's office, Tigo and Ryan visited the school counselor, Mrs. Villerreal, a Hispanic woman with graying hair and a tight smile. They introduced themselves, and Ryan closed the door.

"We have a few questions about Curt and Ian Yeat," Tigo said. "We're assuming you counsel both boys?"

"Yes, sir." She gestured for them to sit and eased into a chair behind her desk. A bowl of chocolate kisses sat on the desktop, which was littered with school paraphernalia.

"What can you tell us about the Yeat brothers? Their grades? Friends? How they get along with other students?"

She stiffened. "I'm not sure I legally have to answer your questions."

Tigo nodded — Ryan's cue to persuade the woman to help them so they wouldn't have to take legal measures.

"Why wouldn't you want to assist the FBI?" Ryan began. "A horrible crime has been committed, and none of us want Curt or Ian to be another stat in an unsolved murder case."

The color vanished from Mrs. Villerreal's face. "I hadn't considered that the bomber might be after them too. I know bodyguards are at the house, but I thought it was just precautionary."

"No, ma'am," Ryan said. "We don't know who the next victim could be."

She gasped. "Okay. I'll help with what little I know."

"Good." Ryan smiled. "Agent Harris will pose the questions, and I'll record your answers. All right?"

She nodded and reached for a chocolate.

"Thank you," Tigo said, his comment aimed more at Ryan than the counselor. His partner knew how to soften tough situations and seldom lost his temper. But when it happened, no one had better get in his way. "Tell us about Curt and Ian."

"The boys make good grades and are likable."

A definite textbook response. "Any behavior problems?"

"Not really." The woman fidgeted in her chair. "That information is confidential."

"Mrs. Villerreal, what are you not telling us?"

The clock on her desk ticked the seconds.

"Do you think the boys could be involved in this?" she said. "I mean, the news says the parents were having problems, and Mr. Yeat had just made a critical business decision that appears to have endangered his family's lives."

"Our concern is for Curt and Ian." Tigo studied her facial expressions. She was cautious and nervous. "Whatever you tell us is strictly confidential."

"But I don't see how I can help."

The woman knew something. Tigo glanced at Ryan.

"This is off the record," Ryan said. "But it's still your choice whether to give us information."

She nodded and rearranged paper clips on her desk. "What I'm about to say is common knowledge to most of us. Nothing documented." She directed her gaze at Ryan, then Tigo. "Ian has a nasty temper, and Curt cleans up his messes."

"In what way?" Tigo resumed the questioning.

"Ian likes to party, and Curt doesn't because he has scouts at every game and wants to maintain that status."

"So Curt follows his kid brother around to keep him out of trouble?"

"Apparently so."

"But Ian doesn't have a police record," Tigo said.

"I wouldn't know."

"What does your information say about altercations?"

She shrugged. "His dad keeps the incidents off his record."

Resentment had to be building in Curt. "Do you suspect an addiction?"

"Not yet."

"Any problems on school time?"

"A few arguments." She swallowed hard. "Ian also threatened a female teacher in the school parking lot last spring. But Curt intervened."

"Was the threat verbal or physical?"

"Uh . . . both."

"Do you have the threat documented?"

She flushed. "Uh, no. Mr. Yeat met privately with the teacher to discuss the incident, and she decided not to file any charges."

Tigo got the message. "What recourse did you take?"

"I initiated a conference with Ian's parents about his aggressive behavior. Mrs. Yeat tended to be more upset than his father."

"What else?" Tigo said softly.

"I shouldn't be saying any of this. I could

lose my job. Mr. Yeat could sue me."

"What happened?" Tigo said.

"They got into an argument in my office. Mrs. Yeat wanted to take disciplinary action, and Mr. Yeat thought a family vacation would help the problem."

Tigo let the silence flow. Giving them any more information had to be her choice.

She cleared her throat. "Mr. Yeat said Ian was stressed by trying to live up to Curt's achievements. He accused Mrs. Yeat of favoring Curt. She accused him of allowing Ian to get away with behavior that would eventually land him in jail. Both left . . . angry."

CHAPTER 12

Kariss helped Vicki load the car with baby Rose's many supplies for the morning excursion. Kariss stretched and watched her sister organize and rearrange toys and extra clothes as though they'd be gone for a weekend instead of a few hours. Kariss referred to packing for Rose as the What-If Syndrome — whatever emergency might arise, its solution had been tucked into the diaper bag or positioned in the backseat.

"I'm so excited to show off my baby girl." Vicki's high school friend and her husband had built a home in a rural section south of Tomball. Kariss questioned who was showing off what. But a precious baby beat four thousand square feet of brick and mortar.

"Is your friend a good cook?" Kariss said.

"Absolutely."

"Better than you?"

Vicki laughed. "You be the judge."

Kariss counted the number of diapers and checked the box of baby wipes. She'd hoped by this time in her life, a little one would be calling *her* mommy . . . possibly three little ones.

"I think we're ready." Vicki rechecked the rear-facing car seat to make sure it was securely fastened.

Kariss feigned a sigh. "Takes longer to get Rose ready than it does me."

"I know what you mean. At least I can put on my makeup while you drive. You had to get up an hour earlier than we did to get yourself beautiful. Then again, I'm a natural."

Kariss frowned, but they ended up laughing. How she loved her sister and treasured their relationship. One day Vicki would have a home of her own. Kariss didn't blame her for wanting independence. But right now, having Vicki and Rose in the same house helped her bear the sadness of losing Tigo and moving on with her life. Selfish, but true. She stopped herself midthought. Had she really lost Tigo, or could something draw them together again? He'd betrayed her trust. Should she have asked why instead of responding in hurt and anger?

"Sis, what's bothering you?" Vicki said.

Kariss opened the driver's door, giving

herself time to construct a reply. A little honesty went a long way. "I'm peagreen jealous over you and Rose. Oh, I know the situation's tough, raising your baby girl alone, but motherhood makes you sparkle."

"Your time's coming. And you will be a great mother."

Kariss hoped it came before her biological clock expired. She'd be thirty-six in May. Of course, she had a textbook of hurdles to overcome first. One of those was the fear of not being a good wife or mother.

They fastened their seat belts, and Kariss hoped the conversation about her personal life was done. She wanted a family. And not just any family, but the one God planned for her. Was it wrong to hope that God might include Tigo? Placing her silver Jaguar in reverse, she backed out of the driveway and headed toward the gated exit of their small community.

"Earth to Kariss," Vicki said. "Avoiding the subject will never make it go away. There's more, and you know it. Yesterday you started to tell me about Tigo, but the phone call from Amy interrupted what could have been a deep discussion. You've held me while I've cried about Wyatt, and it's not fair to shut me out of your pain."

"I miss him."

"Then tell him so."

"I can't. He's hurt. I'm hurt. We're both miserable. It's all in God's hands anyway, and I refuse to lead Tigo on when the situation is out of my control."

"In other words, the ball's in his court."

"Exactly. If reconciliation is part of the plan, then Tigo knows what has to take place. All I can do — all anyone can do — is pray."

"Sometimes God's answer isn't what we want to hear."

"That's what I'm afraid of." Kariss tossed Vicki a smile, one that hopefully said the topic had been flushed down the drain. She turned the satellite radio to a classical station and let Bach soothe her troubled mind.

Kariss drove north on SH 249, noting the light traffic and enjoying the early morning. Gray clouds in the distance indicated rain, but that was January in Houston.

"Thanksgiving night I heard Tigo shout at you," Vicki said.

Kariss's stomach knotted. "What did you hear?"

"Enough to know he was furious."

Kariss tapped the steering wheel. "Maybe you and I will talk later, okay?"

"Sure thing. If you don't bring it up, I will."

"So you want me to blubber all over you?"

"I might have to pay the FBI a visit and take revenge on Special Agent Santiago Harris for making my sister cry."

They laughed, and Kariss knew the subject had been dropped for now. She watched a black Ford pickup in her rear-view mirror. Ever since she'd been chased and kidnapped, she was wary of every vehicle that appeared to be following her. This one had been behind her since before they merged onto the highway. But that was only ten minutes ago — nothing to be alarmed about.

A few minutes later, Kariss turned onto a rural road that would eventually take them to the home of Vicki's friend. The pickup was tailgating them now. The road ahead was straight and clear of traffic. Kariss slowed and hugged the right side of the road so the driver could pass, but the truck stayed on her bumper. His custom rims had extensions that looked like whirling knife blades.

"What is he doing?" Vicki glanced back at Rose. "Did he drink his breakfast? And look at those wheels. Why would anyone sane want those things?"

"I have no clue. Maybe he thinks they're hot." Kariss sped up to see what the other driver would do. He did the same. "Kids call those spinners."

"Whoa," Vicki said. "Straight off a movie screen, sis. Are they even legal? They must stick out a foot."

Acid rose in Kariss's throat as the situation threw her into her nightmare scare zone.

"You have a Baby on Board sign on the back window," Vicki said. "I'm going to get his license plate number and turn him in."

"Good call."

Vicki reached for pad and paper inside her purse. "I think he's laughing. Hard to tell through his tinted window. Does he think this is a game? What a jerk, a bully." She rattled on, her normal method of handling stress. "Speed up again. He's so close I can't see his plate numbers."

Kariss pressed on the gas as Vicki twisted around, but the truck stayed within inches of the Jag's bumper.

"Rats, all I got was V8."

"Don't think he's driving a vegetable truck." But Kariss didn't think any of this was humorous. She turned off the radio.

"I'd call 911," Vicki said, "but what would I say? A driver is tailgating us, and we're nervous?"

"Go for it. He probably has a record."

Kariss wanted to study him but couldn't risk it with a baby in the car. She refused to panic. "Most likely drunk or high."

"Ah, but we're a team." Vicki pressed numbers into her cell phone. "Would you believe there's no signal? I'll take a pic of his truck. That ought to help the cops locate him."

"Maybe we should open our own private-eye firm. Name our own hours." Kariss knew she didn't sound brave or witty.

"You've done everything else, oh fearless one." Vicki turned in her seat again and snapped a pic. "Even things you won't tell me."

"More than I care to remember."

"We haven't gotten to that part of the discussion yet."

"Hey, try my phone. I have a different provider."

Vicki grabbed Kariss's purse and dug out the cell phone before pressing in the three emergency numbers. She relayed their location to the dispatcher, describing how close they were to the county road where her friend lived.

Kariss had experienced too many close calls with unscrupulous drivers to dismiss this incident as a joyrider playing with them. But why? And who? She thought about speeding ahead to turn at the next intersection, but such reckless driving could endanger little Rose or Vicki.

"He's not slowing down." Vicki's voice rose, her attention focused on her baby.

The truck moved into the opposite lane, and Kariss felt relief, believing he was finally going to pass. Instead, he swerved toward them, smacking against the side of the Jag. Metal scraped against metal. Vicki screamed. "Oh, Lord, remember my baby!"

Kariss stomped on the accelerator. She'd bought this car because of its performance. The intersection loomed ahead. If she could just make it . . .

Kariss's prayers came in short bursts for Vicki's and Rose's safety. If she could get away from the truck, her precious cargo would be okay.

The truck rammed into them again, hard. Kariss gripped the steering wheel, attempting to keep her car on the road, but she hit gravel and felt herself lose control.

CHAPTER 13

9:20 A.M. FRIDAY

Tigo and Ryan left the high school en route to Yeat's Commercial Construction. Tigo drove his pickup, his mind going back over the information he'd gleaned from the coach and the guidance counselor — verbal and nonverbal. Had Jonathan really been surprised by Joanna's filing for divorce?

Tigo and Ryan had several hours to pore over the reports gathered from the accounting department and employee records before showing up at the high school in the afternoon.

But first Tigo wanted to interview Jonathan again to confront him about Curt's and Ian's behavior. Maybe it all meant nothing, but his gut feeling about the family hiding issues kept resurfacing. He couldn't ignore it — his sixth sense had helped him solve many crimes.

"This is a mess," Ryan finally said. "What

looked like a simple case of retaliation has exploded. This family has far too much baggage and far too many secrets. Oh, and did I mention the bomb component that has sophistication written all over it?"

"Jonathan's a deacon in his church, and his brother's a pastor. Was he a jealous husband? Did Alexia not belong to him? Did he insist on taking care of his children's discipline? Perhaps he was abusive to Joanna? Linc will be devastated if any of these suspicions are true."

No wonder Tigo questioned the reality of God and the unconditional love he heard about on Sunday mornings. This family had deceit stamped all over it.

"The other investigators believe our bad guy is affiliated with Jonathan's business. They think Jonathan would have tried to talk Joanna out of a divorce instead of killing her."

"I hope so." Tigo toyed with what they knew about the Yeat family. "Would Joanna have told anyone else she planned to take Jonathan's car Wednesday morning? And would that someone have been able to tamper with it before she left?"

"He would have had to have been on the grounds or have had access to the security gate. Look at the facts, Tigo. Whoever did this had to have planned it. People don't stack kilos of Semtex in their garages. This guy planned and executed a murder. Brings us back to who had motive."

"Jonathan reeks of it," Tigo said.

"Interviewing Roger Collins is more my expertise," Ryan said. "Or Carolyn Hopkins, once she's found. You may have written them off as suspects, but I still have my doubts. Think protocol."

"You crave the hard cases as much as I do," Tigo said. "What you need is a good disguise in a sleazy bar. Turn on super bad boy."

"Makes me wonder how I'll tell my kids what I do to solve crimes."

Tigo chuckled. "They'll figure it out. Let's have Collins brought in later today after we finish at the high school."

At Yeat's complex, FBI agents searched accounting and employee records. A team talked to those in the warehouse, while another team posed questions to the employees and subcontractors at the construction sites. HPD worked alongside them with their own investigators.

Tigo had interviewed Jonathan's executive assistant via the phone, but he wanted to talk to her face-to-face. See if she remembered anything. Vanessa Whitcom had worked at Yeat's Commercial Construction for eight years, five of those as Jonathan's executive assistant. According to him, she knew more about the business than he did. Swore she had a photographic memory. Tigo doubted the latter. The woman, divorced and an empty nester, probably just placed all her energies into job dedication. If anyone knew of shady activity at the business, though, Vanessa would be that person.

Tigo entered Vanessa's eclectic office with a large cranberry slush from Sonic. When he'd phoned Jonathan's office about their arrival and spoken to the receptionist, he asked what he could bring Vanessa.

"I heard cranberry is your poison." Tigo poured charm into his words as he handed her the drink.

"Thank you, Agent Harris," the attractive woman said, reaching for the Sonic cup. "What a perfect icebreaker. Pardon the pun. Won't you please sit down?"

Tigo introduced Ryan and closed the door before they sat across from the woman.

"How can I help with your investigation?" Vanessa took a sip of her drink and gave Tigo a thumbs-up.

"The killer is still running loose," Tigo said. "Thought you might be able to recall something we could use in our investigation."

She sobered. "I've been praying for the good Lord to show me something." She pointed to Ryan. "Does Agent Steadman talk?"

Ryan laughed. "When it's necessary. In fact, I'll ask the questions and let the agent with the charm record your answers."

Tigo eased back in the chair and let his partner take over. Ryan and Vanessa had the faith thing in common. Would he ever come to the same conclusion?

Vanessa scooted aside a mound of papers and set the cup on her desk. A heart-shaped dish held red jelly beans, and a zebra clock with pink-and-orange streamers rested precariously on the edge of the desk. Women and their knickknacks.

"Jonathan's a dream boss. Always has been. He's mannerly, gentle, and yet firm when the situation calls for it. I have no idea who would want him dead. Even now, when he's not able to come into the office, his calls are attentive, with concern for all of us running the company."

"Did Joanna spend much time here?"

"A little. She had her charities and her friends."

"We've been told she has sisters. I imagine

127

they spent time together. My wife and her sister talk every day. Volunteer for the same projects at church."

Vanessa's frown confirmed Curt's earlier statement. "Your wife and sister are very lucky, Agent Steadman. But in answer to your question, Joanna and her sisters rarely spent time together. Not sure why."

"I think you are." Ryan's piercing gaze met hers. "I bet you know everything that goes on here and with the family. Jonathan spoke highly of his reliance on you."

She shrugged. "Her sisters didn't care for Joanna, no matter how hard she tried."

"She told you this?"

Vanessa studied Ryan. "Joanna and I were close. We met for lunch regularly. She wanted so much for her sisters to know the Lord so they could be a happy, loving family. But it never happened." She blinked and shivered. "You two have to find her and Alexia's killer."

Tigo had some questions of his own. "What about the divorce?"

Vanessa paled. "That was one thing Joanna hadn't shared with me, and we talked about everything."

"She didn't mention any problems?"

"Spits and spats from time to time. But she loved Jonathan. No, she was *in love* with him. All you had to do was look at them together, and you knew they were committed to each other."

Tigo nodded at Ryan for him to continue. Vanessa seemed more comfortable with him, and they needed any information she could offer.

Between questions, Vanessa and Ryan talked about other topics that would build trust — a photograph of her children, the weather, a book about prayer on her desk. She confided that Pastor Taylor Yeat was her pastor too.

"Are you sure there isn't anything else you can tell us?" Ryan said.

"Nothing out of the ordinary. Whoever said she'd filed for divorce lied."

"Her attorney has a signed document." Ryan's voice softened.

"Then something other than her relationship with Jonathan drove her to the attorney's office. Because their marriage was rock solid." She wrapped her fingers around the Sonic cup. "I would have known."

CHAPTER 14

Vicki's screams pierced Kariss's ears. The car hit the ditch with a sharp jolt that deployed the air bags. The chemicals released stung Kariss's eyes and nose.

She blinked as the car ground to a stop. The windshield had cracked in a spiderweb pattern but hadn't shattered. She whirled around to watch the truck, but it disappeared in a flurry of dirt and gravel. For a moment, she considered pulling out her 9mm and unloading it in the direction of his tires or gas tank.

Not a godly thought, but still true.

Rose.

Vicki.

Dear God, let them be all right.

Grasping the steering wheel for support, she touched Vicki's arm. "You okay?"

Vicki slowly turned toward the backseat. Blood trickled down the right side of her face. "My baby. How's Rose?" Her sister's quiet sobs filled the car. Unfortunately, the car leaned against the ditch in such a way that it was impossible to open the passenger door, but Kariss could still get out her side. "Please, Kariss. Get her out of here."

Kariss pressed the Unlock button on the doors and lowered the windows before turning off the engine. She pushed aside her air bag and tried to release her seat belt. It was jammed.

She reached over to Vicki's side to search through the glove box for a pocketknife, an item their father had always insisted be in his girls' cars. With it, she cut her seat belt and then pushed open the door. If only Rose would scream at the top of her lungs. But there was nothing.

Kariss flung open the rear door, and a muffled cry met her ears. Not a pain-filled sound, but a whimper. Kariss studied the baby's face while reaching for the car seat's Release button, not an easy task with the car leaning on its right side. Kariss held her breath. No blood. No marks.

The little face scrunched into a frown, then a cry. Kariss lifted Rose from the car seat, speaking words of comfort. Not a visible mark on her tiny body. The car seat had done its job. Praise God she'd been strapped in on the driver's side so Kariss could reach her.

"She's fine, Vicki." When her sister failed to respond, the possible extent of Vicki's injuries slammed against Kariss's heart.

Glancing behind her, Kariss saw that an SUV had stopped, and a couple was emerging. But her concern was for her sister.

"Help is on the way," the woman called as she hurried toward Kariss.

Kariss nodded. Vicki had phoned 911 before the pickup had run them off the road. Now the emergency hotline had two calls about them.

Rose looked unharmed, but Kariss couldn't lay her on the ground to check on Vicki. Kariss took a quick peek at her sister. Vicki's eyes were closed, and blood flowed down her face and onto her neck. Had she blacked out?

"How can I help?" the woman said.

Kariss patted Rose's back to calm her. "I'm concerned about my sister."

The man peered through the open driver's door at Vicki. "Wait for an ambulance. She might be badly hurt."

Kariss had thought the same thing. "I wonder how long before help gets here? We called 911 when the pickup was riding our bumper."

"Just a few minutes. It'll come from Tom-ball." He shook his head. "Wish we'd seen what happened."

"I'm just glad you're here now."

"Why don't you let me take the baby?" the woman said. "I have four girls of my own."

Kariss looked into the woman's kind eyes and relinquished Rose, who was still crying. "Thanks. I'm shaking so much I'm afraid I'll drop her. I think she's fine."

The woman cradled Rose. "You get a hold of yourself, and I'll keep little missy company. Do you have a bottle?"

"My sister's nursing her. But she ate just before we left. I'll get her wah-wah from her diaper bag." She gave the woman a smile. "That's what our family calls a pacifier." Kariss reached into the car, her attention flying to Vicki, who was still so quiet and stationary. While searching for the diaper bag, she heard a siren. What a blessed sound. "Help is here, sis. Hold on."

Vicki moaned. "Rose. Where is she?"

Relief lifted a ton of weight from Kariss's heart. "She's just fine. Not a scratch. A nice lady is holding her."

"I hear her crying. Thank You, God."

"I wanted to get you out of there, but the man who stopped to help suggested we wait

133

for the ambulance."

"Probably smart." Vicki had yet to open her eyes. "My head —"

"Hush. The paramedics will fix you up. Save your strength."

"Thanks, sis. You're the best."

Kariss forced a laugh. "Remember how you protested when I spent three hundred dollars on Rose's car seat?"

Vicki smiled through closed eyes. "Yeah."

"You can now write an endorsement for the brand. Probably get lots of good free stuff."

Vicki didn't appear to hear this last comment.

Kariss would find out who had done this. A chill raced up her arms. She didn't care about possible danger to herself, but the driver had stepped over the line when he threatened Vicki's and Rose's lives.

Chapter 15

Tigo's personal cell phone, the iPhone, rang. Seeing the caller was Kariss's father, he explained to Ryan the need to take the call and left Vanessa's office to answer it. Odd for Mr. Walker to call during working hours.

"Tigo, Fred Walker here. Wanted to let you know that Kariss, Vicki, and the baby were in an accident this morning."

Tigo's pulse raced into overdrive. "How bad?"

"The baby and Kariss are fine. Vicki's awaiting treatment for a head wound. She has a nasty bump on her head. We're on our way to the hospital now."

Tigo blew out a breath. "What happened?"

"Some redneck ran them off the road and into a ditch and didn't bother to stick around. Kariss says she's okay, but I have

135

my doubts. Vicki and Rose would come first for her."

Tigo pushed aside his rising apprehension to focus on the situation. "What hospital?"

"Tomball. We've been on the road a little while, but it'll still be over twenty minutes before we get there."

"I'm on my way. Coming from the south-west side of town." Tigo stepped back into the office and motioned for Ryan to join him in the hallway.

"What's going on?" Ryan said.

Tigo told him all he knew. "Vicki's hurt, but Kariss and the baby are supposedly okay. I've got to make sure."

"Go ahead. I'll take care of things here. They were lucky."

"I have to see for myself. Probably wouldn't hurt if you'd pray."

Ryan chuckled. "I'm on it. The skeptic asks for prayer?"

"I'm listening on Sundays. Got to admit, though, just when it all makes sense, I'm confused again. That whole surrender thing goes against the grain of my independent nature."

"Keep at it."

Tigo wasn't sure faith answered the plaguing questions in his life. But Ryan and Linc held stock in prayer, and for them, it worked.

Twenty minutes later, at the hospital ER, Tigo flashed his ID and followed a nurse through double doors into the treatment area. She no doubt thought the accident was an FBI matter. Behind a curtain, Vicki lay on a treatment table with her eyes closed.

A nasty gash near her right temple needed stitches. Why hadn't they taken care of her yet? Kariss sat in a chair holding a baby decked out in pink and lace and some sort of frilly headband. Kariss and Vicki's parents stood by Vicki's bed. Fred held his injured daughter's hand while Ella gently stroked her hair. Tigo planted a kiss on Ella's cheek and patted Fred's back.

"We've been here about five minutes. Did you fly?" Fred said.

"I have my moments on the road." Tigo caught Kariss's gaze. The first time they'd met, he'd been driving faster than Buzz Lightyear on steroids and had cut her off on the highway. A mile later, an officer had ticketed him.

"I remember." Although her hair was tousled, she looked in control and beautiful . . . as always.

"How's the patient?"

"Doing okay. I think she's in more pain than she'll admit," Kariss said. "We're waiting to get her stitched up. They had another emergency just before she was brought in."

Tigo studied Vicki's pale face. "Is she sleeping, or did the doctor give her something?"

"Resting," Kariss said. A hint of pink tinged her cheeks. "I think she used up her energy making sure Rose was okay. I told Dad not to bother you."

"Friends look out for friends."

"Most of the time."

He understood exactly what she meant and focused his attention back on Fred and Ella. "Thanks for the call."

"We knew you'd want to know about the accident, despite our youngest daughter's protests."

Tigo chose not to toss out a sarcastic remark and turned to Kariss instead. "Rose is growing. She's a beautiful baby."

"We're all prejudiced, but you're right." She smiled.

Thoughts about the past slammed against his brain. Why had he been so stupid?

Vicki half opened her eyes. "I thought I heard a familiar voice. Are we having a party?"

"Only when the jerk who did this is arrested," Kariss said.

"I pity him if my sister gets to him first,"

Vicki said. "Thanks for coming, Tigo. I'm fine, really. Just waiting" — pain creased her face — "for the doctor to stitch my head."

"And a room." Fred patted her hand. "Got to run a few tests on little mama. Make sure nothing's knocked loose up there."

A doctor stepped inside the curtained area, a nurse trailing behind, pushing a cart loaded with paraphernalia to stitch up Vicki's head. Tigo seized the opportunity and turned to Kariss. Odd how he needed courage to talk to the woman who occupied his thoughts. "Would you and Miss Rose join me for a walk? Blood makes me squeamish."

Kariss laughed. "Right."

He reached for the baby so Kariss could stand.

"You handle Rose very nicely," she said.

"I handle little girls better than big ones."

Ella and Fred laughed, but Kariss didn't. Once outside the ER, they strolled down the hospital hallway. Tigo continued holding Rose. She felt right snuggled in his arms. To think Kariss had once been this helpless. She could still be helpless, but Tigo wouldn't bring it up.

"Are you in trouble, Ms. Indiana Jones?"

he said. "Or should I ask if you're working on a story that's put you in danger?"

"No, I don't think so." Her voice trembled.

Was it fear he detected, or did she feel uncomfortable with him? "I hear the reservation. Want to tell me about it?"

"I'm tired and angry at the truck-daddy who did this. He was probably strung out. Got scared and took off when we headed for the ditch."

"Your Jag tends to attract attention."

"I should have stuck with my Prius. Vanity took over once the arrests were made last summer."

He remembered the day she'd sold the Prius. They'd celebrated with dinner at Ruth's Chris. "Did you get his license plate number?"

"Only V8. I gave it to the officer who arrived on the scene. Vicki thought she took a pic of the truck with her cell phone. But it's not there. I guess she was too nervous."

He brushed a kiss across the tip of Rose's nose, and the baby smiled. Melted him like butter. "Did you get a look at the driver?"

"Nope. Tinted glass. I thought about trying to stop him before he got away, but I had Rose and Vicki to worry about."

"What would you have done? Chased after the guy with your handgun?"

Kariss rolled her eyes. "Very funny. I was actually planning to shoot out a tire or aim for his gas tank."

"Don't worry, they'll find him. Although I'd like the chance." He forced himself to look into Kariss's brown eyes and realized he couldn't breathe. Facing bad guys was so much easier. "I'd appreciate a call in a few days on how your sister's doing."

"Sure." She winced. "I smell awful from the deployed air bag."

"I thought it was the ER."

"I'd take you out if you weren't holding my niece."

"Then I'm safe."

"Sorry Dad called you."

"No problem." He was glad Fred did. Tigo wanted to be there.

A nurse met them in the hall. "Your baby's beautiful," she said. "She has her mama's hair and eyes." She smiled at Tigo. "I bet you're one proud daddy."

"We're not her parents." Kariss brushed her finger across Rose's cheek. "She's my sister's baby. Thanks anyway. We think she's beautiful too."

Tigo wanted to think they had a future if they could just work through the damage. That they could someday earn that compliment. But he'd have to take the first step.

CHAPTER 16

5:00 P.M. FRIDAY

"So now your wife claims you were at home the morning of the car bombing?" Tigo watched Roger Collins, who had three eyebrow piercings, two piercings on his upper lip, and a safety pin through his ear. Very easy to stereotype him. "New information. Had she forgotten you were there?"

Roger Collins had been brought in before Tigo and Ryan returned from Curt and Ian's high school. Tigo was in a sour mood, regretting the waste of time talking to the basketball team, and Collins wasn't helping his attitude.

Ryan glanced up from his iPad, no doubt reading Collins for signs of deceit. Although the interview was being recorded, the two agents always compared their personal notes with the footage. The FBI interview room was quiet except for the low hum of the heating system.

Collins rubbed his nose. "I was at home with my wife and daughter. Since I lost my job, where else could I go? I was sitting on the patio talking to a friend most of the morning. You know, commiserating."

"A little cold to be on the patio. It was pouring rain that morning."

"It's covered. And the weather fit my attitude."

"Especially if you were planting a bomb in Jonathan Yeat's car," Tigo said.

"No way. I went to prison once. I'm not going back again."

"But you threatened him."

"Wouldn't you if you didn't know how you were going to feed your family?"

Tigo picked up a piece of paper. "I wouldn't resort to murder. Says here you'd like to see him dead."

Collins pressed his fingers into the top of the table, his knuckles white. "I didn't kill anyone."

"How good are you at building bombs?"

"Not good enough."

Tigo glanced at Ryan. "What did you tell me about this man's record?"

"Did time for armed robbery. Pistol-whipped a male clerk behind the counter of a convenience store."

"Hmm." Tigo tapped his pen on the table.

"Did you have a job then?"

"Look, dude. I was living in California. Me and the wife were just married. Had a three-month-old baby girl. Needed cash for food and stuff. But I learned my lesson, and I've worked hard for nearly eighteen months at Yeat's Construction. I'm going to college and making good grades." He pointed a finger at Tigo. "I have an alibi — two of them, my wife and my friend. You're not going to blame me for something I didn't do. My wife's pregnant with our second kid, and the doctors are concerned she might miscarry. I need a job. But note this — I'll flip burgers at Micky D's before breaking the law."

"Maybe you know who did."

He shook his head. "Guys are upset with the layoffs. Some got hot and talked crazy. Me? I was one of them. But I wouldn't murder for revenge. That doesn't put a man back to work when the economy gets better."

"Anybody mention Semtex?"

"No one talked about a bomb or how they planned to get even with Jonathan Yeat. You guys need to talk to someone else."

"Maybe so," Tigo said. "But don't leave town."

Kariss didn't know whether to admire her sister's stubbornness or knock some sense into her. Vicki had refused to be admitted into the hospital. Instead, she insisted the tests be conducted while she was in the ER. Mom and Dad took care of Rose while Kariss arranged to have her Jag towed. She also phoned Babies"R"Us and arranged to have a new car seat delivered to the hospital via taxi. A rental car arrived at the same time Vicki was signing the discharge papers.

"Sis, you've got a mild concussion, and your right eye is turning purple," Kariss said while their dad helped Vicki scoot into the backseat beside Rose. "I really wish you'd reconsider and spend the night here."

"I'll second that." Dad massaged his lower back. Installing the car seat in the rental had been a chore. "I won't sleep a wink wondering if you're all right."

"Dad, I'm a nurse, remember? And I'm quite capable of knowing when Rose or I need medical attention."

"I've made a decision." Mom's brown eyes widened with a familiar threatening look. Kariss had seen that look plenty of times during her growing-up years. "I'm staying at the condo with my girls tonight."

"Good idea," Kariss said. "Mom's even

better at making sure you behave than I am."

"Suffocating attention." Vicki moaned. "Rose's schedule will be a thing of the past."

"That's right. I'm going to spoil both of you." Mom slid into the front seat. "As soon as we get to the condo, I'm putting Vicki to bed and making a pot of gumbo."

"And I'll get my dinner at Whataburger and load up on the fries your mother doesn't let me have at home." Dad double-checked the car seat. "Great to see Tigo today. He's a good man — good enough for a son-in-law in my book."

Kariss's emotions were still playing havoc with her heart. "I don't think so. Too many problems."

"I can feel it in my bones. God's gonna work this out."

If Kariss didn't ease into another subject soon, Dad would be inviting Tigo to Sunday dinner. "He teased me about chasing the driver with my handgun."

"Too bad I didn't see who ran my girls off the road. There wouldn't have been anything left to bury." He shook his head. "Excuse me, Lord, but I'm not feeling too forgiving right now."

"I'm right there in a box seat." Kariss allowed a single tear to drip down her cheek.

Until now, she'd been too angry and concerned about Vicki and Rose to let her defenses down. "That guy thinks he got away, but God knows where he lives." She wouldn't rest until the jerk was arrested.

CHAPTER 17

Tigo and Ryan sat in Linc's office, discussing what they knew about the Yeat bombing. Too many ragged edges had set the stage for a lengthy investigation. More questions and a deeper scrutiny of established facts lay ahead in the days to come.

They'd eliminated Joanna's dress designer as a suspect. She was confined to a wheelchair and depended on her caregiver to transport her to her clients. The woman lived an exemplary life and contributed to many of the same charities as the Yeat Foundation. She'd had no idea anything was troubling Joanna.

Linc stared at an oil painting of Teddy Roosevelt that hung on his office wall, as if the twinkle behind the president's spectacles held answers to the puzzling case. "Strange how you think you know a man, a family, and then you realize the perfect family is waist-deep in mud."

Tigo remembered one of Teddy Roosevelt's sayings — "Speak softly and carry a big stick." That certainly fit Linc.

"Jonathan never mentioned any problems in his marriage. And I never observed any tension between them. Yet I find it hard to believe he didn't know Joanna planned to divorce him." Linc shook his head. "A man knows when the light's out."

"So you think the idea of her having an affair doesn't make sense?" Tigo said. "Ian gave us a good description of the man he'd seen with her. We don't have a solid ID match to anyone in our database, but we're looking for him."

"Guess anything's possible. The man Ian saw at the mall could be a lover. You said Jonathan's assistant, Vanessa, was clueless about the divorce, right?"

Ryan nodded. "You saw my notes from the interview, and her body language didn't indicate she was lying."

"What else do you two have for me?" Linc said.

Tigo nodded at Ryan to continue. His partner was definitely in think mode.

"You witnessed our questioning of Collins." Ryan reached for his iPad and swiped his finger across the screen. "We're tailing him. Carolyn Hopkins hasn't been found yet. Her records state she has family in Arkansas, which gives us a lead." He glanced up from the screen. "But I don't think there's anything solid there unless she's working with someone."

Linc nodded. "Keep on it. Who had access to Semtex or motive to hire a bomber?"

"Semtex is the key," Ryan said. "I've done a little snooping. All the two-bit bad guys out there would have shot or knifed Jonathan. Tigo and I have decided our guy had money. Plenty of it. And that means a vendetta. But the information we've discovered about Joanna confused our theory. I'm not letting go of anything yet."

"I think we're chasing two storms," Linc said.

Tigo nodded. "We're researching every angle. I'll take time this weekend to brainstorm what we do know. See what we've missed or need to follow up on. The gun dealer Hershey may know something." He nodded at Ryan. "Want to question him on Monday?"

"It's a plan."

Linc frowned. "The funeral's tomorrow afternoon."

"I plan to be there." Tigo waved away Linc's protest. "A few things don't add up, and observing the family and friends could answer those questions."

"All right. I'll be doing the same thing," Linc said. "I'll be playing more than one role. This funeral will be hard on my family. Alexia referred to us as her aunt and uncle."

In other words, Linc would not only be at the funeral in a professional capacity but would also be grieving the deaths personally.

"I'll focus on the family," Tigo said. "See if anyone lets something slip."

"Good idea. I'm banking on employees and business acquaintances not suspecting me of gathering evidence. Yvonne and I will be there for the duration, so you and I can compare notes later."

Tigo nodded. "I'm thinking the family will be on their best behavior, and I want to meet Joanna's sisters. Follow up on a few comments Curt made."

"The sisters attend Taylor's church too. Darena and her husband are members. He's a deacon. I'll reserve my opinion of that situation until you meet her."

"Tigo, call me after the funeral," Ryan said. "I'd join you if I didn't already have family obligations."

"Why don't you call me instead? I don't want to interrupt anything." Tigo knew

Ryan and Cindy needed to work through the problem with her mother's care. The couple had lined up a babysitter and planned to spend Saturday night at a hotel.

"Thanks." Ryan gave him a grim look.

Tigo figured the happenings at home must be wearing on him.

Tigo debriefed on the long day. "We visited the high school this morning and again this afternoon to meet with the boys' basketball teams. Questioning the kids was useless. Zilch. The players are a loyal brotherhood, and Curt and Ian are two of their own. None of them spoke a derogatory word about the Yeat boys. Parents urged their kids to share information, but the atmosphere was as if nothing had happened."

"Another dead end?" Linc eased back in his chair.

"Not exactly," Tigo said. "Before we visited with Vanessa, we learned a few things from the school counselor. Ryan has the dialogue in his notes."

Ryan relayed what had transpired. "Usually it's the mother who makes excuses for her child's actions. This time we have a reversal. The counselor told us off the record that Ian threatened a female teacher in the parking lot last spring. Curt stepped in as usual, and Jonathan persuaded the teacher not to press charges."

Linc's features were a mass of frustration. "Don't let this thing slide. My son called just before you two arrived. Gave me an earful about Curt covering for Ian. Confirms what you found out."

Tigo grinned to relieve the tension, which could have been split with an ax. "Curt isn't doing his brother any favors. Neither of those kids are choir boys, are they?"

"Heaven help Jonathan if we learn that one of his sons had a hand in killing their mother and sister."

9:35 P.M. FRIDAY

Kariss pulled her laptop into bed with her and leaned back against a mound of pillows. Exhaustion had hit her early tonight, and she was relieved her mother slept in the guest room near Vicki and Rose. Mom had the baby monitor, so she'd hear any move either of them made. Like a child, Kariss believed having her mother close by meant the world was safe. She knew better, but she'd not go there tonight.

A writing how-to article needed to be edited, but first she wanted to check email. Keeping up with incoming messages could be an addiction. But when they filled her in-box, she found it overwhelming until she responded to questions and concerns. She hadn't posted on Facebook and Twitter about the accident in case the driver of the pickup followed her on social media and was thinking he'd gotten away with his bullying.

She had 123 new messages since early this morning. Not bad for a Friday. Definitely manageable. Fortunately, most made their way into the Junk folder.

Halfway through the list, an email with the subject line of "Amy Garrett" caught Kariss's attention. Perhaps Amy had more than one email address. This one had S. Todd as the sender. Kariss opened the message, expecting to read an insight about the writing project.

You've agreed to write about Amy Garrett's story. Forget it. She doesn't need you or anyone else poking around in her life. This is a warning, and I don't waste words.

Irritation swept through Kariss. She detested anyone telling her what to write or not write. Threats made her furious . . .

though cautious. She responded to the message.

WHO ARE YOU? WHY SHOULD I FORGET AMY'S STORY? ARE YOU A WRITER?

She pressed Send and finished working through the remaining emails. A delivery-failure message popped into her in-box. The S. Todd address wasn't a legitimate address. Now what was that all about? Leaning back against the mass of pillows, Kariss thought about various scenarios. The sender could be someone who worked at Amy's office, a person who cared for her and didn't want Kariss to dredge up old memories. That made sense. The process had the potential to damage the reputation of Freedom's Way.

Kariss thought that scenario made the most sense, and she'd ask Amy about the email when they met tomorrow afternoon. Kariss doubted the Garrett family would make a threat. Even so, she understood that her dogged attitude could get her into trouble, and she'd learned a valuable lesson last year while researching the Cherished Doe case.

Or had she? Here she was again, writing a book from a cold case in which a violent crime had been committed and not paying any attention to the warning signs. But she also believed in helping crime victims find healing, and this was her way of helping Amy and other victims find it.

CHAPTER 18

Tigo stood in the back of the crowded church and scanned those who were attending Joanna and Alexia's closed-casket funeral. Many solemn kids. Three counselors from the school district who were available for grieving students and parents. Many tears.

Jonathan appeared to be holding up. He'd swiped at his eyes a few times, but his brother, Taylor, stood right beside him offering support. The closest thing Tigo had ever had to brothers was Linc and Ryan, and he'd do just about anything for them.

Men and women hugged Jonathan. Curt wept openly, and Ian clenched his jaw. The boys' reactions could be their method of expressing sorrow, or it could mean something else — regret or fear of getting caught. Tigo thought well of Curt, but Ian was another matter. Would the older boy cover up evidence to protect the younger?

Why did Tigo feel this family knew more than they had admitted? Attending funerals wasn't his normal mode of investigation, but his gut was telling him that many of the answers were right there with the Yeats. The killer could be among those gathered in the church, and that knowledge kept Tigo's senses on alert. The investigation had already uncovered a dysfunctional family that held grudges, lived with shame, and hid secrets.

But the immediate family's response to the service wasn't all Tigo was looking for. He had studied the initial video footage of the crime scene and now searched the crowd for someone who might have been at both places. Tigo also planned to attend the meal after the graveside service, which would allow him to mingle . . . and listen.

Media had mixed reports. Some concentrated on an ex-employee who sought revenge, and others focused on Jonathan as a do-gooder who neglected his family. Mike McDougal had taken the latter stance at Channel 5 and in his weekly blog. Tigo had no use for McDougal, whose writing slanted toward defamation.

The explosion occurred one day after

Joanna's appointment with the attorney, a highly reputable man who had an impeccable family law practice. Nothing had turned up there.

Or was there a compelling motive none of them had uncovered?

Tigo's attention shifted to Taylor Yeat as he came forward to give the eulogy. The pastor spoke a few words then stopped, overcome with emotion. He took a deep breath and moistened his lips. A man handed him a bottle of water. After a long drink, he thanked those present for their patience. "Alexia was a blessing to Joanna and Jonathan, a gift to all who knew her. She danced. She sang. She played softball and loved to go fishing. Alexia had her mother's beauty. I . . ."

While Taylor continued to speak as a family member and pastor, Tigo scrutinized the crowd. Grief increased at each mention of Alexia, a child caught in the middle of an ugly plot. Curt broke down. Ian wrapped an arm around his shoulder. Jonathan sobbed, his anguish rising to a thunderous roar.

A child didn't deserve to die before having had the chance to live. How could a righteous God justify this? Tigo focused on Taylor, who struggled through his roles of pastor, brother, brother-in-law, and uncle.

"Joanna and my brother were role models for all of us. Many of you sought them out for counseling regarding anything from finances to parental guidance to marital help. Joanna always had her Bible open with scriptures underlined, but she seldom had to read the passage. She had them memorized.

"Beloved friends and family, today we mourn Joanna's and Alexia's passing and the terrible circumstances that have brought us together. Many of you have expressed the need to have the guilty person found, and I'm right there with you." Taylor wiped his brow. "Joanna would ask us to forgive as Jesus instructed. I admit, it's a difficult task. I'm trying, but I'm telling you it's not easy. We can rejoice in the understanding that Alexia and Joanna are with Jesus, and one day we'll see them again."

In the meantime, Taylor was asking these people to forgive a murderer. Tigo understood the principles of Christianity, and at times he accepted the theology. But the Jesus-in-your-heart seemed to cripple him, as though believers used their faith as a crutch instead of using logic to think through their problems. Tigo's heart beat not with forgiveness but with a resolve to find the killer.

A knot formed in his throat. Linc and Ryan were pillars of strength. But Tigo simply didn't get it, and tragedies like this made him so angry with God. At times he wanted to walk away from finding who God really was and live life his own way. Yet he'd promised his mother he wouldn't give up.

After the graveside service — where Tigo shivered in the January cold for more reasons than the plunging temperatures — he drove to Jonathan Yeat's home for the meal. This would last until midafternoon, but the time would be worth every moment if Tigo found a clue about the person who'd planted the bomb. Outside the gated entrance, he spotted Linc, Yvonne, and their college-age son. He hurried to join them. Because of the crime scene, the crowd had to park on the street and display ID before entering the property.

Tigo again realized his suit coat provided little warmth in the forty-degree temps and freezing rain.

"Did you see anything unusual?" Linc murmured.

"Not yet."

"One of Jonathan's key employees isn't here — his executive assistant, Vanessa Whitcom."

Her absence surprised Tigo after she'd sworn devotion to Joanna and Jonathan. "I'll look into it."

"Are you two talking about the investigation?" said Yvonne, a lovely African-American woman who always reminded Tigo of a runway model. Almost as attractive as Kariss. Now why would Tigo think of her when he had work to do?

"Yes, honey. We're talking about the case," Linc said. "It's who we are."

Yvonne peered around her husband's side and said to Tigo, "I want to talk to you about Joanna. Perhaps later on. I've been trying to make sense of this, and I might have some insight." She smiled at her husband. "This isn't anything you haven't already heard. Sometimes another perspective opens doors we haven't thought of."

Linc squeezed her waist. "Thanks, honey. Go ahead and talk to Tigo now, and I'll begin my own investigation." He kissed her cheek and walked to the house with their son. A police officer stopped Linc, and he pulled the officer aside, no doubt giving instructions about keeping the agents' identification private.

Yvonne shivered. "It's cold. Nasty day for a funeral. Though it's not as if sunshine would have made it any more bearable . . .

Let me get right to the point."

Tigo noticed she used the same verbiage as Linc — probably the years of marriage.

"I want to know the smallest thing, so bring it on," Tigo said.

"Joanna had been distant for the past six months or so. Refused dinner invitations. Said she was worried about Ian. But she wouldn't say why."

That made sense.

"I learned from my own son that Ian had been giving his parents trouble. But I thought Joanna and I were friends. Why wouldn't she tell me about it unless she was embarrassed?" She shrugged. "Joanna prided herself on helping others. Could be she didn't have a solution for him."

"So you think Ian had something to do with this?"

"I hope not. I just wondered if she had information about Ian that she couldn't tell anyone. Maybe he still knows more than he's claimed."

Unless the problem was another man. Joanna could have been seeing another man and then wanted out. The guy could have refused. Tigo would chew on it some more. See where it led.

"One more thing." Yvonne lifted her chin. "She loved Jonathan, and this divorce thing is a cover for something else."

"Any idea what?"

"No. You're the FBI agent. I'm just a woman with intuition. Trouble was brewing in the Yeat household, but I have no clue what."

Another person who shared his suspicions. Once inside the over-ten-thousand-square-foot home, Tigo joined the people clustered in the formal rooms. The kitchen and dining room tables overflowed with food and beverages, and many people stood in line. Tigo paid his respects to Jonathan, Curt, and Ian and then slipped into the background to observe those in attendance. The Yeat men had been given instructions not to give away Tigo's profession. In his opinion, the Yeat men walked a fine line of trust. While Tigo wove through the crowd, he heard sympathetic comments.

"I hate this for Jonathan and the boys."

"Who could have done such a thing?"

"Why haven't the FBI or HPD made an arrest?"

"We need to keep everyone in our prayers."

"I was helping Alexia try out for cheerleading."

Two African-American women stepped outside onto a covered patio. Earlier, Linc had pointed them out as Joanna's sisters. A little cold for a breather unless their grieving needed to be private. After Curt's and Vanessa's comments about the animosity between the sisters, Tigo wanted to hear what they had to say. He grabbed a cup of coffee and exited through the front door, making his way around to the back of the home, where he could hear the conversation.

"I'd give anything to have five minutes with Joanna," a woman said. "Maybe we could've made things right between us. Let go of the past and be real sisters. We were getting close."

"Give me a break, Angela," a second woman said. "You don't think for one minute Joanna lived the holy life. Everything was a front so she could spend money and screw around."

Tigo pressed Record on his Blackberry. The two had already given the case a new slant.

"I admit she had a few faults," Angela said, "but when Dad tossed me out on my rear because I was pregnant, Joanna opened her home and paid my bills."

"A few faults?" the second woman said. "She persuaded you to give up your daughter. You hated her for it."

"Joanna's gone. Why drag her through the mud?" Angela sniffed. A click indicated she'd opened her purse. "My baby was better off in a home with two parents who could provide for her."

"Sure. You keep telling yourself that, and one day you'll believe it."

"Darena, how can you be so heartless?" Angela said.

"I'm just saying I thought Joanna had more sense than to get involved with a low-life who would kill her and her daughter."

"That's enough. This is our sister and niece's funeral. And you're still acting like a fool. Jealous for no reason except that Joanna was beautiful and had a good life. Conjuring up smut today? That's low. One of Jonathan's ex-employees did this, and you're stupid to think otherwise. Jonathan was the target, not our sister or niece."

"I was simply pointing out the facts," Darena said. "You always were the gullible one, swallowing all Joanna's piety. Since when did you become so sympathetic?"

"I should have defended her a long time ago instead of letting you walk all over me."

"Don't tell me you believed her crap too?" Darena laughed.

"She never did a thing to you but try to be a good sister," Angela said. "You're pathetic, and one day you'll get yours. I'm not listening to any more of this." The door slammed.

One of Joanna's sisters despised her. Tigo turned to leave, needing to make his way back into the crowd to talk to the high schoolers. The patio door squeaked, and he hesitated.

"Hey, babe. You doing all right?" The male voice sounded familiar.

Tigo waited a few more moments so he could seal the man's identity. He anchored his back against the side of the house and took a sip of his coffee. Who did that voice belong to?

"I'm fine, sweetheart. My sister is in total denial. Where's your wife?"

"With Jonathan. I told her I needed to check on you, but I can't be gone long. I know you and Joanna had your differences, but this is horrible."

"So the tears were real?"

"Of course. Can't believe you'd ask such a thing."

"I'm sorry." Darena's tone dripped in sugar. "You and I have nothing to fear now that Joanna's gone. Angela has no clue about us."

"It's the only thing about today that eases

my mind. Don't know what I'd do without you."

Tigo kicked at a stone along the path loud enough to create attention. He stepped into the couple's view. Darena gasped. The man took a step backward but not quickly enough.

Pastor Taylor Yeat was having an affair with Joanna's sister?

CHAPTER 19

2:25 P.M. SATURDAY

Kariss drove her rental car into the covered parking garage of the building where Freedom's Way housed its suite of offices. She slid in beside a late-model Malibu and breathed a quick prayer for wisdom. The empty area seemed a bit spooky, though it could just be her imagination heading into overdrive after being run off the road yesterday morning. She felt guilty leaving Vicki at home, but Mom was there and Dad planned to stop by.

The excitement of a new novel and compassion for Amy's horrific experience rose within her. Unusual emotions to feel simultaneously, but they were real. Kariss's personal goal was for each novel she wrote to be better written than the previous one, which meant a more intriguing plot and deepening characterization. Reaching for her purse and hot-pink computer case, she recalled her last meeting with Amy and how well they'd gotten along. Hopefully that camaraderie would continue long after the novel was written.

Amy met her at the building's entrance and ushered her inside. "Good to see you. I've been looking forward to our getting together all morning." Odd how once again Amy's voice and words sounded rehearsed. A quick look into her blue eyes revealed apprehension.

"Are you sure?" Kariss said. "We can postpone this."

"Absolutely not." Amy locked the glass door behind them, then turned to Kariss. "I don't want anyone walking in off the street and thinking I'm open," she said. "You know, free counseling."

Kariss waited while Amy confirmed — four times — that the door was locked. Obsessive-compulsive disorder?

"Excuse me a moment while I inform the security company of your arrival," Amy said, heading down the hallway.

Maybe if Kariss had survived such trauma, she'd be a little OCD herself. After what Amy had been through, it was a wonder she was able to function on any level. Whoever had guided her through her ordeal had to have been a gentle counselor. Perhaps that person had encouraged her to help others too.

While waiting for Amy to reappear, Kariss studied the waiting area. A pair of contemporary, cream-colored sofas, chrome-and-green upholstered chairs, and a massive philodendron filled the room. An abstract painting above one of the sofas, painted in rich blue, green, and red, looked like something Kariss's four-year-old nephew had done with finger paint. Magazines were arranged accordion style, ready to distract an anxious client or simply entertain a reader. Ah, a hint of Amy's personality caught Kariss's attention. A collection of elephants was artfully arranged in a corner display case. The symbolism curled around her heart.

An elephant never forgot.

Amy reappeared, wearing a smile that complemented her designer jeans and green turtleneck sweater. Green was the color of healing and nurturing.

"Are we locked down?" Kariss said, making sure Amy could read her lips.

"We are. No walk-ins today."

"Those who've abused the women you've counseled would be more of a challenge than a suffering client."

Amy nodded. "Right. They're the worst."

"Ever have a problem with hostility?"

"A few." Amy gestured down the hallway. "Right this way. My office is the last one on the right."

"Before we continue, I received an email last night warning me against writing your story. Would you know anything about that?"

"No."

"What about a family member? You said they didn't support this project."

Amy startled. "You're blunt. Is that a writer's trait?"

"Sometimes it's simply research. Before I turned to suspense novels, I wrote women's fiction, and I learned to be straightforward and ask questions."

"I have no idea who'd want to discourage you."

Kariss didn't believe her. "If you did, would you tell me?"

"What kind of question is that?"

"An honest one."

"I'm a woman of integrity. You and I have a business relationship."

Kariss hadn't seen this condescension in Amy at the coffee shop. "How about friendship?"

"I'm sorry." Amy's tensed facial muscles relaxed. "Yes, we all need friends. I've been in a rough place these past two days, and I shouldn't take it out on you." She pointed to facing love seats in pale green, constant reminders of healing and nurturing. Behind Amy's desk hung a pastoral scene of sheep grazing under the watchful eye of a shepherd. Kariss recognized the artist, Larry Dyke. She had two of his prints in her condo.

"No problem. Want to talk about it?"

"Not really, but thanks." Amy smiled.

"So how long do we have this afternoon?"

"As long as it takes. In answer to your earlier question, there have been times men and women who've victimized my clients have sought revenge, which is why security measures are in place and law-enforcement numbers are at my fingertips."

"Have you ever been assaulted by one of them?"

"No. But it only takes one attack to make sure precautions are always in place."

"Do you carry a gun?"

Amy crossed her arms over her chest. "I'd never resort to a weapon. It would shatter my ministry to the hurting. Do you?"

"Yes. I've learned to defend myself. My motto is 'Never again'."

"Ever had to threaten someone with your gun?"

"I killed a man to protect an innocent one."

"It didn't make the evening news."

Kariss forced a smile. "It didn't make my scrapbook either."

"If you need counseling, I can recommend one of my other therapists."

"Thanks, but I've got it handled." Kariss pulled out a small digital recorder and her laptop. "I'll make a copy of our conversation so you can review it later for accuracy."

Amy nodded. Her wan complexion told more about the woman's mood than any words could convey. "Fair enough. I want to tell the entire story, regurgitate the past in one sitting. My brother and parents are great, but they fear for my emotional health and the possibility of my assailant coming after me again."

"I understand. But it's because they love you."

"The attack nearly ended my life, and it deserves to be told in a manner that would reach the most readers. I've done the research. I know a novel is my best option."

"Okay, then let's get started. I'll type while you talk, and I won't stop you unless I need clarification. Can you begin by telling me about your childhood, then move on to what happened the day of the assault?"

Amy took a deep breath. She looked poised, but her lips quivered for a fraction of a second. "I may repeat some things from our earlier discussion, but I want to tell the story in chronological sequence."

"Sounds good. I didn't take any notes when we met earlier."

"My family wasn't and isn't perfect. But after the attack, they worked hard to keep dysfunction tucked away. My dad is a commercial real estate investor, and my mother is an account rep for an insurance company. We did the vacation thing. Birthdays and holidays are still special. My brother and I were encouraged to work hard in school and have friends. Our door was open to the neighborhood kids. After the attack, that continued to give me a semblance of a normal childhood."

"Did your friends treat you differently after the trauma?"

"Not those my own age. But older kids and adults acted as though I were a bubble child." Amy folded her hands. "Most parents couldn't get past the horror or the realization that their child could have been the victim."

Kariss shivered. "What about your brother? Is he married?"

"He was, but it ended in divorce. No

children."

Kariss typed and listened for clues to indicate who may have hurt Amy. Although that aspect of the story had been analyzed by the most experienced criminologists, Kariss couldn't help but wonder if a new detail in the case could bring a cruel man to justice. "Are you ready to describe what happened?"

The color drained from Amy's face.

"Are you sure you want to do this?"

"Yes." Amy laid her hands in her lap. "The day I was abducted from my bedroom is as vivid now as when it happened. It was a Thursday night in mid-May. We'd returned from a school event for my brother, where he'd been a finalist in a science fair and had taken first place. We celebrated with ice cream from Dairy Queen. Mom and Dad were so proud of him. We went to bed like any normal night. I remember looking forward to summer."

Kariss noted Amy's clenched fists.

"I was woken by a hand clasped over my mouth. I could barely breathe. The other hand held what I thought was a knife to my throat. I learned later it was a piece of glass from my bedroom window. Neither my parents nor my brother heard the glass breaking."

Amy paused, and Kariss glanced up from her laptop. A tear slipped down the woman's cheek. "We had a dog, a golden retriever. Her name was Daisy. The . . . the assailant killed her. My dad found her before he realized I was missing."

"Do you want to continue?" Kariss whispered.

Amy nodded. "I simply haven't thought it through from beginning to end for a long time. This is really good for me, I think. Helps me get in touch with what my clients feel."

As if Amy needed to feel additional pain. "Did the assailant say anything?"

"Told me to be quiet or he'd kill my parents and brother. He obviously knew a little about me." Amy moved a magazine on the table in front of her. "He dragged me through my broken window. In the darkness, I never saw his face. Only felt what he did to me and heard his voice." She paused and rearranged the magazine again. "His voice has haunted me for years, and now I'm going deaf. Rather ironic, don't you think?"

The only way Amy would ever be able to identify him was his voice, and she was being robbed of her hearing. Incredibly unfair.

"Are you ready to go on?" Kariss said.

She nodded. "He carried me to a grassy field behind our house. Told me to be still or he'd go back and kill my family. I remember his breath reeked of onions. I've never been able to tolerate them since. Briars scratched my arms and legs, and I heard a siren in the distance. I thought it was someone coming to rescue me. But it wasn't. He talked to me. Told me he'd thought about this for a long time. Said I was a good girl, and that's why I was chosen. He said strange things. I had no idea what he meant. When I was older, I recognized lines from Truman Capote's novel *In Cold Blood*."

Kariss remembered the story about two men who'd murdered a Kansas family. Maybe it was time to reread it. Realization rippled through her. "He could read this, Amy. Do you realize this could force him into a face-off? You could be killed."

"You're overreacting. The man who assaulted me wouldn't read a novel written by a former women's fiction author."

Kariss studied Amy's face. Not a muscle moved. "How can you be sure?"

"If he wanted me dead, he'd have done it a long time ago." Amy stared at the empty hall, then turned to Kariss. "You don't have anything to be afraid of, and neither do I."

Kariss had seen enough danger in the past year not to risk going there again, not for herself or Amy. What would Tigo say? She shoved the thought from her mind and focused on what her heart was telling her. She wanted this project. She believed in it. "When the book is released, we have to involve law-enforcement authorities to keep you protected. Agree or I back out."

Empty moments ticked by while a myriad of emotions crossed Amy's face. "That's your stipulation?"

"Yes."

"Okay. Let's do it. We're running out of time for today."

Kariss hoped and prayed Amy would be safe. "All right. We have more work to do."

"Are you a fast writer?"

Kariss smiled. "Just watch me."

"Okay . . . in the field, he slapped me so hard I blacked out. At least I think that's what happened. Being unconscious was a blessing, because he raped me and slit my throat with that piece of glass from the window."

Kariss's stomach curdled. She focused on the positioning of her fingers on the keyboard to gain control.

"I guess he assumed I'd bleed out, because he left me there. I lay awake, drifting in and out of consciousness. I wanted to go home, but I was too weak to move. God's good, Kariss, because I didn't feel any pain. So I waited and thought about my parents. How much I loved them. And my brother. I prayed, too, and repeated Bible verses in my mind, the ones I'd learned in Sunday school. Strangely, I wasn't afraid. Sometimes I thought someone sat beside me. Maybe an angel. God was certainly there."

Kariss glanced up at Amy, her throat tightening. "I felt God was with me during my ordeal too."

Amy nodded. "This is tough for both of us."

Kariss blinked back tears and typed in rhythm to her rapidly pounding heart.

"The next morning, a couple of neighborhood boys found me. Doctors claimed my survival was a miracle, but I knew God had a special plan for me. I spent the next two months in the hospital having surgeries and learning to talk again. Then years in psychiatrists' chairs." Amy rubbed her palms. "I'm such a bad host. Would you care for something to drink? A Coke or a bottle of water?"

This had to be too much for Amy. "No, thanks. Do you want to call it quits for today?"

"I thought you wanted the whole story. Is

180

there enough material for you to begin?"

How could Kariss talk about plot points, a climax, and story resolution after this painful accounting? "This will be powerful, an inspiration to others. You are a true survivor."

"I'd like to think so."

"And you give me permission to write a climax and resolution?"

Amy leaned back against the love seat. "Use your best judgment in how you end it."

Kariss released her tight shoulder muscles. "As we proceed, I'll need to probe deeper into heart-wrenching areas."

"Bring it on." Amy's lighthearted tone failed to reach her eyes.

Testing time. "What were your thoughts while he carried you to the field?"

Amy swallowed hard. "Before I blacked out, I felt paralyzing fear. I couldn't fight him. But I believed my dad would save me."

"Did you pray about being rescued?"

"Not exactly. I'd argued with my mother about spending the night with a friend. I hadn't —"

The sound of a door opening and an ear-piercing beep signaling the countdown for the security alarm interrupted her. A small box on the table in front of them flashed red. Heavy footsteps pounded down the hallway. Amy blanched. She hurried to the doorway. Kariss grabbed her purse, where she kept her 9mm handgun.

"Baxter, you scared me." Amy placed a hand over her heart.

"Sorry. I used my key. Let me stop this thing." The alarm quieted. "I need to talk to you."

"I'm talking with someone in my office. Can you come back later, or can we meet somewhere?"

"A client on Saturday afternoon? That's unusual."

"No. A friend." Amy, red-faced, glanced at Kariss, then back to the man in the hall. "I could introduce you."

"Sure. Maybe this friend isn't as stupid as you are." His words dripped bitterness. He stepped into her office, his towering frame filling the doorway, so unlike Amy's small frame. Dressed in jeans and a dark-blue pullover, he reached out to shake Kariss's hand, and she introduced herself.

"I'm Baxter Garrett, Amy's brother." Brother and sister shared the same wide-set blue eyes and light hair.

After Kariss introduced herself, Baxter claimed a seat beside her on the love seat. Body odor permeated the air.

"Has she told you about her crazy idea of having her story published?" Baxter said.

"She has." This guy could have sent the threatening email. "You obviously don't agree with the project."

"I don't. I don't want her dead."

"Baxter, this isn't appropriate." Amy touched his knee.

"Save it." Baxter didn't make eye contact, but Amy could obviously still read his lips. "What you're proposing is dangerous. Could get you killed." He noticed the recorder, which Kariss had not shut off. "You're the writer, aren't you?" His nostrils flared.

"I am. I understand your concerns, and I want you —"

"You don't understand squat. This is family business, and I suggest you keep your nose out of it."

The threat fueled Kariss's temper. "Or what?"

He stood and shook his finger in her face. "You really don't want to find out, pretty lady."

Chapter 20

He prided himself on being a true craftsman by designing precision-made bullets that no one could trace. This afternoon he'd perfected the one he'd use for the kill, a hollow-back bullet for his Beretta .40. Perhaps his finest piece of art. Undeniable pleasure, warm and tingling, flowed through him.

He was also an expert in other means of killing — his bare hands, preferably. Unfortunately, those days were gone. Technological advances meant he had to be careful. There were so many ways to trace a person now that he'd considered retiring, and he would once Amy lay cold in a dark grave. But what would he do during idle hours while Michelle slept? For the past few years, he'd gotten by with less and less sleep, until three hours did him nicely. He could possibly work as a consultant and hire himself out to the highest bidder.

Holding the bullet to the overhead light, he considered his expert marksmanship. He'd also developed competitive archery skills, could throw a knife dead center, and had the expertise to build a bomb with plenty of scatter power. His favorite bombs were those that used Semtex. Expensive but worth it. He'd been able to pass on the cost to buyers and recoup his expenses.

Good job.

Perfect.

The voices always confirmed his artistry.

Using strains of E. coli to kill masses of people intrigued him. Lately he'd been working with coral snake venom, and the rhyme, "Red on yellow, kill a fellow. Red on black, venom lack" repeated in his mind. The little buggers were hard to find, since they hid under logs in hot, humid areas, preferring sandy soil around hardwoods. But he'd been lucky and had three good specimens to play with.

He paused. What an ingenious idea. If he hadn't already perfected the bullet for Amy, he could have painted it red and yellow. That would get the attention he deserved. Maybe he wasn't ready to retire yet.

Amy Garrett, PhD, had lived when he'd thought her dead. His fault. And because she'd survived what he believed was a perfect crime, he'd allowed her to live all these years. No one else could claim the title of survivor. She'd fought the odds and won. As always, a quote from *In Cold Blood* reminded him of her.

" 'I didn't want to harm the man. I thought he was a very nice gentleman. Soft-spoken. I thought so right up to the moment I cut his throat.' " He repeated the quote, just like the night he pulled her through her bedroom window.

He chuckled. "I didn't want to harm the little girl." He tossed the copper bullet in his hand and imagined sending it into her head. "I thought she was a very nice little girl. Soft-spoken. Sweet. Innocent. I thought so right up to the moment I cut her throat."

Another matter irritated him. A Kariss Walker had stepped in his way, but he'd devise a plan to stop her too. What a great idea. He could create another bullet like Amy's for her so they'd know no one should get in his way. His and Amy's story was their own private adventure.

He licked his lips and reached for a tall glass of tomato juice.

CHAPTER 21

4:00 P.M. SATURDAY

"I don't scare easily." Kariss wrapped her fingers around the recorder, thankful she hadn't turned it off. She stood and eyed Baxter. "I have a theory about bullies."

"You're not going to make money on my sister. She's not a sideshow freak." Baxter snarled, his wide eyes dilated. "I'm looking out for my sister, something you selfish types wouldn't know a thing about. So gather up your tools of the trade and leave. Don't ever contact Amy again."

Kariss realized her tolerance level had just reached the breaking point. "As I said, I have a theory about bullies. They either have low self-esteem, or they have something to hide." She hoped her words sounded braver than she felt with all the warning flares going off in her head. "Maybe you have both."

"Call it what you want. My sister is the most important thing in my life. My job is to protect her from losers, and you fit the bill."

"So what are you hiding?"

He stepped closer. She trembled, but she didn't back down.

"Baxter, that's enough. You have no right coming into my office and berating my friend."

"He threatened me." Kariss shook with the anger raging through her. She gathered her laptop, purse, and recorder as she attempted to speak rationally. "I've had enough of this family feud." She focused on Amy. "You said your family didn't approve of the idea, and I should have probed that statement further. My fault. But it's quite evident you have a few issues to handle before we can continue your story."

"Smart woman. Good riddance." Baxter's bravado permeated the room.

Kariss took three steps toward the door and then whirled back to face him. "I'm assuming you sent the email last night warning me against writing Amy's story. I don't take aggressive behavior lightly. If I ever hear from you again, I'll press charges." She paused to keep her anger in check. "And I don't make idle threats. I play for keeps."

He chuckled. "Glad you saw the point."

Amy clenched her fists. "Baxter, get out of

my office. Now." She reached toward Kariss. "Please don't go. I can explain."

"Explain what? That your brother needs psychological help? At this point, I wonder if he needs to be locked up." Kariss caught herself before she uttered another word. She couldn't control Baxter's behavior, but she could control her reactions. "I apologize, Amy. I'm angry and need time to cool off."

Baxter blocked the doorway. "Anyone who lives in a fiction world is a nutcase."

"Baxter, leave now," Amy said. "Wait. Give me the keys to my office, car, and my house first."

He pressed a finger against Amy's chest, towering over her. "Once I'm gone, you're on your own. He'll come after you, and this time he'll make sure you're dead."

"Your strong-arm tactics no longer affect me. Truth is, I dealt with what happened years ago. You should have too. Instead, you use my past as an excuse to intimidate me and others."

Kariss understood siblings not communicating well, but these two were drowning in the deep end. What happened to the happy family who tucked away dysfunction?

Baxter pulled out his keys and slipped one off his ring, then another.

"I won't be blamed for this." Kariss kept

her tone soft. "I'm leaving, and you two can work out your differences."

"I'm finished with you, little sister." Baxter palmed a third key into Amy's outstretched hand. "You're an idiot to put yourself out there. Go ahead. Have your story published. Hunting season is now officially open." He swung around, brushing against Kariss's shoulder, and stomped down the hall. The entry lock clicked and the door slammed, vibrating the walls.

Amy turned her attention to Kariss. "I'm so sorry."

"I appreciate your apology. But that was ludicrous."

"May I explain? Baxter has issues." She sighed. "That's obvious. Ten minutes of your time. Please?"

Staying went against Kariss's better judgment, but she didn't want to run into Baxter in the parking garage. She sat and placed her laptop and purse beside her. The recorder continued, and she didn't see a reason to stop it, especially if Baxter returned.

Amy hurried down the hall, no doubt to lock the door. Kariss blinked. Had she heard God correctly about writing Amy's story? She hadn't expected Baxter's response.

Amy stood in the doorway again. "Baxter blames himself for what happened to me. When we were kids, his bedroom was next to mine."

Her parents probably blamed themselves too. "That doesn't give him a license to threaten me. And I have a feeling I'm not the first." Kariss took a deep breath, forcing logic into the conversation.

"You're right," Amy said. "It doesn't give him a license to make life miserable for others."

"How do your parents handle him? Or do they think his behavior is acceptable?" Kariss caught her own sarcasm. "Never mind. I'll listen to your explanation."

"Thanks." Amy sat on the love seat opposite her. "My parents don't approve of his actions, but he's a grown man. I have to be the one to stand up to him. Baxter proclaimed himself my bodyguard the moment I returned home from the hospital. For over two decades, he's taken his role to the extreme. As you can see, I'm not married. Baxter has run off every man who's ever expressed interest in me. He's also destroyed any friendships with other women. I've put up with him for as long as I can. I told him those very words when he blew up about the story idea. But I never expected what just happened. Honestly, he's harmless except for his nasty tongue."

Amy shuddered. "I'm not being honest. He can be physical. But I never thought he'd barge in here and pitch a fit like a toddler." She glanced at the keys in her palm. "It's over. He won't be back. I've never taken such extreme measures before. Finally I've practiced what I encourage my clients to do."

How could Kariss be sure? "I'm the youngest of six, and we've weathered a lot of junk. Someone has to put the reins on your brother. Even if he pushes me to press charges, that will only stop him temporarily."

Amy nodded. "I'll explain his behavior to my parents. They've always encouraged me. I'll make sure he doesn't interfere again."

"How do you plan to do that?" Anger at Baxter rolled through Kariss again. "He's a ticking time bomb, and I don't want to be around when he explodes again."

"My dad could send him out of town to work on a project with one of his investment properties."

Kariss thought about her commitment to write Amy's story . . . and the possibility of helping other crime victims find healing. "That would work."

"Good. Then we're on track again?"

Kariss nodded. But Baxter Garrett was a hot match in a stack of brittle wood.

CHAPTER 22

JANUARY 20
11:00 A.M. SUNDAY

Tigo drove home from Ryan's church more
confused about the faith thing than the day
he'd decided to seek God. Taking time from
his Sunday morning seemed a waste. There
were so many other things he could be doing — sleeping, rereading interviews from
the current case, looking to see if either of
Joanna's sisters had a record, and evaluat-
ing body language from past interviews
while weighing conversations with inter-
viewees.

His dwindling view of God had slid down-
hill after learning Taylor Yeat was cheating
on his wife. Why did a good God allow such
behavior? Two people were killed while a
pastor duped his wife and his congregation.
All that talk about Joanna being such a good
person was a cover-up for his affair with her
sister. The good pastor may have denied to

194

Darena that he wanted Joanna out of the picture, but Tigo believed otherwise.

He pulled into his driveway and watched the garage door open slowly, as if some great unveiling was about to take place. Two mountain bikes perched on the right wall. In the opposite corner stood a workbench Tigo rarely used, covered by tools organized according to the job's requirements. No Tonka trucks or Barbie training-wheel bikes. Nor were there any dents in the garage wall from a sweet wife who miscalculated when to apply the car brakes. All he had was a neat, orderly life that left him alone and miserable.

He had a lawn service.

A housecleaning service.

A reputable dealer to service his car.

A dry-cleaning service to keep his clothes clean and repaired.

Phone service to ensure he stayed connected to the world.

Internet service so he could search out global information.

But he didn't have a service to repair the crack in his spirit.

He understood loneliness, but he knew Kariss couldn't cure the longing in him for something he couldn't name. So he searched and often wondered if God held the missing piece. If God had all this unconditional love, why did He allow countless crimes against the innocent? Or the premature death of Tigo's mother? Or the big screwup with Kariss? All the songs and Scripture and sermons about a great God didn't make sense when violence erupted and tragedies hit. Did Tigo believe in God or not?

He exited his truck and noted chores that needed to be done to keep the garage spotless. But why bother? Who cared? He wasn't simply frustrated — he was furious.

If only he could have a discussion with God, ask Him why He allowed psychopaths and genocides to exist. Or the countless other questions that kept him up at night.

His work phone rang, and he snatched it from the seat of his truck as though the caller were God.

"We located Carolyn Hopkins in Arkansas, and she's in transit back to Houston," an agent said. "You and Special Agent Ryan Steadman can interview her around three o'clock. He's confirmed the time."

"I'll be there. Has she given a statement?"

"Nothing other than she hates Yeat and claims she was driving to see her family during the time of the bombing."

"I doubt her parole officer gave her permission to leave the state. Anything else?"

"She was packing a stolen gun."

"Looks like she just renewed her reservation at the state prison."

Tigo ended the call, dropped the phone into his pocket, and opened the truck door. He could use answers today, beginning at three o'clock.

2:15 P.M. SUNDAY

"Why are you so antsy?" Vicki said.

Kariss swallowed the butterflies hatching in her stomach and smiled at her sister. "Your color is much better today. Having Mom here to keep you in bed was a good idea. Glad she canceled the family lunch today. You couldn't have handled the drive to Texas City."

"That didn't answer my question."

"I told Tigo I'd call. Give him an update on how you were doing."

Vicki tilted her head. "Rose and I are going to nap. We don't need a babysitter. So take your cell phone to your office and be a good girl."

"Easy for you to say."

"I've made a decision."

Kariss lifted a brow.

"I'm not going to bother you about what

happened with Tigo until you're ready to talk."

"Thanks, sis. Probably wouldn't seem big to you, but —"

"Go call him."

Kariss tossed a frown at her sister and headed to her office. After staring at the phone for several seconds, she placed the call. And hoped it wouldn't be confrontational.

"Hey. Can't sleep on a Sunday afternoon?" His familiar voice ushered in sweet memories.

"Too full. Mom made carrot cake, and I ate the last piece."

Tigo moaned. "Okay, you won that round. How's Vicki?"

"Minding Mom, which is worse than taking doctor's orders. Mom's been assigned to bedroom duty since Friday afternoon."

"Good, and thanks for the update. Tell her that mommies and FBI agents have to keep up their strength."

Kariss giggled. She'd missed their talks . . . and the wit . . . and the laughter. "I will."

"Do you still play Word Family?"

"Every chance I get."

"When was the last time you were challenged by a winner?"

Word Family was an app on her phone, a

game they used to play together. "I believe I have the trophy on the last three games."

"I'm out to cut my losses. Be expecting my word. Gotta run to an interview now."

After disconnecting, Kariss gingerly laid her cell phone on the desk as though it were Rose. Sixty seconds later, her phone alerted her to a Word Family play. Tigo had chosen R-E-G-R-E-T.

CHAPTER 23

3:30 P.M. SUNDAY

Tigo watched Carolyn Hopkins, who was seated across from him. The years of drug and alcohol abuse, along with a belligerent attitude that came with a total of six years in prison and an aversion to rehabilitation, had hardened the woman's features. Her bloodshot eyes and slurred speech indicated she'd recently dived into the devil cocaine, her drug of choice, according to her record. This type of interview always challenged Tigo, seeing what it took to draw out the truth. But she'd stretched his patience to the limit. In the past thirty minutes, Hopkins had pleaded the fifth so often, Tigo wanted to toss her rear back in jail.

He gave Ryan a smile before focusing on her again. "You're a lousy liar, Carolyn. Your stories don't line up. Which tells me you're guilty of murder."

Carolyn brushed a strand of strawlike hair

from her face, revealing fingernails bitten to the quick. "I despised Jonathan Yeat, but I didn't plant a bomb in his car."

"What did he do wrong? Didn't he give you a job after you were released from prison?"

Lines splayed from the corners of her eyes. "He paid diddly. Then took the job away. Called it cutbacks due to current economic times."

"What did you do for him?"

"Cleaned toilets and swept the floors. Got paid barely above minimum wage."

Not enough to finance a drug habit. Tigo picked up her work record. "You'd been warned about absences."

"Some days I didn't feel work was important. People shouldn't have to clock in if they'd rather be doing something else."

Tigo had met people with her type of work ethic before. "Did you want Jonathan Yeat dead?"

"Nice thought, Agent Harris, but I didn't do it." She paused and rubbed her nose. "I was on the road to Arkansas for a family reunion." She leaned in closer, giving Tigo a clear view of wrinkled cleavage.

"If you didn't plant the bomb, then who did?"

"Do I look like a walking Wikipedia?"

"You broke your parole by leaving the state, and you have a stolen gun in your possession. That says you know more than you're telling us."

Her lips trembled. "I needed protection."

"From who? Your pimp?"

"Business associates." Beads of sweat broke out on her forehead.

"Special Agent Steadman and I can help you there. Because violating your parole will get you all the protection you need. Even a guard and three squares for as long as you'd like, probably longer."

She played with a strand of hair at her temple. "You think you're so smart."

"I'm sure of it." He watched her gaze dart around the interview room. "Tell me what you know, and I'll see the judge goes easy on you."

"If I had a name, I'd give it to you. But I don't know nothin'."

"What about Semtex?"

"No clue what that is."

"Really? So you aren't going to help us. Hey, I heard you had a kid."

"She's in a foster home where she belongs. So don't pull the 'be a good mama' routine. I'm not buyin' it."

Tigo stood. Pathetic. Carolyn didn't care about anything or anyone but herself.

"We're done here until you're ready to talk."

"You sending me back to Huntsville?"

"A limo is waiting."

"You're signing my death warrant."

Tigo leaned on the table and captured her attention. "Your choice."

She pressed her lips together.

Who was she afraid of? What would it take to make her talk?

5:25 P.M. SUNDAY

Kariss walked through the security gate of her community and returned the guard's wave, forcing a smile she didn't feel. Even with an umbrella, the slow drizzle chilled her to the bone, but it matched her disheartened mood. After her parents had left, Kariss decided to take a walk while Vicki rested and attempt to sort through the thoughts warring against her heart. As the cold splatters of rain pelted her umbrella, she pondered the situation. She'd used Tigo's past to shape her future, but not in the way her loved ones believed.

What if her parents knew the truth about Tigo? She wished she knew the circumstances. Losing a baby and then having his wife leave him had to have been horrible, but why hadn't he told her? Had enough time passed that the two could talk without arguing? Then there was the problem of his lack of faith. Why did love have to be so hard?

Living alone wasn't so bad. Kariss had lived as a single since graduating from college and had adjusted quite well. Her habits were like cured concrete. Those things that ordered her life would be difficult to change. But her life was empty.

She missed Tigo, and swapping words on a phone game wasn't going to make her feel any better. Just before leaving her condo, she'd used the first R in regret to play T-R-U-T-H. Together, she and Tigo sounded like candidates for group therapy. Pulling her phone from her pocket, she typed a text.

WE NEED 2 TALK

When he didn't respond, she walked back to the security gate, where the guard waved at her again.

"Miss Walker, I have a delivery for you," the white-haired man said.

On a Sunday?

"I didn't know anyone had died." He handed her a funeral wreath covered in lilies. "I'm real sorry."

Kariss startled. "There must be a mistake."

"Take a look at the card. Maybe that will help."

She opened the envelope and read the typed note.

"The boundaries which divide Life from Death are at best shadowy and vague. Who shall say where the one ends, and where the other begins?"

Ice pelted Kariss's veins. Edgar Allan Poe.

CHAPTER 24

5:30 P.M. SUNDAY

Tigo sat in his recliner with his secure laptop and listed what he knew about the Yeat bombing. Months before, he'd done this kind of work at his mother's bedside. While she was unconscious, teetering near death, he'd labor over his latest case, often sharing with her what puzzled him . . . and his dilemmas about unsolved aspects. Close to the end, he'd talked to her about Kariss. His mother's inability to communicate hadn't mattered. He knew she cared. Now her absence left an ache in his heart. He missed her and hoped she'd died knowing how much he loved and treasured her.

He glanced down the hallway that led to what had once been her bedroom. She'd wanted him to consider mentoring teen boys who were headed down the wrong path, but he hadn't pursued it — yet. Probably a topic to bring up with Ryan, since his church had a large youth group, and some of the kids lived in Hispanic neighborhoods. Tigo could relate to the pressures, do the big brother thing. Someday soon he needed to act on it.

Turning his attention to the Yeat case, he pushed aside his loneliness to concentrate on finding who'd bombed the car. Forensics hadn't turned up anything further, but the investigators were still sorting through rubble and running diagnostics. This bad guy knew how to cover his tracks.

Before spreading out his notes on the table, he made a list of suspects and noted whether follow-up had been done or needed to be done. The interviews and various reports were only a click away, and somewhere in all of this mess was a bad guy who'd made a mistake.

Angela Bronston — Joanna's sister. Joanna persuaded her to give up her baby. Need to question.

Roger Collins — Ex-con, laid off from work. Unreliable alibi. Being tailed.

Carolyn Hopkins — Ex-con, caught in Arkansas. Hostile. May have information. Currently incarcerated.

Darena Willis — Joanna's sister. Having an affair with Taylor Yeat. Hostile. Need to question.

Jonathan Yeat — Favoritism between his sons caused marital issues. Body language indicates denial of such problems.

Ian Yeat — Angry, rebellious teen. Quarreled with Joanna about unidentified man.

Taylor Yeat — Seemed to grieve for Joanna, but that could be an act. Having an affair with Joanna's sister. Need to question.

The unidentified Caucasian man Ian saw with Joanna.

No one else fell under Tigo's scrutiny. But with the right connections, any of these suspects could have accessed Semtex. Roger Collins and Carolyn Hopkins most likely knew how to make a bomb or had a source with those skills. The other suspects would have had to find an explosives expert to do their dirty work. Tigo's informants were working on leads.

He started another list for anyone who might be withholding information. Two people made that list.

Vanessa Whitcom — Worked for Jonathan for eight years. Joanna's friend. Didn't attend the funeral. Need to question again.

Curt Yeat — Responsible teen who covers for Ian. What's he hiding?

Jonathan didn't have a partner in his firm. The interviews with contractors and sub-contractors indicated an allegiance to a man who'd built his commercial construction company with integrity. Even those companies in direct competition with Jonathan's company cleared investigation. But the killer had overseas connections somewhere.

Tigo rubbed his face, frustrated with the complexity of the case. Going undercover was more to his liking. When he was under-cover, all he had to do was catch someone in the act of breaking the law. He saved his documents and texted Ryan.

SENDING YEAT INFO. CAN U TALK?

N 10 MIN.

A few minutes later, Ryan called. "Who do we interview first?"

"I'm thinking about going to church."

"What?"

"Pastor Taylor Yeat's church. There's a Sunday-night service at seven o'clock."

Ryan chuckled. "Got it. I'll drive. Pick you up in a few minutes. Grabbing my keys now."

"What are our chances of talking to a couple of sisters tonight?"

Tigo heard the hum of Ryan's garage door opening and the sound of an engine roaring into action. "The conversation you overheard was pretty toxic."

"I also want to find out why Vanessa Whitcom didn't attend the funeral. She's a church member too."

"And here I thought you wanted a dose of God's Word."

Tigo smiled, understanding that Ryan wanted him to step into Christianity with both feet. "I'm sure I'll get it. One way or the other."

"I prefer sooner rather than later. Did you see what Vanessa turned over on her desk when we walked into her office?" Ryan said.

"Missed it."

"That's why you have me. You were too busy carrying her cranberry slush and turning on the charm. Anyway, it was a photo of Jonathan, and she laid a pad of paper over it."

"Interesting. This thing weaves tighter and tighter. I wondered if she had more than a loyal interest in him." Tigo typed "Possibly in love with Jonathan" after her name on his list.

"Right. Did Linc have anything to add after the funeral?" Ryan interrupted himself with a moan. "A car's stalled in front of me."

"We have plenty of time. Linc suspected Taylor and his wife were having problems, but he didn't think the man was stupid enough to have an affair, and certainly not with Darena. She must have quite a reputation."

"Gives hypocrite a whole new flair. I hope you aren't judging all Christians from a few rotten apples."

Tigo laughed. "I do understand the difference." He remembered his mother's strong beliefs . . . and those of Kariss's family. "I'm wondering if Darena hated her sister enough to hire a killer. I also wonder if Joanna had approached her about the affair."

"I imagine so."

"We're going to raise a few eyebrows tonight," Ryan said. "Let's find out who doesn't want to cooperate. See you in a few."

Tigo's phone alerted him to a text from Kariss. He typed out a response.

WILL CALL LATER. GOING 2 CHURCH.

He needed time to think about her text.

CHAPTER 25

Kariss dropped the funeral flowers into the trash bin but kept the card. Her insides knotted. Why the flowers had been sent was obvious, and the who was Baxter Garrett. As she walked into the house, she decided she wouldn't mention it to Vicki. She'd just pretend everything was fine. She smiled at her sister, who started chatting away about their parents and Rose.

"With all that's been going on, I didn't ask about yesterday's meeting with Dr. Garrett," Vicki said, changing the subject. She lifted Rose to her shoulder and patted her back. "Did I ever tell you I attended one of her seminars?"

The announcement took Kariss by surprise. "When was this?"

"Last December when you were in New York visiting your publisher. Her talk about dealing with violence helped me forgive Wyatt."

But Kariss wasn't so sure Amy had forgiven her abductor. Yesterday afternoon her tone had been matter-of-fact, even dismissive at times, but Kariss had sensed an undercurrent of raw emotion behind the controlled facade. "I'm glad, sis. She's helped a lot of women."

"Because of her, I decided to continue counseling."

Kariss despised the physical and mental trauma her sister had experienced over the past year — a divorce, an unplanned pregnancy, Wyatt's criminal involvement and subsequent death. Everything. Vicki deserved peace in her life. Kariss could use a little too.

"I wish I could change what happened Friday morning," Kariss said. "My prayer for you and baby Rose is for a sweet life filled with blessings."

Vicki glanced away, her eyes moist. "We can't change the past, so we move on." She lifted her chin. "I'm not frail, and I'm working through my mistakes with Wyatt. The shame and guilt still jump into my mind. Nightmares rake at my heart. It's hard to trust again when you've been hurt." She smiled. "Listen to me. I'm talking in idioms. Like one of the characters in your novels."

She sobered. "Although you've never admitted it and the media reports never indicated it, I know in my heart that Wyatt set you up to be killed." Her expression turned grim. "See, I said the dark ugly for you. No reason for you to harbor guilt either, and don't tell me it's not there."

"It does raise its head now and then."

Vicki dabbed at her eyes. "Sit down before we start behaving like hormonal teenagers again. This all started when I asked about your meeting with Amy Garrett."

Kariss formed words to respond intelligently without alarming her sister. "Not well. There's enough dysfunction in her family to start a reality show." She told Vicki about Baxter Garrett's crazy behavior, leaving out the threat.

"Odd . . . she's the victim, and he's the one who hasn't dealt with the tragedy."

"My thoughts exactly. Strange how tragedy affects people differently. Puzzling."

"Maybe God wants you to be her friend and write her story."

Kariss was glad her sister's suggestion matched her own beliefs. "I agree. Amy doesn't have any close friends. After all, who would she confide in? With her education and experience, she probably wouldn't want to bother anyone with personal problems and wind up looking inept. And she must trust me, because she gave me her personal contact information."

After eating Mom's fried chicken leftovers, Kariss opened her Kindle and read a few more chapters of *In Cold Blood*. Ever since Amy mentioned that her assailant had quoted lines from the novel, Kariss had wanted to reread it.

When the creepiness of the psychological narrative got the best of her, she powered off the Kindle and decided to call Amy. Didn't make much sense switching from a fictional nightmare to a real one, but at least here she might be able to offer a listening ear.

Amy answered on the second ring. "Kariss?"

"Yes. I'm checking on you."

Amy laughed, but it sounded forced. "Thanks, but I'm fine. Good news. My parents promised to keep Baxter away from both of us."

As though their son were in grade school? "You're sure?"

"I assure you, it's handled. He came by my office again after you left, so I called the police," Amy said. "Then he arrived at my front door. Called the police again. Sorry. That's more info than you need."

"No problem. Tell me, what kind of vehicle does Baxter drive?"

"Hmm. Usually one of my dad's company-owned vans. He does the maintenance on various commercial and privately owned office buildings. Why?"

"I thought I saw him, but I must be mistaken. This guy was in a black pickup."

"Oh . . . Baxter has a black pickup."

Kariss's throat constricted. "Special-order rims?"

"Just a plain truck. He couldn't afford anything else."

Kariss didn't know whether to be relieved or continue speculating. Amy could be wrong about the rims. And why hadn't she or her parents tried stopping Baxter in the past?

"Kariss, I'm concerned. You've seen behavior in my brother that no one in my office has a clue about. Please promise this stays between us. My practice could be severely handicapped if any of Baxter's issues leak out."

"Promise. I'm blessed with a sister who not only listens but gives wise counsel. I value my relationship with her, and I hope you can have the same trust in me."

"I do," Amy whispered. "You're an answer to prayer. Strange, but I knew it the moment we met in the coffee shop and split the oatmeal-raisin cookie."

A veil of peace draped over Kariss. "Will you be able to sleep tonight?"

"My door is quadruple-locked." She laughed, but Kariss didn't think it was funny. "And I have a German shepherd, Apollo, who is fiercely devoted."

"I'll start working on transcribing our conversation and get back to you, then."

"Great. You know, in our professions we both have to be cautious. I'm wondering if the woman befriending me wants free counseling, and you're wondering if your new friend wants a free book."

"Or worse yet" — Kariss laughed — "you're wondering whether the woman you've asked to write the next bestseller has a clue how to write."

"I once knew a tarot reader who wanted to offer her services to my clients. Said we could team up and handle all of their issues."

"I was in the bathroom at a writer's conference, and a woman shoved her manuscript under the stall door," Kariss said. "She attached a note written on a piece of toilet paper that said, 'I dreamed I was supposed to give this to you, and you'd help me get it published.' "

The tension between Amy and Kariss had eased. A few moments later, they ended the call with a decision to announce the writing project on Facebook and other social media. Kariss would also contact her agent and ask her to pitch the story to potential publishers. Amy was taking a risk, and she knew it. But courage took many forms, and Dr. Amy Garrett wanted her story written.

Kariss brewed a pot of coffee and headed to her office. She couldn't rest until the conversation she'd recorded was transcribed. In the morning she'd work on deepening characterization and toying with plot.

She glanced at the clock. Would Tigo call? She thought about the lily-covered funeral wreath and the card . . . No point involving him. He might misunderstand.

CHAPTER 26

7:00 P.M. SUNDAY

When Tigo attended the Yeats' funeral, Jonathan's church had been a sea of different faces, ages, and races. Everyone had been dressed in somber, muted colors, and the soft murmurs reflected two tragic deaths. But tonight men, women, and children were dressed in bright colors as though they were a part of a celebration. These were the members of Taylor Yeat's African-American congregation. Ladies with wide-brimmed hats and fashionable dresses, men in exquisite suits and silk ties, and children who looked as if they'd stepped out of a magazine cover.

Not what Tigo expected, but then he hadn't known what to expect. He glanced at his jeans and sports jacket, as well as Ryan's, and realized they were out of place for more reasons than just the color of their skin.

The large crowd hummed with excitement.

"Welcome, brother."

"Good to see you, sister."

Hugs and laughter rose. Tigo had no time to evaluate the mood, because his job came first.

"Ever visit an African-American church?" Ryan said.

"No. Just your church, which has a mix of every race out there and some in between."

"You're in for a spiritual treat. Our church could take notes and double our attendance."

Tigo nodded as though he understood Ryan's comment. But as far as he was concerned, the service tonight was only a way to round up everyone he wanted to talk to in one place.

Tigo and Ryan slid into a pew at the rear of the sanctuary. Linc, who had full knowledge of the agents' purpose, sat with his wife and son in the middle of the sanctuary. Tigo spotted Angela and Darena standing near the front of the sanctuary, behind Taylor Yeat's wife, a short, round woman who had a solid alibi for the day of the bombing. What was her name? He searched his mind's data bank . . . Wanda. Sympathy for what she probably didn't know swept through him, especially when Darena took Wanda's hands and gave her a kiss on the cheek. What a Judas moment.

Joanna's sisters were good-looking women, similar in appearance, with large eyes and high cheekbones. Joanna had been the most beautiful, but was that a motive for murder? After the conversation Tigo had overheard yesterday between the sisters, seeing the two women in church pretend to be devoted family made him question why he was attempting to find God at all. Too bad he didn't have a key to unlock Darena's mind — or Taylor's. Bedroom conversation could be helpful in solving this case.

Vanessa Whitcom belonged to this church as well, but she wasn't here. Maybe ill . . . or guilt-ridden. His critical views of suspects would raise the brows of a few innocent-until-proven-guilty die-hards, but Tigo had seen the result of depraved minds. He didn't trust anyone linked to this case until evidence proved otherwise.

From the moment Taylor Yeat, whom Tigo could no longer refer to as a pastor, stepped up to the pulpit until the final amen an hour later, the charismatic man delivered a resounding message smelling of sulfur. The lively music was entertaining, and Taylor used it to his advantage to highlight strategic points. Oddly enough, the sermon topic was about securing the family unit, a topic Yeat obviously hadn't researched or experienced.

At the close of the service, Tigo and Ryan stepped to one side of the center aisle to wait for Angela and Darena. Linc joined them, but his wife and son exited the church. When the sisters approached, Tigo blocked their path with his ID in full view.

"Excuse me. I'm FBI Special Agent Santiago Harris, and this is Special Agent Ryan Steadman. We're investigating the death of Joanna and Alexia Yeat. We need to talk to Darena Willis and Angela Bronston."

Angela startled. Darena stiffened.

"Excuse me, Special Agent Santiago Harris. I'm Francis Willis. Darena's husband." The man spat each word. "You have no right conducting this business in the house of our Lord."

"Sir, we apologize for the inconvenience," Tigo said, holding back a string of sarcasm. "We can talk here once the church clears, or we can go outside. We can also drive to the FBI office if that suits you. Won't take long."

"Not on Sunday." Francis puffed up his gym-sculpted frame.

"You can bring your Bible." Tigo steadied his gaze.

Linc cleared his throat. "As Agent Harris stated, we don't have to conduct the interviews here."

"I can't believe you approve of this interrogation on a Sunday." Darena tilted her head and glared at Linc. "Of course you do. This is all in the line of duty. Our sister isn't cold in the grave, and you're groping for information we don't have. Is this part of our tax dollars at work?"

"I hope you understand this jeopardizes your position as deacon," Francis said. "Approaching a grieving family as though they're criminals is morally and spiritually wrong."

"Oh, really?" Linc said. "Church is about truth, don't you agree?"

"Pastor Yeat should join us," Francis said. He walked away and soon returned with Taylor, who'd been greeting exiting parishioners. How appropriate to include the righteous pastor. The group followed Tigo, Ryan, and Linc to the front pew.

"Will the interview be conducted separately or together?" Angela's voice quivered.

"Your choice," Linc said. "Agent Harris will lead the interview, and Agent Steadman will take notes. I'm here in support of my agents."

"Let's do it together." Darena swung her

attention to Angela. "You can handle this, honey. We're right here beside you. Did you take a Valium before church?"

Angela nodded. "Just half because I was driving."

Darena handed her a tissue. "We have to stick together."

Not exactly the way she'd spoken to her sister the previous day.

"If you feel at any time that you'd prefer responding privately, let us know." Linc spoke softly but with authority, one of his admirable traits.

"I'm sure there's a good reason for Linc to initiate this questioning on the day of our Lord." Taylor's face was devoid of emotion. "And there's probably safety in numbers."

Tigo would remember the comment. "Do any of you have information about Jonathan's family that you have not yet revealed to the authorities?"

Tigo observed body language — Angela's eyes narrowed for a second before she lifted her chin. Darena gave a wave of denial. Taylor remained stoic.

"Where were you ladies the morning of Wednesday, January sixteenth?" Tigo said.

"I was at my job," Angela said. "I'm a buyer at Macy's, and we were in a staff meeting." She reached into her purse and handed him a card. "I'll call you with those who were in the meeting with me."

Tigo nodded his approval. "Mrs. Willis?" The woman reminded him of a banty rooster, complete with feathers.

"I was at my job, and that can be verified. You, Agent Harris, will hear from my lawyer."

Tigo slid her a smile. "Go for it."

"And I was praying at the park across from my church. Wednesday, you know, and a sermon to give."

"Thanks, Pastor Yeat, for volunteering your whereabouts." Criminals often offered unasked-for information to cover their rears.

Tigo formed his next question. "How were your relationships with Joanna? Were you close?"

Angela's body language displayed grief. "I wish we'd been closer. I could have been a better sister. She never refused me anything."

"We were so close we could tell what the other was thinking," Darena said, and pulled a tissue from her purse.

Francis stepped in front of her. "Can't you tell this is upsetting my wife?"

Tigo ignored him, feeling sorry for what the man didn't know. "Was Joanna the type of woman in whom others confided?"

225

"Always." Angela cleared her throat. "She had a gift for listening and not condemning. Pastor Taylor said the same at the funeral."

Darena wrapped her arm around Angela's waist and glared at Tigo. "If you'd have listened at the service, you'd have heard how Joanna ministered to others."

Angela's eyes glistened. "After my failed marriage, she counseled me on many occasions."

"Do either of you feel you could be in danger as well?"

Both denied feeling unsafe.

"Do you know anyone who may have wanted a member of the Yeat family dead? Were you aware Joanna had filed for divorce?"

"I heard she was having an affair . . ." Darena adjusted her shoulder purse. "With one of the ex-cons who worked for Jonathan." Tigo could practically see her fangs shining.

"No, you didn't." Angela glared at her. "You're making that up."

"Are you calling me a liar in God's house?"

"I am," Angela said. "He would too."

"Why you —"

"Enough," Linc said. "Answer the agent's

question, then take your arguments outside. Or we can escort both of you to the FBI office."

"I have my rights," Darena said. "I don't appreciate being questioned as though I'm a lowlife suspect."

"Ma'am," Tigo began, "I overheard everything you, the good pastor, and Angela said on Jonathan's patio yesterday after the funeral. I could repeat it word for word to refresh your memory." He showed her his phone. "I have it all right here, and I'm all about airing dirty laundry."

"What is that supposed to mean?" Darena clenched her jaw.

"Nothing, unless you have something to hide."

She paled for a second. Then her face reddened. "How dare you eavesdrop on personal conversations and then accuse us of murder?"

"We haven't accused anyone. We're asking questions. Be glad you have an alibi, or I'd have you arrested." Tigo didn't trust her. Taylor's hard swallow clearly indicated fear, but Tigo would analyze it later. "Pastor Yeat, do you have anything to add? You were present during a portion of the patio conversation."

Not a muscle moved on Taylor's face. "I

do not. I believe anything you heard from me yesterday was a means of comforting a family member."

Tigo stared into his dark brown eyes. "Of course. What was the line from the hymn tonight? 'Savior, like a Shepherd lead us'?"

"I'm leaving," Darena said. "If you have any further questions, you can contact my attorney." She made a grand demonstration of leaving the group. Her stilettos tapped an angry message on the wood floor. Her husband followed.

Did she have a leash for him? Tigo smiled at Angela. "Do you have anything to add to the interview?"

Angela moistened her lips. "I'll do anything to help. Since you heard our conversation yesterday, you understand Darena has her difficult moments. I'll be praying you find my sister's and niece's killer soon."

"Thank you for your cooperation." Tigo handed his business card to Angela and gave another to Taylor. "Please contact us with any concerns or information."

Tigo stared at the back of the church, where Darena was shoving past a few lingering people.

Definitely a woman who had something to hide. What else lay beneath her narcissism and her affair with the church's pastor?

CHAPTER 27

Kariss lay in bed and wished she could sleep. Her body ached from an exhausting weekend, but her mind refused to stop spinning. How could so much occur in three days?

Tigo had called after nine thirty.

"Can I get back with you in the morning?" he'd said. "Not sure about my schedule until I get to work."

"It's not important."

"Kariss, anything that connects you and me is important. I owe you an explanation."

"Yes. I need closure."

The ensuing silence had caused her to wonder if she'd made him angry. If he thought one conversation would make things right between them, he could forget it.

"As in 'resolve the problem' closure or 'no

229

chance of us starting over' closure?" he said.

"Tigo, you demand truth in all your investigative work. When you don't get it, you explode in sarcasm and daredevil exploits until you find it. Truth is important to you. And to me. I need you to explain why you kept your past from me."

"I didn't want to deal with it. The situation was over."

"So are we, if that's all you have to say."

He had sighed. "All right. I'll dive into the whole mess."

"Thanks. I'll talk to you tomorrow then." She had ended the call, wanting to scream at him for hurting her. Perhaps exhaustion had more to do with it than anger, though.

Now, as Kariss attempted to drift into sleep's twilight, that place where her mind would completely shut down, her thoughts stayed fixed on Tigo instead.

Seeing him at the hospital had shaken her to the core.

Being near him caused her to question why she'd ended their relationship.

The scent of him and the sound of his voice created a longing so intense, Kariss couldn't think. She wanted to be in charge of her feelings, not overcome by them.

In the past, when he'd been upset with her, his tone had always demonstrated his caring. She missed what they'd had to-gether. If only he'd told her everything about his life instead of omitting the most important thing she should have been told. A failed marriage.

Honesty was so painful.

She swung her feet over the side of the bed and walked to the kitchen for a drink of water, her last-ditch effort to coax her body to sleep. Shadows played across her furniture, conjuring memories of times she and Tigo had spent together. After filling a glass, she stepped into the living room and made her way to the window.

Kariss startled and ducked to the side. Who was standing at the end of her driveway? A man, who had his hands shoved into his pockets, appeared to be staring at her house. Odd. Her community was gated, and she didn't recognize the man's build. He didn't have a dog with him, which eliminated the most obvious reason he would be out at this hour . . .

He nodded, as though addressing her, then walked away.

CHAPTER 28

6:00 A.M. MONDAY

Kariss read the morning news from her iPhone while walking the third mile on her treadmill. It was a great way to surf through the headlines and read the articles that seized her attention while also getting her exercise. She'd love to read good news for a change. Instead, reality ticked on about an African country that was committing genocide among its own people, about a country that threatened the free world with plans to test a nuclear bomb, and about Christians being blamed for the world's economic woes. She hesitated to weed through the articles about the United States.

Her body ached from lack of sleep. In the wee hours of the morning, she'd called the security gate with her concern about the man who'd been in her driveway, but the guard hadn't observed anyone unusual. Those entering the gated community had all been accounted for.

"We have some visitors," he'd said. "Maybe one of them was out walking."

But she'd still been too keyed up to sleep. She'd gotten up to check her security system at least four times and then chided herself for being obsessive-compulsive like Amy.

Kariss turned her attention again to the news on her iPhone. While reading a Houston headline, fear gripped her — "Noted Psychologist's Car Bombed." Blinking, Kariss attributed her rising anxiety about Amy to the weekend's series of one trauma after another. She swept her finger across her iPhone screen to read the full article.

A car bomb detonated at 12:30 a.m. Monday in a Walgreen's parking lot in northwest Houston. No one was injured in the blast, but some collateral property damage was reported. The vehicle involved in the explosion was registered to local psychologist Dr. Amy Garrett. Dr. Garrett is the director of Freedom's Way, a clinic that treats women who have been victims of violent crime. Dr. Garrett, who was inside the store at the time of the blast, declined to comment on a possible motive for the bombing. Authorities are investigating the explosion.

Oh no. Would Baxter resort to hurting his sister? How could Kariss find out if an arrest had been made?

Tigo.

He'd have information about this.

She should tell him about Baxter. She doubted Amy would mention her brother unless she had substantial proof of his guilt, and maybe not even then. Kariss shook her head to dispel the dilemma of letting the authorities work through the matter themselves or contacting the one man whose skills, in her opinion, rivaled any mastermind.

Without another moment of hesitation, she pressed in Tigo's personal cell phone number and powered off the treadmill.

"You're calling pretty early. This must be important." His deep voice caused her heart to work faster than it had during exercise.

"It is. The car bombing early this morning, the one concerning Dr. Amy Garrett? I think I may have some helpful information."

"What do you know?"

She imagined Tigo scrabbling for a pen and any slip of paper that would hold ink. "Dr. Amy Garrett is a new friend of mine.

We're collaborating on a book project, and I have a little insight into her situation."

"Kariss, have you gotten yourself into trouble again?"

Had she? "I don't think so. I was with her Saturday afternoon, and there was an incident with her brother that creeped me out."

"His name?"

"Baxter Garrett."

"Let's hear it."

"I was at Amy's office, talking with her about her story, when he let himself in. He is strongly opposed to the writing project, though it's a pretty amazing account. Anyway, he blew up, and they had a horrible argument. He didn't sound rational."

"Most angry people don't."

She heard a click and envisioned Tigo tapping his pen on a hard surface, probably the kitchen counter. She'd seen him take notes on a paper towel before.

"Tell me all of it," he said.

"Baxter was near violent. Threatened me. I'd received an email Friday night warning me about writing the book, and he basically admitted sending it. I don't know if Amy would ever implicate her brother. But she did tell me she had to call the police on her brother twice later Saturday."

"Could this Baxter be the guy who ran

you off the road?"

"Not sure. Amy told me Baxter has a black truck, but he doesn't have custom rims."

"What are you not telling me?"

What mattered was keeping Amy safe. "I gave Amy my word not to pass on everything she's told me about Baxter. But you might want to talk to him."

"Are you afraid?"

"I can take care of myself."

"Okay." He blew out a sigh. "I'm working on another case, but I'll see what I can do with this one."

"Amy has history," Kariss added. "It's the root of the problem with her brother."

"What kind of history?"

Kariss hesitated, but he could read it all on Amy's website. "A cold case. As a child, she was abducted and viciously assaulted. Left for dead. Never found the man who did it. That's our book."

Tigo moaned. "How do you manage to meet these people? Did you place an ad in the *Gullible Times*?"

"I may have. Makes for great reading. But this one found me."

"Congrats. Brew a pot of coffee. I'll be there in forty-five minutes."

"It's not —"

"Be looking for me so I don't have to ring the doorbell and wake Vicki and the baby."

The phone disconnected. Kariss hurried to her bedroom for a quick shower, wondering if she was looking forward to seeing Tigo or dreading it.

7:15 A.M. MONDAY

The moment Kariss appeared in the doorway of her condo, Tigo's resolve to handle the Garrett car bombing like a routine case vanished. Last summer he'd thought Kariss was hot. He still did. Dark hair and lips that begged to be kissed. He gazed into the pecan-colored eyes that had held him captive since he and Kariss had first met.

The longer he was around her, the more time he craved with her. At the hospital he'd done a good job of masking the feelings that had nearly driven him crazy. But this morning was different. She could have asked him to climb on her roof and knock down a dozen wasp nests, and he'd have done it.

Slow your hormones. You're not eighteen. This is business. Or so he told himself.

"Coffee's ready." Her lips curved into a smile. "Black and strong."

"Thanks." He could handle this — just get the facts.

"I need to thank you for coming over."

"No problem. Strictly business, of course."
She nodded.

They were both liars.

"Come in. I think I heard Vicki and Rose moving about."

"Good. Would love to see them again. Vicki doing all right?"

"She says so, but I'm keeping an eye on her. Still having headaches, but what else would a person with a mild concussion expect?"

"And stitches."

"Oh, she covers them with her hair — as if I could forget."

He followed Kariss to the kitchen. "Is she still whipping up five-star restaurant food?"

"When Rose isn't keeping her busy." Kariss reached into the cabinet and pulled out his favorite supersize black mug that had a picture of a chromed-out Harley on the side.

The gesture gave him hope. If not for today, perhaps tomorrow. She poured two mugs of coffee, leaving room in hers for half-and-half. Her slender fingers wrapped around his mug to hand it to him.

"I made cinnamon rolls."

Her specialty. "Homemade with frosting?"

"Yes. Lots of butter too." She blushed, and he enjoyed every inch of added color.

He wanted to think this was a homecoming, but he knew better.

"Do I hear Tigo?" Vicki rounded the corner wearing jeans and a sweatshirt. Rose was nestled in her arms, wrapped in a pink blanket.

"You do." He held out his arms. "May I hold her? We got along fine at the hospital."

Vicki placed the baby in his arms. Rose was so little, but she already possessed the Walker women's charm. He planted a kiss on Rose's forehead.

"Tigo, are you a baby whisperer?" Vicki's voice rang with laughter.

"Yeah. Gives me a protective feeling, and I know she can't break my heart." He ignored Kariss. Vicki chuckled, but he wasn't going to glance her way either. "She is a beauty."

"Thanks. I doubt you're here to see me or Rose, so I'll grab a glass of OJ and make my escape."

In less than two minutes, Tigo was alone with Kariss, feeling as awkward as a schoolboy. "I need to hear the whole story about what happened at Amy Garrett's office. Word for word. To give insight into the car bombing. I've moved an interview, so we can talk until eight thirty."

"What do you know about the case at this

point?" she said.

"Triggered by a cell phone. No forensic report yet. No one hurt. The blast destroyed the car and caused some property damage. Dr. Garrett has no idea who planted the bomb. All that you can get online."

Her gaze flew to his. "You don't believe Amy?"

He shrugged. "With her profession, she has files full of suspects."

She sat on a stool at the counter, reminding him of a few months before when his world's axis tipped in her direction. She sipped her coffee. "I had an appointment with Amy at two thirty on Saturday afternoon. The first thing that struck me as odd was the number of times she checked the locks on her door and her office's elaborate security system. I assumed the extra precautions came from her childhood experience, but now I wonder who else she's afraid of."

"I googled her earlier."

Kariss took a generous sip of coffee before continuing. Tigo listened, storing the testimony about the volatile brother where he could recall it later.

"I can't give you confidential information, only my observations and what happened to me," she said.

"I'll have her brother brought in for

questioning, and I'll talk to Amy myself."

"Thanks. I don't want to betray her confidence."

Tigo's Buzz Lightyear watch beeped, bringing his time with Kariss to an end. If only she'd express what he saw in her eyes. But she wouldn't, and his idiocy was to blame.

"I've got to go," he said, "but I'll check back with you later." He saw her hesitation. "About the Garrett bombing and our discussion."

She stared into her coffee. "I . . . I admire who she is and what she does. With the bomber behind bars, Amy and I will be able to continue our work on the novel without any more interruptions."

"I understand. If Baxter Garrett contacts you again, let me know." He finished his coffee. "One more question."

"Sure."

"Writing Amy's story seems dangerous. Can I ask you to put it on hold, at least until we nab the bomber?"

"I can't."

"You must have a short memory. It's a cold case, which means the assailant is still out there. Apprehending the bomber won't eliminate the danger."

"I can take care of myself."

"Heard that before." He walked toward the door. "You —"

"Tigo."

The tone in her voice stopped him cold. Did she have to be so stubborn?

"It's my job to make sure the innocent are safe," Tigo said.

She took a breath. "I understand, and I appreciate it."

Real men didn't wimp out over a woman.

Yes, they did.

Tigo still owed Kariss an explanation about his past. He could almost hear his mother's warning. *"Santiago, until your standards are the same as God's, your pride will win."*

CHAPTER 29

9:00 A.M. MONDAY

Vanessa Whitcom nursed a cup of coffee in an FBI interview room while Tigo and Ryan poured their own. Tigo studied the woman. She wasn't a glamorous type, but she was attractive and personable. His mind zipped to other possible situations that could have occurred at her office. Had Jonathan taken notice of Vanessa? Perhaps because he and Joanna were having problems?

Tigo sat opposite her. This time he'd handle the interview. "Why weren't you at the funeral? You'd stated that you and Joanna were close."

"Flu," she said. "Or some kind of bug. Couldn't stop vomiting. Ended up going to the ER." She sat the cup on the table. "Drinking this is a bad idea."

"Which ER?"

"Methodist downtown." She reached inside her purse and pulled out the treatment plan and discharge papers. "I figured I'd be on your most-wanted list."

He grinned. "The FBI's website was calling your name."

"I wanted to be at the funeral. But my stomach objected. Guess the stress threw my immune system out of whack." Her eyes brimmed with tears. "Joanna and Alexia probably think I don't care."

"What about Jonathan?"

"I texted him from the ER about my illness."

Tigo allowed a few moments to pass. "Were you and Jonathan involved?"

The crinkles around her eyes deepened. "Jonathan loved Joanna. Period."

"What about you?"

"My feelings for him are of friendship and respect."

Tigo wouldn't explore her response unless she gave him reason to. She'd been at work the day of the bombing. "What can you tell me about Darena Willis?"

Vanessa shuddered. "She's a b— witch. Lying and manipulating. Borrowed thousands of dollars from Joanna, and I know she never paid back a cent of it."

"What did she spend it on?"

"Clothes, jewelry, credit card debt."

"Joanna was a smart woman. Why would

she give Darena money?"

Vanessa blinked. "Trying to buy her sister's love."

"How did Jonathan feel about the relationship?"

"They argued. He gave in."

Tigo leaned in closer. "What else did they argue about?"

He waited.

Several seconds passed.

"Vanessa, what else did they argue about?"

She toyed with her cup. "I suppose you'll find out about this during the investigation anyway. They argued about Ian. His behavior seemed to be getting worse."

"Why did they disagree?"

Vanessa hesitated before speaking. "Joanna wanted to ship Ian off to a military school. Jonathan couldn't handle the thought. I was caught in the middle."

"Is Ian why she filed for divorce?"

Vanessa reached inside her purse for a tissue. "I doubt it."

"Why?"

"Because Jonathan and Joanna were committed to their marriage and their children." She swallowed. "They were working on their problem with Ian."

So Tigo's suspicions were true. Vanessa was in love with Jonathan. "Is he why you befriended Joanna?"

Vanessa's gaze darted about the room before coming back to his. "In the beginning. But I enjoyed her company and admired her. She had a genuine desire to help others. We became good friends. God put Jonathan and Joanna together." She leaned back in her chair.

"What else, Vanessa? We need to find out who bombed that car."

"Jonathan didn't know everything about her."

"Most men spend a lifetime getting to know their women."

Vanessa stared at her trembling hands. "A man from her college days wouldn't leave her alone. She wouldn't tell me what was going on, but it had to be horrible." Vanessa tucked a wayward curl behind her ear. "He'd been harassing her, and she was afraid. He wanted money. He said he'd go to the local papers with some news if he didn't get it. Said he'd ruin Jonathan's name. Joanna told me last Monday at lunch. The more I think about it, the more I'm convinced that's why she filed for divorce — to save Jonathan's reputation."

Now a few things were starting to click.

When Amy didn't answer her cell phone, Kariss phoned Freedom's Way and learned that Amy planned to be in at ten o'clock. Kariss grabbed her keys. Although their friendship was in the embryonic stage, she wanted to be there for Amy. The car bombing had to have rattled some old fears, and if Kariss was right, Amy would need a listening ear.

Within fifteen minutes, she arrived at Freedom's Way. The office building's parking garage was full, leaving her no choice but to park across the street. A steady rain, cold and unforgiving, beat against her windshield, characteristic of Houston winters. The dampness sent the cold into her bones, and she often thought the freezing temps of the north might be easier to handle. Shouldering her purse and balancing her umbrella, she entered Freedom's Way.

A young woman greeted her. "I'm sorry, Miss Walker," the woman said after hearing Kariss's request, "but Dr. Garrett will be detained until midafternoon."

After writing a quick note to Amy, she exited the building. Holding tight to her umbrella, she hurried across the street.

"Don't know when to quit, do you?"

Kariss swung around to face Baxter Garrett, who was still dressed in the same dirty jeans and dark-blue pullover from Saturday afternoon. He smelled rank. Stepping closer, he invaded her personal space.

"Excuse me?"

He lifted his chin. "I don't appreciate your turning my sister against me."

"You accomplished that all by yourself."

"We were fine until you contacted her about writing that book."

"Get your facts straight. She contacted me."

"I hate a liar. This is the last time I'm warning you to stay away from my sister."

Kariss's knees weakened. Where were the police when she needed them? "And if I don't?"

He smiled from the corner of his mouth. "I'm not stupid enough to say what. But your pretty face might not look so good. Only a warped mind would use what Amy went through to make money."

"Don't you have a job?"

"Looking down on me with your so-called success won't stop me."

She moved her right hand toward the top of her purse. Her 9mm handgun lay just inside. "I told you last time what I'd do if you persisted with your threats. So now you can tell your pathetic tale to the police or the FBI."

Baxter's hand flashed out. He gripped her right arm and squeezed. "You need to learn a lesson, and I'm just the man to do it."

Kariss dropped her umbrella. Keeping her right arm close to her body, she swung the heel of her left hand into his Adam's apple. Baxter lost his grip on her arm and stumbled backward onto the pavement.

"Think about that before you decide to teach me a lesson." With water dripping from every inch of her, Kariss picked up her umbrella. "Do you want more?"

Baxter attempted to stand.

"You're pathetic." She slid into her car and locked the doors. She wondered whether to contact the police or phone Tigo.

The latter won out. Tigo already knew the situation and had Baxter's name. After all, bad guys were his area of expertise.

CHAPTER 30

"What has the FIG turned up about Joanna's college days?" Tigo stepped into Ryan's cubicle, wishing the Yeat case was solved so he could move on.

Ryan's brows were drawn tighter than stretched rubber bands. "I'll get it when you do," he snapped.

Tigo shook his head. "Sorry. My mind's occupied with too many things."

Ryan gave a half smile. "Didn't mean to bite your head off. Cindy's birthday is Friday, and I haven't bought her anything. I'm thinking it should be more of a peace offering, what with the decision we need to make about her mother." He rubbed a hand over his bald head. "Sit down and counsel me."

Tigo slid into a chair. "Flowers, jewelry, and chocolate."

Ryan frowned. "Which one?"

"All three. Can't miss with that. Might even get you out of the doghouse."

"It would be worth it, no matter the strain on my wallet. Okay, a dozen red roses, a garnet necklace, and Godiva chocolates."

"She'll be butter in your hands. Take her to dinner too."

"Experience speaking?"

Tigo scowled and didn't attempt to hide it. "Not lately. But it's supposed to charm the ladies."

Ryan sighed. "It's been so hard to discuss the situation about her mom with the kids around. We've resorted to email, which lacks that personal touch. And our night out didn't happen because the babysitter canceled. So I've lined up things for Saturday — birthday and getting our marriage back on track." Ryan jotted down a few things on a pad of paper. "But back to you. You're distracted, and I know you saw Kariss this morning."

"I did, but it's the Yeat case that's driving me nuts. We've hit one snag after another. But I think Vanessa gave us a good suspect."

"Ian saw Joanna with a man, and she refused to discuss it. Then she tells Vanessa about a guy from her college days harassing her. She files for divorce on Tuesday and is killed the following day."

"Could Jonathan have been the target?" Tigo said. "A way to keep Joanna in line?"

"Maybe. I think we have our man, especially if the artist's sketch IDs him."

"I told Kariss I'd work on the Garrett bombing case." Tigo switched topics. "I already called Ric Montoya, so I won't be stepping on HPD's feet. We're good there."

"We? How did I get so lucky?" Ryan said. "And how did Kariss get involved?"

"The Garrett woman is a friend." Tigo shoved aside his feelings for Kariss so he could focus on the case objectively. "The two are collaborating on a book. Cold case."

"Sounds like déjà vu to me."

"She's too smart to knock on danger's door again." Tigo wished he believed it. But when it came to championing a victim, Kariss was the first to bat.

Ryan raised a brow. "So you believe in Santa Claus and the Easter bunny too?"

Tigo's iPhone rang. Kariss. He figured she must want information about the bombing. He responded with his best professional voice — for Ryan's benefit.

"Tigo, I need your help." Her voice sounded shaky. "I'm in over my head. Can't figure out how to handle this mess on my own." She paused briefly. "If you're busy, I'd appreciate a call back later."

But his attention had zeroed in immediately. "What happened?"

"I went to Amy's office to see if I could do anything to help. When I left, Baxter Garrett came breathing down my neck. He threatened me and grabbed my arm. Said I needed to learn a lesson. I defended myself. Anyway, I'm ready to file charges and get that menace off the streets."

"HPD wants to bring him in for questioning anyway. Where are you now?"

"Home. I wanted time to think before calling you."

"I'll be there after work. By then I'll have more information."

"Would you rather I contact HPD? I know this is out of your jurisdiction."

"You did the right thing. Stay put today. I mean it. No detective work. Don't answer the door or the phone unless it's someone you know."

"Okay. Thanks."

Tigo dropped his phone back into his pocket. "Amy Garrett's brother just stepped over the line. He assaulted Kariss."

"Is she okay?"

"Says she is."

"Sure you don't want me to handle it?"

Tigo grinned. "And ruin my chances to get back together with her?" He clenched his fist, realizing his anger could affect his judgment. "Baxter Garrett has no idea how tough I can be."

Their Blackberrys sounded with an incoming message from the FIG. The message informed them that Joanna Yeat had worked for an escort service while in college. She'd also done some modeling for the same company. The photographer was David Smith. An alias. No known address. No social security number. Possibly linked to other crimes.

"Blackmail," Tigo said. "I want to talk to this guy as soon as we can find him."

11:30 A.M. MONDAY
Kariss poured a glass of blackberry-sage iced tea and walked into her office. Depression hung over her like a shroud. The idea of staying home while her mind raced faster than the Indy 500 had no appeal, but her other choice fell off the deep end of common sense. She'd tried to call Amy again, but there'd been no answer. Baxter's unexpected presence at Amy's office building had shaken Kariss, but she did know how to take care of herself. Still, chasing down trouble usually meant trouble ended up chasing her — with deadly intent.

Could Baxter have been the driver of the

pickup on Saturday morning? That meant he'd been waiting for her to leave her gated community. Eerie thought. Premeditated aggravation . . . if there was such a thing. But Amy had assured her that Baxter's truck didn't have custom rims, so it couldn't be the same one that had landed Vicki in the ER. What about the funeral flowers and card? And the emails? Kariss was fishing for answers but not getting any bites.

The thought of Baxter harming his sister made little sense, unless his disturbed mind believed this was the only way to convince her she needed protection.

Kariss shuddered. Weird people were capable of bizarre behavior. The media reported on tons of them. The FBI had files filled with information about them.

Okay, so what could she do to occupy her mind before Tigo arrived later this afternoon? Her editor wanted her to brainstorm a stand-alone novel involving the Border Patrol in Texas. And she wanted to explore an ending to Amy's story. But she couldn't concentrate on either one. Vicki planned to take Rose to a late-afternoon doctor's appointment . . . which meant Kariss and Tigo would be alone.

She had to stay focused on anything but giving in to how she felt about Tigo.

What if his explanation for his deceit made sense?

What if he'd made the decision to follow Jesus?

Kariss wished her writer's mind would stop exploding with what-ifs.

After updating her Facebook status and re-tweeting a mention on Twitter, Kariss typed up a blog post about eccentric behavior in characters. Once she was done with that, she decided that making a batch of oatmeal-raisin cookies would keep her mind off Baxter and Tigo. She could smell the cookies now, made with real butter and extra cinnamon. Her cooking attempts were a disaster, but baking she could do.

First she'd check email.

Her agent had received a contract offer for Amy's story. Wonderful news. The novel had potential to help other victims of violent crime and give Amy some closure. Ultimately, though, Kariss knew Amy's nightmare wouldn't end until the case was solved and the assailant was brought to justice. Amy wanted her story told to help other women, but Kariss hoped the novel might somehow lead to a break in the case.

Kariss scrolled through her in-box and spotted a message from sender J. T. Ripper. It had been sent at 11:43 a.m.

You made a mistake going to Amy's office today. I'm watching. You're stupid, Kariss Walker. Keep it up, and your career will be over.

Baxter had just made another huge mistake. Kariss's fingers pounded the keyboard.

How am I making a mistake?

She pressed Send, but the message was instantly returned with a delivery-failure notice. Another email sailed into her in-box from J. T. Ripper.

Don't you wish you knew what was going on? Leave Amy alone. She's mine.

Rubbing her arms, Kariss walked to the window and closed the drapes. Baxter Garrett had more than a few issues. Tigo would want to know about these emails too. He'd trace them and end Baxter's little tirade.

CHAPTER 31

12:30 P.M. MONDAY

Tigo frequently needed information found only on the streets, but his informants often needed a little encouragement. This was especially true of the man who'd helped the FBI save Kariss's life and close down a gun-smuggling operation last summer. A face-to-face accompanied by cash for past services would sweeten the conversation.

Tigo and Ryan left the FBI office dressed in torn jeans, black T-shirts, and baseball caps. Tigo drove his latest junk heap, a '77 Ford Taurus he'd named Swiss Cheese because of all its bullet holes. He drove to the southeast part of town to talk to Hershey, the informant, who operated a gun shop. Sometimes legal and sometimes not. The man had skirted the law with his gun trade for the past decade. Supposedly he'd ended his lucrative career of modifying vehicles so they could transport illegal weapons into Mexico, but Tigo would tackle the downside of Hershey's dealings another day.

Outside the gun shop, African-American gang members played rap and talked trash. Every nerve in Tigo's body was on alert.

"I love this part of our job," Ryan said.

"Don't you know it."

"Want to take on a few of these guys?"

Tigo chuckled. "Hershey might not appreciate us running off his customers."

With their Glocks tucked into the waistbands of their jeans, Tigo and Ryan exited the car and buzzed the alarm for Hershey to unlock the door. Once inside, Tigo waited for his eyes to adjust to the lack of light.

"You're bad for business." Hershey's voice came from a rear corner.

"Hey, Hershey," Tigo said. "Miss me?"

"Come back in six months and ask me again."

Tigo laughed. "Turn on a light so I can see your ugly face."

"Yeah. At least I got friends."

"Mine don't have records." A light flipped on. Hershey leaned against a dirty glass display case and waved. "I see you brought your partner, the one who always has his fingers resting on his Glock."

Ryan laughed. "You got my game."

Tigo stepped up to the counter and slipped Hershey his payment.

"What's up?"

"Who's selling Semtex now that Pablo Martinez is dead?" Tigo said.

"Ask me something easy."

"You're the expert."

"Not this time. But I'll see what I can find out."

"We also want to know who's buying."

"That'll be harder."

"You'll figure it out."

"What I do know is this guy covers his tracks and eliminates the source."

"All we need's a name."

"Call me in a couple days."

"How about tomorrow?" Tigo said.

Hershey shook his head. "I'll call you."

Tigo nodded toward the door. "What's going on outside? I counted a dozen men, all gang members. Are you having a sale?"

"Nosey, aren't you? Couple of guys killed in a fight last night. Gang stuff. Does that suit you?"

"Maybe. Find out who's selling and buying Semtex, and I'll add a few more dollars to the next envelope."

Hershey smiled, but it didn't reach his eyes. Never did.

Tigo had received a text about the FBI picking up Baxter Garrett at eleven thirty that morning, but he and Ryan had been busy until now. Garrett had been in a black pickup outside of his sister's office in a no-parking zone. When he emerged from his truck, he took a swing at a female agent.

Not good for a man who'd possibly bombed his sister's car.

Nor was it good for a man suspected of running a car off the road and threatening a woman.

Tigo and Ryan met with Garrett in an interview room. The suspect reeked of body odor, and his clothes were covered in mud. Garrett was tapping his hand on his knee. He crossed his legs. The tapping continued. He uncrossed his legs. Sweat dripped down his face.

After Tigo introduced himself and Ryan, he offered Garrett a bottle of water.

"Why am I here?" Garrett uncapped the bottle. "I didn't do anything."

"You've been a busy boy," Tigo said. "And you need a fix."

"What are you talking about?" Garrett spat the words.

"What's your drug of choice?"

Garrett smirked. "What I do is none of

your business." He took a long drink of the water.

"Wrong answer, buddy. We have a list of questions." Tigo picked up a printout of Garrett's priors. "You've been arrested for possession and assault and battery. Got a temper, I see."

"I was never convicted. Do I need my lawyer?"

"Your choice."

Garrett narrowed his brows. "Bring on your questions. I haven't done anything to break the law."

That's a joke. "Let's start with Friday morning around eight twenty. A black pickup ran a car off the road. Happened in the Tomball area. The car contained two women and a baby. Where were you?"

Garrett twisted in the chair. "Running errands for my father. Documented and witnessed. I'll even give you the numbers to reach the witnesses."

Tigo vowed to follow up personally. "You own a black pickup."

"So do lots of other people."

True. Tigo's truck was black. Most guys preferred black because it gave off a mysterious, macho image. But Garrett's truck had a dent in the right rear bumper. Unfortunately, it didn't have custom rims, and the license plate numbers didn't contain a V or an 8. "We'll need to check out your alibi. Let's move on. You threatened Kariss Walker on Saturday afternoon and assaulted her this morning. Explain that."

Baxter leaned in. "For the record, on Saturday I simply gave her my opinion about her writing my sister's story. This morning she assaulted me for no reason."

"According to Miss Walker, Saturday's opinion escalated to a few threats, and this morning you grabbed her." Tigo narrowed his eyes. "You said you were going to teach her a lesson."

"She lied." He nodded at Tigo and Ryan. "We were chatting. Friendly. Joking around. And it was raining. She started to fall, and I reached to help her. Just being a gentleman. This will end up biting her in the rear. I'm filing charges against her."

"She beat you to it. We saw the email you sent her."

Garrett lifted his chin. "I didn't send her an email. She thought it was me, and I let her believe it. Helped my case."

"Your case?"

"Exploiting my sister's tragedy makes the Walker woman no better than the cops who failed to bring in the guy who hurt her." Garrett's entire body shook. He opened his mouth to continue speaking but couldn't utter a word.

"Why did your sister phone the police twice on Saturday afternoon?"

"We . . . we had a misunderstanding. But we worked it out."

Tigo picked up the police reports. "Not according to Amy Garrett's testimony. What were you doing outside the office building of Freedom's Way this morning?"

Garrett sneered. "Duh. It's my sister's office, and whoever bombed her car might be hanging around."

"Finding him is not your job."

"Well, the authorities didn't find who slit her throat when she was a kid, so I don't have any reason to believe they'll find who planted the bomb in her car."

"Did you do it?"

Baxter pounded the table. "Are you deaf? I'm her brother. I protect her. It's what I do."

"Calm down, Mr. Garrett." Tigo had seen that wild look plenty of times before, and it read clearly unbalanced and addicted.

"Someone forced my sister to make those calls. She'd never have contacted a cop about family business. We handle our own problems."

"What kind of problems?"

"That's none of your business."

"It became our business when Dr. Garrett's car was bombed and you assaulted Kariss Walker and then resisted arrest."

Baxter scowled. "That Walker woman is behind this. Fine. My folks will bail me out." He pointed at Tigo. "Kariss Walker is a moneygrubbing user. Why didn't the cops pick me up instead of you guys?"

"Guess you're just lucky."

"I want to talk to my lawyer."

Tigo would do everything possible to keep Baxter off the streets for a few days, but he'd probably be out on bail in twenty-four hours. "Understand you will appear before a judge for assaulting Miss Walker."

"Right. You're wasting taxpayers' money running down an honest man. I'm my sister's bodyguard. I clean up what your type fails to."

CHAPTER 32

4:15 P.M. MONDAY

Kariss listened to her cell phone ring for the third time in the past twenty minutes. She knew the caller. Both previous times he'd left a voice message, but if she turned off her phone, she might miss something important. There was only one way to stop this annoyance.

"This is Kariss Walker."

"Ah, the great writer emerges to respond to the peons of the universe." Mike McDougal never failed to deliver a heavy dose of arrogance. "I knew I'd get your attention sooner or later."

Preferably never. "What do you want? Aren't you busy enough with Channel 5 and your blog? What's that called? *McDougal Snorts?*"

"Very funny. *McDougal Reports* is up to ninety thousand followers."

"Are there ninety thousand people in the

Houston area with poor taste? Make it short, Mike. I have things to do."

"And to think, I called just to see how my ex-girlfriend was doing after her car accident."

His syrupy words hadn't worked for a long time. "I'm fine, thank you."

"I saw you were run off the road. Who'd you tick off? I bet you're onto another story. I heard the execs at Channel 5 tried to get you back."

"They tried, but I was afraid you'd have to work for me."

"You're running down a big one, aren't you? Is this one as good as the Mexican gang and gun-smuggling case?"

Kariss wasn't going to discuss any of the past or the present with Mike, but with him, anything but his agenda was a moot point.

"We'd make a good team again. Remember when I helped you learn the ropes for Channel 5?" he said.

"Not interested. And for the record, I made my own way."

"You were green and naive, Kariss. You owe me for your career. All of it."

"Your ego just popped a blood vessel in your brain."

"Are you still seeing that FBI/bodyguard type?"

Now what did she say? "My personal life is none of your business. So —"

"You must have broken up. I'm so sorry. Not really. How about dinner? You can tell me all about it. I might even let you cry on my shoulder. Or more, if you're sweet."

The thought of Mike's hands on her made Kariss cringe. "No thanks. This conversation is over. Don't call me back."

"Will I need to write about your cold treatment on my blog?"

"Go for it. Won't be the first time." Kariss ended the call.

Mike called back, leaving a message again. Three calls later, Kariss finally turned off her phone. No doubt their conversation would be twisted into an unflattering, libelous blog in the next *McDougal Reports.*

4:30 P.M. MONDAY

Tigo stared at his computer screen as though the answers to all his problems would magically appear. He didn't know what irritated him more — Joanna's and Alexia's unsolved murders or Baxter Garrett's threats to Kariss and his possible involvement in running her car off the road. Both involved crimes against the innocent, and Tigo hadn't managed to nail anyone for either case. The best he could hope for was a quick lead from Hershey.

Glancing at his Buzz Lightyear watch, he saw that time had raced ahead while he'd been accomplishing nothing. He pulled up the Yeat case to look for missing pieces. Ryan had agreed that the sisters needed to be interviewed separately. One of them might reveal something about Joanna's college days.

So might Jonathan. What Tigo and Ryan had learned would devastate the strongest of men. How could a woman keep that kind of secret from a man she supposedly loved? But then, she'd filed for divorce, and he claimed to have no previous knowledge of her discontent either.

Tomorrow they'd also need to talk about Ian's problems, even though the thought of Ian planning a horrendous crime could destroy what was left of Jonathan's family. Tigo alerted Ryan of his plan to phone Jonathan about their newest findings, and his partner joined him.

"Maybe we'll get a handle on this today," Tigo said before pressing in Jonathan's cell number.

"A lead would be good," Ryan said. "I feel really inept right now."

"I'm itching to go undercover, to get in a good fight."

Ryan laughed. "Be at my house tonight and watch my two kids when it's time for homework."

Jonathan answered on the second ring.

"We have a new development," Tigo said.

"An arrest or a suspect?" Jonathan sounded weary.

"A suspect. This is of a sensitive nature. Are your sons with you?"

"No. They're with a tutor, trying to keep up with their classes. What's this about?"

Tigo took a breath. He'd invested a lot of time and energy into this case, and it kept getting worse. Plus, he'd allowed himself to become personally involved. Definitely a flaw. But Curt and Ian might never recover from this tragedy. "What do you know about Joanna's college days?"

"Nothing really. We met four years after she graduated."

Tigo figured as much. "She worked for an escort service owned by someone who called himself David Smith. He also photographed her."

"Escort service . . . What kind of photographs?" Jonathan's words seemed forced, as though he'd guessed the truth.

"The kind you wouldn't want your sons to see."

A heavy sigh, then a cough. "Joanna

became a Christian during the last semester of her senior year in college. She asked me once if I wanted to know about her past. I said no. Didn't matter who she was then."

Tigo could only imagine how Jonathan felt.

"Are you sure you have the right Joanna?" Jonathan's voice cracked.

"Our source is accurate. Recently David Smith had been in contact with her. Made threats. It was possibly the man Ian saw her with."

"God have mercy on this family." Jonathan paused, probably allowing the news to sink in. "Can you keep this from the media? I can't let Curt and Ian find out."

"We'll do our best. No guarantees."

Jonathan moaned. "That means I need to tell them. Some of her mood swings and behavior the past few months are making sense now."

"Care to explain?"

"Lack of interest in family activities. Depressed. Pulled back from her church and community work. Distant from me."

"Darena and Angela are next on our list to call."

"Doubt if they know anything, considering their relationship with Joanna — or lack of. But if they do, I want a full report."

Tigo wouldn't tell him about Joanna confiding in Vanessa. "I'll tell you what I can."

"I'll be at your office in the morning. I want to see the official report for myself."

"How about one o'clock? The morning's tied up. Do you have a bodyguard? We don't want you taking any chances."

"I do."

Tigo ended the call, then contacted the FIG. He wanted the man who called himself David Smith found.

His next call was to Darena, the cold-hearted woman who'd latched on to Pastor Taylor Yeat. Questions needed answering, and Tigo wanted to show Ian's sketch of the man to her and Angela.

"Darena, this is Special Agent Santiago Harris."

"What do you want? I'm about to leave work."

"Good afternoon to you too. I need to see you at our office in the morning."

"I work, remember?" The sarcasm was toxic.

"Be here at seven thirty. I'll write you an excuse."

"Wait. What is this about?"

"It will be in your best interest to be here."

"I intend to bring my husband and our

attorney."

"Good for you. Do they know about your affair with the good pastor?"

Darena cursed.

"See you in the morning with your party face," Tigo said.

After scheduling Angela and Taylor for back-to-back interviews after Darena, he typed an email to keep Linc informed of his findings.

"At least the morning will be entertaining," Ryan said. "I think I could write a movie script from those three."

"Wouldn't make the Hallmark Channel."

After answering some emails and taking care of some paperwork, Tigo gathered up his things and headed to the parking lot, en route to see Kariss. On his way, he phoned Jonathan again.

"Agent Steadman and I would like to go through Joanna's belongings," he told Jonathan. A thorough search had already been conducted, but in view of new information, another look made sense.

"I understand." Weariness was heavy in Jonathan's voice. "When did you have in mind?"

"Is eight thirty tonight all right? With your permission, we want to search through Alexia's personal items too."

"Whatever you think will provide answers. But I admit I haven't been in Alexia's room since it happened."

"You won't be alone."

"Are you a believer, Agent Harris?"

Tigo nearly moaned. "I meant Ryan and I will be with you."

CHAPTER 33

5:15 P.M. MONDAY

Kariss had spent the rest of the day in her condo just as Tigo had instructed. Not unusual, since many days she worked on her latest novel, wrote blogs, responded to email and social media, and became totally immersed in whatever project needed to be completed. But staying in on those days were her choice, and today's mandate made her feel agitated. For a while, she shoved Baxter Garrett and the culprit who'd chased her off the road from her mind. But she couldn't chase away the idea of Tigo making a second visit today — not for a moment.

When a knock alerted her to his arrival, she nearly tripped over her own feet getting to the door. This had to stop or she'd be in his arms. The Kariss of a few months ago would have welcomed him into her home and heart without reservation. But not today. No matter how much she cared for him.

No matter how much she wanted him.

No matter how much she knew he felt the same.

No matter how much she inched toward love.

She couldn't.

The deceit keeping them apart would be tough to resolve, but they were about to tackle it. If this relationship was going to take the next step, then honesty had to reign. Taking a deep breath to slow her pounding heart, she opened the door.

"Hey." Tigo wore a smile that would have melted a glacier. His five o'clock shadow made him look all the more appealing. "Your friendly FBI agent is here to check on you."

Irresistible. A hero better than any she could create. "Come in. No problems since this morning."

Tigo stepped inside, her senses drowning in his presence. The moment she breathed in his intoxicating aroma — a fresh out-doorsy scent that reminded her of a wild ride on a motorcycle — she had to put on the brakes.

"Can I get you an iced tea or coffee?"

"No thanks. I'm good." He grinned, and

her stomach fluttered like a teenage girl's. "Baxter Garrett is under arrest."

"Great news. He's a loose cannon." She gestured toward the sofa. "Do you want to sit down?"

"How about dinner?"

Her attention flew to his handsome face.

"We can talk about the Garretts on the way there. And our situation at the restaurant." His eyes said so much more. "I have an eight thirty appointment, so we have until eight."

She could handle dinner away from her condo. A good choice. "Okay. I'll grab my purse." She headed toward her bedroom.

"You look great. Those jeans were always my favorite."

She whipped around with a smile, warmth flooding her cheeks. How old was she again? "Thanks."

"Do you remember the first time I asked you to dinner, and you gave me permission to access your laptop?"

She laughed. "I do. That's when you found out I'd gotten in too deep while researching a cold case, and now it's part of our book." She realized she'd used the word "our." Too late now.

"Do I need to take a look at your laptop again?"

"There's nothing there that points to danger."

"Kariss, this is me. Tigo. The guy you can't fool. I can read you like a bestseller. You're knee-deep in trouble. So what's up?"

"I'll tell you in the truck." Good. Stay in control.

Once she'd snatched up her purse and her resolve to learn the truth behind the emails, she left a note for Vicki. Before she and Tigo had even driven through the security gate, he repeated his question.

"So what's up?"

"I received another email this morning at eleven forty-five. Tried to respond, but it came back undeliverable. I assume Baxter wanted to make sure I understood his concern."

"He was picked up at eleven thirty this morning."

She frowned. What did it mean if Baxter hadn't sent the second email? Shivers crept up her spine. "Well, he sent the first one."

"Denied it. But I expected that."

"An email can be written and then sent at a specific time."

"Right."

"What did Baxter's body language say?"

"He might have been telling the truth about the email."

She studied Tigo, wanting to ask more questions but knowing he wouldn't violate FBI procedures. "There's something else."

"Spill it," Tigo said.

"Sunday night I received a funeral wreath with a typed note."

Tigo immediately pulled the truck into the nearest parking lot, which belonged to a shopping strip. "Why didn't you tell me this earlier?" He took a deep breath. "What did the card say?"

"It was addressed to me, and it had an Edgar Allan Poe quote on it. Something about the shadowy boundaries between life and death." Kariss was amazed at her control. "I phoned the floral shop. A man wearing a baseball cap that hid his face walked in and paid cash for it."

"I'd like to see the note."

She reached inside her purse, retrieved the note, and laid it on the center console. "I'm sure it was Baxter."

He opened the note and studied it. "Hard for me to believe Baxter is this smart. Doesn't strike me as the poetic type." He stuck it in his pants pocket. "I'll keep the note for now. See what I can find out."

Tigo drove them to a popular seafood restaurant and escorted her inside. Kariss hoped the hum of voices filling the room would hide the secrets of her heart. She focused on the Cajun decor mounted on the wall — a life-size stuffed alligator, a rusted canoe, a single oar, and a chipped sign that read "Gumbo and Dirty Rice."

"Do you remember this place?"

"Sure." How could she forget any of the places the two of them had frequented together?

Tigo wore khakis and a light-blue shirt under his brown jacket. Casual yet professional. She realized he'd fit anywhere, but maybe not with her.

She ordered Chilean sea bass with lump crab gratin, sautéed spinach, and roasted tomatoes. He ordered blackened catfish with shrimp, oysters, and crawfish in a lemon-butter sauce, served with fried rice and extra jalapeños.

"And a bowl of seafood gumbo," he said to the young man taking their order. "Can you toss a few jalapeños in there as well?"

"You have a cast-iron stomach," Kariss said once the waiter disappeared.

He leaned on the table. "But my heart's soft as putty."

"Is it, Tigo?"

"I blew it with us."

"So then why are we here?"

He drew in a breath. "You're not making

this easy."

While they waited for their food, Kariss asked questions about Baxter to avoid the dead silence and awkwardness of their situation. She wanted their relationship to work, but she was afraid of getting hurt again. "I'm assuming Amy was right when she talked about his temper?"

He nodded. "With his dicey attitude and past record, I'm surprised he hasn't done time."

"Maybe his dark side is revealed only when it comes to his sister, and he's simply overprotective."

"He claims to have an alibi for Friday morning, by the way."

"If the Garrett family's as dysfunctional as I think they are, they'll probably cover for him." She regretted her judgmental thoughts. "I'm sorry. I've never met the older Garretts. I have no clue what they're like."

"We'll look into them and their son. But unfortunately, his license plate doesn't have a V8 in it, and other than a dent in the rear bumper, there was no sign that the truck had recently been in an accident. We've also confirmed that it doesn't have custom rims."

More bad news. "So Amy was right about the custom rims. But if it wasn't Baxter, then who was it?" She shook her head. "Of course you don't know."

"What have you done to make someone angry enough to possibly want you dead?"

She startled. She hadn't considered anyone wanting her dead, just deterred from writing Amy's story. Tigo was overreacting. "Could this be carryover from the gun-smuggling case?"

He lifted a brow. "Those guys are either buried or in jail, so they couldn't have run your car off the road. Bad guys play for keeps. If they wanted you dead, they wouldn't have run you off the road and then left without making sure they finished the job."

Oh yes, she recalled the repercussions of upsetting the wrong people.

"I'll rest my case on your observations — for now," Tigo said. "But what about the emails? Would you forward all of them so we can put a trace on them?"

"Sure." Kariss reconsidered the content of the emails and grew perturbed at her lack of sleuthing skills. "I must be losing my touch."

He smiled. "What have you put together?"

"The emails sent from S. Todd and J. T. Ripper? Sweeney Todd and Jack the Ripper slit their victims' throats. The sender must have thought he was being clever. That pattern also fits the sender of the card and funeral wreath."

"More evidence of someone's instability. Garrett probably arranged to have the second email sent at a designated time. Ties in too closely to his sister's attack." Tigo took a long drink of iced tea. The look of desire he gave Kariss made her shiver. Especially since she felt the same. She stared at the canoe displayed on the wall . . . it had a huge hole and no bucket.

Her iPhone buzzed, alerting her to a Facebook post. In an attempt to keep her feelings for Tigo at a distance, she took a glance. "Amazes me the number of weirdos roaming the streets. Mike McDougal is one of them."

"What now?"

"He tagged me regarding his latest blog. Why can't the man leave it alone? Find another female to exasperate."

"He can't get you out of his system. You've handled him before and done a fine job."

She frowned. "Right. He called today wanting information about the accident. Warned me about my lack of cooperation."

"Oh, let's hear the blog post. It'll give us some comic relief."

Kariss doubted Mike's blog would offer

any humor, but she brought it up and dived into his latest post.

" 'Houston's own Kariss Walker, *New York Times* bestselling author, has proven again that her past friends are exactly that — the past. Upon learning she'd been in a hit-and-run accident, I called to make sure she was okay. I wanted to check to see if she was hurt or needed anything. What a waste. She tossed me off like yesterday's trash. I'd seen her in December at Houston's Annual Authors' Dinner, and she'd ignored me then too. Odd, she didn't have her FBI bodyguard boyfriend with her at the event. Probably why she wore a low-cut, red-sequined gown and a come-on look that said she was single again. Saw her alone at a New Year's Eve gala as well. Whoa. Short and black. The sirens went nuts. In any event, Ms. Walker's attitude will one day cost her admirers. Could be today.' "

Tigo chuckled. "I missed the red-sequined gown and the short, black getup?"

"Neither was cut low." She shook her head. McDougal infuriated her. "Just simple evening dresses."

"Did he ask you out, or shouldn't I ask?"

She wanted to smack the smirk off Tigo's face. "He did, but I was strong and didn't fall for his charms. At least he doesn't know about my friendship with Amy Garrett, or he'd be after an exclusive."

Tigo studied her. His face softened, indicating his teasing had vanished. "Kariss, why do you think you're being targeted? The sender of those emails is aligning himself with villains who enjoyed a neck spray."

"No clue. That's your department." She remembered what Amy had said about her assailant quoting lines from Truman Capote's *In Cold Blood.* The email sender's names . . . Fiction . . . A man who read stories about violent crimes . . .

No, that wasn't possible. Why would he know about her or have her email address? She wouldn't even mention it.

Tigo reached for her hand. The moment his fingers touched hers, she slid her hand back. Burned. Every definition of the word raced across her mind.

"Sorry." He picked up his glass again, but it didn't reach his lips. "Is there someone else?"

How could there ever be? "No. Just me and my laptop. Living in a fiction world keeps me busy." She wanted to laugh but couldn't.

"I miss you, more than I ever thought possible," he said. "What I wouldn't give for an opportunity to start over. To show you I can be the man who makes you happy." He sighed and set the glass on the table. "I want to tell you the truth — about everything."

She missed him too, ached for him. But she chose silence.

"Kariss, we can't keep running around the track. To make things work between us, we've got to jump the hurdle." He leaned back in his chair. "Let me tell you what I do know. I've read enough of the Bible and listened enough in church to understand that you'd never consider a serious relationship with a guy who doesn't share your beliefs. But even if I became a Christian this very minute, it wouldn't make any difference if I couldn't tell you why I kept my divorce from you."

He'd said it. The big ugly. She nodded and noted the thickening in her throat.

"I hurt you, and I'm sorry. I don't know what I was thinking." He brushed his hand through his hair. "I kept putting it off. Then it was too late. You found out from Linc."

Kariss knew this was hard for Tigo, but she wouldn't interrupt or talk about Linc's role.

"The Monday after Thanksgiving, he told me what happened," he said. "I was down. Told him we'd split. He said he'd told you it had been a long time since he'd seen me happy. Thanked you. Told you that after Erin lost the baby and divorced me, I'd lost focus. That I'd headed off to Saudi."

"You can't blame Linc."

"I don't. Only my own stupidity."

Why did Kariss fear losing Tigo by asking for more information? She couldn't lose someone she no longer had. "Do you want to continue?"

"No. But I will. There's a lot at stake." He sipped his iced tea. A frown creased his brow. "I could use something stronger, but liquid courage isn't my poison anymore."

Kariss wondered how the rest of the story would affect her heart.

"Erin and I met in college and married two weeks after graduation. We were young. Thought a good time in bed was the basis for life. We argued right from the start. Sarcasm was at an all-time high. Within the first year, we got pregnant. My dad hadn't been there for me, and I refused to be the same as him. So I tried to keep our marriage afloat. Really tried. Later I learned Erin had given up on the marriage before she even learned about the pregnancy. Then she miscarried." He drummed his fingers on the table. "When the doctor released her from the hospital, she went to a hotel. While I was at work, her parents drove in from

West Virginia and moved her home with them. That's it. Pathetic, huh?"

"No, Tigo, it's not. When did you plan to tell me?"

"No idea." He moistened his lips and returned to his story. "I called her cell a few times. Called her parents' home. But no one ever returned my messages. The divorce papers came. I signed them. Got drunk. Signed up for a security job in Saudi, making use of my experience in the marines." The pain in his eyes matched the hurt she was attempting to hide. "I didn't fight hard enough for my marriage." He paused. "I was afraid of getting hurt again. The truth doesn't set anyone free. It only makes bad issues stink."

"I would have listened."

"I know. So what's the verdict?"

Kariss wanted a relationship with Tigo. But God wanted one more.

CHAPTER 34

8:15 P.M. MONDAY

Tigo shoved the situation with Kariss into a holding pattern until he could think through his options — and their talk. Her eyes said they still had a chance, but he had work to do on himself. He knew it, and he avoided it. Seeing a shrink was not his style. Probably his so-called pride.

Linc and Ryan had given him the same advice — God would help him if he opened his heart. Canned response. But if Tigo gave up searching for meaning in his life, he'd break his promise to his mother and never have a relationship with Kariss. Was God blackmailing him, or was this indecision and doubt part of the process?

Driving to Jonathan Yeat's home, where he'd meet Ryan, Tigo shifted into agent mode. He knew it was unlikely they'd find anything of note among Joanna's and Alexia's personal belongings. Investigators from the FBI and HPD had searched every corner of the house and found nothing pointing to the bomber. Computers and other communication devices had been confiscated, imaged, and returned. Every cabinet and drawer emptied. And all of it had yielded nothing. But a killer had been successful in snuffing out two lives, and Tigo couldn't rest until the person was found.

Tigo greeted the guard at the community gates and showed his ID before driving through. He parked his truck outside the Yeat entrance and surveyed the crime scene while he waited for Ryan. When Ryan arrived, they walked to the house together, where Jonathan greeted them at the door. The man had aged in less than a week. Traces of gray wove through his closely cropped hair, his face looked haggard, and his shoulders slumped. Still he welcomed the agents inside his home. Always the gracious host.

"Can we talk in my study?" The creases on his forehead were new. "I haven't told the boys what I learned from you today, and until I make peace with it, I can't expect them to understand this new . . . devastation."

"Jonathan," Ryan began, "unfortunately,

there's been a media leak. Sources tell us they've learned about Joanna's past. Media outlets will break the story by morning."

The man paled. "That means I have to tell my sons tonight."

Behind the closed doors of the study, Jonathan sat at his desk and stared at a photo of his now-shattered family, a replica of the same portrait that hung in the foyer.

"A man believes he knows his wife." Jonathan's voice quivered. "Loves her. Trusts her. And then his whole world collapses. I should have asked about her past when she offered, but it didn't matter then. I've discovered more about Joanna since her death than I ever did while she was alive." He glanced up. "Have you located David Smith?" Tigo could see the man was nearing a breakdown.

Tigo nodded at Ryan to field the question.

"Not yet. David Smith is one of several names this man has used. Our people are working on it. Have you uncovered anything?" Ryan said. "A receipt? A questionable entry on a credit card statement? Do you recall any conversations with Joanna that didn't make sense?"

"Nothing. She didn't talk much about her life here before we met. Our conversations were more about her growing-up years in Memphis. She attended college in Houston. We met at church while she was working at the medical center downtown. Then her sisters moved here seven years ago, and the chaos began."

"How did their move change things?" Ryan's gentle voice seemed to help Jonathan relax.

Jonathan folded his hands on the desktop. "Joanna's mother died, and the sisters relocated here with their father. It was Joanna's idea so the family could live closer. We paid all the relocation expenses." Bitterness dripped from his words.

Did Jonathan regret his marriage? Certainly the heartache would leave a question in any man's mind.

"Was their father at the funeral?" Ryan said.

"He died about three years ago. Heart attack." Jonathan lifted a bottle of water to his lips. He drank in fully, as though it would give him new stamina. "I appreciate your tag-team approach. Tigo, you're all about the facts. Ryan, you take a gentler approach, and you're a man of God. It's not surprising Linc says you two are the best." He blew his nose. "I'm okay. Today's been the worst since the bombing, but I'm committed to whatever it takes to find out who stole my girls' lives. I firmly believe I was the target, but I know the investigation has to look at every angle."

"Thank you, Jonathan." Ryan smiled. "We're not the bad guys, and we're glad you see that. We have another tough question for you, so brace yourself."

Jonathan lifted a brow. "All right."

"Ian has a reputation for being rebellious. We understand you and Joanna didn't agree about disciplinary measures."

Jonathan's eyes sparked. "Guess the FBI finds out everything people try to hide." His words weren't harsh but were filled with passion. "I was the lenient one." He paused. "Lately I've been thinking about things. Regarding Ian, she may have been right. He's the middle child. Doesn't know where he fits." He lifted his chin. "But my son would not have attempted to take my life or his mother's and sister's."

"We understand, but we'll need to talk to him later about the man he saw with his mother. That man might have been David Smith." Ryan nodded at Tigo to take over.

Tigo hesitated over the direction his questioning needed to take, but the more they learned about Joanna's personal life, the sooner the current suspects could be narrowed and possible new ones added. "What else can you tell us about Darena and Joanna? Why didn't they get along? Other than Joanna attempting to break up Darena's affair with Taylor."

"One dirty mess after another. Knew you'd find out about it sooner or later." Jonathan frowned. "Darena was jealous of what Joanna had, every aspect of Joanna's physical, mental, and spiritual well-being. But my girl never gave up. Loved her sister unconditionally, even when Darena spit in her face."

"Do you think Darena despised Joanna enough to kill her?"

Jonathan picked up the photo of his family. "I've thought about it. She definitely has her own agenda." Contempt curled the side of his mouth.

"The bomber was a professional."

"Darena could have hired him. I've seen her in action . . . But murder is a terrible accusation. I did a little research about Semtex," Jonathan said. "Points more to the bomb having my name on it. Or was that a ruse to throw off investigators? I'm so confused."

"We'll get the answers." Tigo needed to probe further. "We wanted to hear from you about your brother and Darena."

"How did you find out about those two?"

"I overheard a conversation the day of the funeral."

"Joanna tried talking some sense into Darena. Her husband adores her, and he's a good provider. But he lets Darena walk all over him. When Joanna got nowhere with her, I asked Taylor about his unfaithfulness. He said God had put him and Darena together." Jonathan sighed. "Probably a direct quote from her. My brother knows the consequences of sin. I threatened to go to his wife but didn't follow through."

Tigo listened while Jonathan complained about Joanna's sisters — their selfishness, their repulsive behavior, how they used Joanna. He despised them both.

"Now Darena has her clutches in my brother, a man of God. The church will crumble when this surfaces . . . I'm sorry. This isn't your problem." Jonathan pushed back from his desk. "It's time to go through Joanna's and Alexia's things."

Tigo studied the anguish on Jonathan's face. "It's not our purpose to invade your privacy. We'll work fast."

Jonathan stood. "One more thing you should know . . . The last time Joanna talked to Darena about her affair with Taylor, Darena said she'd see Joanna dead before she allowed her to ruin her life."

Tigo tucked the statement into his arsenal of questions for Darena's interview in the morning.

Jonathan opened the office door. "I've been sleeping in the guest room since the bombing. Been in the bedroom only for clothes. It feels haunted to me." He gasped as though reality had suddenly plunged into his heart. "I'll do anything to get to the bottom of this."

Joanna and Jonathan's master bedroom was bigger than Tigo's living and dining rooms combined, and he had a large home. Windows lined a circular sitting area that overlooked the pool outside, which allowed natural light to focus on a bed that appeared larger than a king. Shades of dark orange and gold added to an opulent feel. A foot-wide wood molding framed a hand-painted ceiling.

Whoa.

Tigo couldn't imagine such luxury . . . But wealth may have cost Jonathan the lives of his wife and daughter. The investigation could still lead to a disgruntled worker or someone in competition with Yeat's Commercial Construction. If someone had been plotting to kill Joanna for a long time, he couldn't have anticipated the exchange of cars the morning of the bombing. So many scenarios.

"Just do it." Jonathan shoved his hands into his pants pockets. "Maybe an item will trigger a memory. The mattress has already been flipped and the bedding analyzed."

Tigo didn't comment on the latter statement. Slipping on latex gloves, Tigo and Ryan painstakingly sorted through each drawer assigned to Joanna. Undergarments were neatly folded. Everything was in place. They repeated the procedure with Jonathan's drawers. Nothing out of the ordinary. No receipts or purchases. No perfume or jewelry items that Jonathan didn't know the origin of. When they asked Jonathan about an anniversary necklace containing a diamond surrounded by their children's birthstones that he had given Joanna five years ago, tears filled his eyes.

A hidden vault behind a picture didn't offer any leads either.

"I have a safe-deposit box that you're welcome to search," Jonathan said. "I went there today to see if I could find anything of question. Found nothing that would help you. According to bank records, I was the last person to examine the contents."

Tigo wished he'd accompanied Jonathan to the bank. "Did you have your bodyguard take you?"

"No. Drove myself."

"Jonathan, your sons need you."

"Sometimes I don't care. Being strong has lost its significance."

Ryan searched through Jonathan's closet while Tigo conducted the daunting task of examining Joanna's massive wardrobe. He went through every pocket. Even the designer hangers the clothes were hung on must have cost more than his shirts. But at least Joanna had been organized, so the process took less time than Tigo originally anticipated.

A bazillion pairs of shoes were displayed by color on a lit wall, and Joanna'd had almost as many purses. Tigo began with the shoes simply because those were the least likely places to hide something.

Thirteen pairs later, Tigo reached inside a running shoe, the right one. Nothing. When he searched the left one, he found a tiny piece of paper lying flat between the laces and the shoe tongue. A telephone number had been scribbled on it. Odd that no one had found it before.

"Jonathan, do you recognize this number?"

He looked at the paper and shook his head. "It's Joanna's handwriting. I could enter it into our computer and our cell phones for a match."

"Go for it."

A few moments later, Jonathan returned. No match.

Tigo flipped open his phone and pressed in the number. The number had been disconnected. He dropped the paper into a plastic bag to analyze later. Joanna's cell phone records might have this number listed. Maybe it was the same one. A job for the FIG.

A couple of hours later, nothing else suspicious surfaced in Joanna and Jonathan's room. Nothing led Tigo and Ryan directly to a possible killer.

Alexia's room was typical for a girl her age — posters of Justin Bieber, stuffed animals, pink and turquoise decor. One end of a white dresser displayed an open music box with a tiny African-American ballerina. At the other end was a stack of DVDs.

"We're finished here. It's nearly midnight," Tigo said. The agents left the room, and Jonathan closed the door behind them. "I know it's late, but can we talk to Ian?"

"I'm sure neither of the boys is in bed. I can guarantee it. No one's sleeping in this house. Do you mind waiting a minute? I've got to tell them about their mother before it hits the airwaves."

"Jonathan" — Ryan touched Jonathan's shoulder — "you've had to unload some heavy stuff on your sons lately. Do you want us there with you not as agents but as friends?"

Good idea. Tigo wanted to read their reactions, see if either of the boys let something slip. The thought had a callous edge to it, but it was the truth.

Jonathan glanced out a window facing the gate where the car had exploded. "I thought I was a stronger man than this. If both of you could be there, that would be great."

In the kitchen, Tigo and Ryan gathered at the table with Jonathan and his sons. The boys were pale, their eyes dull. Though they'd been in the home's expansive game room, they gave no indication that they'd been enjoying themselves. Jonathan dismissed the bodyguard while they talked.

"Agents Harris and Steadman gave me more information about your mother. Information you boys need to hear," Jonathan said.

"Can't be any worse than what's already happened." Ian's antagonistic attitude hadn't lessened. "What is it this time? Oh, I know. She worked for the CIA."

"Dad, let's hear it." Curt rubbed his face.

"I don't want to find out something about Mom from the news."

"I don't want any of us finding out information about her through the media. No matter how heartbreaking." Jonathan's soft response indicated his tender regard for his sons. "This one may unlock the identity of the killer." He rubbed his palms. "While your mother was in college, before she became a Christian, she worked for an escort service and posed for pictures . . ."

"What kind of pictures?" Ian clenched his fists.

"Do I need to spell it out?" Jonathan said.

Ian exploded in anger. "You mean you didn't know?"

"She never told me." Jonathan buried his face in his hands. "The FBI uncovered it today."

Ian pounded the table. "Did she and Alexia have to die for us to learn this stuff? Did . . ." His voice trailed off. "That makes me sick. My mom . . . a slut."

Curt's fist smacked against the side of Ian's face. Ryan caught Ian's chair before it sent the younger teen backward onto the stone floor.

"Don't you ever talk about Mom like that again," Curt ground out. "She came to the Lord and never turned back."

Ian jumped forward, but Tigo grabbed him.

"Boys!" Jonathan's voice thundered. "Fighting doesn't change any of this."

"He hit me." Ian whimpered.

"Be glad it was your brother instead of me." Jonathan grabbed Ian by the shoulders. "Now, I'm telling you, if you ever speak of your mother with anything but love and respect again, I'll ship you off to military school." He released the boy, disgust evident on his lined face.

"I'm sorry, Ian, Dad." Tears filled Curt's eyes, and his facial features contorted. "I lost my temper. Sometimes I can hear her laughing or smell her perfume. This afternoon I reached into the dryer and pulled out a sweater that belonged to Alexia. I can't believe they're gone."

Jonathan touched Curt's shoulder, and Curt clasped his father's hand.

"Dad, I want the killer found. Maybe it's the guy Ian saw at the mall."

Ian rubbed his cheek and glared at his brother. "So what?"

"Ian, if he's found out you saw him, then your life could be in danger too." Jonathan's gaze went from one boy to the other. "The authorities will put this together soon."

"I appreciate all you've done." Curt

reached up to shake Tigo's hand, but Ian resumed his stoic demeanor. "I know kids give cop types a hard time, but I see you care about us. And I want to believe you'll find the killer soon. You're all the hope we have."

Ian snorted, but Curt didn't look his way.

"Hey, either of you ever need to talk about school or this or anything, you have my card with my personal cell number. I know your dad has professional counselors for you, but I still want to make the offer," Tigo said.

"I don't need anyone." Ian's voice rose. "Except a new family."

Had this kid always been so belligerent? "I have a few more questions for you."

"I don't feel like answering anything," Ian said. "I'm tired of all this crap."

"Ian, please, son. These men need your cooperation," Jonathan said.

"Whatever."

Tigo pressed on. "When you saw your mother and the man at the mall, what was going on?" He probably could have worded that more delicately.

Several seconds passed before Ian responded.

"All right," Ian said. "They were arguing, but I couldn't hear what they were saying. Mom talked and cried. At the time, I thought she might be upset for other reasons. Now I wonder if the way he shook his finger at her and scooted back his chair meant something else." His tough-boy image dropped, and he choked back a sob.

"Any mention of money?"

Ian shook his head. "I just said I couldn't hear them. Besides, if this guy was threatening her, why didn't she tell someone?"

"Maybe to protect all of us." Jonathan's morose tone seemed to punctuate the Yeat mood.

"Do you have a name for the . . . man she worked for?" Curt said.

"Yes." Ryan took over the conversation. "But it's fictitious. Our sources indicate he's wanted for other crimes and possibly used other aliases."

"Son." Jonathan turned to Ian. "Do you remember your mother calling this man by name?"

Ian swiped at his nose. "No. But these agents should still be able to do their job."

"They are doing their best. So is HPD." Jonathan draped his arm around his younger son's shoulder. "I'll get you an ice pack. You've offered more information than anyone else has. I'm so proud of you."

"Right," Curt said with a huff. "As always, he's the good guy."

"That's enough." Jonathan furrowed his brow. "Your brother's hurting, and part of the problem is you."

Curt took a step back and then left the room. Jonathan didn't try to stop him or follow.

CHAPTER 35

Darena arrived alone for her 7:30 a.m. interview. She'd apparently had second thoughts about bringing her husband and attorney with her. Her dress was short, her heels were spiked, her earrings dangled on her shoulders, and she wore more makeup than a streetwalker. Tigo escorted her to an interview room, where Ryan waited.

"I don't have time for the attitude you've been using lately," Tigo said. "According to Jonathan, the last time Joanna talked to you about ending your affair with Taylor Yeat, you said you'd see her dead before she ruined your life."

For the first time, Tigo detected remorse in Darena's dark eyes. But for what? Tigo wondered. Had she planted the bomb? Or did she regret her affair?

"Ridiculous. She was my sister."

306

"But did you threaten her? Special Agent Steadman is waiting to record your answer."

Darena pursed her lips. "Her demands made me angry. People say things they don't mean when they're upset."

"And some people follow through." Tigo tapped his pen on the table. "When a woman and child are blown to pieces — and there's little left to bury — angry words ramp up to a motive for murder."

"I did not kill my sister and my niece." She turned to Ryan. "Make sure my statement is recorded verbatim, Special Agent Steadman. And since this is being videoed, you have my denial in two places. I detested Joanna and her righteous facade, but I didn't kill her. Neither did I hire someone to plant a bomb in her husband's car."

Tigo smiled. "I appreciate your answering the question before Special Agent Steadman or I posed it."

Her gaze filled with animosity. "I'm a proactive kind of woman, but I suggest you find the killer instead of wasting innocent people's time. My taxpayer money is footing your salary."

Tigo had heard that remark three times in the past two days, and he didn't like it any better than the first time. "Your conversations with Taylor after the funeral indicated deceit, hatred for your sister, an affair with a married man, and relief that she was dead. I don't play games."

"Are . . . are you planning to arrest me?"

"Should I?"

Fear seeped from the pores of her skin. "Please . . . I'm a married woman. My son is only eight years old. This would destroy my husband. Think about the scandal. Taylor's ministry would be over."

"I don't care about what this means to your life. Neither do I care about your husband's or Taylor's reputations. That's your problem. What I want to know is why you had a bomb planted in Jonathan's car."

Darena stood, trembling. "I'm innocent."

"Sit down, Darena." Ryan stood, eye to eye, his voice calm. "We're not done yet." He nodded at Tigo, definitely a role reversal in their typical interviewing process. "Do you have more questions, Agent Harris? Or do you want to arrest her now for the murder of Joanna and Alexia Yeat?"

Darena slowly eased into the chair. Her lips quivered. "I'll help in any way I can."

"That's better," Ryan said. "Any more outbursts, and you'll need to contact your lawyer."

"What other questions do you have, Agent Steadman?" Darena had obviously stepped down from her queenly role.

"What do you know about Joanna's college days?"

"Nothing. She only visited us in Memphis a few times."

"Were you and Joanna as close then as you were at her death?"

A single tear slipped down her cheek. "That doesn't deserve an answer."

"Agent Harris, take over. Talking to this woman is a waste of time," Ryan said.

Desperation crept into her face. "Joanna never talked about her life before Jonathan."

"Does the name David Smith mean anything to you?" Tigo said.

She shook her head. "Was that a boyfriend's name?"

"He's a photographer. Entrepreneur type."

"Why don't you interrogate him?"

"We will."

She tilted her head. "Why do you care about a photographer? Joanna detested having her picture taken. Most of the time, Jonathan had to pose for social events by himself." She gathered her purse. "Are we finished? I need to get to work."

"Just one more thing." Tigo took out the sketch of the man Ian had seen with his mom and slid it in front of Darena. "Do you recognize this man?"

She glanced at it, then looked at Tigo. "No I don't. So is that it?"

"Although your charisma is hard to resist, you're free to go."

Darena glared at him as she stood, then headed for the door.

"Don't leave town," Tigo said. "I'd enjoy taking your mug shot for the media."

Angela arrived shortly after Darena left, but Tigo and Ryan received no new leads during their interview with her.

After she left, Taylor Yeat entered the interview room with the composure of a man in control. He wore his rehearsed answers better than a new suit.

"I've heard enough," Tigo said after listening to Taylor for too long. "You can brag about your ministry until this time tomorrow, but it doesn't change your motive to see Jonathan or Joanna dead."

"Jonathan? He's my brother. You —"

"He confronted you about your affair with Darena, but you blew him off. How did his confrontation make you feel? He's a deacon in your church and has the power to make sure you never preach again. Joanna went to Darena and tried to put a stop to your affair. Multiple reasons to find someone who has access to Semtex."

"Try again, Special Agent Harris." Taylor

nodded at the glass window. "I know this is being recorded and that a couple of experts are watching the interview. I also know you're looking for a man from Joanna's past. And her past is filled with dirt. This is just a cheap shot, since you can't find the real killer. I'm not drinking the Kool-Aid."

"Might get you further than communion wine."

Taylor's nostrils flared. "How dare you speak disrespectfully about the Lord."

"You accomplished that feat all by yourself."

"I've had enough. I refuse to tolerate any more of this interrogation without my lawyer present." Taylor's voice bounced off the wall.

"This isn't a hearty-amen audience. Did you have your sister-in-law and her daughter killed? Or was that bomb meant for Jonathan?"

"No." Taylor gritted his teeth. "I'm a man of God, not a murderer."

"I know my Bible, Mr. Yeat," Tigo replied. "King David claimed to be a man of God before he killed Bathsheba's husband. The prophet Nathan had to set him straight. Don't leave town."

Kariss left her condo so the cleaning crew could work their magic and Vicki could spend time with Rose. The maids usually dusted and vacuumed Kariss's office first so she could get back to work, but today expediency wasn't foremost in Kariss's thoughts. She needed to pound the pavement and think through what it meant if Baxter wasn't the perpetrator of the threatening emails or the card and wreath. If he wasn't guilty, she had reason to be cautious.

She stepped down hard from the curb and lost her footing, landing on her hip. Fiery pain shot up her leg. Kariss took a moment to make sure she hadn't broken anything, then slowly stood. She'd certainly have a huge bruise, but she'd survive. Walking would still help her think through her dilemma and ensure her leg didn't stiffen. Sometimes Kariss thought she added dimension to the word *klutz*.

Ignoring the ache in her hip, she walked on and allowed her thoughts to turn back to the emails. Who had taken the time to compose them? And why? Why would that person not want to receive her response? If the intent was to intimidate her, the sender hadn't accomplished his or her purpose yet. Was the whole anonymity thing in place to protect Amy?

Deterring Kariss from writing the book made little sense, because Amy would keep looking until she found a writer who agreed to her terms.

Amy . . . They'd chatted on the phone, but Amy had been distant. How could Kariss soften her? The woman came with baggage, but she was an inspiration to every person who'd ever faced death and emerged victorious.

Kariss wondered whether Amy's assailant had been keeping tabs on her, charting her professional successes. It wouldn't be difficult. Amy was a high-profile figure in the community and didn't shy away from public appearances. He could be lurking in the shadows watching her every move. He might even know about the book she and Kariss were working on.

Kariss suddenly thought of an email that had been sent to her shortly after she'd met with Amy the first time. She'd deleted it without a thought. The subject line had read "True Story Alert," and the message had been an Agatha Christie quote — "If you place your head in a lion's mouth, then you cannot complain one day if he happens to bite it off." When she returned to her condo, she'd retrieve it from her Deleted folder and look into it further.

Kariss stopped at the security gate and greeted the guard. Pulling a wrapped cream-cheese-filled brownie from her purse, she slipped it onto the counter of his security booth. He was a sweet man. Always looked out for those in the condo community.

A chill filled the humidity-saturated air, and Kariss slipped her hands into her coat pockets as she walked across the street into an adjacent neighborhood. Dirty clouds hovered and threatened rain. *Threaten.* That word again. Kariss couldn't get it out of her mind.

She shivered, but her reaction had nothing to do with the weather. She strolled past homes with staged lawns and magazine-cover architecture. Every pine needle and leaf had been raked by some magical hand, commonly referred to as lawn-care providers.

She picked up her speed as she passed a home that housed a German shepherd behind a wrought-iron gate and brick wall. Dogs were the one angst in life Kariss hadn't conquered. She'd been bitten as a little girl and had never been able to forget the experience.

"It's only me, taking a walk," she told the barking dog. She hoped her voice sounded more confident than she felt.

An eerie sensation swept over her, and she turned to look over her shoulder. No one was following her. She'd been reading and writing too much suspense. Some of the TV series were even worse, with their vivid shots of gory crime scenes. When she didn't close her eyes fast enough to avoid the blood, she dreamed about it. Or the imagery brought on the nightmares.

The dog's deep-throated growls could be heard all over the neighborhood. Heaven help her if the animal got loose.

Across the street, an old man limped, somehow managing to keep pace with her.

So that's what was holding the dog's attention.

The man had his hands shoved into his pockets, and he wore a cap pulled down over his ears as though the temps were in the twenties instead of the forties. After her fall a few minutes ago, she could identify with an uncomfortable gait. The man glanced her way and stopped. She shivered, as though he might be a menace. Nonsense. Maybe he'd lost his way, wandered from home. Possibly an Alzheimer's sufferer.

"Do you need help?" she called to him.

He merely stared, as though looking through her. An inexplicable fear crawled up her spine. If she knew any of the people living in these homes, she'd knock on a door. She reached for her phone. Dead. Why hadn't she charged it?

The man limped across the street toward her. His scruffy beard, combined with the hat he wore, hid his face. Beneath his coat, it was obvious he was a broad-shouldered man. What was she thinking? Paranoia had definitely set in.

"Are you lost?" she said.

He laughed and continued toward her.

Kariss hurried forward, her heart thumping against her chest, the pain in her hip increasing. Surely she was overreacting, a combination of the unexplained threats and the dog's growls.

"Kariss." His voice sounded strong.

She whirled around.

" 'The past is a foreign country: they do things differently there.' "

She sucked in a breath. It was a quote from L. P. Hartley's book *The Go-Between.* A coincidence?

He knew her name.

He'd been following her.

He'd quoted a line from a novel . . . like Amy's attacker.

The urge to run spurred Kariss forward though her hip felt as if it were on fire.

She'd thought that when adrenaline flowed, everything else escaped the senses. But not this time. Tears sprang to her eyes, but she forced herself to keep moving.

Where was he? If she turned to see if he'd gained ground, she'd surely fall.

Did she feel his hot breath on her neck, or was it her imagination?

Her complex's security gate loomed in sight.

"Kariss, running from me will never save you."

Chapter 36

"How do you eat hot sauce on everything?" Ryan pointed to Tigo's rice, where he'd added his favorite hot sauce. "I need a TUMS just inhaling the fumes."

"Keeps my body moving. Makes me want to dance." Tigo gestured around the Mexican restaurant, one of his favorite places. The hum of voices and the strum of a Spanish guitar combined with the spiciest hot sauce on the planet suited him perfectly. His mom had had a recipe straight from Argentina, but Tigo hadn't been able to duplicate it.

"Never mind what it does to me," Ryan said. "Note that you're the only one pouring liquid fire on your food."

Tigo laughed. "You complain every time we eat here, which is about once a week. Don't I accommodate your craving for Chinese?"

"That's different. It's healthy. Vegetables." Ryan folded his fajita and licked his fingers. "Hey, I gotta hand it to you."

"For what? My increasing need for hot food?"

Ryan tossed him a disgusted look. "Not food. The way you gave Taylor Yeat a bit of theology."

Tigo chuckled. "My mother made sure I knew those stories inside and out."

"Do you think Darena's guilty?"

Tigo added sugar to his iced tea. "Her body language didn't say deceit to me. Just arrogance. But we're all about protocol and following through."

"Explain why —"

Their Blackberrys simultaneously alerted them to a notification from the FIG. Tigo pulled his phone from his shirt pocket, and Ryan did the same.

"We have the forensic report from the Garrett bombing," Ryan said.

"I've had my fill of car bombings lately." Tigo read through the report. "You've got to be kidding." He met Ryan's startled gaze.

"Semtex used in both bombs?" Ryan settled back in his chair. "Same color and gauge of wire. Cell phone trigger."

Tigo read the report again. Slower. He needed to digest the implications. Think beyond Joanna and Alexia Yeat's killings to a psychologist who'd survived a childhood attack — a woman Kariss was writing a novel about. "This changes everything."

"Sure does," Ryan said. "Let's have them box up our food."

"Great idea. I want to get back to the office." He caught Ryan's frown. "What links these bombings to our bad guy? Is he hired out?"

"I've got to think about it. Need more information. And we need to study the forensic reports side by side."

Tigo tried to get their server's attention as impatience wove a familiar path through him. "The Yeats and Amy Garrett made the wrong people mad, and there's a connection somewhere."

"Could Joanna have seen Amy Garrett for counseling?"

"She was dealing with Ian's behavior, and she and Jonathan didn't agree about how to handle it." Tigo finally got the waiter's attention. "Then there's the issue of whoever met her at the mall."

"Let's find out if Joanna was a client at Freedom's Way."

The two paid their bills and left the restaurant. Once they were in Ryan's car, Tigo phoned Freedom's Way, hoping to catch Amy between appointments. Instead, he reached her answering service and left a message, mentioning he was from the FBI.

Linking Joanna to Freedom's Way didn't explain why Kariss had received threatening emails. These had to be separate incidents. But Tigo didn't believe in coincidences. Never had.

Tigo punched in Jonathan's number.

Jonathan picked up before the call went to voicemail. "Hi, Tigo. Let me get to my truck for privacy. I'm outside one of my warehouses talking to a foreman. Before you ask, I do have a bodyguard with me."

"Glad to hear you're taking precautions. We have a new development."

Jonathan moaned. "My brother's calling me. I've ignored his last two calls. Is it okay if I take his call while I walk to the truck? Call you back in a few?"

Tigo assented and then turned to Ryan. "Taylor's phoning him. That should be a prized conversation."

"Taylor has his pockets stuffed with answers, but Jonathan's onto his bad habits," Ryan said. "From the looks of Darena's husband, he could easily tear Taylor apart."

"Fear does weird things to a man, and Taylor has plenty of reasons to be running scared."

Ten minutes later, Jonathan phoned Tigo. "I hear you talked to my brother this morning." He chuckled. It was the first time Tigo had heard Jonathan show any signs of amusement.

"We did," Tigo said.

Jonathan sighed. "I hate this. I just want it to end."

"What did your brother have to say?"

"He mostly raved."

"Do you think he could be involved in the bombing?"

When Jonathan didn't respond, Tigo repeated the question.

"I don't know. I'm going to say no. Taylor may be caught up in lust for Darena and may have messed up covering his tracks, but he wouldn't plan a murder. Darena, on the other hand, is capable of anything. I told Taylor the same thing. Maybe he'll get smart and leave her. Who else knew we switched cars that morning? Ignore me. I'm rambling."

Tigo listened and then shifted focus. "I have a question. Was Joanna receiving counseling from Dr. Amy Garrett of Freedom's Way?"

"Not to my knowledge. But she could have kept that from me too. I've heard of the organization. Even contributed to last year's fund-raiser. Why?"

"On Monday morning, a bomb exploded in Dr. Amy Garrett's car. She wasn't in the vehicle. The bomb was identical to the one that killed Joanna and Alexia."

"Why can't you find this guy?"

Tigo wanted to say the bomber had thought through every detail of his crimes. But why make himself and Ryan look like kindergarten agents. "We're getting closer, Jonathan."

"Not close enough."

1:30 P.M. TUESDAY

Kariss exited the expressway and drove to the city jail. She'd wrestled with the visit all morning, but she needed answers before contacting Amy. If Baxter knew more than what he'd told the authorities, then her job was to appeal to his cocky attitude and hope he offered the information. He might even confess to knowing the identity of the old man who'd followed her. She'd already thought about the fact that the stalker could have been in disguise. His voice had been strong . . .

"Why did you want to see me?" Baxter spoke through the phone on the opposite side of a Plexiglas wall.

She stared into his dark-rimmed eyes. He

323

needed meds or a fix, and he'd get neither in jail. "Amy made the decision to have her story written long before she contacted me. You know your sister well enough to understand her determination. Have you threatened her too?"

He curled his lip. "Amy gets weird ideas. Can't believe everything she says."

"Give me an example."

He moistened his lips. Kariss had wanted to believe his mind was clearing and he'd be rational, but nothing indicated any change. Did he think that Amy had fabricated parts of her story?

"Let me give you another news flash. Her attacker quoted from a novel," he said.

"Oh, I've read the reports, and I plan to use those quotes in my novel."

"Your type disgusts me."

"I'm really afraid, since you're in jail and facing charges." She laced her words with contempt and leaned closer to the shield separating them. "Are you working alone?"

Baxter laughed. "Wouldn't you like to know? You'd be amazed at what can be accomplished while I'm in here."

Chapter 37

5:15 P.M. TUESDAY

"Why haven't you called the police?" Vicki pointed to Kariss's cell phone. "That man approached you hours ago. I'm furious, sis. Why did you wait so long to tell me about it?"

"I didn't want to alarm you. What would I say to the police? 'An old man followed me'? 'And by the way, he knew my name'?" Kariss paced her living room while Vicki fed Rose. If only the answers would fall into her brain. She'd certainly not tell her sister about any of the other happenings nipping at her heels. "Maybe you're overreacting. I mean, I was the evening newscaster for Channel 5 and have since written a few bestsellers. The man probably recognized me."

"Have you lost your mind? Will I read about your death on my iPad?"

Motherhood had definitely made Vicki

hormonal. "Calm down. I'm fine, and you're blowing this way out of proportion."

"Do you think I can be duped so easily? Have you forgotten what happened Friday morning? Has it occurred to you this could be the same guy?" Vicki's brows narrowed. "And don't tell me it was Baxter, because he's in jail. What have you gotten yourself into?"

She wondered herself, but she wouldn't admit it to Vicki. "Sis, you're overreacting."

"This scares me, Kariss."

Kariss's mind zoomed in another direction. Her decision to not contact the police now looked insensitive. Jeopardizing her own life was a choice, but putting her sister and niece in danger was selfish. "I'm sorry. I don't see what I can do. I have no proof or reason to believe the man intended to harm me." But she had a gut feeling otherwise. Especially after seeing Baxter today . . . But he could have been bluffing.

"What happened when you ran back to the security gate?" Vicki said.

"The man had a bad limp, so he wasn't able to follow." The man had laughed — but Kariss wouldn't tell Vicki about that. Neither would she tell her about his final words.

"This isn't a scene from one of your books."

Kariss's gaze flew to her sister's face.

Vicki positioned Rose and patted her back. "When you got yourself into trouble before, I knew nothing about it until you were nearly killed. I've seen you in action. Remember? You have this stupid wild streak that defies danger. You think you're all street-smart with your self-defense expertise and your concealed handgun license, but you're not Superwoman." Rose startled at her mother's outburst.

Kariss stared. Who was this woman? Had someone taken over her sister's body?

"This time I'm sharing your house," Vicki said. "My child will not get caught up in your antics. Call the police or Tigo, or I'm moving in with Mom and Dad tonight."

Kariss moistened her lips and stared at her phone. She understood Vicki's ultimatum. Her sister had every right to make the demand.

Contacting the police meant explaining the entire situation about Amy and her brother. That left Tigo, and there was so much stuff between them — stuff she didn't want to contemplate until everything calmed down around her. Baxter had implied that someone outside the jail could be working with him, but she didn't have proof.

Kariss took a deep breath and faced reality. Scary things had been happening since she'd agreed to write Amy's book.

"I'll call Tigo."

5:40 P.M. TUESDAY

Amy Garrett returned Tigo's call shortly after five forty. He introduced himself and requested an interview.

"Special Agent Ryan Steadman and I have a few questions about the car bombing," Tigo said. "What time are you available this evening? We can meet you at your office or ours."

"My office," she said, punctuating her words with ice. "We're open until nine, and my last appointment ends at eight. Have you arrested the person who bombed my car?"

"Not yet, but our investigation has uncovered additional information. Will you be alone?"

"Three other counselors are scheduled with clients. Is there a problem?"

"For your own protection, I recommend not working alone late at night until a suspect is apprehended."

"Excuse me? My building has a security officer. I'm capable of conducting my practice without assistance from the FBI."

Tigo bristled. Uncooperative people made his job doubly hard. "Dr. Garrett, our job is to keep people safe. I'm offering advice to protect you from whoever tried to kill you."

"The car blew up in front of Walgreens while I was inside buying a sleep aid. Did you note the time? It was a random act."

"A random act? What if someone had been walking by the car? Or the bomb had been triggered during the day?"

"I understand you have a job to do, Agent Harris, but I won't live my life in a cave because someone is unhappy with me. I meet disgruntled clients and those who don't appreciate my work all the time."

"This is more than an unhappy client. This is someone sending a warning."

"I've been threatened before. Probably a man who's upset because I suggested his woman not take any more abuse." The phone clicked in his ear.

Great, a martyr for the cause of victimized women. No wonder Tigo had a headache.

Tigo and Ryan worked until after six thirty, then grabbed a couple of cheeseburgers and fries before driving to Amy Garrett's office.

After Tigo and Ryan displayed their

badges, Dr. Garrett checked the door locks four times. Kariss had indicated the woman had an obsession with locked doors, and her actions proved it. But Tigo understood. If he'd had her past, he might surgically attach an MK-38 to his body.

Dr. Garrett showed them to her office, where they seated themselves on facing sofas. Shades of green dominated the area, including the live plants and pictures on the wall. Tigo explained his and Ryan's method of conducting an interview.

"I apologize for my rudeness earlier," Dr. Garrett said after telling them about her near-failing hearing. She clasped her hands. "It's been a stressful week so far, and I took it out on you. But I am adamant about not hiding from anyone. Life's too short to live in isolation."

"Keep in mind our role." Tigo made sure to face her so she could read his lips. "I'm far too busy to investigate your murder. So I'll get right to the point. Do you remember the car bombing last week that killed Joanna Yeat and her daughter?"

"I do," Dr. Garrett said. "A tragic situation. But I fail to see how it's related to me."

"The bombs were identical."

Amy's face blanched. "Are you saying the same person blew up both cars? How would

330

you know?"

"He left his signature." Tigo explained Semtex and the two bombs' similarities. "Both bombs were triggered by a cell phone of the same make and model."

"Agent Harris, this doesn't make sense." Her lips quivered for a tenth of a second before she seemed to gain control. "I've never met Joanna Yeat or any member of her family."

"She's never been a client of Freedom's Way?"

"I'm positive we've never counseled her. I remember all my clients' names. It's who I am. Don't you remember all your cases?"

His headache mounted. "I do my best. Would you mind checking?"

She hesitated. "I'm never wrong when it comes to remembering names. But if you'll give me a moment, I'll check my client files." She rose and walked to her desk, where the computer sat.

Tigo waited, checking his Blackberry for updates, then his personal cell phone. Kariss had texted him, asking him to call when he had an opportunity.

Dr. Garrett cleared her throat. Perfectly poised, she nodded at her computer. "Agent Steadman, Agent Harris, Freedom's Way has never counseled anyone by the name of Yeat."

"Could we see the list?"

"For you to access my files, you'll need a subpoena."

"If you've never seen her, what is there to hide?"

"My clients trust me. Confidentiality. Fear. Surely you understand."

He knew the law, but it never hurt to ask. "Do your clients ever use aliases?"

"That's their choice. We don't take insurance, so Mrs. Yeat could have chosen to keep her identity private. Our purpose is to treat the individual, not check their name." She remained seated at her desk.

Didn't she realize the FBI was here to protect her?

"I appreciate your taking time out of your evening, but I can't help you with Mrs. Yeat's case."

Tigo glanced at Ryan, a signal for him to take over. This woman needed kid gloves, and Tigo was quickly losing his professionalism. Courage and strength were admirable traits, but failure to avoid danger was like touching a downed power line.

"Dr. Garrett, we want the same things you do." Ryan's calm tone did nothing to relax her rigid body. "We have valid reasons to find this person. The Yeat bombing left a widower and two teenage boys without a mother and sister. We have signature crimes with both car bombings, and we're looking for a link to make an arrest."

The lines around Amy's eyes softened. "It's . . . extremely sad."

"We have a photo of Joanna Yeat," Ryan continued. "It might sharpen your memory. Perhaps you met her at a conference and counseled her there." He pulled up a photograph of Joanna and Alexia on his iPad and stood to show her the pics.

"I'm sorry. I don't recognize the woman." Amy lifted her chin. "Having her as a client might have helped you solve both bombings. But even if she had been a client, I couldn't allow you to see her files."

"There is a connection with the cases," Ryan said. "We simply need to find it."

"What does this information mean for me?"

"The danger is imminent. Agent Harris and I recommend you take advantage of the FBI's protective-detail program."

"As in a bodyguard?" Amy bristled as though she'd been offended. "I've made it clear how I feel about hiding from anyone or anything."

"A car bomb is a threat to lives and

property," Tigo said. "A deadly one. It's not our policy to recommend a bodyguard, but we can provide protection by arranging for you to stay at a hotel or safe house with agents until this is over."

She stood. "It's not necessary."

"What are you not telling us? Is the bombing a reminder about an event from your past?" Tigo captured her attention and held on. "You of all people understand the intricacies of an evil mind."

She opened the door to her office. "Gentlemen, I have more important things to occupy my time. I appreciate your stopping by, but I can't help you. I repeat, I don't want any law-enforcement types hovering over me."

"You might not be so lucky the second time. Inconvenience or your life?" Tigo stood. "You need to decide. Agent Steadman and I will be in contact." He handed her his card. "Think about it. Who's going to help these women recover from tragedies if you're not around? Our protective-detail program will keep you safe until the person is arrested, and you can resume your work. Your clients need you."

"No thanks. Bullying me into closing my office while you run around looking for clues is not the answer. Excuse me. I have work to do before going home."

CHAPTER 38

10:25 P.M. TUESDAY

Kariss yawned and stared longingly at her bed. She'd turned back the covers in anticipation of the moment she could crawl under the warm blankets and let exhaustion take over.

Tigo hadn't returned her call. He must be working late, possibly undercover. It was one of the things he loved about the FBI. Vicki had been correct in one evaluation — Kariss did enjoy a taste of danger, and she understood Tigo's quest for the same thrill. One of the many things they had in common. Kariss was such a mess when it came to analyzing her feelings for him. She danced around the truth as though she'd be burned if the flames touched her.

Kariss had never expected Vicki to give an ultimatum, but she couldn't blame her sister. Rose needed to be protected from the evils of the world, and last Friday morning had proved how evil the world could be. Contacting Tigo was the prudent response, and if telling him about this morning protected those she loved, she would swallow her pride and do it.

After brushing her teeth and washing her face, she crawled into bed with the latest issue of *Writer's Digest*. Several articles had been dedicated to the craft of fiction, and she was particularly interested in one that focused on viewing setting as an antagonist.

Unfortunately, she couldn't concentrate. With one hand on her cell phone, she allowed her eyes to close. The lamplight shone in her eyes, ensuring she wouldn't sleep. She'd simply rest.

Her cell rang, jarring her from a deeper sleep than she'd anticipated.

"Kariss." The familiar voice caused her heart to beat faster. "I know it's late, but I didn't know if your message was urgent."

She was instantly alert. "Thanks. I appreciate it."

"I woke you, didn't I?"

"It's okay. I have the light on, but I must have dozed off anyway."

"Do you still get nightmares?"

She wouldn't lie. "They're not as frequent as before."

"What's going on?"

She'd already rehearsed what to say, and the words came easily. After relaying the story, she added, "The odd thing is, he used my first name and quoted a line from a novel."

"Kariss, I've read Amy Garrett's case." His voice was solemn. "This is not some lunatic fan who wants to have a little fun with an author. He either knows the case history, or he's the man who attacked Amy years ago. You must have realized this."

"Crossed my mind." But she didn't want to think about what it could mean. Denial of danger had gotten her into trouble before . . .

"Someone needs to write a novel about you. What was the quote?"

" 'The past is a foreign country; they do things differently there.' "

"Never heard it before. But I also don't like Baxter Garrett's intimidation and his veiled threat about using an outside connection to help him get his point across." Tigo sighed, and Kariss could imagine the lines deepening across his forehead. "It rings too close to Dr. Garrett's case. In view of her cold case, alluding to the past implies more than I care to get into right now."

"But it was supposed to. That's Baxter's way of bullying people."

"Thank you, Dr. Walker."

"So what do you suggest?"

"Don't take any walks without your gun. And take an advanced course in self-defense."

"Very funny."

"Have you spoken with Dr. Garrett this evening?"

"No. Why?"

"Here's a little tidbit for you. The person who bombed Jonathan Yeat's car is the same person who bombed Amy's car."

She gasped. "What's the connection?"

"How about don't get in the same car as Amy Garrett?"

Tigo wasn't divulging a thing about the investigation. "Do you think last Friday morning and today are linked?" she asked.

"Maybe. Did you get a pic of the old man?"

"My phone was dead." She let a sliver of regret creep into her words. "If anything comes to mind, I'll call."

"Why don't you and Vicki take a vacation until this is over?"

He and Vicki must have been on the same wavelength. "I could send her and Rose to our parents."

"Good idea. How about you? I'd rather see you out of the state. Isn't there a writer's conference going on somewhere? What about visiting your agent or publisher in New York?"

"You should know by now I'm not a runner. If someone wants to find me, they can."

"Not if you let the FBI handle it."

Acid rose in her throat. "Not yet. I'd rather be in my own home and simply take precautions when I venture out. If I've upset someone, they'll have to get over it."

"Right." He growled the words. "You keep telling yourself that, and maybe a rabbit will jump out of your hat. You and Amy Garrett are walking a tightrope."

"Tigo. It's my choice."

"I've heard you use the same line before, and you nearly ended up dead."

"I make my own decisions. Good night."

CHAPTER 39

Kariss was into the fourth mile on the treadmill when her cell phone rang. She hoped it was Tigo. Hanging up on him had given her a sleepless night and more heartache. Caring for him was easy. Swallowing her pride meant digesting a horse pill. He only wanted what was best for her, and she'd reacted in her typical stubborn, reckless fashion. Now to confess that.

But one glance told her he wasn't the caller. She should have felt relief, but regret took its place.

"Good morning, Amy. How are you doing since the bombing?"

"All right." Amy's voice had that curt, emotionless tone — as in ultraprofessional — that Kariss had heard on more than one occasion. "Are you running?"

"Yes. I'm on the treadmill."

341

"Can you talk?"

"I'm a multitasking junky." So much so that she'd already shed a few tears for a man she couldn't have, but she knew who had the real answers to that dilemma.

"First I need to apologize for not returning your calls." Amy sighed. "I'm not normally so unprofessional."

Nice change of pace. "Thank you. So what's up?"

"I won't keep you, but I wondered if we could meet for coffee this afternoon?"

"I could after three thirty. Around four?" She slowed the treadmill's pace to 4.2 miles per hour. "Is everything okay?"

"It will be. Want to meet at Starbucks? I'll spring for the cookie." Amy's words were kind, but Kariss heard the tension in her voice. Someday she'd find a way to melt Amy's facade.

"What's wrong?"

"Got a visit last night from two FBI agents regarding the car bombing, and I have to make a tough decision. Need to discuss it with someone who's been there."

"What did the agents want?"

"They offered some suggestions."

"Like what?"

"I don't want to discuss this over the phone."

"The FBI is committed to keeping us safe. Who were the agents?"

"Special Agents Steadman and Harris. Do you know them from your experience?"

Now she understood why Tigo had called her so late. "I do. They're good men."

"I'm not so sure."

"Okay. When we meet later, we can talk about your dilemma."

Kariss had a decision to make too, and prolonging it only stirred her emotions. After ending the call with Amy, she pressed in Tigo's number, wishing she'd taken the time to consider how to word her apology.

"Good morning, Miss Walker. Had your coffee yet?"

"I had that coming." He could say so much more, but she hoped he didn't. "I apologize for last night. I'm sorry for being obnoxious when you were only looking out for my welfare."

He chuckled. "I didn't get much sleep either."

She turned off the treadmill. "We're like two lit fuses of dynamite."

"In more ways than one."

She wasn't going to give him the pleasure of a response.

"Will you consider a vacation?" he said.

"Depends on what happens with Baxter

Garrett. Vicki and Rose are leaving this morning to stay at our parents' until this is over. Keeping company with me can be hazardous to anyone's health." She kept her tone light.

"What about you, Kariss? I need to know you're out of harm's way too." His gentle tone caused her to shiver even though she was covered in sweat.

"I carry a gun, and I'm not looking for trouble."

He blew out an exasperated sigh. "Talk to your parents. Get their take on the situation. For that matter, pray about it. Okay?"

"I will. I promise. Amy Garrett told me you met with her. She wants to get together."

"We asked her to take advantage of FBI protection. Both of you need to be tucked away. When are you meeting?"

"Four o'clock this afternoon at Starbucks."

"Toss out a convincing reason why she needs to accept protection. I don't like how any of this is going."

"I'll do my best."

"Be safe and drive yourself. And check in with me after your meeting so I know you're okay."

"I will, Agent Harris."

"Good. Gotta run. Have a meeting with Linc." Tigo ended the call before she could think of something witty to say. Good thing. She was ready to invite him for coffee.

CHAPTER 40

He'd waited twenty-three years for Amy to make the ultimate mistake. He'd allowed her to roll the dice while he adjusted the pieces on her game board of life. Finally she'd grabbed hold of greed and proved his point. Stupid woman. She should have died after he'd finished with her long ago. But he'd always kept tabs on her in case he needed to set the record straight after that first failed attempt that May night so many years ago.

We told you she'd slip. Kill her and be done with her. She's lived on borrowed time too long.

Did Amy think a novel about her escape from death would rise to the level of his accomplishments? He had ways to circumvent so-called law-enforcement investigators, and he'd get away with one more crime.

Amy had struggled through the years to

make something of herself, and he'd observed it all. Her fancy PhD degrees meant accomplishment to some people, but not him. Survival instincts were the best traits. In a Vietnam prison, he'd managed to out-think the torture experts and had learned to be cunning. The enemy had been his best teacher, driving home the cliché that only the strong survive. That's when the voices had first begun, and he'd always be grateful.

Why did Amy think her story would ever rival those of the great storytellers? If she'd chosen Cussler, King, Koontz, Patterson, or any true male author to write what happened back then, he might have let her foolishness slide. But Kariss Walker and her novels weren't masterpieces. They were trash. What did a woman know about executing procedures for a crime?

He'd been patient and covered his tracks more than once. All his victims had died. He caught himself. The Yeat bombing hadn't turned out exactly as planned, but the results suited his purpose.

In his pocket lay two perfectly crafted bullets with his signature so the cops would know that a mastermind had achieved a perfect crime. He dared them to find him.

Today would end it for Amy and Kariss,

and then he'd creep back into his world, where no one ever suspected him of anything more than devotion to his frail wife. The latter was true.

Exiting his wife's car, he stepped into a downpour. His mind raced with what made accuracy important — wind speed and direction. Today the cursed rain played against him, but he'd make allowances. He'd be close enough to ensure both bullets found their victims.

CHAPTER 41

4:00 P.M. WEDNESDAY

Kariss slid into a parking space outside Starbucks at the same time Amy drove up. The blinding rain slapped against the windshield of Kariss's rental car while the wipers ran a marathon. She'd be glad when the repairs to her Jag were completed. At least nature's display this afternoon didn't include thunder and lightning. Electrical storms ranked number two on Kariss's list of personal fears. Dogs were number one. She grabbed her purse and laptop, then huddled under her umbrella while Amy locked her car doors and checked the driver's and left passenger's doors — four times. That seemed to be the magic number.

"The coffee and cookies had better be fresh." Kariss shivered in the damp cold.

The women hustled across the parking lot, sidestepping puddles on the way. Kariss opened the door of the coffee shop and held it for Amy. She hadn't observed how frail Amy's frame was until this moment. The problems of late must have been wearing her down.

"Mmm. I can smell the coffee already." Amy smiled, but a deep V was etched between her brows, and the dark circles beneath her blue eyes added years to her lovely face — a face that reminded Kariss of the late Princess Grace of Monaco.

How sad that Amy had to rely on Kariss's listening ear when they'd only known each other such a short time. Kariss would try to persuade her to leave town or seek FBI protection. Tigo always said the bad guys thought they'd never get caught, and that's when they made mistakes. But until the FBI found the bomber's weak point, Amy should be sunning on a beach or skiing down a slope — anywhere but Houston. She had to be on emotional overload, especially with Baxter and his stint in the city jail.

The rich, intoxicating aroma of coffee pushed the chaotic world aside. Let the rain drench the outdoors.

The coffee shop, with only two other tables occupied, was the perfect spot to talk. If a mention of the book came up, Kariss would let Amy know that she'd drafted the first chapter while adding detail to characterization. Much still needed to be done to the plot, and Kariss had to steal moments to work on it.

After Kariss and Amy ordered their coffee and decided they each needed an oatmeal-raisin cookie, they claimed a small bistro table along the window of the cafe. Huge raindrops crashed against the pane and raced downward, with more chasing after them. Definitely the perfect place for Kariss to write a suspenseful scene after their discussion.

Kariss watched the steam rising from her mug before focusing on Amy. "You mentioned Special Agents Steadman and Harris had visited you."

Amy took a sip of coffee and stared into her mug. Was she thinking about the conversation with Ryan and Tigo, or was she savoring the hot brew? The woman was hard to read. Perhaps that trait came with her profession. "The FBI has asked me to take advantage of their protective-detail program," she finally said, meeting Kariss's gaze.

"So is the decision you need help with whether to stay in Houston under the protection of the FBI or to take a vacation until this is over?"

Amy broke off a piece of her cookie. "I

don't want to consider either one. I refused the offer last night, but then I kept thinking about it all day today. Special Agent Harris made an insightful comment."

Kariss envisioned Tigo in his professional mode, either incredibly charming or scaring Amy into compliance. "What did he say?"

"Simple, really. In short, I can't counsel clients if I'm dead." She sighed. "I was afraid Baxter was about to be implicated in the bombings. How horrible for my family if he were to be accused. He can be a handful with his issues and addictions, but murder is another matter. Our parents might never recover. As you can imagine, my family harbors guilt and blame because of my attack, so I've decided —" Amy reached for her purse and accidentally sent it tumbling to the floor. As she bent to retrieve it, her coffee took a dive. Kariss rushed forward to grab the cup before it could spill on Amy.

A pop and a sharp pain attacked Kariss's senses. The left side of her head stung.

A woman screamed.

Another pop pierced the air.

Amy pulled Kariss to the floor.

Tables crashed.

Kariss gripped her throbbing head and felt the slimy liquid she knew was blood.

Tigo glanced at the time on his computer. If he didn't come up with an excuse soon, he'd be stuck going to the Wednesday night church service with Ryan — again. Not that the preacher was boring, but Tigo always felt trapped in the pew. Which was a joke. A daredevil FBI agent shouldn't feel intimidated by a building full of Christians, but Tigo was. He felt like the congregation all had a secret and he'd missed the initiation.

He scrolled through the FIG's latest information. Nothing had turned up for the source of the phone number found in Joanna's tennis shoe, and it didn't match the unidentified number on Joanna's call list. Neither Curt nor Ian recognized the number, or they refused to acknowledge it.

Those two boys didn't ring true. Curt seemed to have his head on straight, except for cleaning up Ian's messes. Tigo had heard through Linc's son that Ian had threatened to take out one of the kids at school for slandering his mother.

When Tigo was a kid, he'd longed for a large family — lots of aunts and uncles with a dozen or more cousins. The Yeat situation had convinced him those childhood dreams would have been a nightmare if they'd come true. Most of the Yeat family relatives had motive to see either Joanna or Jonathan dead.

Unanswered questions ticked through Tigo's mind. Who'd planned to murder Jonathan or Joanna Yeat? The same bomber had blown up Dr. Amy Garrett's car. What linked the bombings and why? Semtex could only be bought for the right price by people outside of the U.S., which eliminated disgruntled Yeat employees. If those who'd been laid off had money to buy expensive explosives, they wouldn't care about losing their jobs. Conspirators could have pooled their resources for vengeance, but that was highly unlikely. And with Dr. Garrett's bomb a match, he could eliminate those who did business with Jonathan.

He pulled up his original suspect list and his current notes.

Angela Bronston — No longer a suspect.
Roger Collins — Not a suspect but being tailed.
Baxter Garrett — No longer a suspect.
Carolyn Hopkins — May have information. Currently incarcerated.
Vanessa Whitcom — Not a suspect.
Darena Willis — Not a suspect.
Curt Yeat — Not a suspect but could have information.

Jonathan Yeat — No longer a suspect.

Ian Yeat — Not a suspect but could have information.

Taylor Yeat — Not a suspect.

Business associates and competitors — Nothing there.

David Smith — Strongest lead in case.

Tigo's phone rang. The number told him it was an informant.

"The guy you call David Smith? The one in the sketch? Frequents a bar called the Stragglers near the ship channel. Goes by the name of Wesson."

Tigo was itching to go undercover, and now he had the chance. "Thanks."

The call disconnected. He needed a break, and this looked like it.

"Tigo, there's a problem." Ryan stood in the doorway. His face wore the look of bad news. "Just checked the latest HPD report about a shooting at a Starbucks across from the Crystal Point Mall. A hunch told me to call Ric Montoya. He confirmed that it was Kariss who was shot."

Tigo rose to his feet, his pulse racing. "How is she?"

"Stable at Crystal Point Methodist Hospital. Scalp wound. Dr. Amy Garrett was with her."

Tigo grabbed his keys and phones. "I've got to get to the hospital. What happened?"

"A shooter from the parking lot while she and Garrett were inside. A few people inside, but they didn't see a thing due to the rain."

"This guy is good." Tigo tripped over his chair in his haste to get out of his cubicle. "I'll call you as soon as I know she's okay."

"Don't think so. I'm driving."

Tigo threw him a quick glance. "No deal. I know how to get there in a hurry."

Ryan blocked the cubicle's entryway. "Preferably in one piece. This is a personal situation, Tigo, and you have big stakes in it. I'll drive, and you can contact the hospital for an update if it'll make you feel better."

Tigo knew his heart overrode his good sense. If he had any sense at all when it came to Kariss. It hadn't been that long since he'd gotten the call that his mother was dying. He had the same sinking feeling now. "Okay. We're wasting time."

God, I'm begging here.

Once in Ryan's car, Tigo phoned the nurse in the ER and gave him his FBI credentials. The nurse reported little more than Tigo already knew.

"The bullet grazed her head. A few sutures," Tigo told Ryan. "She's stable."

"Good news." Ryan passed two cars and a semitruck. Rush-hour traffic streamed bumper to bumper.

"Can't wait to get my hands on the police report," Tigo said. "But that'll come soon enough. What do you think this means? Your head is clearer than mine right now."

"I'm thinking."

Tigo had worked with Ryan long enough to know he'd already formed his own opinion. "You tell me first. I'm the one who needs to get past the shock of Kariss being the target of a killer. Again. Didn't we go through this last summer?"

"She must be a slow learner."

"That's what scares me about her. She seems to have no fear."

Ryan cocked his head. "Look who's talking."

"But I'm trained."

"Point taken," Ryan said. "Okay, here goes. Kariss has gotten herself involved in a situation where someone is seeking revenge. Baxter's still in jail. Can't be him. He gave Kariss the impression that someone's working with him on the outside, but I doubt it. He's a loner and doesn't have the money to pay a hired gun. Simple answer. The shooter has to be the same perp who bombed the Yeat and Garrett vehicles."

"And ran Kariss off the road. And sent her emails and a funeral wreath." Tigo's mind switched into crime-solving mode. "I'm past thinking it's a previous employee or anyone who might have had a grievance against Jonathan. Although Darena and Taylor have motive, I don't see a connection to Dr. Garrett. I need a subpoena to look at her list of clients."

"Darena could have seen her for counseling. Talked about Taylor and used an alias. But she doesn't come across as a woman who wants help."

Tigo detested the woman. "Good call. Then there's David Smith. But unless he's older than what our sources indicate, he'd have been a young teen when Amy was attacked."

"Can't talk to him if we can't locate him."

"We might have already done that. An informant called me, and we have a lead on him. I want an opportunity to question him. That's all."

Ryan fixed a stare on him. "What are you really thinking?"

"Here's my best shot. I think both of us are ignoring the elephant in the driver's seat," Tigo said. "My gut is telling me that the man who assaulted Dr. Garrett twenty-three years ago is the bomber and the man who shot Kariss. I think he moved up from attacking little girls to making bombs."

Ryan nodded. "Maybe. But why did he target the Yeat family? And why is he after Dr. Garrett now, when he had twenty-three years to kill her?"

"Maybe he had no reason until now. What's happened that might have changed his mind?" Tigo had the answer the moment he uttered the words. "The book. He's afraid of Amy Garrett's book."

"If Dr. Garrett hasn't gone to the police before now with new evidence, what would make the book so threatening?"

"Fear of getting caught. Think like a psychopath, Ryan. This could be cat and mouse for him. In his mind, the job is unfinished."

"Possibly. Not sure I agree. I think the original target was Jonathan Yeat, and somehow he's tied to Amy Garrett."

Tigo disagreed, but he needed proof to show that Jonathan and Amy shared a common enemy.

"Your silence tells me you don't agree," Ryan said. "So what do you say we keep this to ourselves until we investigate the shooting today?"

"Good idea. Then we can talk to Linc this afternoon." Tigo pressed in Fred Walker's number. This had to be hard on the older couple — first Vicki, now Kariss.

"I have a question," Ryan said. "Shall we talk to Dr. Garrett's parents for another possible connection?"

"Make the arrangements, and let's do it."

Fred answered the call. "Hello?"

"This is Tigo, and I'm on my way to the hospital. What can you tell me?"

"We're just now leaving Texas City. All I know is Kariss's been shot. Don't know anything else." Fred's voice trembled.

"The ER told me that the bullet grazed her scalp. The wound was sutured, and she's in stable condition. That's good, Fred. I'll call you once I'm there. Tell Ella not to worry."

"Fat chance. What has my little girl gotten herself into?"

Tigo wished he had an answer. "The shooter won't get away with this. I promise." He disconnected the call. What wasn't he seeing in these cases?

CHAPTER 42

5:17 P.M. WEDNESDAY

Tigo hurried into Crystal Point Methodist's ER while Ryan parked the car. He had to put cuffs on his temper. Frustration and concern for Kariss made a volatile brew. He should have insisted she stay at home and not meet with Amy. But she probably wouldn't have listened anyway. They were two stubborn women. He planned to give both of them another dose of reality if the shooting hadn't done the trick.

But first he had to make sure Kariss was okay . . . stable. A bullet had grazed her temple.

After he flashed his ID at the reception desk, a nurse escorted him to the treatment area. A police officer and Amy stood on opposite sides of Kariss's bed. The officer scribbled on a pad, no doubt pumping the women for answers. Tigo focused on Kariss. The color of her face matched the sheets,

361

and the left side of her head was bandaged. Blood had seeped through. Two IV bags dripped into her right arm. All of Tigo's irritation melted in a pool of compassion that quickly turned to anger. Whoever had done this would pay.

Tigo showed the officer his ID and informed him of Ryan's coming arrival. Then he stepped past the officer and bent over Kariss. "Hey, babe. How are you doing?" The words were out before he could hide behind his tough-guy image. Let the good Dr. Amy Garrett think whatever she wanted. Analyze that.

Kariss's lips inched into a smile. Her eyes were glazed, hopefully from the medication and not from pain. "I'm fine. Just . . . just trying to help the officer."

Tigo nodded a hello to Dr. Garrett, whose stoic persona matched her demeanor from last night's interview.

"The FBI's working this?" the officer said.

"It's linked to the Yeat bombing case that we're partnering with HPD on," Tigo said. "Detective Ricardo Montoya can confirm. After you speak to him, we'll need to see the police report."

The officer pulled out his phone. He moved from the curtained area, leaving Tigo a moment to talk to Kariss. "What did you do this time? Why weren't you wearing a Kevlar helmet?"

Kariss's smile grew. "Didn't match my outfit."

He wanted to kiss her, do anything to make the shooting go away. "Do you feel like talking about it?"

She nodded. "Got in the way of a bullet. Grazed my head. Nothing to dig out like in the movies." She peered around him. "Hey, Ryan. So I have two special agents —" She drew in a quick breath.

"Aren't they giving you pain meds?" Tigo touched her forehead and brushed back a damp curl, being careful not to venture too close to the bandage. He wrapped his hand around hers, and she didn't resist.

"Just before you came in. They put it into the IV. I'm waiting for it to take me into la-la land."

"Kariss," Dr. Garrett said, her shoulders arched like an angry cat's, "you could have told me that you and Agent Harris were friends."

"I wanted you to listen to Tigo as a professional first," Kariss said. "I planned to tell you during our discussion."

"You expect me to believe that?"

"I have no reason to lie."

The renowned doctor needed a little help

with her bedside manner. Tigo bit back a caustic remark. "Does our friendship make any difference?"

"You and Kariss deceived me."

"I don't think so." Tigo swallowed what he wanted to say. "Our relationship goes back a long time. I tend to be her bodyguard."

"Right," Kariss whispered. "More than that. More . . ."

Were those her words or the pain meds talking?

Dr. Garrett cleared her throat. "Agent Steadman, what information do you have regarding the shooting?"

No doubt the woman remembered Ryan's manners were a little more genteel than Tigo's.

"Investigators are combing the area," Ryan said. "We need to ask you some questions, if you feel up to it."

She wrung her hands. "I apologize for my abruptness. It's not my normal mode of conversing during stress."

Tigo had yet to see an amiable side of the woman. "A shooting can do that," he said.

"Dr. Garrett," Ryan said, "can you tell us your version of what happened?"

"I can. Please call me Amy. I'm so sorry. I know this is my fault. I shouldn't have asked

Kariss to join me for coffee." She drew in a breath. "Honestly, we were there to discuss your suggestion about my taking advantage of a protective detail."

The shooting proved the two women were a hair too late for FBI protection.

"I understand the officer has questioned you, but do you mind repeating the series of events that led up to the shooting?"

"I'll do all I can. We arrived in separate cars for a four o'clock appointment. The rain was coming down in sheets, so I don't think either of us noted anything unusual in the parking lot. We bought coffee and two cookies, then sat at a table near the window."

"Anyone else in the coffee shop?"

"A couple across the room, and two women at another table. All of them were seated near the bakery display. I don't remember any particulars, but an officer took their information."

"Good. So you were drinking coffee, and someone shot Kariss."

She shook her head. "Not exactly. I accidentally knocked my purse onto the floor. When I bent to pick it up, I tipped over my coffee. Kariss reached to help, and that's when she was shot."

So Kariss had taken a bullet for Amy.

Realization caused Tigo's gut to churn. "Did she stand to grab the cup?"

"Leaned over the table. It all happened so fast."

"I know we were lucky," Kariss whispered, as though reading Tigo's thoughts.

He squeezed her hand. *Thanks, God, for looking out for these women.* He caught himself. It was the second time he'd prayed today.

The officer reentered the room. "I've verified the information with Detective Montoya." He handed Ryan the report. "You'll find this interesting."

Tigo studied Ryan's face. Not a muscle moved. Then a twitch. "What does it say?"

"The bullet came from a Beretta 90-Two .40 S&W. The shooter used a hollow-back bullet." Ryan paused as if in thought. "Says here the lab almost missed the signature. When it peeled back on impact, a name etched on the inside was revealed . . . Amy. A second bullet was lodged into the floor and had Kariss's name inscribed the same way."

Amy gasped. "No. This isn't the way it was supposed to happen."

6:00 P.M. WEDNESDAY

Despite the sharp pain and waiting for the

366

meds to kick in, Kariss sensed anger pouring through her veins. Had Amy set her up for some freak power play with the assailant? Before she could pose a question, Tigo was on it.

"What do you mean 'This isn't the way it was supposed to happen'?"

Kariss stared at Amy. "Answer him."

"If anyone was to get hurt, it was supposed to be me," Amy said.

"You haven't answered my question." Tigo appeared in control, but Kariss heard the underlying fury in his tone. "Had you been threatened before the shooting?"

Amy stiffened. "No. I . . . I just think I'm living on borrowed time."

"Do you know more about the bombing than you've relayed to law-enforcement officers?"

"No." She rubbed her arms.

"Do you have information about the Yeat bombing?"

"No. I've never met Joanna or Jonathan Yeat."

"That you are aware of."

"I'm positive." Amy reached for a tissue in her purse. "I feel like anyone who gets close to me ends up getting hurt."

"Feelings, Dr. Garrett? Those might work in your office, but not here. I exist on facts."

"I don't have anything to tell you."

"Don't or won't?"

As much as the ache in Kariss's head consumed her, she was coherent enough to recall that Amy had seemed evasive from the beginning. On more than one occasion, her words had sounded mechanical . . . rehearsed. Kariss had been left with more questions than answers, and yet she'd agreed to help Amy tell her story. Maybe she deserved to get shot for her own stupidity.

"Ditch the feelings and give me an answer." Tigo glared at her. "What did you mean by your original statement?"

Amy toyed with her bracelet. "I never figured Kariss taking a bullet for me into the equation. I only wanted to draw him out with the book. Period."

"Draw who out?"

"Wait just a minute," Kariss said. "I believed you when you said you wanted to write this novel to help other women who have been victims of violent crimes. When were you going to tell me your real motive?"

"When you agreed to write my story." Amy's gaze darted around the room. "But the appropriate time to tell you never came."

"I asked you specifically about the assailant reading the book, and you dismissed the idea. You claimed he wouldn't read a novel written by a women's fiction author. And what about that line you fed me about being a woman of integrity?"

"I lied." Amy raised her chin. "I'm sorry."

"Is that what you'd have said for my eulogy?"

Tigo held up his hand. "Look, we can't stop this man if we don't have the truth," he said. "Do you realize an innocent woman could have been killed, not to mention yourself? What about Joanna and Alexia Yeat? How many people need to be killed or wounded before you realize the seriousness of the situation? You, Dr. Garrett, are withholding information essential to an FBI investigation."

Amy reached across Kariss's bed and jammed her finger into Tigo's chest. "You have no idea what this is about. No clue. Maybe my brother's right."

Tigo's face flushed red. "How?"

"You haven't caught this guy in twenty-three years. What makes you think you can now?"

Kariss fought the sleep enveloping her. Did Amy care more about finding her assailant than who might be killed in the quest to do so?

CHAPTER 43

Tigo glanced around his living room, everything orderly and in place. Exasperation ate at the lining of his stomach. The intricacies of the two cases baffled him, and he needed to clear his head. Snatching his keys and a coat, he headed for the door. His mind wouldn't let him rest until today's shooting and the two bombings made sense.

Keeping Kariss safe was his mission. But he'd failed.

Outside, under a veil of blackness, he walked the streets of his neighborhood. The only sounds were an occasional barking dog or a vehicle driving past. The lights from other homes were slowly being turned off for the night.

If only Tigo could figure out the key players. Too many people had motive and too few had the means. But only one person shook hands with both crimes.

Amy Garrett hid behind the walls of her past. From what he'd seen, she tore them down only to build another one. And Tigo didn't need to be a shrink to diagnose her condition. Her demons clung to her PhDs and allowed her to help others while she continued to suffer the consequences of her childhood.

Amy's parents had arrived at the hospital around seven o'clock. Calm people. No pretense in their body language. Genuinely concerned about their daughter and Kariss, a woman they'd never met. Neither of them had done business with Jonathan or Joanna Yeat. When he and Ryan questioned them about Baxter, regret filled their words. Their plans were to have him enter rehab upon release from jail. But Tigo still needed to investigate the older Garretts. At this point, he needed every detail covered.

He stuffed his hands into his pockets and walked on. He understood Kariss's desire to befriend Amy, although he didn't agree with her rationalization. She had compassion for what happened to Amy as a child, more than most people . . .

His thoughts drifted back to last summer, when he'd begun working with Kariss as a favor to Linc. During her days as a news anchor for Channel 5, Kariss had helped

Linc solve crimes by reaching out for public support. One of her reports had been influential to Linc's career, which led to his current role as Special Agent in Charge of the Houston FBI office.

At the time, Tigo couldn't think of a worse assignment than helping a woman write a suspense novel. He'd even referred to it as babysitting a diva. Kariss's book was based on a five-year-old cold case about a little girl named Cherished Doe who'd been starved to death, her body discarded in a grove of pine trees. The case had touched all those who'd learned about the crime, including Tigo. He'd kept the child's autopsy picture and often reviewed the case in hopes of finding a reason to reopen it. As Kariss had examined the facts for her novel, she'd gotten involved in the research. Danger stalked her . . . nearly killed her. That's what Tigo feared now — Kariss again walking the line with a crazed killer linked to Amy Garrett and the Yeats.

At a street corner, he stopped to examine how he felt about the renowned Dr. Amy Garrett. She had lied to Kariss about her true motive for writing her story and had knowingly put Kariss's life in danger. Kariss insisted she'd known the risks involved in writing another cold case novel but had jumped in with her laptop anyway.

God, will You protect her?

He'd done it again. Prayed as though he believed in a deity . . . who cared.

Questions continued to bombard his mind like mosquitoes buzzing around a stagnant pond. But he couldn't drive them away because he didn't have the answers. What about the nutcase Baxter Garrett? Were the older Garretts withholding information?

Tigo crossed the street and continued down the other side toward home. He was cold and still didn't have any answers. He was convinced that the car bomber in the two incidents, today's shooter, and the assailant in Amy's cold case were the same person. But how was Tigo going to pull it all together? How could the assailant have known about the book project if he wasn't close to Amy?

The book . . . As Tigo entered his home, he wondered if Amy had mentioned the book on social media. He went to his laptop and checked her Facebook page, skimming through the many posts.

"*New York Times* bestselling author Kariss Walker has agreed to write my story."

Amy had purposely baited her assailant, and Kariss had taken the fall. What was the woman thinking? He respected Amy's determination, but he also wanted to shove her into a box labeled "Selfish."

On Amy's Facebook page, other posts referenced conversations between her and Kariss. Today she'd announced to cyberspace that the two were having coffee at a Starbucks, and she'd indicated the exact location. She'd sent the shooter an invitation.

Tigo checked Kariss's Facebook page and saw she'd announced the book project but hadn't given any details.

Tigo grabbed his keys and laptop. If he was going to be up all night, he'd rather work beside Kariss at the hospital. At least he could help her if she needed anything. He wanted to be there when she opened her eyes, to see if a light for him still shimmered in those brown pools. He'd seen it before, but he hesitated to give his heart away again, considering what happened with Erin. But Kariss was different — full of life and spunk and so unlike Erin. If only Tigo could be the man Kariss deserved.

He couldn't hold her and kiss away the problems. But tonight he'd watch over her.

JANUARY 24
2:30 A.M. THURSDAY
Long after midnight, the hospital hummed

with activity. Staff talked and laughed, ignoring the courtesy of providing a restful environment for patients. The sound of footsteps echoing down the hallway never ended. But Kariss slept anyway.

A police officer, courtesy of HPD, stood outside her door in case the shooter decided to finish the job. Tigo wouldn't let anyone who planned to hurt her inside the room, which was the reason he'd chosen to sit facing the door. He studied the woman who'd captured his senses. In the shadows, with a hint of illumination streaming across her features, her beauty held him captive.

Earlier, when the ER had been full of officers and family, she'd protested against spending the night. But her dad and Vicki had been the voices of reason, and she'd relinquished. Not many days ago, Vicki had won the argument against an overnight stay in the hospital. But she hadn't been shot.

Tigo wanted to touch Kariss's hand but was afraid it might wake her, so he turned his attention to finding out who was behind the crime. The hospital staff provided him with a code to get onto their Internet so he could establish an encrypted VPN connection and search the FBI-secured sites.

Tigo had requested a list of every woman who'd ever been counseled at Freedom's

Way or attended a conference. Fortunately, Amy had agreed to the request earlier in the evening and had forwarded him the files. Scrolling through the names, he found that Vanessa Whitcom and Joanna Yeat had attended a women's conference a year ago at Houston's First Baptist Church, where Dr. Amy Garrett had spoken three times over the course of a weekend.

The FIG never stopped working, and information continually streamed through his Blackberry. Right now it was showing him that none of the women who'd sought counseling from Dr. Amy Garrett had criminal records.

Voices in the hallway brought Tigo's attention to the door.

"Sir, you cannot enter this room," the young female officer said.

"I have to see Kariss Walker. It's important," a male voice said. "I'm a reporter for Channel 5. See? Here's my ID."

Disgust washed over Tigo as he closed his laptop and stood. He recognized McDougal's voice.

"I repeat." The officer's voice demanded attention. "You cannot enter this room. If you don't leave now, I'll have to detain you."

"Oh, we can work this out. How about a crisp hundred-dollar bill? Just between you and me."

The officer picked up her radio and asked for backup.

Tigo leaned against the doorway and smiled at Mike McDougal. "The officer asked you to leave. Now I'm telling you. Or should I assist HPD in making an arrest? Sounds tempting, since there's a bribe involved."

McDougal raised his hands. His lips curled, a giveaway for his contempt. "Hey, I'm just looking for a story. Heard my good friend Kariss had been shot, and I wanted to get to the truth."

"At three in the morning?" Tigo jammed his hands into his jeans pockets. "I'm sure if she wants you to gain any more notoriety than you already have, she'll call."

McDougal's eyes narrowed. The man was easier to read than a comic book. "Do you have any idea what I could do to destroy the public's view of the FBI? I know how badly you thugs want to look good in the community."

"I've read your blog. This is the real scoop, McDougal. I'm not denying you a story. The people of this city have a right to know what's going on. My problem is when you attempt to undermine law-enforcement mandates in a manner that doesn't reflect the integrity of Channel 5 and choose to break the law."

"Your day is coming. One day Kariss will toss you out like three-day-old trash. Then your bodyguard days will be over."

"Out of here. Now."

The two backup officers arrived. McDougal offered a mock salute and moved down the hall. Tigo turned to the police officer. "I have no doubt you could have handled him. He and I just have some history. It's all about his name on the next story."

"No problem. But I was itching to handcuff him."

"Do us all a favor. If he returns, haul him in."

"And throw away the key," Kariss said quietly. "Talk to me, Tigo. Why are you here?"

3:15 A.M. THURSDAY
Kariss needed rest to heal, but she wanted to talk to Tigo. Their last conversation about their relationship had exposed the truth, but nothing had been resolved. At least in words. One of Vicki's comments wouldn't leave Kariss alone — "It's hard to trust again when you've been hurt." That was Tigo's fear, and instead of addressing it, Kariss had swept it under a rug.

"Do you feel like talking?" she said.

He chuckled. "I'm here for whatever you need."

"That's loaded."

His hand tightened around hers. "What's inside that pretty head?"

"Us."

"Can't think of a better subject." He hesitated. "Unless I've hit ground zero."

"I think we're halfway up the peak."

In the shadows, the lines on Tigo's face softened. Not everyone saw this side of him. His Buzz Lightyear image wouldn't permit it. "Where do I stand?"

"I miss you. We could try again. Date. Slowly. Go to church together."

He nodded. "I keep hoping God will text so I'll know He's real."

"Then it's not faith."

"You have a point. I've heard that as long as I'm searching, God will find me."

"I've never stopped praying for you." Or caring.

"Thanks."

Kariss more than cared for Tigo, but his failed marriage stopped him from giving his whole heart to her or God.

Both of them needed patience with a heavy dose of prayer.

CHAPTER 44

Kariss waited for her doctor to release her from the hospital. She'd been poked and x-rayed and stitched. Not all in that order. But after she had awakened in the middle of the night and found Tigo at her bedside, the hospital routine didn't seem to matter so much. Maybe she'd simply been vulnerable, but hearing his voice and seeing him towering in the doorway had eased away the pain.

Though she was alone now, she wouldn't forget his tenderness or the sacrifice of sleep he'd made for her.

"We can't give up on each other," he'd whispered just before leaving earlier this morning. "Believe that, Kariss."

A tear had trickled down her cheek, perhaps an emotional response from the medication. "I —"

"You don't have to say a word." He leaned

over the bed. "I know your heart. I see what you feel in your eyes. We'll get the junk behind us and move forward together. Just don't give up on me."

She swallowed the lump in her throat. "I won't."

"I can't do the Jesus thing unless I feel it's real."

"I understand . . . Thanks for being here. Not just for taking care of McDougal, but for everything."

"How could I sleep when I'm concerned about you?"

She clamped onto her lower lip to fight the tears threatening to flow. She despised weak women. "You must rehearse what you say to me."

"It's part of the package." He smiled. "Even the things you don't want to hear. But you are the bravest woman I know."

"I don't feel brave." Her determination to take care of herself had failed miserably, and Tigo deserved her cooperation. "I'm thinking about taking residence at a hotel for a few days, the kind with a pair of FBI agents assigned to keep me safe."

He planted a kiss on her forehead. "That makes me one happy man. I'll make the arrangements when I get to the office. Remember Jerry Reiner? I'll find out if he's

381

available. He has a new partner, and the two work well together. Call me when you're released, and I'll have them take you home and wait at the condo while you pack."

Hours later, Kariss regretted agreeing to protective detail, but Tigo had seemed at peace with her decision. She would do this for him, even if hiding was a coward's way out. Closing her eyes until the pain meds took effect again, she thought about their sweet early morning hours together.

She heard a knock and turned to see Amy standing in the doorway. Kariss hadn't decided how she felt toward the famed psychologist now. She pointed to a chair beside her bed, the one Tigo had occupied hours earlier.

"I wasn't sure you'd see me." Amy scooted the chair away from the bed.

"The jury's still out. A little truth would go a long way."

"I suppose."

"You suppose?" Kariss's head throbbed. Or was the pain due to stress? "Have you been using me as bait?"

Amy moistened her lips. "No. His anger should be aimed at me and only me. I fought the odds and won. Every day he lets me live is a bonus day. I never thought he'd target you."

Kariss attempted to manage her anger. "That's rich, Amy. Oh, and what about endangering the lives of my sister and niece? How do you explain that? Or doesn't it matter as long as you exact revenge? That's what you really want, isn't it?" Kariss endured another jolt of pain, but it didn't bridle her tongue. "Says a lot for your Christian testimony. Do you encourage deceit in your counseling?"

Amy glanced at the door, and then her eyes shifted back to Kariss.

"Stay right where you are. I want to see your face when you answer me. Don't even think about leaving. I'm in the mood to chase you down the hall."

Amy wrung her hands. Kariss had seen that mannerism before. The first time, it brought pity. No more. "Answers," Kariss said. "I deserve honesty."

"I'm trying."

"Try harder."

"Now you sound like Agent Harris."

"He's a good teacher. Look, I've been run off the road. My loved ones have been hurt and frightened. I've been threatened and followed. Now shot. I think you hit the bull's-eye by using me to draw your assailant from his hole. Maybe he's under my hospital bed. Maybe I was just plain stupid to agree to this writing project."

Amy's eyes pooled.

"Don't turn on the waterworks, Doc, 'cause I'm not buying any of it. What have you not told the FBI, HPD, or me? Where is the logic in holding back information from those who want to help?"

"I didn't think." Amy buried her face in her hands. "I'm sorry. Really sorry."

The tone of her voice told Kariss to back off. Amy was sincere. "If you're serious about the apology, then you need to tell Tigo and Ryan everything. What about Sergeant Bud Hanson? The man is haunted by this crime too."

"Bud called me this morning."

"What did he suggest?"

"To do the protective-detail thing. Toss the book idea. But I can't. It just delays things."

"I took yesterday very personally. You have a death wish?"

"My motto is walk with courage and put fear on the run."

"And you counsel women who've been victimized? I understand you've helped many women, but I wouldn't recommend you to anyone." The longer Kariss talked, the more the pain in her head intensified, as though the meds had forgotten their job. "The FBI is working with HPD to solve this crime. They're close to solid answers. The best thing you can do is cooperate. That includes telling the whole truth. Is Baxter more involved than you've claimed?"

Amy's eyes flared. "Why does he need to be brought into this? He's ill and needs to be hospitalized. He's not a murderer."

"I'm not beyond believing he knows more about who assaulted you than you care to admit."

"He doesn't know a thing. He simply has issues . . . issues that could be resolved if the assailant were caught. I need to go." She stood abruptly. The woman's emotions seemed even more scattered now.

"I want the truth. Or I'll tell the FBI you're withholding information."

"All right." Kariss saw fear in her eyes. "Emails. I received two threatening emails about pursuing the novel. They came after I posted on Facebook. I kept them. Not sure why. When I responded, the messages came back undeliverable."

"Novel quotes?"

Amy nodded.

"Me too. You're afraid and playing Miss Independent, and it's going to get you killed. Look, I'm mad, but I'm still your friend, and self-reliance and stubbornness are traits I'm quite familiar with. Sometimes we have to let others help."

Amy nodded, but she remained standing.

Kariss pointed to the chair again. "We can talk through this. You thought a novel would bring the assailant into the open. Into a showdown. Well, it worked. But it backfired."

"When Special Agents Harris and Steadman explained the car-bombing links, all I could think about was how much bolder he'd become." Amy shrugged. "But I've never met Joanna or her daughter."

"But his boldness means that his chances of getting caught are exponentially greater now." Kariss poured hope into her words. "I've been down this road before. It's not pretty, and it's not one you want to walk alone."

"But everything that's happened means he's closer to me than I thought. I . . . I could know him. See him every day."

"Do you suspect anyone?"

"No, and I analyze every male I see. Sad but true. He's probably a pillar of the community, and I haven't the sense to recognize it."

Perhaps Amy was right . . . Could the assailant be someone respected in the community? Kariss inwardly startled.

CHAPTER 45

Tigo welcomed Ryan inside his cubicle. "You heard the news?"

"Hard to believe that Amy and Kariss are planning to share living quarters while in protective detail," Ryan said. "That should be interesting. Odd, since last night I thought Kariss was going to climb out of bed after Amy."

"At least we'll be able to keep them safe until this guy's found," Tigo said. But he shared his partner's skepticism about the two women getting along. Both were strong personalities — stubborn and opinionated. He respected that about Kariss, but the two women together could be . . . volatile.

"Sounds like a combo for trouble," Ryan said. "Let's hope Jerry and Hank are up for it."

"Right. We'll see how long it lasts. Kariss can't handle being confined, and she's too

388

curious to just let us work through the case. I'd rather toss her in jail."

Ryan chuckled. "Are you jealous of Amy?"

Tigo lifted a brow. "I might be." No point in telling Ryan that he'd spent the night at the hospital.

"Thought so. Where are they?"

"Locked down at an extended-stay hotel off FM 1960 near I-45 north. Hope those two don't try something stupid." Tigo yawned. "Every hour they take advantage of the program brings us closer to the guy who thinks he's outsmarted us. But we both know what Kariss is capable of."

"You two need to get back together so you can keep tabs on her . . . activities."

"Don't think that would stop her. But we're talking."

Ryan leaned on Tigo's desk. "Hey, that's great. Didn't mean to pry."

"No problem. What she doesn't know is I'm more determined than she could ever be."

Ryan grinned. "So what's on our list?"

"Got a lead on a man who might be David Smith. Works on an offshore rig. Fits the MO — rough, rowdy, a drinker. A week ago, he bragged to some buds that an old girlfriend had been killed in a car bomb."

"Where'd you find him?"

"At a bar near the channel called the Stragglers. Bartender's an informant. I'd shown him Ian's sketch." Tigo handed Ryan his handwritten notes. "He now goes by the name of Cohn Wesson and has other aliases. He's wanted for a handful of crimes. Murder stretches what he's done in the past, and I have no idea how he fits with the Garrett bombing."

Ryan studied the pic of Cohn Wesson, possibly David Smith. "Blond, blue-eyed. From the size of his shoulders, he's probably a bodybuilder. Mouthful of white teeth, so he must be good with his fists. Let's check him out tonight."

"I'll flip for steaks." Tigo needed to get his mind in the game and off Kariss. "Then we can check on Smith and Wesson."

Ryan chuckled. "He probably thought he was clever with his aliases. More like an ego trip."

10:00 P.M. THURSDAY

Tigo assessed the smoky bar, taking in the characters — and they were characters. Hadn't seen that many tattoos in one place since he helped bring down one of Houston's largest Hispanic gangs. He and Ryan fit right in. His partner wore a wool cap pulled over his bald head and had added a long scar to his left cheek — to make him look extra mean. His five o'clock shadow added to the effect. Ryan often took on a tougher persona when working undercover. It made for interesting conversation with the bad guys.

Tigo was using a wide prosthetic nose, plenty of bling, and a black leather jacket, a hoodie underneath.

Kariss would have loved this place, a great setting for one of her novels. But Tigo couldn't think about her right now. He needed to concentrate on sorting out those who'd welcome a good fight and those who were there to drink. A mix of tobacco and weed weighted the air along with the stench of unwashed bodies.

Tigo and Ryan made their way to the end of the bar, close to an exit but where they could still watch both the front and rear doors. The bartender who'd provided the information worked his way to their end.

"Where's Wesson?" Tigo said.

"Standing at the other end of the bar, wearing a brown leather jacket with a rebel flag on the back. He's had plenty to drink, but he holds his liquor. Doesn't miss a thing, so I'm sure he's spotted you. Two of his buds from the rig are with him."

"Does he know we want to talk?"

"That's all you."

Tigo slipped the bartender an envelope, cash for his tip. He and Ryan made their way toward the man who might be behind the car bombings and shooting. Wesson had sidled himself up to a blonde whose flaxen hair didn't blend with the harsh lines etched into her face.

"Wesson?" Tigo said. "Or is it Smith?"

The man turned and sneered. "What's that supposed to mean?"

Tigo pulled out his ID and discreetly flashed it. "We need to talk."

"Can't you see I'm busy?"

"It'll have to wait, dude. We have some questions. It'll only take a few minutes, and then you can continue your business with the lady."

Wesson's jaw tightened. "What's this about? Who are you?" Two men stepped up next to him.

"Call off your dogs, or the three of you will face FBI arrest," Tigo said.

Wesson hesitated. No doubt he was packing.

"I wouldn't reach for a weapon if I were you." Ryan's voice registered barely above a whisper . . . a deadly one. "Hate to tell your boss he can find you at the morgue."

"They come with me."

"Then they'll go down with you," Ryan said.

Wesson glanced around. "All right. Let's talk outside."

Tigo and Ryan stayed on Wesson's heels on the way to the front entrance. About ten feet from the door, Wesson bolted, grabbing a person on each side of him and shoving them in Tigo's and Ryan's paths, sending bodies flying in every direction.

The agents stepped over the bodies and ran after him. Wesson headed for a motorcycle.

"Stop! FBI! You know what happens if we pull our weapons."

Wesson slowed and raised his hands.

"On the ground." Tigo kept his firearm aimed at Wesson as the man lowered himself to the pavement.

"I haven't done anything." Wesson tossed in a few curses to emphasize his point.

Ryan cuffed him, then pulled a .38 Special and a pocket knife from inside Wesson's jacket. "We're taking a trip to the other end of town. You can cool off in custody. See if it improves your attitude."

"I know my rights."

Ryan chuckled. "Let's go talk about it. We've identified three aliases, and you're

wanted in two states for assault and robbery."

"Wrong guy. You don't know what you're
talking about."

"Convince us," Tigo said.

11:50 P.M. THURSDAY
Back at the office, Tigo, Ryan, and Wesson
sat in an interview room. Tigo observed
Wesson, whose fury had escalated since
they'd gotten to the office. "This will go a
lot easier if you cooperate."

When Wesson didn't respond, Tigo dove
into questioning. If the suspect didn't
request a lawyer, Tigo wasn't going to waste
time. "You've used the names David Smith,
Cohn Wesson, and Alex Winchester. I bet
you think you're clever. Our report says
your real name is Jarod Mason from Beau-
mont, Texas."

Wesson leaned back in the chair, wearing
the same sneer they'd seen earlier. "The
FBI's getting pretty smart. But a man has
the right to use whatever name he chooses."

"Especially if you're going to beat up a
convenience store clerk and rob an eighty-
year-old man."

"I didn't do either of those. Someone set
me up."

"Do you think we'd haul you in here if we

394

didn't have evidence? Do you want to make a deal or not?"

Wesson glared. "What do you want to know?"

"Joanna Yeat was recently killed in a car bombing along with her daughter. We understand you threatened her. What can you tell us about it?"

Wesson rubbed the back of his neck. "I met with Joanna a few times, and we had words, but I didn't kill her. And I don't kill kids."

"What was your relationship with her?"

"We knew each other a long time ago."

"Involved?"

He chuckled. "I helped her get through college. Saved her from asking her family for money."

"You don't have the professor look," Tigo said. "What did you do?"

"I helped businessmen get dates with her."

"What else?"

"Took pics. She was my model."

"What kind of pics?"

"The kind that pay big bucks. What do you think?"

"So you took porn shots of Joanna."

"It's called art."

"So is drawing in mud. When did you last see her?"

"A few weeks ago. Don't remember the date."

"Yes, you do."

"Uh, a Saturday afternoon."

"Where?"

"At a mall."

Ian hadn't lied. "What was the occasion?" Tigo leaned in. "Rich woman who refuses to hand over a few dollars spells murder to me."

"I had nothing to do with her death."

"What happened at the mall?"

"She was supposed to bring me something, but she forgot."

"Were you blackmailing her?"

Wesson narrowed his eyes. "She owed me."

"How much?"

"I asked for one mil to keep her secret."

"About the photos?"

Wesson smirked. "What of it? I have a right to earn a living."

"I bet." Tigo showed him the phone numbers found in Joanna's tennis shoe and on her cell phone records. "Are these your numbers? Burner phones?"

Wesson narrowed his gaze.

"Do you want to be arrested for murder?"

His gaze darted. "Yes. Those are both mine."

"Where were you the morning of Wednesday, January sixteenth?"

"At home minding my own business."

"What's the address?"

The man rattled off the numbers and street name. Ryan cleared his throat and glanced up from his iPad. "That apartment complex closed a year ago. Try again."

"Oh yeah, that was my previous address. I'm sharing a trailer house in Galveston with a friend."

Ryan typed in the information. "The property belongs to the owner of the park. So you live alone?"

"With a friend, a lady friend. She'll vouch for me on the sixteenth."

"Name," Tigo said. "We want to call her. Now."

"Can't help you. She's working."

"You mean you don't have the number or you're lying?" Tigo waited, not moving a muscle. Wesson squared his jaw in a stare down.

"Which is it?"

"We're separated at the moment."

Tigo laughed. "I think we have our bomber, Special Agent Steadman."

"Wait." The man whipped his attention from Tigo to Ryan. "I didn't blow up the Yeat car."

"Where are you keeping the Semtex?" Tigo said.

"I don't have any of the stuff. Look, you can't pin this on me."

"We can if you're guilty. We have witnesses who saw you with Joanna at the mall, and the testimony says you two were arguing. Then she's killed. Give us a full confession, and things will go easier."

"I don't know any more than what I heard on the news." He rubbed his forehead. "Search my place. You won't find any explosives."

"Since when does a smart man store kilos of Semtex in a trailer?" Tigo said. "Did you bomb Dr. Amy Garrett's vehicle too?"

The man shook his head. "Never heard of her. I'm innocent."

"Maybe you'll remember after a few days in jail." Tigo picked up his Blackberry. "I'll check on your reservation."

CHAPTER 46

The hotel felt like a prison.

Kariss was accustomed to her own bed in her own home, and the unfamiliar sights and sounds of the two-bedroom hotel suite contributed to a sleepless night. The heater rattled, reminding her of an old man's bones, and the smell of it when it kicked on reminded her of couples' activities that were better left unsaid. Long after midnight, she gave in and took a pain pill to ease the throbbing in her head. But sleep never came. Just when she felt herself easing into oblivion, something in her brain snapped . . . a thought . . . a reminder that this wasn't her home.

Or did she spend the night restless because of the circumstances? Last summer she'd refused when Tigo insisted she take a vacation until the bad guys were apprehended.

And she'd been nabbed by a Mexican gang who had wanted her dead. Nearly succeeded in killing her too.

Now she wanted to pull on her tennis shoes and go running.

She wanted to go out for breakfast.

She wanted to catch a sale.

What about church this week?

And she was being incredibly selfish.

Tossing back the sheet and the blue-and-gold-flowered quilt that matched the one in Amy's room, Kariss swung her legs over the side of the bed and took her bad attitude to the kitchen. She'd brought coffee from home, and right now she needed a strong cup. Her gaze settled on her Bible, which rested on the counter. Certain she'd be convicted for her less-than-admirable thoughts, she considered skipping the morning's reading and study. With a sigh, she snatched up the leather-bound book. What else could she do at four in the morning? Drink herself into a caffeine high and continue to stress about her situation? Why not talk to the One who had it all under control?

She glanced at Amy's closed door and hoped her suitemate slept until noon. Most of Kariss's ill mood was spelled A-M-Y. Kariss had forgiven her, but she hadn't gotten past her frustration at being betrayed.

She'd brew the coffee and take a fresh cup to both Jerry and Hank, who were keeping vigil in their car in the rear parking lot. According to a text from Tigo, the two had just come on duty at three, so she could at least show some hospitality. Then she'd read her Bible — perhaps the passage about the Good Samaritan . . . as soon as she decided whether she was the victim or the one who did the bandaging.

Restlessness had settled into her bones and rocked her equilibrium, and this was only the first morning of solitary confinement.

Fifteen minutes later, Amy emerged from her room. Dressed in a white robe, she appeared to survey the room. One glance at the dark circles beneath her reddened eyes revealed her equally sleepless night.

"I just made a pot of coffee." Kariss rose from the sofa. "I'll get you a cup."

"I'd take something stronger if you had it, and I'm not a drinking woman." Amy slumped into an upholstered chair and wrung her hands.

"Need a shrink?" Kariss hoped a light tone would help Amy focus.

"How about a little sympathy for my situation?" Amy snapped. "After all, I've lived with this for a while."

All thought about the Bible reading a few minutes ago did little to stop Kariss's anger from sizzling like bacon. "How about a little sympathy directed this way?"

Amy's head jerked up. "I'm the one who had a bullet with my name on it."

"And I took it, Dr. Garrett. Not to mention narrowly escaping another bullet that had my name on it. What am I? If you're accustomed to having those around you tread in ballet slippers, count me out. I've forgotten how to pirouette."

Amy opened her mouth, then shut it abruptly. "I'll get my own coffee."

"Look, we've got to get along or this won't work. I have my laptop and can disappear into my room. No problem. Working on your novel is therapeutic. But we do need to occasionally communicate. We're supposed to be helping the investigation and working on our friendship."

Amy sloshed the coffee while pouring it into her cup. "I'm sorry. Lately those seem to be my two favorite words. But you're right. I'm used to others catering to me. Other counselors can see my clients today, and you can write, but neither will help get us out of this mess. I hate this game. Twenty-three years I've waited for him to surface, and now I'm terrified."

"Might change the ending of the book."

"You and Agent Harris fit together well. Your remarks remind me of scraping chalk."

"Because they're true? They make you think?"

"Both. I respond better to people who offer encouragement and compassion."

"Your choice, Amy. We can make the best of our situation or argue like two junior high girls." Kariss noted her own empty cup. "What quotes were in your emails?"

"Two from *In Cold Blood.* I've read the book at least a dozen times trying to find a clue to the assailant's identity."

Kariss cringed. "I'm sorry."

Amy returned to the chair. "You see, I'm a fraud. I counsel hurting women and give fancy speeches, while inside I'm an emotional cripple."

"I'm not your family or a staff member," Kariss said. "Friendship isn't a one-way street."

"You remind me of my old therapist," Amy said. "She wouldn't take excuses either."

"Maybe you should call her."

"She died."

Pity seeped into Kariss's heart as she went and filled her coffee cup again. But not enough to turn her into a doormat. "Do you want to wait this out in separate rooms?"

"Not sure."

"If we don't kill each other first."

Amy smiled. "I deserved that. Truce, okay? Let me drink this coffee and take a shower. Then we can talk."

"Here are my thoughts," Kariss said. "I can't sit here and wait for the FBI and HPD to solve this case. Nor do I want to munch on M&M's or play word games on my iPhone."

"I'd rather crawl in a hole and die." Amy's voice was laced with acid. "I've lived my life looking over my shoulder and waiting. I'm tired of it."

"I have an idea." Kariss lifted her cup to her lips and took a sip of coffee while studying Amy. "Facebook got us both into trouble, right?"

"What are you thinking?"

Kariss grinned. "Consider social media's ability to spread the word while you take your shower."

9:30 A.M. FRIDAY

Tigo, Linc, and Ryan stood in front of the squad board labeled "Semtex Bomber." The details and photos of the victims were posted for agents to brainstorm the next step of their investigation. Unfortunately, they still didn't have substantial evidence for any of the suspects.

"Baxter Garrett couldn't have shot Kariss," Linc said. "David Smith/Wesson might have threatened Joanna, but he has a solid alibi during the time of the shooting. We're missing something. Maybe a few coincidences are clouding the picture."

Ryan pointed to Joanna's picture. "Makes sense that Joanna filed for divorce to protect her family and get enough money from the settlement to pay Wesson off."

"We haven't found the right bad guy," Tigo said. "We haven't dug deep enough to find the real motive that links both bombings. Amy was a child when she was assaulted, and Joanna was in her midforties when the bomb took her life. I don't see anything linking the two women. None of our suspects are old enough to have assaulted Amy, which makes me question how many persons are involved."

"Jonathan's pressing me," Linc said. "Last night at a deacons' meeting, he and Taylor had an argument about the budget. I thought the two were going to take a punch at each other. Oddly enough, Francis Willis took Taylor's side. Wonder how long that will last."

Tigo sighed. "I know I suspected Jonathan in the beginning, but not anymore."

Linc stared at the board. "He tugged at his ear more than once during the argument, and he was distracted, angry. I think the unsolved murders and dealing with Joanna's involvement with an escort service is driving him near the edge." He nodded. "Then there's Ian."

"Want us to talk to them again?" Tigo said.

"Jonathan's at work, and the boys are in school. There's a game tonight too." Linc hesitated. "Let me do this. I don't think for one second that he's a part of this. I'll talk to him when we're finished here — away from our office and his."

"I've been thinking," Tigo said. "If I could get Curt away from his family and buds, he might open up. I offered him a way out if he ever needed to talk. Seemed receptive. Ian, on the other hand, had no interest in even listening to my offer."

Linc studied the squad board. "Jonathan said the boys refused to see counselors. Both said it was too soon. Slim chance of either of them opening up to an FBI agent, but I'll mention it and see if anything happens. It's far-fetched, but it could bring us closer to ending this case."

Back at his desk, Tigo considered calling Kariss to see how she and Amy were handling the situation. Instead, he decided that when this was over, he'd order a dozen roses for each woman — red ones for Kariss and yellow for Amy. Once they recovered from being holed up together, they'd think he was the best agent in Houston.

He suspected both women had long since regretted agreeing to a protective detail. They were probably bored. But Kariss could write and do the social-media thing. He checked her Facebook page but didn't see anything alarming. Then he checked Amy's page. He didn't expect to read anything after he'd lectured her about informing followers of her every move. But she'd been at it again.

"What is she thinking?" Tigo was certain everyone within earshot heard him. What were those two women planning this time?

Bestselling writer Kariss Walker and I have spent the last few days outlining the ending of our novel. I'm thrilled with the story. We plan to use everything that happened to me, including a few details that are not in the records. But we need feedback. What are your thoughts? Should we keep the truth intact or give the information to law-enforcement officials who are working my case?

Did Amy and Kariss really want to know Tigo's thoughts about their ludicrous idea?

"What's up?" Ryan stuck his head into Tigo's cubicle. "I heard your eruption."

"Our daring doctor posted an update on Facebook. Take a look."

Ryan read the post. "Do you see where this is going? My bet is Kariss instigated this."

"Definitely her MO. They're trying to shine a spotlight on this guy again. Brilliant — as long as it doesn't get them killed."

"Can we lock them inside a vault?" Ryan crossed his arms over his chest.

"I'm considering spending my nights on the couch of their hotel room."

Ryan lifted a brow. "Convenient. Plays into your personal plot too."

Tigo frowned. "I'm thinking about their welfare. What would you do if the woman you cared about was in danger? And not for the first time?"

"I'd be all over it. Give it a try. I'm warning you, though — she might throw you out."

"Wouldn't be the first time." Tigo laughed. No point in getting upset about Kariss's latest antics. She had her own mind, and he understood her drive to help Amy.

"Thought you'd want to know. Taylor Yeat just called me."

"How do you rate?"

"I think he's afraid of you."

Tigo laughed again. Comic relief was good for the soul. "He should have seen your disguise last night. It even scared me. So what did he want?"

"Permission to leave town. He wants to visit a church in Mobile that may extend a call."

"Not sure what that means."

"A church there wants to meet him. Hear him preach. See if he's a good fit. Taylor said it was a last-minute thing and wants to fly out tonight."

"Is his wife going?"

"He wasn't sure. She might be needed at home for their three kids."

"How convenient. What about Darena?"

"He claims to have backed away from the relationship. Maybe he's finished looking at greener pastures before his wife leaves him and his ministry is ruined."

Tigo considered his lack of respect for the man. "I think he found the greener pastures grew over a septic tank. I commend the guy if he's trying to clean up his act. Not sure how I feel about him leading a church after what he's done. Would he tell a prospective congregation about his affair?"

"Who knows? So should I call him back, get the info on Mobile, and give him an okay?"

"Sure. If he doesn't make it back Sunday night, we'll know he's guilty." Tigo tapped his pen on the desk and snatched his Blackberry. "I'm calling Darena. See if she's in on this."

But Darena didn't answer at work, at home, or on her cell phone.

"Let's check the airlines. Make sure this isn't a lover's weekend," Tigo said.

The day had gone from stressful to complicated. Tigo wanted to see Kariss and find out what she and Amy were up to, but now he needed to check up on an immoral pastor and attend a high school basketball game.

CHAPTER 47

4:40 P.M. FRIDAY

Kariss had checked Amy's Facebook page numerous times for a comment that would lead them to the man who wanted Amy dead . . . and possibly Kariss too. Only well-wishers had responded. A few suggested an ending for Amy's story, while others recommended the story be told in its entirety. All the responses encouraged whatever means available to ensure that Amy's story was told. Kariss's page had been tagged but was devoid of negative comments that could have revealed the assailant.

To say she was disappointed barely touched the surface of Kariss's feelings. Her head pounded, and she wanted to think something good had come from Wednesday afternoon.

In short, the idea had gone south, and Kariss was bored from her fingertips to her toes. A wild-boar hunt on horseback sounded appealing, but she'd probably have to settle for a game of Monopoly. She clenched her jaw . . . claustrophobia was a terrible foe.

Earlier she'd passed a little time by inviting the agents inside for lunch. Of course, protocol kept them on task, but they were able to talk. Jerry had two girls in high school. His partner's story, however, had a sour taste to it. Hank had just gone through a stressful divorce. His wife couldn't handle his commitment to the FBI. He'd joked about the agents' demanding mistress. It made Kariss think about Tigo. She didn't look at his career as competition. Perhaps it was a challenge during difficult times, but it had never appeared to be a battle of priorities.

After the agents returned to their car, Kariss worked on the second chapter of Amy's story. Concentrating was another matter. Amy stared at her own computer screen, seemingly in another world, while Beethoven's Fifth sounded faintly from her PC.

Kariss waved her hand to get Amy's attention. "Tomorrow I'm going home," she said. "This is nuts."

Amy frowned. "You're asking for trouble, and you're sending me and the FBI mixed messages."

Ah, Amy was back in therapist mode and making too much sense. "Maybe so. But this isn't living."

"Day one, Kariss. You'll get used to it. I thought we'd talked this out. Do you want me to get my notes? You gave your word to Tigo, and then you talked me into it too."

"I remember what we said. My point is, I don't want to get used to this . . . to this confinement. I'll take my chances in my gated community behind locked doors with my 9mm."

"Owning a gun didn't do you any good at the coffee shop. If someone wants you dead bad enough, a security gate isn't going to stop him."

The voice of reason held far too much truth. Kariss paced across the small living area floor. Before she could respond intelligently, someone knocked at the door. A moment later, her fingers touched the knob, but caution sent a warning signal to her brain.

When she looked through the peephole, she saw no one. "Jerry, Hank?" When neither of the agents responded, she repeated her question.

When there was still no response, she moistened her lips and went to retrieve her gun from her purse.

"What are you going to do?" Amy whispered.

"Use this if I need to."

"There are two trained FBI agents in the parking lot assigned to protect us. Stay inside where you belong."

"I don't understand why someone knocked but hasn't answered. They should have identified themselves. Maybe it's housekeeping." She pulled her phone out of her purse as she was grabbing her gun and called each agent's cell phone. Neither man answered.

She swung toward Amy. "I'm going to check on Jerry and Hank."

"You're crazy. What if they're apprehending someone?"

"I have my weapon."

"You're not writing a story, Kariss. You're living a dangerous one."

"Good line, Amy. I'll remember it." She glanced at Amy's frown. "I'll be careful. But I can't sit inside and do nothing. I'm not wired that way."

"Then you need to call an electrician."

Kariss tucked her phone into her jeans pocket. "Another great line. Thanks. Seriously though, God's writing our life stories. It will be okay."

The moment Kariss stepped onto the balcony that overlooked the rear parking lot, she felt relief. Jerry and Hank were in their car, so she waved. When they didn't wave back, she ventured down the steps. They were probably on their phones or something.

The agents were parked two rows back, because it gave them a wider view of the area. With long strides she walked to the car.

Jerry's head was slumped against the steering wheel. Blood matted his gray-white hair. Hank leaned back against the head rest, his throat cut. A piece of folded paper had been stuck in his mouth.

CHAPTER 48

Tigo learned that Taylor Yeat's trip was legit and that he was maybe taking a step in the right direction, since his wife was accompanying him. They must have found someone to watch their children. He hadn't found out anything about Darena, since she had a habit of not answering her cell phone. According to Jonathan, she had her moods.

His personal cell phone rang. Kariss. Did he really want to talk to her after learning about the Facebook post? But what if someone had posted a lead? At least she was safe in protective detail.

When his cell rang the third time he pressed Talk.

"Tigo . . ." Kariss's shaky voice brought him to attention.

"What's wrong?"

"Jerry and Hank, the agents assigned to us . . . They've been murdered. Hank's

416

throat was slit, and Jerry was shot in the head."

Tigo's insides curdled. "Are you sure?"

"I saw them. There's no doubt."

"Did you call the police?"

"Amy has 911 on the line. We're inside the room."

Good men . . . gone. "Are you two okay?"

"Yes. We didn't hear any shots. That means a silencer, right?"

"Probably. Kariss, don't open the door unless you're sure it's the police." He stuffed his work phone and keys into his pants pocket. "Take a deep breath."

"I'm trying to stay calm, but all I can see is . . . them."

He raced down the hall to the parking lot. "Thank God for keeping you and Amy safe." He meant every word.

"There was a note, but I haven't touched a thing." Her voice cracked. "Someone knocked at our door, but when I asked who was there, no one answered. It must have been the killer . . ." Her voice faltered. "Tigo, I hear police sirens."

"I'm on my way. Don't let Amy end the call to the 911 operator until the police arrive." Throat slit . . . an echo from Amy's past?

"Okay," Kariss said. "I'm hanging up now.

417

Amy's not doing well." The phone clicked in his ear.

Tigo pressed in Linc's number.

"You're on your way to the crime scene?" Linc said.

"Yes. Haven't talked to Ryan yet."

"I'll handle it and send him your way. Call me the moment you arrive. I'm on my way to visit Jerry's and Hank's families. I've known these agents for years. Makes me furious."

"I was closer to Jerry than Hank, but I want this guy found. Today."

"Right. What matters now is finding out how the killer knew where we'd hidden Kariss and Amy. And how did he manage to take down two agents?"

Tigo had one thought. "He could have followed the women when Kariss left the hospital and then waited for the right opportunity. With the way he killed Hank, I'm convinced he's the same man who attacked Amy twenty-three years ago. This killer is patient, and I think the book project brought him out of his hole. What I don't understand is why he left a note but didn't break into their room."

"Maybe he was interrupted . . . Amy Garrett must be an incredibly strong woman. Think of what she's lived with all

418

these years. For that matter, Kariss is no quitter. This whole thing has me baffled. We know it's connected to the Yeat case, but how?"

"Linc, he must have a cache of well-thought-out moves, or he'd have been caught a long time ago."

"I think our bad guy isn't on our list of suspects. You and Ryan have done a fine job, but all we've come up with are dead ends. We've got to rev up the investigation. Bait the killer. Put some pressure on your informants. Do whatever it takes."

"Yes, sir. He stepped on personal ground when he killed agents."

"It got personal for me a long time ago," Linc said. "Kariss got in over her head — again. Remember that I've known her longer than you have. But you do know she challenged some rough characters publicly when she worked at Channel 5. That tenacity of hers helped us solve crimes, but it also gets her into trouble."

"Don't I know it." Tigo's mind whipped into overdrive. "I bet Carolyn Hopkins knows something. Her body language communicated more than animosity for Jonathan. She was scared — fear like a billboard."

"When did her body language alert you?"

"When I mentioned Semtex. I don't think she had a part in the bombings, but I bet she knows who did. She claimed to carry a gun for protection from business associates."

"Anyone else?"

"I wish." Tigo pulled onto US 290 and headed toward FM 1960.

"Hold on a minute. The FIG is calling me." Linc cut out and returned to Tigo in less than two minutes. "We received an untraceable phone call about five minutes ago. A man claimed to have murdered Jerry and Hank. Dared us to find him, then hung up."

A calculating killer. A psychopath. Highly intelligent and cunning. A hunter. The worst of his traits was no guilt or shame.

9:00 P.M. FRIDAY

Kariss watched Tigo and Ryan reexamine their notes about Jerry's and Hank's murders. The words written on the piece of paper in Hank's mouth repeated in her mind — "I am a sick man . . . I am a spiteful man." A quote from Fyodor Dostoyevsky's novel *Notes from Underground*.

The assault twenty-three years ago victimized Amy, but the assailant's thirst for blood had swept to others. Fortunately, Vicki had seen the need to go stay with their parents, but Kariss realized the rest of her family would need to stay away from her too. Who else was on the death list?

With the guilt raging through her, Kariss couldn't look at Tigo or Ryan. They had been sitting in the living room of her condo, attempting to persuade her to allow the protective detail to continue guarding her. But she'd refused until she was exhausted. Amy had left after the police finished at the crime scene, claiming she was heading home and wanted to be left alone.

Two men were dead, men who'd been dedicated to their profession. Their vacant eyes would haunt Kariss for a long time. Jerry had been a Christian, but Hank had had no use for faith. She should have talked to him more about the ways of God and His love. Would the agents' families and friends blame her and Amy? How did the families live with this part of an FBI agent's job? Who was ever prepared for a violent death? A manual hadn't been written with twelve steps for walking through the murder of a loved one. This time it was two highly respected men who'd given the ultimate sacrifice, but what if Tigo were killed in the line of duty while protecting Kariss? How would she forgive herself?

Today was the end of a protective detail for her. She'd take her chances alone. Now to persuade Tigo, who paced the floor.

"So you and Amy have given up on FBI or police protection until this is over. Kariss, you know where this kind of thinking gets you." Tigo focused on her. "Have you forgotten what violent men are capable of?"

She remembered the consequences of choosing to break the law . . . and she remembered the blood. "This time I didn't go looking for some crazed killer. He found me."

"Amy was acting as a willing magnet with her Facebook posts, and you knew about them."

"No one else is going to die on my account."

"Brave words won't remove the danger," Tigo said. "You're wading in an alligator-infested swamp."

"The solution is simple. I'll post a retraction of Amy's last Facebook post on both our walls. I'll just say we decided not to reveal all of the details of the crime."

Ryan rubbed his face. "You don't think the killer is smart enough to figure out what you're doing?"

She wished the two agents would simply leave. She had plenty of things to do, one of which was working through the sorrow and grief of what happened to Jerry and Hank. She wanted to run five miles on the treadmill — sweat, figure out the best way to help the victims' families . . . and pray.

She turned her attention to Ryan, because looking at Tigo would cause emotions to surface that she hadn't dealt with. Every day she prayed for his salvation, and today was a grim reminder of what could happen to a dedicated agent.

"I know you want what's best for me and Amy," Kariss said, "but backing away from protective detail makes sense in view of the two dead men."

"Your refusal of further protection means those agents gave their lives for nothing," Ryan said.

His response caused Kariss's chest to ache, as though someone were ripping at her heart. "It means I'm smart enough to understand the value of human life so no one else is killed in the line of duty."

"What if Amy doesn't make it home alive?" Tigo said. "What if her pride gets her killed?"

Kariss knew Tigo cared . . . understood he was trying to break down her stubbornness. "She promised to email me when she arrived home."

Turning to her laptop, she brought up her email again. She'd checked it repeatedly throughout the day, but there were still many unread messages. Mostly junk from people who were vested in themselves and their pitiful products. She scrolled through the list, looking for a message from Amy. Then an incoming message caught her attention. In capital letters, the subject line read "I'M NOT FINISHED YET."

"What's wrong?" Tigo said.

Could he read her that well? "Maybe nothing." She clicked on the message. Tigo peered over her shoulder, his breath warm against her neck.

TODAY WAS A HINT OF WHAT'S TO COME. TWO MORE POINTS FOR MY SIDE. SMART GIRLS DO NOT ANSWER THE DOOR.

The sender's email was stalker@killu2 .com.

"Scare tactics are for bullies," Kariss said, despite her trembling.

"This guy doesn't let up," Tigo said. "We'll trace this."

"Weren't the other emails sent from separate public libraries?" Kariss said. "Bogus addresses?"

"They were." Tigo placed his hand on her shoulder. "Doesn't mean he won't make a mistake. Forward the email to me, and we'll get an agent from cybercrimes on it."

Kariss did as he requested and bid the turmoil whirling inside her to vanish. "You two can get back to work. I'm home and I'm okay."

"What if I camp here in the evenings?"

Tigo's persuasive tone would not change her mind. And his suggestion would raise another set of problems. "Inappropriate. And the killer hit in the afternoon today. If —"

Tigo's and Ryan's Blackberrys sounded.

"I'll get this," Ryan said, then walked to the kitchen. "Whatever the situation, it concerns both of us."

"Your pigheaded attitude could drive a man to drugs." Tigo shook his finger at Kariss. "I can't keep this man from getting to you if you don't let me do my job."

He could be the third death if she allowed him to play bodyguard.

"I have a cabin in the mountains of Utah," he said.

"I have a beach house in Florida. No plans to visit either one."

Ryan returned from the kitchen. "We have an urgent request for an interview."

She felt relief, at least for the moment.

Until Tigo shot her a look that should have frightened her. "Alarm the house after we leave. Don't go anywhere. Don't answer the door unless it's me. Don't step outside, and stay away from windows. We're not finished with this conversation."

Chapter 49

11:05 P.M. FRIDAY

Tigo learned that the interview request was from Curt Yeat, and he wanted to talk to Tigo. At first he thought the kid had information about the case, but Curt was merely acting on Tigo's offer to listen to him, which Linc had passed on.

Why wasn't he out with his buddies on a Friday night after a basketball game?

After checking his Blackberry, he saw that Curt's team had lost by twenty-five points, though the other team had been predicted to lose. Tigo had witnessed Jonathan's favoritism toward Ian on two occasions and figured Curt probably needed a listening ear tonight.

Curt chose to meet him at a Starbucks near the Yeat home. He sat with three guys, jock types. The rich smell of coffee teased Tigo's nostrils, but his prime concern was Curt and why he wanted to talk. Tigo wove through the busy crowd that brimmed with voices and laughter to a corner table facing the door.

Curt stood, his features stoic. "Hey, Tigo."

Obviously the kid didn't want his buddies to know Tigo's FBI status. Tigo grinned and shook Curt's hand. "You guys mind if an old guy joins you?"

One of the other guys, an African-American kid, pointed to a chair. "We can handle it."

"What do you want to drink?" Curt said.

"Venti, black."

Curt disappeared, giving Tigo time to scrutinize the others — a glum trio. "You guys basketball players?"

"Supposed to be," the African-American kid said.

"Heard about the game tonight. What a bummer."

"We were supposed to take 'em," a white kid said.

"Curt's not doin' so good," the African-American kid said. "Coach Ofsteller blamed him."

Now Tigo understood. "Why's that? Aren't you a team?"

"Curt's our best player." The white kid glanced toward Curt. "Ever since his mom and sister were killed, his game's been off.

The coach really got up in his grill."

"What did he say?"

"Here he comes."

Tigo reached for his wallet, but Curt stopped him and set the coffee on the table. "I can afford it."

"Thanks. You ready?" Tigo said. "The late movie starts in twenty minutes."

Appreciation sparked Curt's eyes. "Yeah." He nodded at his friends. "Talk to you later."

Outside, Tigo pointed to his pickup. "Anywhere you want to go? Or do you want me to just drive?"

"Just drive. And thanks for not giving me away in there."

"No problem."

"Glad you look like a regular guy."

It had been a long time since Tigo had thought about peer pressure. "I do try to fit in."

"Do you ever do the undercover stuff?"

"Sure. Happens to be part of my specialty."

"Disguises too?"

Tigo laughed. "I have a closet full."

"What's the biggest case you've ever had?"

He thought about the latest case he'd solved. "Last summer was interesting. Helped bring down a Mexican gang that was involved in white-collar crime and gun smuggling. Drugs and prostitution too."

"Wow. What did you do? I mean, what was your disguise?"

Tigo chuckled. "If I told you that, I'd —"

"I know. You'd have to kill me. But being an FBI agent sounds exciting. Maybe something I could do. Maybe even find out who killed my mom and sister." He shrugged. "Not that you aren't doing your job."

"It's all right." Sympathy spread through Tigo. Poor kid. Only a junior in high school, with his whole life before him, and dealing with unexplained deaths.

"I remember your mom died not so long ago. What about your dad?"

"My folks divorced when I was a kid. He's not in the picture," Tigo said.

"I was lucky there. But I wish I knew who the killer was."

"Hey, we're closing in on a suspect."

"Are you feeding me trash?"

Youth and their bluntness. "The guy's bombed two cars using the same explosive. I imagine you heard about the similarities from the media. He also killed two good FBI agents today. He's getting bolder, which means he'll get sloppy."

"I . . . I read about the other bombing. I'd never heard of Dr. Garrett, and neither had my dad, except to give her money. I'm sorry that I don't have anything new to tell you. Just wanted to talk. Thought I'd feel better after we got rid of the bodyguard, but I don't. I just feel sick all the time."

"I'm listening."

"Not sure I know where to begin."

"Try me."

"Ever play basketball?"

Tigo shook his head. "Soccer in middle school and high school."

"Were you good?"

"Not sure. Got stuck being the goalie. But the discipline was good. I hear you're the best on the team. Do you like basketball?"

"Most of the time."

"What position?"

"Forward. I used to be good, but lately I stink."

"Winning or losing is a team effort."

"Not according to the coach."

"What did he say?" At least Curt was opening up. Surprising, since teens were notoriously close-mouthed with adults. But the kid had just lost his mother.

Curt rubbed the back of his neck. "Oh, you know coaches. They say some pretty weird stuff."

"Like what? I've heard it all. My soccer coach used to cuss at us in Spanish and

English at the same time."

Curt laughed. He relayed what Coach Of-steller had said. Cursing put it mildly. Tigo understood coaches often used intimidation to make players angry so they would try harder. But what the coach had said to Curt had no place on any playing field or court.

"I think you should let your dad know what he said about your mother and sister." Tigo waited for Curt to comment, not sure if the kid would voice his real emotions.

"I can't. He's having a hard time with Ian."

"So you're going to let your coach talk to you like that?"

"What I want is the bomber found. I'd like to kill him with my bare hands," Curt whispered. "Cut his throat and hack him into pieces."

Whoa. That was harsh. What was simmering beneath the surface? "I've been mad a few times in my life. If it was something I couldn't do a thing about, I resolved to get over it. But Curt, your coach shouldn't have pulled your mom and sister into the equation."

"He's a jerk. Replacing me with a sopho-more. At least that's what he said tonight. Not sure I even care. If I hadn't planned on a basketball scholarship, I'd quit."

Jonathan Yeat could well afford to send his son to college. "Not sure if a free ride's worth putting up with your coach."

"I don't want Dad to pay a cent for my education. Rather do it myself. My SATs are good. I applied at UT. Thinking either basketball or my grades will get me in."

"I understand. A man wants to pay his own way. What do you plan to major in?"

"Engineering."

"Heard it's tough to get in there. Your SATs have to be better than good."

"I suppose. Counselor says I should hear soon. My calculus readiness scores were okay."

"Let me know what happens," Tigo said. "Was your dad at the game tonight?"

"Ian was upset about something, so those two went to a movie instead."

"I see." Did Jonathan have any idea the barriers he was building with his older son?

"Mom and Alexia always went to my games, but Ian's the middle kid and has problems." He sighed. "You can take me back to Starbucks."

"Are you sure? I'm in no rush. Your buds think we're going to a movie."

"I'll make up something. Need to get my truck."

Tigo sensed the kid was embarrassed by

his confession. "Okay." He pulled out his business card. "I know I gave you one of these before, but here's another one. It has my personal cell number on the back. Call me anytime."

"Thanks. I feel a little stupid right now." He blew out a sigh, no doubt aimed at himself.

"Don't."

"Thanks. I'm having trouble sleeping. Can't stop thinking about Mom and Alexia. I really want that guy found. Promise me you won't stop until you get him."

"You got it. Do you need to talk to someone who specializes in grief counseling?"

"Not really. Dad suggested it, but I'm not ready. Uncle Taylor offered, but what he preaches and what he does are two different things. Heard him and Dad get into it about Aunt Darena. My uncle's an idiot."

Touché. "Tell me about your truck."

"It's a black Ford. Dad bought it for me last summer. Mom bought me custom rims after the results came back from my SATs."

Custom rims? Tigo didn't want to go there. "She must have been really proud of you."

"I guess. Anyway, got to pick out those awesome rims."

Tigo couldn't get to Starbucks fast enough.

JANUARY 26
3:11 A.M. SATURDAY

Kariss wanted to sleep. Wanted to forget about the day and let exhaustion and her whirling mind rest. Odd how the wee hours of the morning when the world was quiet brought out her real fears, as though a monster lived in her closet. Or in the next room. Actually a monster stalked her memories in the form of . . . dead bodies. How did law-enforcement officials handle the sight of blood? Kariss could write it, but experiencing it made her squeamish.

She longed for someone to talk to, but who at this crazy hour? Vicki would listen and offer sound advice, but sleep was precious to a new mommy. Tigo would want to come over, to fix it. He'd probably bring a roll of duct tape to ensure that very thing. And if he came, she might cave in to his growing list of what he wanted for her — and them.

So she went back to praying for everyone concerned, including the law-enforcement officials and the man who'd destroyed so many lives. Lately she'd begun to pray for the family who'd lost loved ones by the same bomber. She didn't know the Yeats, only that they were wealthy and contributed to many charities. A few ugly details about Joanna Yeat's past had been tossed out. Kariss could only imagine how her family felt after learning about their mother's previous life. The media said that one of the ex-cons Jonathan Yeat had laid off had probably planted the bomb. But Kariss knew that Amy's attacker had to be the one who had bombed Joanna Yeat's car. And killed Jerry and Hank in cold blood. And sent her those threatening emails. Still the bombings were connected. But how . . . and why?

She and Amy had decided to call the novel *Shattered,* which was exactly how Kariss felt right now. Not that she'd admit it to anyone.

Tossing back a blanket, Kariss walked through her condo to the kitchen for a glass of water. The drapes were closed as Tigo requested, but she couldn't resist a peek. Nothing stirred in the shadows. She remembered the man she saw in her driveway earlier in the week. Tomorrow she'd tell Tigo about it. What would she do if someone emerged now? From the way the killer operated, he didn't lack in the organization and planning arena. Finding a way inside her home would be simple for him. He'd just cut the wires to her alarm system and let himself in. She'd have no warning of the bomb or bullet or throat cutting. A nightmarish thought, but realistic. Did Amy feel the same way?

Despite their differences, she and Amy preferred to confront their problems instead of hiding. Which made staying inside her condo feel like a prison.

"Bring it on," Kariss whispered into the darkness. "I'll give you a good fight."

CHAPTER 50

Tigo reviewed Carolyn Hopkins's recorded interview for the second time while he waited for her arrival. He wanted to reevaluate her nonverbal communication. Deceit crept through her body language. She knew something about the Yeat car bombing, and her efforts to conceal that knowledge rode a tailwind of fear. During the initial interview, her feet had angled toward the door as though she might make a run for it. She'd paused in her conversation, leading him to believe her thoughts ran with the truth while her mouth uttered denial. She also played with her hair, and her nail biting could either be a habit that stemmed from drug use or another sign of lying.

Ryan stepped into the interview room. "Hopkins is being brought to us now. Did you see anything else?"

"Enough to confirm that my initial in-

438

stincts were right. She knows something, but she's more afraid of her so-called business associates than she is of the FBI."

"I noticed the typical signs too. Hard to tell since she was high. Must have taken a hit right before she was picked up."

"After sitting in jail, she'll need a fix. I want to question her about a few other things too. She talked about packing a handgun because she needed protection. Let's probe that further." Tigo considered the woman's lengthy record. "Why don't you question her this time?"

"All right." Ryan handed Tigo his iPad. "Hope you can take notes as well as I can."

"Watch me. Lightning fingers here."

The door opened, and Carolyn Hopkins was ushered inside. Her features were more drawn than during the previous interview, and she'd definitely lost weight.

She glared at Tigo. "Why do you want to talk to me again?"

"It's your delightful company."

"Liar. I have things to do."

"You mean chattin' with all your friends in jail? Braggin' about all the money you almost made?" Tigo pointed to the chair. "I'm letting Agent Steadman talk to you today. He missed out last time."

Tigo sat beside Ryan on the opposite side

of the table.

Ryan leaned back in his chair and crossed his legs. "We believe you know more about the Yeat car bombing than what you told us."

"What makes you think that?" She shifted in her chair.

"One of your friends indicated otherwise."

"No one knows anything about it."

"You're the only one who has information?"

She coughed. "Can I have some water?"

Tigo bit back a remark. The cough was fake.

"We'll get you something in a few minutes. What do you know about the Semtex bomber?" Ryan said.

"Nothing."

"Now, Carolyn, let's get past the lying and help each other."

"What's in it for me?" Her time in jail hadn't changed her priorities since their last meeting.

"What do you want?"

"To visit my daughter, I think." She nodded as though attempting to convince herself. "If I don't make an effort to see her, she'll be put up for adoption."

"Is that what you want?" Ryan said.

"I'm not sure." She stared at her hands.

440

"I have a daughter," Ryan said. "A son too. Carolyn, you have to choose what's best for her."

She pressed her lips together. "Probably not being associated with her mother. I don't want her using drugs, sleeping around . . . in jail and afraid."

Ryan leaned forward. "Then you know the right answer."

She nodded. "If I help, will you talk to the judge? I hate being back in prison."

"Yes. We'll see if the sentence for breaking your parole can be shortened. What's important here is stopping the Semtex bomber before anyone else is killed. Remember, one of the victims was an eleven-year-old girl. We also think he assaulted a nine-year-old girl twenty-three years ago."

A muscle twitched in Carolyn's right cheek. "He raped a child?"

"And slit her throat. Left her in a field to bleed out, but she survived. It was her car in the second bombing."

Carolyn stiffened. "My daughter's six. She's in a good foster home. They put her in a private school, and she's even taking dancing lessons."

"I understand the family wants to adopt her."

Carolyn nodded. "They don't have any

kids. Think of my little girl as their own. I know they'd never let anyone hurt her."

"Neither would the parents of the other two little girls. Carolyn, we need to stop this guy before any other innocent children are killed."

Indecision rolled over her face. Ryan glanced at Tigo, but he wanted Ryan to finish the interview. His gentle mannerisms had accomplished more than Tigo had expected.

"Okay. All I know is Pablo Martinez sold Semtex. I don't know who bought it or why he wanted Jonathan Yeat dead."

"So Jonathan was the target? Not his wife and daughter?"

She glanced away. "Yes," she whispered. "Pablo's dead too. Made me wonder if the bomber killed him. He could come after me too."

Tigo remembered his stake-out the previous Wednesday — the way Pablo Martinez, Pablo's girlfriend, and another gang member had all had their throats slit. Their autopsies had also shown heavy doses of cocaine and alcohol.

"Is that why you left the state?"

She rubbed her hands together. "I made a few other people upset too. Friends of Pablo."

"What did you do?"

"Not do. Just kept a little of what I'd been selling. They took it personal."

"No one will find out where we learned this. But we need a name."

"Can't help you there. If I knew, I'd tell you so he wouldn't hurt any other little girls."

Tigo believed her. Ryan had used a good angle, playing on Carolyn's concern for her daughter and linking that to the young crime victims. Although they'd learned Jonathan had been the target, Tigo sensed the letdown to his toes. With Pablo dead, all they had was the source of the Semtex and that it had come from Mexico.

"You heading home?" Tigo said to Ryan after Carolyn was returned to custody. "Isn't tonight Cindy's birthday celebration?"

"Right. I've arranged for a sitter to stay until Sunday evening. Maybe our getaway will work out this time. We still haven't had a chance to talk through the situation with her mother." Ryan smiled. "But it might have already worked out for the best."

"How's that?"

"The kids told us last night that they want to share a room so their grandma can live with us. The two figured out how to divide one of the bedrooms in half."

"Sounds like the perfect solution."

"I think so. They offered the sacrifice we didn't want to ask of them. Cindy's mom has less than a year, so it will work out."

Tigo grinned. "Now you can give Cindy those presents and get your hero status back."

"Hope so. Say, I'm glad you and Kariss are talking. I hope it works out."

"I should have told her about Erin right from the start, but I kept putting it off. Had no idea where the relationship was going." How much about himself did Tigo dare reveal? "Didn't want to get hurt."

"I understand. But it hurt you in the end anyway."

"Tripped over my own ego. With Kariss, I felt myself getting . . . too attached. So I couldn't tell her. Didn't want to disappoint her." He shook his head. "Not one of my better decisions. But it's all laid out there now."

"Great. So —"

"Yes, the faith issue needs to be resolved. But I'm on it."

"I was about to ask about your meeting with Curt Yeat."

Tigo felt foolish. "Okay, Agent Harris, get your mind on your job," he said. "Curt's a good kid. Showed me his truck. Had some great rims that Joanna bought for him, but not the kind we're looking for. He seemed to appreciate my taking an interest in him. His game's off, and the coach told him to stop using his mother's and sister's deaths as an excuse to play like a — Never mind. Even on my worst days, I don't use that kind of language."

"Where was Jonathan?"

"Babysitting. He has one son who matters to him, and it's not Curt."

CHAPTER 51

Cat-and-mouse games intrigued him. Nothing boosted his adrenaline more than when he followed a victim to learn his or her routine. The voices helped him look for opportunities to make personal contact, adding a unique touch to the soon-to-be murder. Gave a whole new meaning to hands-on learning.

He'd spent some time with Jonathan Yeat, but then his wife and daughter made the mistake of getting into Jonathan's car. He'd triggered the bomb before he realized who was inside. But other opportunities would come. Patience was his one virtue. He'd already paid a visit to Jonathan this morning as a little surprise.

Years ago he'd seen Amy playing with her brother. He'd talked to her for a few minutes, knowing then what had to happen. For some victims, he looked forward to seeing

446

the flicker of recognition before he made the kill. Amy and Kariss Walker fell into that category.

Power — and the prospect of blood — kept him excited about each kill . . . and planning the next one. Yesterday still had him smiling. Distracting the FBI agents with his old-man ruse gave him an edge. And he'd have had the women if a maid hadn't interrupted his carefully laid-out plans.

Now he needed to head over to that Walker woman's so-called gated community. What a front for the rich and famous. The security was nothing more than a uniformed guard operating a gate, requesting IDs, and using a cell phone as a deterrent. Probably had 911 on speed dial.

He chuckled. He knew right where she lived. Had even been in her driveway.

She should have figured out he played for keeps. The bullets with the women's names etched inside them should have been a clue. Although with the rain Wednesday afternoon and the women's sudden movements, he'd unfortunately missed. If it hadn't been for the cops and the FBI agent, he'd have had them at the hospital. Dressing in scrubs nearly got him into the Walker woman's room. But she'd been surrounded.

He hated failing, which meant the Walker woman and Amy would have to die in a special way.

It's okay. You have an even better plan. Have we ever failed you?

Oh, the comfort of his voices.

Too bad about Amy. He'd begun to admire her spunk before she decided to challenge him with a novel. She'd obviously studied his habits and knew his appreciation for fine works of fiction. The Walker woman had a suspense novel coming out in the fall. He might read it and post a review on Amazon. But she'd be dead long before then.

He backed Michelle's four-year-old Camry from his garage. How he'd love to have a new car, a sporty model to zip around town in, but anyone who knew his pay grade would be suspicious. Soon he'd have what he deserved, and as long as he continued to listen to the voices, he'd have everything he ever dreamed of.

Looking at his house, he noticed it needed a paint job again. The humidity in Houston guaranteed peeling. He wished he lived in a better neighborhood instead of this cracker box, which was stuck in the middle of a crumbling subdivision. The only thing he could do to improve his property was use landscaping to set it apart. Hard to keep his money tucked away when he could be enjoying the good life.

Making bombs had become quite lucrative. A few more, and he could move to London. The city intrigued him because of the unsolved murder cases, especially the famed legends of Jack the Ripper and Sweeney Todd. He could live there in luxury and further his career with prospects from European countries and the Middle East. An occasional bomb to a gang or a terrorist group based in the U.S. didn't satisfy all his needs. He wanted more — more money, more bodies.

His phone rang, and he saw the caller was his wife. He smiled. She was one good woman. "Hi, honey."

"Just wanted to tell you good morning and thanks for letting me sleep in."

"My pleasure. I'm out running errands. Anything I can do for you?"

"Not a thing. How about steaks for dinner? I'm feeling stronger today."

"For sure. I'll grill them."

"I love weekends with you. We have a couple of movies we haven't seen yet. Do you want to watch them after dinner?"

"Excellent. Someday I'm going to make your life easier. Love you." He disconnected the call as he pulled in front of that Walker woman's gated community. Loving his wife kept him sane. They'd met in college, and she was the only woman who'd ever made him feel loved . . . respected. She'd even waited for him when he was a POW in Vietnam.

A few minutes later, the Walker woman pulled out of the subdivision. He followed several yards behind her, traveling north on State Highway 249. There were more pine trees here, and the cattle grazing beside the highway was uniquely Houston. He liked the area where he'd abducted Amy — more rural and rolling.

When the Walker woman turned into the parking lot of a shooting range, he laughed out loud. His 9mm was in his glove box, which he could hold on to while making the acquaintance of one of his next victims.

After waiting a full ten minutes, he exited his car and entered the building. People crowded the area, but the woman was alone in an empty lane. Seeing her bandaged head gave him a moment of irritation, but he released his pride over a missed opportunity to accomplish what must be done. He stood back and watched her shoot several rounds. She was using a 9mm too. A conversation starter.

A few minutes later, she glanced behind her, no doubt sensing his presence. Removing her ear protectors, she nodded at him. "Do you need something?"

"No, ma'am. Just admiring your shooting. You must practice a lot."

"Every chance I get."

A looker, but those large brown eyes wouldn't save her. "I should tell my wife. She usually comes with me, but today she had errands. She says a woman needs to know how to protect herself."

"Smart lady."

"Say." He hesitated. "Are you Kariss Walker, the writer?"

She smiled. "The same."

"I thought so. My wife reads your books. We both do. She'll be so sorry she missed you." He tilted his head. "You used to report the evening news for Channel 5, right?"

"Right."

"Read how you helped the FBI solve a cold case last summer."

"That's not exactly accurate. I got in over my head in research, and the FBI saved my life. The book will be out in October."

"Great. We'll have to preorder it. I'll leave you to your target practice. Nice talking to you. Wait till I tell my wife." He patted his shirt pocket. "Doggone it. I left my phone in the car, and I wanted to surprise her."

Kariss reached into her purse. "You can use mine." She handed it to him and then replaced her ear protectors.

While she resumed target practice, he stepped into the hallway and quickly downloaded a custom app onto her iPhone that would enable the microphone and automatically send an audio feed, as well as her GPS coordinates, directly to his computer.

He could now follow her online until the time was right. No more leaving work early or lying to his wife.

CHAPTER 52

11:45 A.M. SATURDAY

From his truck, Tigo pressed in Kariss's number. He considered showing up at her doorstep, but he needed to make sure she wasn't distracted or upset with an untimely arrival.

"Hey, you busy? This is Tigo."

She laughed. "I know who you are. What's up?"

"I have something to discuss and wondered when I could come by."

"I'll be home in about ten minutes."

She wasn't at home? "I specifically asked you not to leave."

"Calm down. The doctor gave me clearance to drive. I feel fine. The pain meds are on the kitchen counter, untouched, and —"

"I don't care about your pain tolerance." Tigo's voice rose with each word. "I care about you staying alive." The killer was out there, and Kariss kept insisting upon taking

453

foolish chances. "I worry about you."

"No need to. But in answer to your original question, you can stop by anytime."

"What about now? I could bring lunch. Panera is on the way, and I remember your favorite salad."

"Okay. I'll see you in a few."

Tigo had come up with another idea for keeping her safe, and he'd need more than a truck bed of charm to make it happen. After picking up their lunch and showing his ID at the security gate, he parked in front of her condo.

Kariss met him at the door wearing a dazzling smile, which he hoped stayed intact. A blue sweater and designer jeans hugged her curves in just the right spots.

"I'm starved," she said, motioning him toward the kitchen. "Went to the shooting range this morning without breakfast."

Why was he not surprised? "How'd you do?"

"Good. Getting better."

He thought about bringing up the fact that her excellent marksmanship had saved his life last summer, but he needed to dive into another matter. They sat at the kitchen counter to eat, but his appetite was zilch.

"Go ahead and eat," he said. "I need to ask you something." He swung his bar stool her way.

"You're wearing your serious face. I hope this isn't a lecture."

"No. It's a proposal."

"Interesting." She stabbed a piece of apple in her salad.

"Would you consider letting me stay here in the evenings if a female agent joined us?"

"Tigo —"

"Hear me out. We could spend hours talking, everything from us to theology. Even do a Bible study together."

She eyed him with a tilt of her head. "Are you trying too hard?"

"Possibly."

"Who's the female agent?"

"You know her. Hillary —"

She lifted a finger. "It won't work for more reasons than I care to list. Hillary and I don't do well together. Is there a new development in the investigation?"

"Jonathan Yeat found a package outside his front gate."

Her eyes widened. "A bomb?"

"A note that proves his family's tragedy and your connection to Amy Garrett are related." He touched her face. "It said you wouldn't be writing Amy's story, and if Jonathan wanted you to write his story, that wouldn't happen either. All of you will be dead."

After Tigo left, Kariss sat in her living room and thought over his words. Nothing changed her determination to help Amy tell her story, but now she needed to take precautions. Precautions that wouldn't involve Tigo and Hillary spending their nights in her condo.

During her musings, a text came in from Amy.

N THE MOOD TO COOK. DINNER @ MY PLACE 2NITE? 6?

GREAT. I HAVE UR ADDY

Perhaps getting away from her whirling thoughts and her raw emotions about Tigo would give her new insight. Shortly after five thirty, Kariss followed her GPS instructions to a relatively new subdivision in northwest Houston. It was a lovely area with three-quarter-acre lots and mature trees. Amy lived in a one-story brick home in the subdivision's cul-de-sac. It was strange to be invited to dinner, but Amy's loneliness became more evident each time she and

Kariss were together. Since they'd survived two dangerous situations, a bond must have cemented her trust in Kariss.

Amy's manicured lawn was a work of art, and Kariss could use the vibrant pink and purple pansies near the front door as a conversation starter. She rang the doorbell and heard a dog bark, the deep growl vibrating to her toes. She realized it must be Apollo, Amy's German shepherd. Kariss hoped her host remembered her fear of dogs. The sound of locks unlocking reminded her of Amy's obsession with security. What would she do in a fire?

The door opened, and Amy held on to Apollo's leash. The large, snarling dog looked as though he'd enjoy Kariss's leg as an appetizer.

"He'll be fine once he gets used to you," Amy said.

Kariss's heart felt as if it would burst from her chest. "Can you put him in another room?"

The dog attempted to lunge at Kariss, but Amy held him tight. "Are you that afraid of dogs?"

Nausea had set in. "I am. But if it's too much trouble, we can go to a restaurant for dinner."

"I'll put him in my bedroom." Leaving

Kariss standing outside, Amy closed the front door and — from the sound of things — secured all the locks.

This might not have been one of Kariss's best decisions.

A few moments later, Amy went through the unlocking ritual again and opened the door. "Won't you come in?" Dressed in jeans and a green turtleneck sweater, she looked relaxed.

Kariss stepped inside and waited while the door was relocked and an alarm system was enabled. The foyer opened to a spacious living and dining area with a glimpse of the kitchen to the far right. Kariss admired the cream-colored upholstery, dark hardwood floors, a grand piano, and many pictures and figurines of elephants. "You have a beautiful home."

"Thank you. It's my haven."

"And you have another collection of elephants here, like the ones in your office." Kariss wondered if her theory was true.

"Elephants never forget."

"Vengeance?"

Amy tilted her head. "Justice. Did you know elephants use their feet to listen? They pick up vibrations of other elephants through the ground. Interesting, don't you think?"

"Unusual."

"And their hearing is poor despite their large ears." Amy pulled her hair back, revealing her own large ears. "Elephants and I have much in common."

Kariss grinned. She stood in front of a picture of an African elephant, a majestic animal with huge tusks. "I learn more about you each time we meet." Kariss pointed to the piano. "What's your favorite type of music?"

"Jazz. Straight out of N'awlins." Amy's pronunciation of New Orleans caused them both to laugh. Amy could write her own blues.

"Maybe you'll play for me sometime?"

"Sure. It needs tuning badly. That's one part of my hearing that isn't gone yet. The woman who tuned it for years has retired, and I haven't a clue who to contact." Amy shrugged. "I'm leery about having strangers in my home."

No surprise there. "My cousin Lance tunes pianos. I'll give you his name before I leave tonight."

"Great. Come into the kitchen, and let's chat while I put the finishing touches on dinner."

Kariss followed Amy into an area that any gourmet cook would have envied. She'd be sure to tell Vicki and Tigo about it. Copper-bottomed pans hung from an island work-station. A six-burner gas stove hugged the wall. Stainless-steel appliances sparkled, and there was a coffee machine that rivaled the ones at Starbucks.

"Whoa. You must cook to relieve stress."

"Not really. I made the investment for resale value. Good staging in the event I want to move."

"It would sell me, and I don't cook, only bake. I smell something yummy. Is it but-ternut squash bisque?"

"Ginger-carrot. Is that okay?"

"Perfect. What can I do?"

"We're having hand-pulled chicken-salad croissants and wild-greens salad with straw-berries and a zesty dressing. All I need to do is put the croissants together and ladle our bisque into bowls. Ah, but first I should show you my garden."

Kariss joined Amy at a wall of windows in the living room. The professionally designed backyard was a gardener's dream. A high stone wall surrounded an area of lush grow-ing plants. Even in the dead of winter, the area looked inviting.

"You're looking at my corner of paradise," Amy said. "It's where I go when life stresses me to the max. Not the kitchen." She smiled. "My bedroom faces there too. Apollo's in my room right now, and I'm sure he's sitting in front of the bay window."

Kariss smiled. "I can see why both of you enjoy it. *Southern Living* could feature your garden."

The courtyard was paved in slate pavers. A huge oak tree in the corner reminded Kariss of an umbrella as it shielded blooming impatiens, ferns, and other shade-loving plants. A round wrought-iron table and cushioned chairs sat in the middle of the courtyard, urns of plants adding color to the paved area.

Kariss turned so Amy could read her lips. "How do you keep this so beautiful?"

"Many hours of hard work. It's well lit, and I often work either late into the night or early in the morning."

"You do all of this yourself? Why not hire a landscaping service?"

"I don't want anyone back there. I even make Apollo use a fenced area to the left of the house for his business. You see, there are only two ways in — through my back door or through the garage."

"You should be very proud. Your courtyard is incredible. Do you have good neighbors?"

"Perfect. The couple on the right spends the winter months and most of spring in

Colorado, and the lady on the left is elderly. Nothing behind me but a creek."

Kariss wondered if the door to the courtyard had multiple security locks. Probably so. She glanced at the windowed wall and saw it was taped and wired in every corner and along the sides.

"Let's eat," Amy said. "I've never invited anyone to share a meal but Baxter or my parents. You're a first."

"I'm honored."

"You were right. I need a friend, and I have to take powerful steps to show I can be successful. You're very good for me, and it's time I practiced what I preach to my clients."

Poor Amy. Living her whole life in fear and caution had robbed her of the joy of having friends. But Kariss was proud of her for finally taking a step in the right direction.

CHAPTER 53

Tigo refused to attend church this morning. For almost six months, he'd sat on a pew beside Ryan and his family. He'd read the Bible and attended Bible study classes. The choice humans had to make between living in dependence on God or living their lives separate from Him plagued Tigo. At times he believed God answered prayer. But today he felt more alienated from Him than ever before. Emptiness filled him.

His bitterness grew each time he considered the Yeat case and the situation with Kariss. The connection? What was the connection?

How could Tigo commit his life to a deity who allowed killers to go free? The dichotomy between a loving God and what was going on in the world around him wasn't logical. Tigo wanted to believe. If

463

only God would give him a reason why all this was happening.

He paced his kitchen, a cup of coffee on the counter and another one on the table. Both cold. Misery swept through him. He needed to do something physical — something to get his mind off life. Free his head so all the pieces could come together in a landscape that made sense. Trail-biking should do it.

Grabbing his keys, he headed to the garage. The thought of leaving his helmet at home crossed his mind, but he'd promised Kariss he'd wear it. She'd seen his daredevil antics in action, not understanding that his DNA nudged him to attempt what others thought ridiculous.

Gray clouds threatened rain, but in his mood, he didn't care. A chill caused him to head back inside for a sweatshirt. After pulling it on, he received a text from Ryan.

WILL MISS U N CHURCH

Anything he'd say would sound pathetic, so he didn't respond. Shaking off his less-than-stellar feelings about his life, he raised the garage door. Near his subdivision, a twelve-mile bike trail wound through trees, across a creek bed, and over roots and bumps. Just what he needed. When his emotions were outpaced by physical exertion, he'd head home and reanalyze why his life hadn't turned out the way he'd planned.

The first three miles of the trail brought back memories of sharing this ride with Kariss.

"Watch that turn," he'd said.

"I see it."

"Slow down for the curve."

"No problem there . . . I'm still waiting for this to be fun."

"Stay with it. You're with me, remember? This tough FBI agent will keep you safe."

"Safe isn't the problem. It's the throbbing in my thighs and the ache in my back."

"But you're strong."

"Did I mention the mosquitoes?"

They'd laughed and repeated the same conversation during the next ride.

On the fourth mile, the rain started, wet and cold. Suited Tigo's current views about life. He took a narrow path down a muddy creek bed and up the other side, maneuvering the bike away from a tree trunk. His swerving caused his right pedal to scrape against a small tree, and he went airborne, flying over the handlebars and crashing to the ground. His breath left him in a whoosh. He struggled to regain his composure, glad he was alone. At least he wouldn't end up being the brunt of a joke. Or, worse yet, having someone snap a pic and post it online. As it was, he might have bruised his ribs or broken a bone, just from riding a bike. How humiliating.

Tigo moved his head first. A dull throb at the base of his skull was probably only the beginning. The rain's momentum increased and splattered his face. He had to get up before he drowned.

I'm a weenie. Buzz Lightyear would be ashamed.

A glance at his bike revealed a twisted wheel. His bike was unrideable. Probably not even pushable.

A rustle made him glance to the left. A rattlesnake emerged six inches from his leg. Too close for him to avoid it. Even though he was sure nothing had been broken, he didn't dare attempt to move from the rattler's path.

Tigo blinked. The weather was cold for snakes. It started slithering over his left leg, sending caution shooting through his mind. Wide-eyed and motionless, he felt the snake gliding over his leg below his kneecap and begin its ascent over the other. Helpless. The rain soaked his clothes while his pounding heart resembled a racehorse on steroids.

Are you listening now, Tigo?

Where had that voice come from? Tigo lay quietly . . . The snake covered both his legs, effectively paralyzing him. He waited for venomous fangs to sink into his flesh.

Do I have your attention?

Humbled and ashamed, Tigo recognized the voice that was whispering to his soul.

I'm listening.

In an instant, all manner of reasoning escaped him. His focus rested on the awareness of God's presence. Even the snake's precarious position on his legs slipped from his mind. In its place, guilt pelted him with reminders of the times he'd insisted on doing things his way. All his life, following God's commands had been like ordering à la cart. He'd made his selections based on what made sense to him.

For the next few moments, scenes from his life marched across his mind — the countless times he'd been snatched from death's path. And had taken credit for it. Those events that had led him to be called a superhero and daredevil now held a miraculous, almost reverent significance. He'd been preserved from harm more times than he could count. But for what purpose?

Jesus in his heart. How many times had he scoffed at this phrase, declared the speaker weak, childish. Tigo didn't need a crutch. If the solution to a problem evaded him, he'd find the answer on his own.

"Lord, I'm sorry." His words were whispered, yet they rushed from his lips as though he couldn't speak them fast enough.

The cold rain continued, still soaking him, but the magnitude of what had happened surged far beyond the narrow path with the little tree that now bore scrape marks from his bike pedal.

A new life.

Purpose and meaning.

No longer alone.

Peace. What a strange sensation.

He opened his eyes to see the snake had disappeared . . . gone like the sin that had infected his soul. Who would have ever thought Special Agent Santiago Harris would reach out to God and grasp the hand of the Creator?

Ironic.

Humorous.

Symbolic.

Time to move on. He carefully moved each arm and leg and found that his body hadn't given up on him. As he slowly rose to his feet, sharp pain burst from his rib cage, from the bones that protected his heart.

Thank You, God.

The long, cold walk in the rain would give him time to think. Truth . . . a lifelong quest, but he was up for it. He'd hit his head, but he understood what had taken place.

Once home, he'd call Kariss. She should be the first to know.

3:45 P.M. SUNDAY

Kariss saw the caller was Tigo. Sweet man. Every moment she spent with him convinced her that she was in love with him. But the thought twisted at her insides. There were too many obstacles for both of them to overcome. She'd lain on the sofa most of the morning, dealing with a horrible headache that had made her physically ill. It was from overdoing it yesterday.

Her phone rang again, and she tossed aside the ice pack. His call could have something to do with Amy's assailant. She pressed Talk.

"Are you staying warm in this cold and rain?" she said and then inwardly groaned. Not a good question considering their quasi-relationship.

"That's loaded, but I'm trying. Do you have a few moments for me to tell you about my day?"

"Sure." She could hear the excitement in his voice and wondered what had caused it. A grocery list of things tumbled through her mind. Had the case been solved? Had an arrest been made?

"I didn't go to church this morning. I was too angry at God. I felt that He'd kept me out of the loop on far too many situations. Instead, I went for a trail-bike ride."

"In this rain?" She'd stayed home from church too.

"It wasn't raining when I left." Tigo continued his story, telling Kariss about his fall and the rattlesnake — which he had decided was a speed bump to get his attention — and the whisper of God.

Kariss gasped. "God spoke to you?"

"Twice. It wasn't an audible thing, but a heart thing. So I listened. I figured since I couldn't go anywhere, and I was at the mercy of a rattler, I could take a moment to hear what He had to say."

"And?"

"I was reminded of my lousy relationship with Him."

Kariss sobbed. She'd known God would find Tigo because he'd been seeking Him. "I'm so happy for you."

"I'm a slow learner. But I got the message this morning. Even downloaded it into this tough skull and heart."

Kariss's mind soared with what this meant. She could deal with all of their past, present, and future problems if his heart belonged to God. "Have you told Ryan?"

"Called you first. I had to take a shower and a nap when I finally got back to my house. If I didn't look so beat up, I'd ask you to dinner."

She startled. "How badly are you hurt? How did you get home?"

He chuckled, the deep-throated sound unique to the man she loved. "Uh. I walked."

"In this rain? Did you break anything?"

"Just my bike and my pride."

She stood from the sofa, noting that her head no longer made her queasy. "I bet you're hurt more than you're telling me. And after being drenched in the cold and rain, you'll probably contract pneumonia. Have you been drinking hot tea?"

"You mean the bitter herbal stuff that tastes like what the Hebrews sprinkled over the Passover lamb?"

She bit back a laugh. Oh, how she treasured their banter. "Precisely. It's good for you."

"No, I haven't. I swallowed a couple of Tylenol with a glass of orange juice."

"I'm coming over."

"Not a good idea. It's not safe."

"But I have a weapon."

"You're no match against a determined killer, Kariss."

"You can't change my mind. I'm on my way."

"I wish you'd reconsider."

"Do you have untreated cuts? Need stitches?"

"No, but I'm hungry."

"I'll stop at Panera and get some chicken-noodle soup and whole-grain bread."

"We need to buy stock there. By the way, I prefer white bread and a cinnamon bun if they still have any this late in the day."

"Just healthy stuff for you."

"But isn't cinnamon good for you?"

"Not when it's mixed with butter and sugar."

He laughed. "I could use a treat."

"You'll have my company. I'll be there in about thirty minutes."

CHAPTER 54

Kariss pulled into the driveway of Tigo's large home. He'd bought the stately two-story brick house about eight years ago after he'd returned from Saudi Arabia to take care of his mother. She'd had a stroke, and her condition had worsened when she was diagnosed with a cancerous tumor on her kidney. Shortly thereafter, his old college friend, Linc Abrams, had recruited him for the FBI. To ensure his mother received the best professional care available, Tigo had overseen around-the-clock nursing care. And a dozen red roses arrived in her room every five days for the remainder of her life.

Tigo was a complex man who had a tender side that many of his FBI friends failed to see. His mind fascinated Kariss. He was a troubleshooter who couldn't rest until crimes were solved and the people responsible placed behind bars.

She took a deep breath. What should she say to the man who'd stolen her heart and had now given his life to Christ? Congratulations? We'll be in heaven together? Peace, brother? Her emotions were so frayed, she feared she'd simply cry. And the good Lord knew that when Kariss Walker cried, her nose put Rudolph to shame, and her splotched face resembled a bad case of measles. None of the dainty, nose-dabbing feminine responses she'd seen in other women — she sobbed and hiccupped.

But she wanted to see his face, his eyes. And tell him how truly happy she felt. Opening the car door of her rented vehicle, she cringed at the creak. She hoped her head healed faster than her Jag, which would be in the shop for another week before the repairs were completed.

She could do this. Be his friend and let God guide both of them.

Tigo must have been standing near the window and watching for her arrival, because he opened the door before she had time to ring the doorbell.

She hid her shock. His handsome face was void of stress lines, and his eyes held a peace she couldn't express in words. He did have a huge Buzz Lightyear bandage on the top of his right hand, but he wore an incredible smile.

"How's the patient?" she said.

"Much better now. Got my heart right, and the rest of my battered body will heal." He took the bag of food and set it inside the door. He opened his arms, and she stepped into his embrace. His arms were as strong as she remembered, but now he had the power of God flowing through his veins.

She sniffed. "I told myself I wouldn't cry."

"Why not? Will it spoil your makeup?"

"Of course." She let the comfort of his arms soothe her a while longer. "I'm so proud of you."

"You mean that I'm an idiot, and it took wrecking my bike to get the message?" He stepped back. "Come on in before my neighbors video us and we find ourselves on Facebook, Twitter, and YouTube."

"Or worse — *McDougal Reports.*"

The familiar smell of his leather furniture mingled with the scent of rich coffee.

She'd come home.

She'd missed this house.

She'd missed him.

"I just made coffee." He held her hand, and she didn't pull away.

"Smells wonderful."

He laughed. "I hope heaven has a Starbucks." He limped toward the kitchen, her hand still clasped in his, and his left hand holding on to the Panera bag. "I'll get us coffee. Still have your diva cup."

"Wrong, Agent Harris. You've been injured, and I'm supposed to be taking care of you."

He pointed at the food. "You brought chicken soup and bread."

"White bread. Just this once. And a cinnamon bun."

"Maybe I'll be hurt for a couple of days," he said.

"You're incorrigible." She nodded to punctuate her remark but couldn't resist reaching out to touch his face.

"I see something special in your eyes."

She shivered. Hiding her feelings from Tigo was getting harder. This time she wouldn't let him go. But what if he'd been so burned in his first marriage that he couldn't make a commitment?

"Do you remember when we first met?" he said.

"You hated me."

"I thought you were hot." His impish grin caused her to giggle. "Can I say that?"

"You're still a man." She took a breath and headed toward the kitchen. "I'll pour the coffee."

"Better add a few ice cubes to mine."

She needed an iceberg. "Did you phone Ryan?"

"Yes, and Linc. But I didn't tell them I'd wrecked my bike or about the snake. Couldn't ruin my image."

"Ah . . . blackmail?"

He frowned. "You wouldn't."

"I'll name my price and let you know."

He slowly eased into a chair in the kitchen. "It's strange how what I'd read and heard all my life now makes sense. Feels good. Real good. I still don't understand why He allows evil. Guess that understanding will come with age. And I can't imagine sitting in church or Bible study not watching the clock so I can get out of there. But knowing me, I'll probably relive a few of those times."

"We all do." She poured their coffee — hers in her diva mug, his in a Buzz mug. "Sorry you had to get banged and bruised to realize the truth of God's love."

"In the great epic of life, it was worth it."

"Are you getting philosophical?"

"Not exactly. I'm looking to the future."

Her heart nearly leaped from her chest. "Do you have half-and-half?" she said as calmly as she could.

"Always, Kariss. I've had a carton in the fridge since last Thanksgiving. When it went bad, I bought another one. And another. There's also mocha creamer in there. Replaced it a few times too."

She flashed a watery look his direction. What more could she ever ask for than a man who showed so much caring?

He chuckled. "Are you getting emotional over a coffee additive?"

She lifted her chin. "Maybe. Tell me about your injuries."

"My hand and my ribs."

"Don't you think you should see a doctor?"

"I have my own personal nurse."

"That's Vicki. I'm the other sister. By the way, I called her on the way here. Had to tell her about you."

"Is she going to name her next baby after me?"

"She already thinks you're a saint. I talked to Dad too. He was hootin' and hollerin' like a Cajun with a kettle of fresh gumbo."

"Your dad's a man's man. Your mom's great too. Do you suppose she'll make me my own carrot cake since I'm on her side now?"

"I'm sure she will." Kariss opened the Panera bag and spread their dinner over the kitchen table, keeping the cinnamon bun in the bag so Tigo wouldn't eat it first.

Once they were seated, he took her hand. "Should I ask God to bless the food?"

That was a first. "Sounds like step two."

So he did. After thanking God for the food, he ended the prayer. "Thank You for not giving up on me. Kariss too. Amen."

She reached for her coffee, laden with half-and-half and a dollop of mocha creamer.

"Before you got here, I was remembering some of our past — the good times," he said.

"As in the time I destroyed your head-phones?"

"You warned me about the electricity thing."

She took a spoonful of soup and held up a finger. "Remember when you and Ryan rescued me from the Arroyos, when you were in disguise?"

"You thought you'd been traded off to a couple of bad guys involved in white-collar crime."

"I was so scared. When I found out it was you, I thanked God all the way home."

"I should have listened to you and Ryan then."

"In your own time, Tigo."

"I bet Mom is smiling, glad to hear her bullheaded son finally listened."

"I'm sure she is."

He grabbed a generous hunk of bread. "You, dear lady, used to make fun of my Buzz Lightyear watch."

"That hasn't changed. And your T-shirt and your plastic dish, cereal bowl, and note-pad."

He laughed. "I'm in my second child-hood."

"I doubt you ever left."

"I admit, some things stick." The teasing left his face, and he took her hand. "Does this mean we have an even better chance to work out our differences?" His ardent gaze bored into hers, and she couldn't deny her own heart.

"Some of our differences are what we admire about each other."

"I hear a hesitancy in your voice. Can this superhero fix it?"

"Confession time for me too. All my life, I've been an overachiever. The grade A student. The 4.0 college grad. The news-caster who earned national awards. The bestselling writer." She sighed. "I have to do my best in everything or I feel defeated. What if I disappoint you while we're work-ing on our relationship?"

Tigo stood, drawing her to her feet. "I don't expect perfection, never did. We'll both mess up at times. We're not kids, and we're both set in our ways. But I believe we can work through the challenges."

She blinked back an unbidden tear. But maybe that tear was one of relief as she realized that she and Tigo might really have a future together. He circled his arms around her and kissed her. His lips caressed hers, lingering, intense. She struggled not to forget her own name as she melted in his embrace. "Challenge number one is how you make me feel this very moment."

He released her. "Guess I'd better munch on that cinnamon bun."

Tigo's Blackberry rang. Concern creased his brow. "It's Jonathan. I'd better take it."

Kariss touched his arm and walked into the living room, hoping this call would have helpful information about the case. Needing to keep her mind busy, she studied the titles in his bookcase. So many biographies, something she'd need to remember at gift-giving time. If they made it that far. She learned a little more about him with each title — John Adams, Winston Churchill, Albert Einstein, Benjamin Franklin, Thomas Jefferson . . .

"Hey, sorry about the interruption," Tigo said.

She spun to face him. "No problem." She stared into the eyes of the man she loved, the man who'd stolen her heart. "Anything you can tell me?"

He limped her way. "It's sensitive, but I can tell you. It may hit the media anyway." He reached for a strand of her hair. "You are one huge distraction."

"Thanks." She kissed the hand beside her face. "Are you going to tell me?"

He grinned at her, then shook his head. "Not good. Jonathan caught Ian clearing out cash from the home safe. Nearly ten grand."

She gasped. "Did Ian say why he was stealing it?"

"Something about being tired of all the crap about his mom's and sister's deaths."

"Do you believe him?"

"When it comes to Ian, I don't believe anything. But you didn't hear that from me."

Chapter 55

Once he heard Michelle's even breathing, he rolled out of bed and walked to her side. He tucked the blanket under her chin and covered her ears. She'd been having a restless night until he gave her a sleeping pill. If only he had more years with her instead of months . . . weeks. Doctors at MD Anderson said her cancer had metastasized beyond medical treatment. They'd told him that all they could do was provide pain medication. Help her endure dying.

Until his wife breathed her last, he'd love her and make her remaining days comfortable. Hospice had been recommended, but he didn't want anyone invading his privacy or taking care of Michelle.

He crept through the house, into the kitchen, and outside to his workroom behind the garage. Pressing in the padlock's code, he glanced behind him to be sure he was alone. Not that he expected anyone to be around at three fifteen in the morning. He slipped inside the shop and locked the door behind him. Ah, his private sanctuary, where he allowed his other life to fill him with satisfaction. Inside the windowless area, he flipped on a light.

His prized vehicle was his truck, which stayed parked in his garage most of the time, covered and shining. Removing the custom rims had made him sick, but they were the one thing that could trace him to the Walker woman. Glad he'd had the foresight not to drive the truck to work.

You're a smart man. No one will ever catch you.

Thank you.

But it's true. We know it, and that's why we help you see what needs to be done.

Photographs of Amy filled a bulletin board. She'd been the first to appease his craving for blood. The voices had urged him to take pictures before leaving her to bleed out, but he'd ignored them. Now all he had were memories of his failed attempt to kill. While she recovered in the hospital, cops had been planted outside her room 24/7. Sergeant Bud Hanson stuck in his mind, a man obsessed with the freckle-faced little girl. The cop had devoted his life to solving a crime, but he would never succeed.

As Amy had grown into a teen and then a woman, he had stalked her, always hiding in the shadows. He'd attended her high school graduation and snapped a picture of her smiling as she accepted her diploma. He'd managed to take pictures of her college graduation but not of her accepting her master's and doctorates. Regardless, he had plenty of photographs to show what she'd done with her life. Amy should thank him for allowing her to live this long.

Other crime scenes decorated other bulletin boards. Most were newspaper clippings, because he couldn't always get his own pics. Cops and investigators were getting smarter . . . interfering with his process. But they'd never outsmart him.

One bulletin board was now devoted to pics of Kariss Walker. In the beginning she'd simply been a curiosity. He remembered her reporting days and admired her guts in reporting tough stories. Unfortunately, she'd gotten in his way. Both Amy and the Walker woman needed to be eliminated before the cops were onto him. That should have happened last week. Well, the women had had a few bonus days.

He powered up his computer and clicked

on the site that allowed him to overhear what was happening in the Walker woman's life. All afternoon and evening, he'd longed to scan through her recorded phone calls, hoping the custom app worked as well as the ads claimed it would. The device even recorded on-site conversations as long as she had her cell phone close by.

What he heard was worth the wait. The conversation at Amy's house was priceless. As he listened, a plan formed. He'd need a little time to work out the details, but opportunities to bring both women together marched across his mind.

Later he laughed at the FBI agent doing the faith thing. Christians . . . they made him want to spit. He'd had his fill of them, wanting to get his wife into church. Hell was right here on earth, watching the woman he loved die in front of his eyes. Almost as bad were the POW camps in Nam.

"Honey, we won't be able to travel, to see the world," Michelle had said after her final prognosis. "Promise me you'll visit Rome, Paris, and London. Pretend I'm with you."

"It won't be the same."

"When you least expect it, I'll touch your hand. We've been planning these trips much too long to simply cancel them."

He kissed the top of her bald head. All those chemo treatments for nothing. Yes, he'd travel abroad — with or without her. Loving her meant abiding by her wishes even if she wasn't physically beside him. She loved him and proved it every time she looked at him. Unlike everyone else in his life. His parents had disowned him for enlisting. That's why they were dead. The American people had deserted him, scorned his torture and his sacrifice. But Michelle clung to him all the more. She'd saved him from insanity. But soon she'd be gone.

All he'd have left were his friends. The voices.

CHAPTER 56

Tigo breathed in too deeply and winced in pain. He hoped no one had been walking by his cubicle when he nearly cratered. The clinic had bandaged his ribs this morning, but no one would be able to tell, since he'd worn his sports jacket. He'd refused to tell the doctor how he'd hurt himself.

"Just put in the records that I parachuted from a plane yesterday and landed in a tree."

"Is that the truth?" the doctor said, his pen in one hand and Tigo's chart in the other.

"Not exactly, but it beats what really happened." And here he was — a new Christian having a problem telling the truth. Must be a process.

An hour and two extra-strength Tylenol later, Tigo was trying to figure out if Ian knew more about the bombing than he'd let on. After last night, the authorities suspected the kid was more involved than he'd said.

Ryan stood in the doorway of Tigo's cubicle. "Got your text. What's happening with Ian?"

"You don't want to know."

"Try me."

Tigo leaned back in his chair and then quickly straightened.

"Are you all right?"

"Sure," Tigo said. "Shortly after Jonathan called me about Ian stealing from him, he called back to say he was sorry that he'd bothered me. He'd handled the situation."

Ryan shook his head. "Let me guess where this is going."

"Father and son are going to buy a car today. No school or work for either one. Jonathan thinks Ian needs a little extra attention to help him through this critical time."

Ryan snorted. "He's using his mother's and sister's deaths to manipulate his father. The kid needs what Jonathan refuses to give him. What happened to consequences?"

Tigo raised a brow. "I doubt if either one can pronounce it. Curt's the one who needs a break. Jonathan's closing words hit the father-of the-year award."

"I'm almost afraid to ask."

" 'If Curt wasn't an overachiever, Ian wouldn't resort to drastic means.' "

"Do you think Ian orchestrated his mother's death, since she wanted to send him to a military school?"

Tigo hoped not. "Linc plans to talk to Jonathan and Ian tonight. But hey, we have another lead. Hershey called with a name. Tell Cindy you won't be home until late tonight."

9:30 A.M. MONDAY

Usually Kariss had already checked and responded to her email by this time of the morning, but she'd stayed at Tigo's late and ended up sleeping in. So sixty-five emails graced her in-box. Most were junk, but she still went through the process of checking the sender and subject line of each one, always looking for another email that might offer a clue.

Her publicist had a request from *Writer's Digest* to conduct an interview. Nice.

Vicki'd sent a photo of Rose in a gorgeous pink sweater and hat. Very cute.

Facebook informed her of seventeen comments on her author page. Hmm. A few comments about her novel project. Back to email.

An inquiry from a reader who wanted a

customized bookplate.

Seven junk emails. Delete.

A message from S. King with the subject line "Do you read Stephen King?" She opened it, thinking it was from a friend in Tennessee who had the same initial and last name.

"THE THING UNDER MY BED WAITING TO GRAB MY ANKLE ISN'T REAL. I KNOW THAT, AND I ALSO KNOW THAT IF I'M CAREFUL TO KEEP MY FOOT UNDER THE COVERS, IT WILL NEVER BE ABLE TO GRAB MY ANKLE."

Kariss shuddered. She performed a quick Google search and discovered that the quote was from the foreword of Stephen King's *Night Shift.* She stared at it for several moments before making a decision. Pressing Reply, she typed a message.

STEPHEN KING IS A MASTER WRITER. WHAT DOES THIS QUOTE HAVE TO DO WITH ME?

She pressed Send, but her message came back undeliverable, as usual. Less than five minutes later, another email landed in her in-box from S. King.

I'M REAL. YOUR NIGHTMARES ARE EYE CANDY COMPARED TO WHAT I HAVE PLANNED FOR YOUR FUTURE.

Her stomach churned with terror. Tigo needed to know about S. King's messages, but rather than call him, she'd simply forward the two messages. She didn't want to alarm him with her trepidation, and her voice would be a dead giveaway.

CHAPTER 57

Kariss analyzed the book cover for the suspense novel she had coming out in October. The editor had sent it earlier this morning, and Kariss had viewed it at least a dozen times. Something about it didn't say "bestseller" — not that a cover established that status. The hero's complexion was darker than she'd pictured, and the heroine's nose reminded her of a ski slope. The hint of lavender bothered her too. She'd envisioned orange-red tones in a black background to bring out the suspense aspect. She composed a note to her editor and copied her agent.

The four walls of her condo were driving her crazy. She had to do something. An idea popped into her head. And it was safe — if she chose a public place more popular with women than men. Even Tigo would agree no one would be in danger.

She phoned Vicki.

"Can you get away today for a late lunch about one o'clock and some shopping?"

"Sounds wonderful. Let me ask Mom if she minds keeping Rose." A few moments later, Vicki confirmed. "Where should we meet?"

"How about the Cheesecake Factory at the Galleria?"

1:00 P.M. MONDAY

At the designated time, Kariss met Vicki at one of their favorite lunch spots. They were quickly seated at a booth and ordered salads from the menu's light side.

"Want to split a piece of cheesecake later?" Kariss said.

Vicki frowned. "I just lost twenty pounds and managed to fit back into my jeans, and you want to split a piece of cake?"

"Half isn't as bad as the whole thing."

"Okay, I'll nibble. How was your evening with Tigo?"

Kariss was still basking in his decision to follow Christ. "Very nice. I get weepy thinking about it."

"What about your relationship?"

"We're working on it." Kariss eased back in the booth. "I realized something about myself."

"Which is . . . ?"

"I love Tigo. But I'm not so sure he feels the same way about me."

"Oh, he does." Vicki's brown eyes sparkled.

Kariss felt a hint of irritation. "What makes you so sure?"

"The way he looks at you and cares about your needs. He might not be able to admit it to himself yet, but he loves you."

"His ex-wife hurt him badly."

"I understand, sis." Vicki took a sip of water. "I'm right there with him."

Kariss would wait as long as it took. Tears pooled in her eyes as she studied her sister. She prayed her sister would find a man who would be her best friend and love her and Rose more than himself.

Vicki lifted her glass of water for a toast. "Here's to good men who love Jesus." She tilted her head. "Are you staying safe with your latest book project?"

Vicki and the rest of her family knew a little bit about what was happening but certainly not all of it. And Kariss had no intention of telling them. "Tigo says the FBI will have it solved soon."

"Between now and soon is what bothers me — and the whole family."

Kariss's cell phone rang. Tigo. "There he

is now. Excuse me one second."

Vicki gave her a goofy smile.

"Hey, I got your email," he said.

She swallowed. "Any luck with it?"

"A public library on the west side."

That meant he couldn't trace the user any further — not easily anyway. "I'm having lunch with Vicki at the Galleria. Should I step outside?"

"Do you mind?"

She excused herself and walked outside into a chilling blast of air. "Do you want to stop over tonight?"

"Can't."

"Undercover?"

"Uh. Yeah."

"Buzz is at it again . . . Seriously, though, be safe."

"I'm not concerned about me. Can I arrange for a protective detail beginning today?"

Kariss despised the thought, but she needed to start thinking about what her safety meant to him. "Have I been foolish in meeting Vicki here?" She knew the answer before he spoke it.

"Not one of your best choices."

Guilt crawled into her heart and stamped "selfish" where "protect" had once been for her loved ones. Jerry's and Hank's deaths were still fresh . . . raw. "Tigo, I don't want to cause you to worry. Neither do I want anyone else hurt or killed. I'm sorry for putting you through this. What about Amy?"

"She refused."

"I —"

"Honey, finish your lunch. There's only so much you or I can do regarding Amy. Tell me where you are, and I'll send a couple of agents to follow you home. I know this is tough, but it'll be over soon. Will you do me a favor?"

"Sure."

"Can I have your Apple password? That way I can enable a 'Find My iPhone' app and keep up with you on my Mac. I know you value your privacy, but this is important."

Kariss didn't need to think twice. "Okay. Makes sense." She gave him her password.

"Thanks. I'll check back with you later."

She dropped her cell into her purse and went back inside. Taking a drink of her iced tea, she looked around. She noted no one around her who looked suspicious. Specifically, none of the men appeared to be killers. She'd already come to the conclusion that the person causing havoc in her life had to be the same man who'd assaulted Amy twenty-three years ago.

"Sis, are you okay?"

Kariss smiled. "Sure. I need to postpone our shopping trip. Tigo thinks it's premature for me to be out in public."

Vicki wagged her finger. "I know there's plenty you're not telling me. Please, from a sister who loves you dearly, consider leaving town."

"Maybe you're right."

Vicki handed her a folded beverage napkin. "A man stopped by the table while you were gone. Said he was a fan and wanted you to have this. Sweet man. But I don't trust anyone in your current situation."

Kariss opened the napkin. A typewritten note on a slip of paper fell out.

"To a predator, fear indicates weakness." — Dean Koontz

CHAPTER 58

Tigo had begun to think Hershey wasn't going to come through with information about who was the new supplier of Semtex, but the FBI had finally gotten a break. He and Ryan were heading into the southeast section of town, where Mexican gangs warred for their piece of the city.

"You look mean tonight," Ryan said, bringing Swiss Cheese to a stop at a red light. "Good thing I'm driving."

"I want this case solved."

"So do I. Can I offer a word of warning?"

"The same one you gave me when Kariss was kidnapped?"

"That's it."

Tigo nodded. "My head's on straight. I've been through boot camp."

"The tattoo helps."

Tigo laughed and glanced at his left forearm. "Thought it would make me more

499

intimidating. Buzz doesn't fit well in these situations."

"Rattlesnakes are deadly."

"Gotta do something. I don't have your shoulders."

"Good genes. Hey, is the ear implant working?"

"Yeah. Do you tell Cindy when we do this?"

"Only that I'm going under," Ryan said. "That's our unspoken communication for her to pray. Then I call when it's over."

"When this is finished tonight, I'll tell Kariss about the implant. That should give her reassurance that I can hear and listen to backup when working undercover."

"We walk a fine line of protecting the women we love while ensuring our cover."

"I never said I was in love with her."

Ryan chuckled. "Didn't have to. From the moment you saw her last summer, living solo ended."

Tigo hadn't even adjusted to being Christian yet, and Ryan was tossing another curve ball.

"Have you checked backup in the last few minutes?" Ryan said.

Tigo pulled out his cell. "Are you getting nervous in your old age?"

"Cindy's pregnant."

"Congrats. I think."

"We planned it. Glad we got the mess straightened out about her mother. But after this one, we're done."

"I think you claimed the same thing after Cindy announced she was pregnant the last time."

"Now I'm serious. Three kids in college means years of undercover work."

"That's what got you there."

Ryan laughed and pulled into the gravel parking lot of a Mexican bar called *Diablo's Esquina* — Devil's Corner.

"Glad you added a little makeup to your white face, gringo," Tigo said. "Hate to have to save your rear."

"You watch your own and find out who's dealing Semtex."

"Yes, sir. I aim to please." Tigo scrutinized their surroundings. "Do you suppose Linc got any information about Ian today? Last night he refused to talk about why he was stealing his dad's money or why he had a bag packed. Oh, he was high too."

"Some parents are pillars in the community but don't see the problems in their own backyards."

"If and when the time comes," Tigo said, "I plan to be there for my kids. By the way, I applied for a job at Quantico. Thinking about reliving my wild days through training recruits."

"You want to break up the team? Oh, I get it. You're thinking about tossing me for another partner."

"You could teach at Quantico too."

They exited the car and walked to the door of the bar. Three men stood in their way. Each had a skull tattooed on his forehead. No doubt they had the word *Skulls* tattooed across their backs as well. But Tigo wanted the one they called Spider. "Looking for Araña," Tigo said.

"Está ocupado," a thick man answered.

"So he's too busy to make a little money?" Tigo said in Spanish.

"What are you looking for?"

"That's between him and me."

"I do his talking for him." The man was obviously Araña's captain.

"I only do business face-to-face." Tigo nodded at the door. "If you don't mind, I'll wait inside while you decide." He prepared himself to slam a few punches or pull his Glock.

"Let them by," the captain said to the two guarding the door.

Inside, Tigo's eyes adjusted to the darkened bar as he and Ryan wove through the crowd to a place where they could watch the exit, entrance, and everything in between. On a raised platform in the center of the room, three topless girls moved their bodies to a South American beat. Some patrons watched with bored interest. Others drank and stuffed money into G-strings. Tigo ignored the entertainment. Disgust best described how he usually felt about what the women did, but now pity filled him.

"Those girls need a job," he said.

"And clothes," Ryan said.

"And a bath." Guess he was a new man.

Over an hour and a half later, the man they'd spoken to at the front door stepped into the bar. The bartender pointed toward Tigo and Ryan.

"Ready to roll?" Ryan whispered.

"Yep. Got my fightin' jeans on."

The man sidled up to Tigo. "He'll be here in twenty minutes. This had better be good, or you're a dead man."

"Your boss better bring what I need, or he'll end up a dead man for braggin' about something he doesn't have."

"Hablas mucha para no ser nadie." Big talk for a nobody.

"Shows how ignorant you are, or you'd know who I am," Tigo said.

"You bleed out just like anybody else."

The man sneered and walked outside.

Shortly after, the Skulls' current leader walked into the bar with his bodyguards. King Araña had a small but deadly following. His face and record were on a squad board as the man suspected of murdering Pablo Martinez and his girlfriend and bodyguard, a move that slid him into position to take over Martinez's role. Araña was known for his charm. He was a ladies' man who'd probably gotten to Martinez through the girlfriend's sister.

"You want to see me?" Araña said. A four-inch gold cross hung around his neck.

"In private," Tigo said.

Araña pointed to a far table. "My office."

Tigo and Ryan followed him and the captain from outside. They ordered *cerveza* from a long-haired girl who was probably still in her teens.

"I'll get right to the point," Tigo said. "I'm looking for Semtex."

No sign of emotion creased Araña's face. "What makes you think I have a source for explosives?"

"Hershey told you to expect me."

"How much do you need? I might be able to find you some for the right price."

"Enough to take out three SUVs. Five kilos."

"Busy, aren't you?"

"You used to bigger customers?"

"Always."

"Supply me with this, and I'll be back for more."

"Maybe." Araña had more missing teeth than kids in an elementary school.

"When can I get my hands on it?"

"Thursday night. Here. About eleven. Fourteen K. In twenties. Park in the rear."

"That's more than the going price."

"Take it or leave it. And come alone." He nodded at Ryan.

"Entiendo." I understand.

Tigo and Ryan left before the waitress brought their beer.

This sting operation had the potential to solve four murders and rid the streets of Semtex. Now to see if Araña had the real stuff.

CHAPTER 59

JANUARY 29
1:10 A.M. TUESDAY

Kariss had yet to fall asleep. Tigo hadn't called, and as much as she prayed for his undercover work to be in God's hands, she still couldn't let go of the fear — and the image of Jerry's and Hank's dead bodies. To make matters worse, two agents were inside her condo. A man and a woman. She knew both — Hillary, who had dreams of publishing a fantasy novel, and Scott, an avid sports enthusiast. They had the night shift, the hours when two-thirds of violent crimes occurred. But whoever was after Kariss and Amy didn't follow the typical MO.

Thinking about the killer's intelligence was driving Kariss crazy.

And then the note left at her table this afternoon . . .

Why didn't Tigo call?

She wanted to check on the agents. Tossing back the quilt, she grabbed her 9mm and phone while making her way to the living room.

Hillary and Scott looked at her in surprise. Kariss realized how ridiculous she looked in her pink, ruffled pajamas, gun in hand.

"Is something wrong?" Hillary said, muffling a laugh. "Or have we been set up for a photo shoot?"

"I can't sleep. Keep thinking about Hank and Jerry."

Hillary sobered. "I suggest putting the gun away and crawling back into bed before you hurt yourself."

Feeling the sting of Hillary's reproach, Kariss stepped back into her bedroom. Hillary wanted to discuss her new novel idea after she was relieved of her duties at 7:00 a.m., but Kariss knew the woman needed to do a lot of work to make her manuscript semi-presentable. Hillary's latest idea was about a futuristic world where oversexed dragonflies took over the universe. When Kariss had hesitated in agreeing to the meeting, Hillary had become defensive. That probably explained her condescension.

Kariss's cell phone rang, and she nearly dropped her gun. Tigo. Finally. She needed to get used to this. Her prayer life just doubled.

"Hey. Sorry it's so late." He sounded alert. Excited. His adrenaline must have been flowing.

"Did you get what you went after?"

"I think so. We'll wrap things up on Thursday."

She calmed at the sound of his voice. "Can I tag along for research? I'll wear a disguise so I fit in." He moaned and she laughed. "Just wanted to give you a bit of yesterday."

"It wasn't so long ago. The answer's the same as it was then."

"Maybe you could tell me about it afterward."

"Over dinner? Give you all the chilling details?"

"Sure. I'll write them into my next novel." She inhaled, gathering courage to tell him about this afternoon. "He was at the restaurant today."

"How do you know?" His low voice indicated his uneasiness.

"What happened?"

Her cell beeped, indicating another incoming call. "Someone's calling me."

"Recognize the number?"

"No. Whoever it is can leave a message."

"Answer it. I'm right here. Could be important."

"All right." She clicked over.

"The agents in your house look real good. I'll leave 'em alone tonight. But when I'm ready, not even Tigo can stop me. You looked real pretty today. Hope they bury you in purple."

Chapter 60

When Tigo arrived at the FBI office, Darena was waiting in an interview room with Ryan. She claimed she couldn't hold back the truth any longer. Taylor had orchestrated his brother's murder because Jonathan had threatened to tell the deacons about his and Darena's affair. That Joanna and Alexia had died instead was an accident. Based on Darena's signed statement that Taylor had begun planning to kill his brother weeks before it happened, agents had been sent to bring him in for questioning. Tigo knew Darena hadn't uttered a word of truth, but they had to follow protocol.

"Now you can put him in jail where he belongs," Darena said. "Poor Jonathan and my nephews can put this tragedy behind them." Syrup dripped from every word. "I can't believe I fell for his inappropriate advances and lies."

"We can't make an arrest based solely on your statement," Tigo said, noting her flirtatious body language, which reminded him of the last time she was at the FBI office.

"Why not?" Her tone changed to ice. "I told you what he did."

"We need corroborating evidence to show probable cause before seeking a warrant."

Some cases intrigued Tigo. They challenged his instincts and his ability to move among the unsavory characters of Houston. But the bombings and subsequent murders were headaches. He turned his attention to Darena. "What about Dr. Amy Garrett? How does Taylor fit into her car bombing?"

Darena didn't miss a beat. "He found out I was seeing Amy for counseling. I told him I wanted to end our relationship and work on my marriage. But Taylor refused to end it and blamed Jonathan."

"There's no evidence of your visits to Freedom's Way."

"I used a different name. Even disguised myself. Went during my lunch hour." Her mouth twitched. Contempt. "I heard Dr. Garrett was recently involved in a shooting. Taylor is insane."

"Facts solve a case," Tigo said. "Not the word of one person."

She slammed her palm against the table. "While a murderer goes free?"

"Ma'am," Ryan said, "we appreciate your information, and we will look into it."

Darena scowled. "Am I being dismissed?"

Tigo smiled. "We'll contact you if necessary."

"My family needs closure. It infuriates me to see how inept you are. Aren't you supposed to protect the community?"

"Sorry to disappoint you."

After Darena left the FBI building, the agents questioned Taylor.

"She lied," Taylor said. "I confess to having an affair, but not murder."

"Then why did she come to us?"

"Because I broke it off. Confessed the whole thing to my wife." His shoulders fell. "Darena doesn't take rejection easily. She can be . . . vindictive."

Tigo had no doubt about that. After Taylor was released, Tigo joined Ryan at the squad board. Relief normally came with more insight into a case, but not this time.

"I believe Taylor," Tigo said. "We've done all the legwork on him already, and he's not a suspect. Darena is out for revenge about something."

"I agree." Ryan shrugged. "But we have

to follow protocol and check out her claims."

"What a waste," Tigo muttered as they walked toward their cubicles. "Has anyone contacted Wanda Yeat?"

"Not yet. The media is all over it. Darena must have leaked Taylor's questioning. Our media coordinator didn't have time to put together a press release before the news broke on Channel 5." Ryan glanced at Tigo. "Want to guess who reported it?"

"McDougal?"

"The one and only. He was all over the FBI's failure to solve the case."

At his cubicle, Tigo called the church office for Wanda Yeat. Again he received the answering machine. Jonathan didn't know how to locate her either, and her cell phone went directly to voicemail.

None of this added up.

Taylor would have been seventeen years old if he'd assaulted Amy twenty-three years ago.

Taylor didn't have a gun registered in his name.

And he neither read crime novels nor owned a black pickup.

In the middle of Tigo's pondering, Wanda Yeat returned his call. She'd heard the news about Taylor's questioning on the radio while driving to church after volunteering at a soup kitchen. Then she'd checked her phone messages.

"I'll be right there," she said.

"I'm sorry to interrupt you," Tigo said. "If you have time, I can ask questions over the phone."

"Sure. Taylor and I expected Darena to pull something after Taylor broke off their relationship. She even called me and said she wasn't finished with him. I suppose if I didn't have an alibi during the time of the bombing, she'd be accusing me too."

Darena in full swing.

Wanda sighed. "Taylor thinks he deserves whatever happens because he's disappointed God. But my husband didn't murder anyone, and I'm not going to stand by and do nothing while his name is smeared across the media."

"Did he have any connections to Freedom's Way and Dr. Amy Garrett?"

"Not to my knowledge. Agent Harris, I've known about this little party for several months. I'm mad. Real mad. But I love my husband, and I believe we can weather this. The innocent victims are the children involved. Did Darena tell you she's pregnant and claims Taylor is the father?"

Now everything with Darena made sense.

Kariss read about Pastor Taylor Yeat's questioning about the bombings on her iPhone. She should have been elated, but she'd reported on enough crime in the past to understand that important details could be missing. Seeing that McDougal was the first to break the story, she doubted its validity. A pastor of a megachurch? A man beloved by his congregation? She didn't think so.

She pressed in Tigo's personal cell number, knowing if he was busy, he'd call her back.

"Hey," he said. "I suppose you saw the news."

"Is it over?"

His hesitation told her the truth. "I'd like to keep you in protective detail a little longer. Our guy's still on a mission."

Her stomach did a flip. "What about Pastor Yeat?"

"According to his wife, he was conducting a funeral when you were having lunch with Vicki, and he was in bed when you received the call last night. Wrong guy, in my opinion."

Kariss attempted to keep frustration from seeping into her words. "This is hard, Tigo. My mind is screaming for answers, and I know you're bound to secrecy. When's it going to end?"

"Maybe tomorrow night we'll be closer to more answers."

God, help me be the woman Tigo needs. "Be careful."

"I don't sell ice cream for a living."

"One of the things I . . . like about you." She started to say "love."

"Can I stop by later, and we'll have dinner?"

"Where?"

"I'll bring something to cook."

She sighed. One more night at home. "I'm not a coward, Tigo. I can't sit back and wait for you and Ryan to stop this crazed killer. If he wants me or Amy or anyone else, he'll find us."

"One more day, Kariss. Maybe two. But we're so close I can smell him."

CHAPTER 61

Tigo drove to the bar where he and Ryan had met Araña earlier in the week. Tigo checked with backup, considered all the things that could go wrong in the next few hours, and confirmed alternate plans. Ryan's earring mic and Tigo's implant ensured communication.

The familiar race of adrenaline kept Tigo hyped up, but he also sensed a twinge of something else — concern for all the gang members and those being recruited into the gangs. Kids as young as junior high looked up to these guys and did whatever was necessary to be a part of the group. Tigo couldn't drive all the gangs off the streets, but he could do everything within his power — with the help of some divine power — to eliminate key figures.

"You're quiet tonight," Ryan said.

517

"Just thinking through what we need to do."

"The stakes are raised when loved ones are affected by our choices."

Tigo grinned. This time the love thing from Ryan didn't grind at his nerves. "The part of me that doesn't mind taking risks, stepping into whatever role is needed, just went into hyperdrive. I want to take Araña alive. Find out who he's selling to. Then I toss in the God thing. A strange mix for a man who's always been a loner."

"How's that working for you?"

"Think Buzz Lightyear taking off in a quest for truth."

They arrived at the bar at 10:45 and parked in the small parking area behind that bar that only had one way in. Gang members and those who lived outside the law filled the dingy building. Dancers moved to deafening music, only their alluring smiles free. Araña's man stood near the left back corner of the room with at least three other Skulls. None of the other agents were posted inside. If Tigo and Ryan got into trouble in here, they were on their own until backup arrived.

Not the first time.

The captain moved toward them. *Suponía que vienen solos.* You were to come alone.

"You have your men. I have my captain," Tigo said in Spanish.

The man sneered and returned to his post. Once in his corner, he made a call. No doubt to Araña.

At 10:55, Araña stepped in with his royal entourage — men whose rap sheets would have filled a volume the size of *War and Peace.* Kariss's literary phrases had begun to rub off on Tigo.

Showtime.

Araña wove through the crowd, greeting some select few. A dancer bent to kiss him, and he took his liberties. Pancho Villa had no less a following. Thirty minutes later, Araña's captain summoned Tigo and Ryan, along with three of his men, into a locked back room that contained a single metal shelf and a desk littered with paper.

"Quién es este hombre?" Tigo nodded at the captain in question, asking who he was.

"Conejo." Rabbit.

"What makes you think we have a deal when you were supposed to come alone?"

"I don't do business without my captain."

Araña referred to Ryan as something less than a male.

Tigo nodded at the door. "I'll take my business to Mexico. Money's the same color. Get more respect there too. We had a deal — five kilos of Semtex."

"Pat them down," Araña said.

As expected, Tigo's and Ryan's guns, knives, and cell phones were confiscated.

"Where's the money?" Araña said.

"In the trunk of my car."

Araña nodded toward the door leading outside. Tigo and Ryan followed Conejo and Araña. The buy was a gamble. The gang's plan could be to kill them once Tigo handed over the cash, or they could consider him a market for their explosives. Since Hershey had given Tigo and Ryan references, including bank accounts that backed up the paperwork, Tigo was hoping for the latter.

In the dark parking lot, an SUV sat running with its engine facing the only exit. The driver must have been ready to roll at a moment's notice. That part was covered by other agents. Without weapons, surviving the buy appeared risky. All Tigo could do was trust that backup had them covered.

Tigo opened Swiss Cheese's trunk, its creaking muffled by the sounds coming from the bar. He lifted a backpack onto his shoulder. It contained $14,000 in twenty-dollar bills. "I want to see the Semtex."

Araña gestured to the pickup. "Of course. Do you think I'd cheat you?"

Tigo chuckled. "I know your reputation. Thing is, you don't know mine."

"Fourteen K is hardly worth my time."

"Depends on how fast you can supply me with explosives."

Araña stared at him in the shadows.

"Did you bring it or not?" Tigo said.

Araña pressed the fob, and the rear opened. Conejo reached inside and pulled out a box. Tigo chuckled again . . . The packages reminded him of bread wrappers.

Araña leveled his gun at Tigo's face. "I think you set us up."

Tigo sneered. "What makes you think that?"

"One of my men saw you at Pablo Martinez's apartment after his little accident."

Tigo grabbed the man's wrist and shoved the slide back on Araña's semiautomatic. He pressed his thumb against the palm of Araña's hand, forcing him to drop the gun. With one foot on the gun, Tigo twisted Araña's hand behind his back while holding the man as a barrier against the shooters behind them. Araña's free elbow hit Tigo's chin before he spun around to level a punch into Tigo's gut. On his way to the ground, Tigo grabbed the semiautomatic. A knife sunk into his right side, sending bursts of pain through his body. Tigo aimed and fired into Araña's chest, propelling the man backward.

The one man who could have led them to the bomber was dead.

Chapter 62

Tigo's side felt as though someone had seared his flesh with a hot poker, but he refused to give in to pain meds. Working on the case meant more than sleeping through the day because of a little knife wound. So he plodded on with the pain, the uncomfortable bandage that covered seven stitches, and his regret about the outcome of the sting operation.

While he'd lain unable to move, backup had shot it out with Araña's men. Now most of them, and their leader, were in the morgue. The only man who'd survived last night said Araña had killed Pablo Martinez. He provided enough detail for Tigo to believe him.

Ric Montoya at HPD phoned while Tigo worked on an EC — an electronic communication report to pay informants.

"You and Ryan will want to talk to a guy who walked into the downtown station at midnight and confessed to killing Pablo Martinez, his girlfriend, and his bodyguard. Says he's Mario Ruiz. We have fingerprints for a B and E, but that's it. I didn't have the heart to tell him Araña's dead. He claims to know you, Tigo. Said he gave you information when you were working on the gun-smuggling case with the Arroyos last year."

Interesting. The men Tigo had talked to back then were either in prison or dead, but he'd play. He didn't recognize the name. "Does he want to cut a deal?"

"Maybe."

"We're on our way."

Ryan joined Tigo a few minutes later, and the two drove downtown. When they arrived, Tigo and Ryan faced a Hispanic man they'd never seen. His shaved head bore a botched tattoo of crossbones . . . an Arroyo wannabe. From the loss of hair and teeth, it looked as if the man had experienced the downside of meth.

"I hear you want to see me," Tigo said, then introduced Ryan and their roles in the interview. "So you're wanting to cut a deal?"

The man brushed his fist across his nose. "I'm confessing to Pablo Martinez's murder and the others with him that day. But I also

524

have information about a couple of car bombings. Will my cooperation be noted on my records?"

"Depends on the information. Let me hear it. For the record, Mario, I've never met you."

"We talked last summer."

The man lied. He must really want into the Arroyos to take a murder rap. "Right."

"Word is, an older white guy builds good bombs using Semtex."

Mario could have heard about this from the media. "Where does he get it?"

"Smuggled from Mexico."

"Did the Arroyos provide it?"

"Does it matter?"

The man's cocky attitude wasn't working. "What's the bomber's name?"

Mario stared at Tigo, then Ryan. "I want a deal."

"Not until we get a name."

"I have rights."

"Suit yourself. You'll be tried for three counts of murder." Tigo smiled at Ryan.

"We could let Mario go and see what Pablo's gang does to him," Ryan said. "The Skulls have been out to replace the Arroyos for a long time."

"Do it." Tigo nodded. "I'll make a call and let them know where we dropped off our friend Mario."

Ryan stood. "Yeah. He's wasting our time."

Mario sneered. "You made your point. I don't have a name, but I know a few other things."

Ryan picked up his iPad, and Tigo turned back toward Mario. "I'm ready. Better make it good."

"They call him Coach. Looks clean. A book addict."

Media had already picked up on the note left in Hank's mouth. And when the news leaked information about Dr. Amy Garrett, a reporter had researched her past and hypothesized that the assailant had returned to finish her off. But Mario did offer some new information. "What else?"

"That's it."

"Tell you what. Sit in jail a few days, and we'll see if this leads anywhere."

Once Tigo and Ryan were alone, Ryan voiced his doubts about Mario's claims. "I'll run it through the FIG. The Coach aspect is new, but I doubt it turns up anything that we don't already know."

3:15 P.M. FRIDAY

After lunch, Tigo sat in his cubicle and searched the FBI's database for suspects.

Nothing turned up. A white guy they called Coach who liked books. What kind of books? What kind of coach? A present occupation? A past one? A nickname that meant nothing?

He doodled the word *Coach,* turning the letters around to see if anything surfaced. A coach who built bombs. Possibly a military background or a job that had kept him out of the U.S. Tigo twisted his Buzz Lightyear watchband while impatience gained momentum.

He made his way to Ryan's cubicle.

"Ryan, I need to bounce a few things off you."

The agent swung around. "Want to take a walk? I need some fresh air."

The two fell into step and made their way outside to an area often used for press conferences. The FBI emblem engraved into the stone wall signified the hard work and sacrifice of every agent.

"I think whoever we're looking for is at least forty-five years old. At forty-five, he'd have been in his early twenties when he attacked Amy. My gut tells me the Yeat boys are connected, but they aren't old enough."

"Remember the first interview when Ian stormed from the room? Taylor and Jonathan trailed after him. When the boys learned about their mother's past, Curt left the room in a huff, but no one followed."

"No surprise there's favoritism there. But neither of us saw any signs of those boys wanting a parent dead. Too much grief." Tigo's thoughts swept to his and Ryan's trip to the Yeat boys' high school. "They have a coach."

"But most of these crimes were committed during school hours."

Tigo crossed his arms. "But it's all we have to go on." He toyed with what he did know. Jonathan and Joanna argued in the school counselor's office over Ian. The kid took off when bodyguards were assigned to his house. He got caught stealing from his dad. Joanna had wanted to put him in a military school, and Jonathan thought their son needed relief from stress. Still felt that way.

"What are you thinking?" Ryan said.

"Hear me out, then you can toss my idea," Tigo said. "Curt plays the role of the big brother. He said so. He's covered up for Ian's temper and who knows what else. So who did he have to talk to about the dysfunction in his family?"

"Most kids that age share more with friends than adults. But Curt's mature. Would he have voiced his feelings to his mother?"

"I don't think so. If Jonathan and Joanna quarreled about Ian, I doubt Curt would have gone to either of them with how he felt about his brother. He put himself into the role of 'the strong one.' So he would have chosen the next most-respected adult in his life — but definitely not Taylor. From what we've witnessed, Taylor catered to Ian too. That leaves the only other person who'd take time to advise him."

Ryan stopped. "The basketball coach — Frank Ofsteller."

Tigo nodded. "What do we know about him? Could he have been the one who assaulted Amy Garrett twenty-three years ago?"

The vertical crease in Ryan's forehead deepened. "It might fit," he said.

"Remember how he tore into Curt when the team lost, the same day Jerry and Hank were killed? If I'm right, it would make sense that he was so upset with Curt. Especially if he'd killed two men earlier in the day. But what would his motive have been?"

"Let's dig into his background. If he's our guy, then the motive's there. But what about the timing? Ofsteller has responsibilities at school."

"Good point. His attendance needs to be verified," Tigo said.

"Pretty far out there . . . but maybe."

"I'm not suggesting Curt had any knowledge of what happened." The more Tigo talked, the more he believed he was pursuing the truth. "Or maybe I don't want to think he knew about it. But I'm wondering if the coach could have heard enough about Jonathan's inability to deal with Ian's rebellion and decided to take action, not knowing Joanna would take the car that morning."

"He's near retirement age. Winning is important. Amy Garrett would be as well, if he fits the twenty-three-year-old crime."

"I think he could, Ryan."

"Have you contacted the FIG for a background check?"

"I have. Does this make sense to you, or am I fishing?"

Ryan pointed to Tigo's Blackberry. "If it makes you a candidate for a little white jacket and sedatives, I'm with you. Let's get on it. I'll contact the school and check the dates and times of the other crimes."

"I'm going to call Curt. See if I can talk to him after school. Maybe it's only the pain in my side and my cracked ribs, but I think we're onto something."

Thirty minutes later, Ryan entered Tigo's cubicle. "I think we hit pay dirt."

Tigo's attention flew to him. "What did you find out? Curt's already left for an away game."

"Coach Ofsteller's free periods, nine thirty to eleven thirty, coincide with the supposed old man who approached Kariss. He also left school early the day of the shooting and on the day Hank and Jerry were killed. And he left school the day Kariss had lunch with Vicki. In every instance, he said his wife had a doctor's appointment. I learned from the guidance counselor that she's dying of cancer, and the school has accommodated him on several occasions. He comes and goes as necessary. What did you find out?"

"I uncovered some history on Ofsteller. Vietnam POW. Spent eighteen months in a prison. Tortured. Treated once in a military hospital in '75 for depression — PTSD."

"Adds up," Ryan said. "All of it."

"We have enough to bring him in for questioning. Don't suppose the guidance counselor knew the name of his wife's doctor."

"Not in the records. Here's another bone for us. Coach Ofsteller teaches American literature."

Tigo glanced at his watch. Four fifteen. The basketball game was in Huntsville.

CHAPTER 63

10:30 P.M. FRIDAY

Tigo had requested permission from Jonathan to drive Curt back to Houston after his game. The elder Yeat appreciated the offer and stated he wouldn't be going to the game. Ian needed some father-son time.

Tigo made a note to reschedule dinner with Kariss and let her know he had a lead on a new suspect. He wet his lips while shoving anticipation from his mind. This case could end tonight, but he needed a clear head.

After a late start and an accident on I-45 North, Tigo arrived at the game just after halftime. He cornered the assistant coach and learned that Coach Ofsteller had left after the first quarter, claiming his wife was in critical condition and needed to be admitted to MD Anderson.

The cancer care center had Michelle Ofsteller in their system as an outpatient for chemo and radiation treatments. Her doctor hadn't been in contact with either Frank or Michelle since her previous visit over two weeks ago. While Ryan and a team of agents searched for the coach and his wife, Tigo would probe Curt for more answers. The team had won, and several parents planned a victory party in Houston. Tigo would get Curt to the celebration in plenty of time.

"What's up?" Curt said once they were driving south on I-45. "Have I done something spectacular to get an FBI escort to the victory party?"

"You scored the most points tonight."

"Thanks. But I'm a smart guy."

Tigo lowered the volume on a popular radio station, one he'd learned was Curt's favorite.

"Wait a minute," Curt said. "Is Dad okay?" He whirled toward Tigo. "Is that why you arranged this? Nothing's happened to him or Ian, right?"

"They're fine. Don't worry. I just have a few questions for you. The questions may sound strange, but your answers will help me and the other agents working on the case." Curt would see right through any distortion of the truth, and he deserved the truth anyway. "I have two reasons for coming to you — I want to be your friend, and

534

I want to find out who killed your mom and sister."

"Okay. I can buy that."

"Before all this happened, who did you talk to — your dad or your mom?"

Curt stared out the passenger window.

"Tough question, Curt?"

"Kinda. Mom and Dad had their hands full with Ian."

"What about your buds?"

"Nah. They think I have it together. Rich dad. Church. School stuff." He shrugged. "I used to talk to Coach Ofsteller. But not anymore."

"Yeah? Did you tell your dad what he said?"

He shook his head. "Didn't see any reason."

"Curt, does your coach teach any of your classes?"

"American lit."

"Is he a good teacher?"

"I guess. He gets salty."

"How so?"

"Some days he acts really weird. Probably because his wife's dying of cancer."

"That would put me in a bad mood."

"I thought it was a lame excuse, until Mom and Alexia were killed."

"Does your coach talk about his wife?"

Curt nodded. "Mostly stuff he remembers before she got sick. Dad's started talking about Mom and Alexia and the things they said and did. So I guess it makes sense." He rubbed his face. "Are you any closer to finding the guy?"

"Narrowing it down." Tigo swung him a look that conveyed his commitment. "I keep my promises. Whoever did this won't get away with it."

"I believe you. But I'm angry. Can't sleep 'cause I just want to see that person dead."

"Don't seek revenge. Revenge solves nothing. Justice ensures no one else will be killed."

Curt clenched his fist. "I want him to hurt . . . to suffer. No mercy."

Tigo understood exactly what he meant. "Let God in. He's the only One who can help."

"So you're an FBI agent who believes in God?"

"I do. But it took a long time for the message to sink in."

"I gave up on the faith thing when Mom and Alexia were killed."

"Think twice about that. Unload the bitterness before it destroys you," Tigo said.

"I hear enough stuff like that from my dad and Uncle Taylor."

"Then let's talk about something else."

"Okay."

"Tell me, what's Coach Ofsteller's method of teaching American lit?"

"He tosses out lines from books."

Bingo. Tigo gripped the steering wheel. "What kind of books?"

"Mystery and suspense."

"Try me."

"His favorite quotes are from Truman Capote's *In Cold Blood.*"

11:45 P.M. FRIDAY

Tigo met Ryan at Frank and Michelle Ofsteller's home. Backup waited behind them and circled the house. Tigo rang the doorbell and knocked, with no response. Their weapons were drawn.

"Michelle Ofsteller's not at MD Anderson," Ryan said. "They're either inside or gone."

"Let's go." Tigo gave the signal and kicked in the door. Pain raced up his wounded side, and he bit back the verbal agony. "FBI!" Would he ever learn to remember his abused body?

The team searched every room, but the small, one-story house was empty. Signs of someone ill living there were evident — a hospital bed in the master bedroom, a lap table, an uneaten bowl of chicken-noodle soup. Sundry medications, both prescribed and over the counter, sat on the kitchen table.

"Nothing here," Ryan said several minutes later. "No weapons or indications of violence. What did you find?"

Tigo picked up a prescription drug bottle. "These are old. Ofsteller must have taken his wife with him, along with her current meds."

"What about suitcases?"

"An agent found a duffel bag in the bedroom. Gym stuff. I went through it. Nothing there. No luggage." Tigo drummed his fingers on the table. "Did you see the black Ford pickup in the garage? Scrapes on the right side. No rims, but they could have been removed."

Ryan picked up a popular novel and showed Tigo a page containing violence that had been highlighted. "We put out an alert for all law-enforcement officials. He's been on their radar since ten o'clock."

"Long enough for him to get a head start to where he was going. Don't think he'd head for an airport. He's too smart for that." Tigo focused on the meds while his mind raced. "We got close, and he ran."

"Let's wake a few neighbors. Maybe they

left a pet with someone . . . Told them when they'd return," Ryan said. "And let's call the school principal."

An agent stepped inside the house. "Take a look at what we found in a padlocked workshop."

Tigo and Ryan entered a small building behind the garage that reeked of a psychopath. Bulletin boards showed pics and stats of previous crimes — all unsolved or with arrests made that didn't allude to the source of the bombs or the killer. What seized Tigo's attention were the Amy Garrett photos that ranged from a freckle-faced little girl of about six to one taken recently. The snapshots supplied a time line depicting milestones in Amy's life and appeared to have been taken by the coach. Another bulletin board contained information about and photographs of Kariss. Tigo's stomach rolled, and he fought back the urge to destroy them.

"He takes pride in stalking his victims," Tigo said. "At least those he kills himself." The glass container holding three coral snakes didn't help his attitude.

"Here's a pic of a dead woman HPD closed as a suicide," Ryan said. "He's circled the investigation report from the *Chronicle*." He shook his head. "Her overdose of sleeping pills may not have been her idea."

Tigo read a few newspaper clippings on a wall area designated for bombings. "One of these occurred in New York. Another in Atlanta. He's obviously making a few extra bucks selling bombs or bomb components."

Ryan pointed to a corner where ten kilos of Semtex were stacked in opened wooden crates. "He has plans. No wonder he has this building temperature controlled. Probably humidity controlled too."

Tigo tore into a crate and found truck rims matching the description Kariss had given. While the other agents confiscated evidence, took fingerprints, and photographed the area, he called Kariss. Her sleepy voice gave him a measure of comfort.

"Hey, babe. Sorry to wake you."

"What's up?"

"We know who's responsible for all the crimes, but we don't have him in custody yet."

"Oh, Tigo. Is it nearly over?"

"Almost. Stay inside your condo and don't answer the door until we get this wrapped up. Okay?"

"I'm in bed with no plans to leave."

"Should have the arrest made before sunrise."

"Is this the same man who attacked Amy?

What else has he done?"

Tigo moaned. "You know I can't tell you everything. Be nice to the agents invading your privacy, and I'll make you the best dinner in town."

"It's a date."

"I'll talk to you when this is finished." He ended the call, relieved she'd be safe until Ofsteller was arrested. No point in alarming her with the psychopath's identity. Coach was on the run with his wife, which meant Kariss and Amy weren't in danger.

CHAPTER 64

Frank slid three dollar-size pancakes onto a plate beside two pieces of crisp bacon. Michelle probably wouldn't take more than a few bites, but he'd coax her into eating more. After adding an orange slice and cherry, he admired the presentation. She used to do this for him. Except she'd have bowls of blueberries, strawberries, and pecans alongside warm maple syrup, real butter, and homemade whipped cream. Those were the days when the two of them stole away moments together — hiking, horseback riding, long walks — when cancer was a disease others got. Those were the days when he could push aside the voices in his head. Except for his obsession with Amy.

He picked up the tray and walked down the hallway of their cabin near Lake Conroe. With the FBI snooping around his business, he'd decided to lie low for the weekend and think through what needed to be done. The FBI had gotten close, but law-enforcement types were bloodhounds. The custom app he'd downloaded onto that Walker woman's iPhone had kept him one step ahead of them. He simply had to throw them off the scent.

We're right there with you, Frank. You have a job to do today, and it will be your finest piece of work.

He lingered to view the pictures mounted on the hallway wall, photos of him and Michelle. Soon she'd be gone, and he'd invite the voices to completely possess him instead of giving them control only when life became unbearable.

"Sweetheart, I have your breakfast." He entered the shadowed room wearing a smile meant only for her.

He opened the curtains to allow sunlight to brighten the room. Lines plowed her pale face, adding years to her age. He didn't need to ask if she'd had a bad night. He'd heard the moans, and the torment was his fault. His insistence upon coming to the cabin had exhausted her. He'd wanted to hold her all night, but his touch seemed to agitate every nerve in her body. So he'd lain awake and begged any deity — if there was one — to ease her suffering. Even if it meant losing her.

"Pancakes . . . my favorite." She smiled. "Thank you, dear. I know you have a busy day ahead of you."

He lightly kissed her lips. They had once been soft and sweet, but now they were cracked and tasted of bitter medicine. "Just a couple of errands and a trip to Home Depot. I want to repair the cabin's roof before the next rain."

It's time to go, Frank.

Michelle nodded and brushed a thin hand across his cheek. "Have a wonderful time."

He left the cabin and drove toward Amy Garrett's home. The voices were laughing.

Although Frank had made this drive many times over the past few years, today he had a purpose, thanks to Kariss Walker and the app he'd installed on her phone. Oh, the things he learned in the wee hours of the morning while Michelle slept. Neither the Walker woman's so-called God nor her FBI agent could save her now. Thanks to Kariss, Frank had devised a plan to rid the world of the two women who'd interfered with his ordered life.

He pulled up next to the curb and grabbed a small black bag. No one would ever suspect him. He'd offered a private seller one hundred dollars down on a used car to take it for a test drive and mechanical check this morning. The guy had even let him take the car last night, with proof of ID. Fake ID, of course. He couldn't be too careful.

He'd driven the car back to the cabin and changed the license plates so he wouldn't have to do it in the morning. The car would be returned to the owner while Amy's and Kariss's bodies were still warm. If he ran into any problems, he'd just tell the guy that the mechanical check took longer than he'd anticipated.

Brilliant idea, Frank.

Frank forced control into his anticipation and rang the doorbell. The dog inside growled. The animal had every reason to protest.

He stood in front of the peephole so Amy could see him. "Yes, can I help you?"

"I'm Lance Walker, Kariss's cousin. I hear you're looking for a piano tuner."

She hushed the dog. "I didn't make an appointment. Just called for information."

"Right. I had an appointment in the area and thought I'd check in." He gave her a mock salute. "I've caught you at a bad time. I'm sorry. Just call the number on the card when you're ready." He turned to leave.

"No, it's okay. Kariss said you were excellent. Come in." The rattle of locks made him grin. Always four, Amy.

"Your dog?"

She blinked. "He's really harmless."

He grimaced. "I've been bitten a time or two, and I don't care to repeat it. Know what? I'll send one of my associates to tune your piano. I've made a nuisance of myself this morning. Again I apologize for the inconvenience."

"I'll put Apollo in my bedroom."

10:35 A.M. SATURDAY

Hiding out was simply too hard on a beautiful Saturday morning.

Kariss read the recipe for the third time. She could do this. Tigo would be there for dinner, and she wanted to surprise him with a decent meal. Nothing grand, just tasty. The marinade for the salmon was simple, and she had all the ingredients from when Vicki and Rose had lived there — lime juice, olive oil, fresh garlic, and ground pepper.

Her cell phone rang, and she slowly picked it up. What did "mince" mean? And what was lime zest? She brought the phone to her ear.

"Hi, Kariss. Did I catch you in the middle of something?" Amy said.

"Absolutely not. I'm bored out of my mind."

"Can you . . . come over? I want to talk about the book." Amy sounded nervous, as if she needed company more than a discussion about their writing project.

Although two agents were guarding her condo from the inside, Tigo had said an arrest would happen before sunrise this morning. She respected his position and concern for her, but staying inside for one more day was torture. Meeting with Amy wouldn't take long. She could drive herself there and be back in a couple of hours.

"Kariss?"

"I was just thinking about you. Hold on a minute while I walk to my office for privacy." Once there, she closed the door. "I could probably dismiss the agents and drive over. Are you okay?"

"Bad morning, and I've remembered a few things about the novel." Amy's shaky voice proved she needed a friend.

"Tigo called last night and said the FBI planned to make an arrest by sunrise, so we have reason to celebrate."

"Wonderful news. I . . . I never thought the pastor could have been involved. I'd heard him speak before losing so much of my hearing, and I admired his delivery. Now

I'm excited to get the book written." Amy's words didn't sound like her. It was as though she was reading them from a script.

Kariss thought about her cooking project. She wasn't domestically wired. Never had been. Never would be. So why was she trying to please a man who already cared for her despite her challenges with a frying pan?

Kariss lifted her chin. "I'll be there within the hour. Hope I can get away without a tail."

Tigo didn't pick up her call. Perhaps he was sleeping in after a hard night. "This is Kariss. I know you won't approve of what I'm about to do, but Amy wants me to run by her house to talk about the book. I'll catch you later. Oh, I'll have my cell, so call or text if you need to."

She grabbed her keys and headed to the kitchen, where she could exit to the garage.

"Where are you going?" Hillary said.

"Got an errand to run."

"I don't think so. My orders are to protect you, and that means you stay inside. Whatever you need, we'll get it handled."

Kariss wished Hillary wasn't so stubborn. "How are you going to stop me?"

"Common sense, Kariss. Something you don't have much of."

Insults wouldn't stop her. "I'm dismissing

both of you."

"Our orders come from the office."

"Protective detail is voluntary. We're done here. I appreciate all you've done. Really. And I'll call you about your new writing project."

Hillary picked up her phone. "Famous last words before your blood is splattered all over Houston."

Now Kariss was angry. "You're wrong. Tigo told me an arrest would be made before sunrise." She hurried to her car.

CHAPTER 65

Kariss pulled in front of Amy's home. Tigo had called within five minutes of her starting her car. She knew what he was going to say, which is why she'd call him back from Amy's house. She grabbed her purse and laptop as a spurt of relief shot through her. With the assailant found, Amy would have multiple reasons to be grateful. This would give the two women time to work on their friendship. Kariss believed Amy had been put into her life so she could show Amy the meaning of real friendship, even when it was hard.

She strolled up the walkway and again admired the meticulous lawn. Ringing the doorbell, she heard Apollo in the distance. At least he wasn't at the front door, which meant Amy had already put him in another room. How thoughtful.

The familiar sound of locks met her ears.

When the door opened, Amy looked pale.

"Are you all right?" Kariss said.

Amy nodded and stepped aside, her invitation cold and formal. "Come in."

"Thanks for putting Apollo in another room."

Amy swallowed. "I'm sorry."

For what? "This is fine. I needed an excuse to get out."

The door closed behind them, and the door locked four times. That's when Kariss saw him. The man from the shooting range.

"Hi, Kariss. Welcome to the last chapter."

12:00 P.M. SATURDAY

Tigo checked his voicemail in the middle of running down leads to find Frank Ofsteller in hopes that Kariss had returned his call. He'd thought he had the situation under control, but her dismissal of protective detail made him furious. When he attempted to call her, she didn't pick up. He'd tried Amy's cell phone and landline as well, but she didn't answer either. His sixth sense partnered with fear. What were they doing?

Further research had revealed that Michelle Dennison owned property and a cabin near Lake Conroe. Dennison was Michelle Ofsteller's maiden name. FBI and HPD were on their way to the cabin, and

Tigo and Ryan led the team.

In a secluded area nestled in the trees, a rustic cabin appeared. Tigo and Ryan approached the door. When no one responded, they forced entry. A frightened woman, too frail to rise from bed, screamed.

"FBI, ma'am. Are you Michelle Ofsteller?" Tigo said.

She nodded. "Has something happened to Frank? Has he been hurt?"

"Where is he?"

"Running errands. What's wrong?"

"Can you reach him by phone?"

"I don't understand." Her face turned a deathly shade of gray.

"I think you do," Tigo said.

"He's done something bad, hasn't he?" she whispered.

She knew. At least she suspected something. "We need your help."

CHAPTER 66

12:15 P.M. SATURDAY

Kariss had studied enough crime cases to know the man waving a knife in her and Amy's faces wouldn't hesitate to use it. His eyes widened, revealing the whites, demonstrating his rage. She had no doubt he'd thought through every detail.

A gun rested inside the waistband of his jeans, and Kariss's 9mm sat in the bottom of her purse, which he'd taken. When her phone, and then Amy's phones, had rung, the man pulled the landline's cord from the wall and then stomped on their cell phones. Apollo's barks were deafening.

"Thank you, Kariss, for allowing me to use your phone at the shooting range. Your generosity allowed me to install a custom app that permitted me to use the phone's mic as a bug and the GPS to track your location. Without your cooperation, this would have been much harder." He searched through her purse for her weapon. When he found it, he grinned. "I'll keep this."

Tigo had installed software to trace her on his computer, and she had told him where she was headed. Hope rose, but she needed to stall the man holding them captive until he arrived. "What's your name?"

"Coach will do."

"The FBI knows who you are."

"Right. Remember, I heard all of your conversations. They don't have a clue who I am. As you can see, it's after sunrise, and I haven't been arrested. Guess Tigo lied to you."

Kariss needed to get close enough to use her self-defense skills, but the man had positioned Amy in front of her. The knife looked . . . wicked.

"Why did you attack me?" Amy's voice quivered. "I was only a little girl."

"He deserved it."

"Who? Surely you don't mean Baxter. He was just a boy."

Coach swore. "Your father was a conscientious objector to the war."

Amy startled. "Yes, he lived in Canada for a few years until he could return."

"Right. In 1977, all the cowards were pardoned."

"My dad's not a coward. He simply didn't agree with the war."

Coach smirked. "His kind turned up their noses at those of us who fought. I survived eighteen months in a Vietnam prison while your daddy smoked pot and sang stupid freedom songs."

"You're wrong."

Coach slapped Amy's face, sending her sprawling backward into Kariss's arms. "He refused to give me a job. I'd have even cleaned toilets for one of his buildings, but he claimed he didn't need any help, and he knew I was a vet. Had hired tons of them. Blame him for what happened to you. Not me. If he'd done his duty instead of dodging the draft, I might not have ended up in the torture chambers of Nam. My wife and I might have had our own children. He deserved to feel some of my pain. The one thing he could have done for me after the war, he refused to do."

Amy's eyes widened, and her eyes filled with tears. The missing pieces of her shattered life had slipped into place.

"Please, let me get some ice for her face," Kariss said.

He laughed. "This is only the beginning. By the time I'm finished with you, pieces of your bodies will be all over this house. I have plans for the afternoon." His phone rang, and he yanked it from his shirt pocket. For a moment, a flicker of something that didn't resemble a rabid dog crossed his features. "Yes, sweetheart. Home Depot didn't have what I needed. Might take me a few hours. I'll make it up to you."

Kariss urged Amy to stand.

Coach aimed the knife at Amy. "What?" He lifted his chin. "Where did you get that idea?"

He said nothing for several seconds, but the lines of his face hardened. "You know better. I'd never hurt anyone. Is someone there with you? Cops? FBI agents?"

Tigo had put this all together. Coach's phone was on, and that meant he was being traced.

His gaze darted about the room. "Don't say another word, Michelle. Those men are phonies. If they broke into our home and went through my shop, then we'll file charges against them. They —" He swore and turned off his phone. "You can't trace me."

But he was wrong. Now to stall him until help arrived.

Kariss recalled that Amy kept the door to her backyard locked. If they could get there, maybe they could escape to the garage, or if they couldn't, at least they'd be separated from Coach until Tigo arrived. And he would rescue them.

While Coach fumbled putting his phone back into his pocket, Kariss grabbed Amy and raced to the rear of the home. Cursing sounded in their ears. She whirled Amy around to face her. "Unlock the door. I'll try to stop him."

His footsteps pounded on the hardwood floors and then the tile.

Amy lunged ahead and pulled one latch.

Then the second.

The third.

Coach yanked on Kariss's arm. She turned and kicked his kneecap, giving Amy a few precious seconds to release the fourth lock and open the door. Amy burst through the door. "The garage door is locked from the inside," she said.

Kariss darted after her, but Coach grabbed the door before it closed.

"Fine," he said from the doorway. "There's no pain you can inflict that I haven't gone through in Nam. This just makes it more interesting. If either of you screams, I'll kill the other."

12:33 P.M. SATURDAY
At first Michelle Ofsteller defended her

557

husband. She claimed Tigo's accusations were ludicrous and her husband was a gentle man. But when she learned about the contents of his workshop, she confessed that Frank had mental issues stemming from the Vietnam War. She agreed to call him, talk him down from whatever he'd planned, and allow the FBI to trace his call.

Frank's GPS signal pinpointed Amy's address, confirming what Tigo already suspected. He made sure agents were en route to the scene, then sprinted for his truck, leaving Ryan with Michelle.

Tigo tried to calm his thoughts as he sped toward the city. Had he become a Christian only to lose the woman he cared for? No, loved. Why had it taken this nightmare to realize it?

Where was God?

CHAPTER 67

Kariss searched for ways to deter Coach. Stalling him became the focus of every moment. Under knifepoint, he'd ordered them to the left corner of Amy's yard, where the back door wasn't visible. Not sure why. Maybe because of Apollo, who could see everything that was happening from the bedroom windows. As though Coach wanted the animal to suffer too.

Amy's haven had become their death chamber.

If Kariss could inch closer and catch Coach off guard, she'd have a chance to overpower him. Tigo was coming. She knew it. She felt it.

"Your wife must be a wonderful person," she said.

"She waited for me while I was in a Nam prison. When I came home and everyone treated me like scum, she was proud." His eyes warmed. "She worked while I went back to school."

"You made a tremendous sacrifice for your country."

He lifted a brow. "I know what you're doing, and I'm not buying. Step back, or Amy here will bleed out in front of you."

Amy trembled.

"Yeah, you ought to be scared. Remember twenty-three years ago? I let you live."

"You left me to die."

Coach leaned closer to both of them, but not close enough for Kariss to do anything without endangering Amy. "I followed your life from the moment I learned you were in the hospital. I allowed you to get all those fancy degrees. Thank me for your success. No one else."

"God has protected me," Amy said.

"Then where is He now? Preparing to watch your life stain the grass red?"

Kariss had to do something, anything to keep him talking. "Your wife wouldn't want you to do this."

A hint of remorse passed over his face, but as quickly as she sensed a change, any semblance of a rational man vanished.

"You're a coward. A sniveling bully. An animal," Amy said.

" 'From time to time, I do consider that I

might be mad. Like any self-respecting lunatic, however, I am always quick to dismiss any doubts about my sanity.' Koontz is brillant, don't you think?"

Kariss wondered if she should contradict Coach's statement with another of Koontz's quotes, but she feared inciting him.

"You *are* insane," Amy said. "And you won't get away with any of this."

"Amy, please," Kariss said, but the woman couldn't read her lips. What would it take to send him over the edge? One of them would be killed while the other watched. "Why did you kill Joanna and Alexia Yeat?"

He smirked. "The bomb was intended for Jonathan. The man has nearly destroyed Curt's chances for a basketball scholarship by making him be Ian's daddy. The man has no guts. Joanna knew what the younger kid needed." Coach slipped the knife into a sheath on his belt and whipped out his gun, a Beretta .40, complete with a silencer. "This will help me keep my distance from you and your fancy martial arts. We're done talking. Amy, come to me now."

Amy hesitated.

Where were the sirens?

He pointed his weapon at Kariss. "You choose, Dr. Garrett."

Amy took a small step toward him, followed by another, and another, until Coach seized her wrist.

The sound of shattering glass pierced the air. Apollo had broken the bedroom window and raced toward Coach and Amy. Teeth bared, the shepherd leaped into the air. The coach whipped his pistol in Apollo's direction.

Amy screamed.

The pistol fired.

Apollo bit the man's arm as he fell to the ground. He whimpered, blood streaming from the side of his body.

Kariss rushed forward and struggled for the weapon, but Coach refused to let go of it or Amy. He whipped Amy around, using her as a shield and aiming the Beretta at her head, eliminating Kariss's opportunity to bring him down with a kick or a punch.

Coach's left arm bled through his sweatshirt. He had to hurt. A quick glance told her Apollo was alive but of no help.

"Back off, Kariss. Do you want Amy's death to be your fault? I'm counting to three."

Amy's eyes widened, but with it came a look of resolve. "Don't listen to him," she whispered. "Come after him. I don't care about me."

"One."

Apollo moved. The poor animal struggled. "Two."

Dear God, help me. Kariss heard a door open . . . Or was it her imagination?

"FBI! Put —"

Apollo lunged at Coach's leg, throwing him off balance. Amy broke away and stumbled over to her dog, her sobs filling the air. Coach regained his footing and took a step toward Kariss. He raised the Beretta. "This is for you. Amy can watch you die."

Coach startled. Kariss heard the pop of a handgun. She grabbed his pistol as he fell backward. His lifeless eyes bored into hers while blood pooled on the ground.

It was over.

Tigo raced toward them with other agents. Weapons were drawn, but the danger was past.

Trembling, Kariss tore her attention away from the dead man to Amy, who cradled Apollo's head in her lap. God had used the dog to save their lives . . . the animal Kariss had feared.

"Kariss, are you okay?" Tigo's voice gave her strength.

She handed him Coach's pistol. "I think so."

He wrapped his arms around her. She was home. Safe.

Chapter 68

Kariss snuggled close to Tigo in front of a fire in his living room. Pillows braced them against an old trunk that served as a coffee table. They sipped hot coffee and stared at crackling gas logs. Silence had fallen on the two, but Kariss didn't mind. Being comfortable without conversation was part of a growing relationship. Questions dropped into her mind about so many things.

"What will happen to Michelle Ofsteller?" she said. "She's alone and dying."

"She has a brother in Milwaukee, and he'll be here tomorrow."

"Did you call him?"

"Yeah. I feel sorry for her . . . Anyway, the brother and his wife plan to take her into their home."

"You're a good man, Special Agent Santiago Harris."

"Gonna keep me?"

"Thinking about it."

He squeezed her shoulder. "Do you think Amy will ever be able to put this behind her?"

"I hope so," Kariss said, sympathy pouring through her. "She no longer has anything to fear. Her attacker will never hurt anyone again."

"Sergeant Bud Hanson from the Conroe Police Department spent most of the evening with her and her parents."

"I met him. He said he'd never give up." Kariss remembered the older police officer's determination.

"I've felt that way about a few cases. Sometimes the facts keep me awake at night and nearly drive me crazy."

She took his hand. "Amy told me that Mike McDougal contacted her for an exclusive."

"What did she tell him?"

"No deal. She's not a fan of *McDougal Reports*. Not sure why the station still has him on their payroll. Except people tune in to see how obnoxious he can be. Comic relief keeps their ratings up."

"I've wanted to punch his arrogant face a few times."

"Me too. But not doing it makes us better

people."

"I'll need to remind myself of that. When we drove Amy home from the veterinarian's, she still secured all four locks on her door. Her OCD habits will be hard to break. Do you suppose she'll be all right without Apollo until the vet releases him on Tuesday?"

"Her mother's going to stay with her," Kariss said. "Amy's a survivor. She'll figure out how to overcome her problems. Have you ever heard her speak to hurting women?"

Tigo kissed Kariss's nose. "No. Hasn't been one of my assignments."

She laughed. "My point is, she knows how to reach out and encourage hurting women to be strong and seek counseling. My prayer is she finally takes her own advice."

"Helping you write her story should help."

"Ah, for both of us. I plan to call my counselor tomorrow to work through my part."

"Maybe you can get over your fear of dogs. Did I see you petting Apollo?"

Amazing how the animal had saved her and Amy. "I changed my mind about him. He's not so bad."

"So I can buy you a German shepherd puppy?"

She shook her head. "I'll take a rain check for now. Tell me about Jonathan Yeat."

"He expressed his gratitude for all we've done to find his wife's and daughter's killer. He included you too."

"I feel sorry for his sons."

"Curt blames himself for taking Ofsteller into his confidence. Can't imagine the guilt. But he's strong and understands what responsibility and maturity mean, and I want to think he'll make it with counseling. Ian really needs help. We'll see if Jonathan finally gets it. His favoritism led to their tragedy. They'll need therapy to survive. But I think the knowledge that Joanna wanted the best for her family — even if it meant being separated by a divorce — is the best legacy she could have left them. All she wanted was to protect those she loved." He paused. "Loving someone means always being ready to sacrifice for that person's good."

Kariss fought against the emotion tightening her throat. "Tigo, you live and breathe to protect others."

He smiled. "I'll remind you of that the next time I forget to tell you some thug knifed me."

She stroked his face, remembering how she'd reached to hug him and learned he had stitches — again. "My hero needs to be more careful, but I know better. I'll add you to every prayer list I can find."

"Make sure you're on the list too." He kissed her fingers. "You, my dear Kariss, have the same daredevil gene."

"Maybe so."

Kariss treasured this time with him. One day she hoped to reveal her heart. "Tell me about Pastor Taylor Yeat, especially since Joanna's sister accused him of murder."

Tigo nodded. "She had her own agenda."

"They were having an affair?"

"Yes. When he chose to work things out with his wife, Darena decided to get even." Tigo hesitated. "She's pregnant and says he's the father."

"Ouch. That makes the situation even stickier."

"Especially since Taylor had a vasectomy after his last child was born and he's agreed to a paternity test."

Kariss pressed her lips together. "When a man of God falls, people can be unforgiving."

"He's resigned his pastoral position and plans to take a secular job in Alabama. Wants to put his family and his relationship with God back together." Tigo smiled. "I heard him preach, and he's good. Maybe he'll return one day."

"What he's doing now is biblical. How it should be. Our first priority is our relationship with God."

"I'm learning. Have miles to go. I heard Taylor say it was 'time to get off the cruise ship and board an aircraft.' "

Kariss snuggled against him. "We all have a long way to go. And I can see a huge change in you. You went to see Jonathan and talked to his sons. That's commendable. Then you spent time with Pastor Yeat and his wife. And you were busy until after midnight finding a nurse to take care of Michelle Ofsteller."

He planted a kiss on her nose. "Ryan told me that when I realized life wasn't about me, I'd know God had impacted my life." He took her hand. "What else can you see?"

Her pulse quickened. What she thought she was seeing could be her imagination. Fictionalizing things was her specialty, after all. "What do you want me to see?"

"A reflection of you." He moistened his lips. "Kariss, I'm in love with you. Am I alone?"

Kariss caught her breath, letting his words encircle her heart. "No, Tigo. We're in this together."

CHAPTER 69

APRIL 6
6:30 P.M. SATURDAY
Kariss lit the candles on the dining room table and adjusted a rosebud stem. Tigo had sent a dozen of the most delicate red roses and baby's breath in a crystal vase. The scent of rosemary chicken baking in the oven, parmesan risotto, freshly baked yeast rolls, and a spinach salad with almonds, blueberries, and strawberries awaited them. And she'd prepared it all by herself, including Mom's carrot cake.

Her phone beeped.

SHOULD I BRING CARRYOUT?

WE'RE GOOD.

ANTACID?

U R PRESSING UR LUCK

She laughed. Since he'd admitted he loved her, their relationship had been sealed. No doubts for either of them.

The doorbell rang, and she hurried to answer it. Would the sight of him always make her this crazy? She hoped so.

"Do you always have to look so good?" he said, and walked inside.

She stepped into his arms. "Every writer has to be onstage at all times. You know, the paparazzi are everywhere."

"Hey, do I smell real food?"

"It's for my FBI agent."

"Me?"

"Absolutely."

"Smells wonderful. When will it be ready?"

"About twenty-five minutes. Do you want to kiss away the minutes?"

"Nope." He picked Kariss up and carried her to the sofa. Once seated, with her securely on his lap, he kissed her, taking her breath away. "I had a reason for this, but now I'm having trouble remembering why."

"That's okay. I'm comfortable."

"You're very distracting."

"Good. Any other complaints?"

"A huge one." Not a muscle moved. "This is serious."

She laughed. "Okay. Bring it on."

"I love you."

"I know. I love you too."

"Would you reach into my right jacket pocket and get something for me? My arms are busy holding you."

She pulled out a box that had Buzz Lightyear's picture on it. "Did you get me a watch to match yours?"

"Do you have a problem with that?"

Cute idea. "No. All we need are matching T-shirts."

"Next time. Open it and see what you think."

Kariss opened the box and gasped. A diamond ring glittered. "Tigo. . . ."

He laughed and planted another kiss on her lips. "This is where I'm supposed to ask you to marry me."

"Don't."

"Kariss?"

"I want to ask you."

He grinned. "Sounds easier than my way."

She sat up straight. "Santiago Miguel Harris. Would you make me the luckiest woman in the whole world and marry me?"

"How long do I have to answer?"

"Ten seconds. Then the question self-destructs."

He kissed her again, his warm lips telling

her what she wanted to hear. "If my time's not up, I'd like to take you up on that offer. I can't imagine another day without you in my life." His eyes were glistening. He took the ring from the box. "Before I slip this on your finger, I want you to see the inscription."

She looked inside the band and read the tiny etching. *To infinity and beyond.* Through tear-rimmed eyes, she fought back the emotions that flooded her heart. "If Buzz approves, then slip it on."

So Tigo did.

He drew her closer, and she snuggled against him, his heartbeat steady and strong in her ear.

"Now I have a question," he said.

"I'm listening."

"How do you feel about a move to Virginia?"

"Are you getting transferred?"

"Not exactly. I'd like to train recruits at Quantico."

"Honey, don't do this because of me."

"I'm doing it for us. I've thought about this for the past several months. I like mentoring and training. But what about your family?"

"Our family." She kissed his cheek. "Hey,

you're not going anywhere without me. I'm ready for the next adventure."

NOTE FROM THE AUTHOR

Dear Reader,

Thank you for reading *The Survivor.*

Using a solved cold case from Houston's FBI records as the basis for my story was incredibly difficult. My character Amy's experience happened to a real little girl who survived a horrible attack in much the same way. Thanks to her memory of the attacker and a sketch that was given to an artist, the man was arrested years later.

Writing the first section of *The Survivor* left me emotionally drained. I thought of the real little girl, of the long night she waited in a field to die, and how she worried about her mother. Even now, her courage fills me with emotion. God had a plan for her life, just as He has for each of us.

I touched on many issues in this book as I strove to write realistic family dynamics in the midst of tragedy. Our lives are all about relationships and the people placed on our paths. We are to love and not smother, give and not take, sacrifice and not demand. I hope you look at your loved ones with more thankfulness and joy. Treasure them. Keep them in your prayers, and always let them know you love them.

DiAnn Mills

DISCUSSION QUESTIONS

1. Horrible tragedies either draw families closer together or tear them apart. Jonathan Yeat grieved, yet he had his sons to consider. Did he make good choices?
2. Dr. Amy Garrett was highly respected. Unfortunately, she walked in fear. Have you ever known anyone who needed help but didn't know how to get it?
3. Tigo wanted something seemingly beyond his reach — his relationship with Kariss restored. How would you have counseled him?
4. Jonathan Yeat believed in giving back to the community, but he lacked leadership in his home. What Bible hero had the same issue? What could Jonathan have learned from this hero?
5. Sometimes when those in ministry fall, others can be unforgiving. Pastor Taylor Yeat made a mistake. How would you feel if you were a member of his church?

6. Kariss sensed that God wanted her to write Amy's story. She discounted the danger until it was too late. How would you have advised her when the story idea was presented?
7. What characteristics did Kariss and Tigo share? What characteristics were different?
8. Kariss had a difficult time keeping her word when it came to staying inside her condo for protection. Do you agree with her rationale?
9. Tigo had kept a part of his past secret from Kariss. How do you feel about keeping secrets from someone you love?
10. Curt Yeat ignored his own needs because his family lived in turmoil over Ian's rebellion. Have you or anyone you know ever been in a family situation such as this?
11. Have you ever considered being a special agent for the FBI? Why or why not?
12. Do you think Kariss and Tigo will spend a happily-ever-after life after saying "I do"?

ACKNOWLEDGMENTS

Amy Wallace; Beth Patch; Eriko N. Valk, PhD; Evelyn Gutierrez; Julie Garmon; Karl Harroff; Lena Flores; Mona Hodgson; Shauna Dunlap, FBI Houston media coordinator; Shonda Savage; Tama Westman; Tanner Holley; Tom Morrisey; and Victor Moreno.

ABOUT THE AUTHOR

Award-winning author **DiAnn Mills** is a fiction writer who combines an adventure-some spirit with unforgettable characters to create action-packed suspense-filled novels. DiAnn's first book was published in 1998. She currently has more than fifty books published. Her titles have appeared on the CBA and ECPA bestseller lists and have won placements through the American Christian Fiction Writer's Carol Awards and Inspirational Reader's Choice awards. Di-Ann won Christy Awards in 2010 and 2011.

The employees of Thorndike Press hope you have enjoyed this Large Print book. All our Thorndike, Wheeler, and Kennebec Large Print titles are designed for easy reading, and all our books are made to last. Other Thorndike Press Large Print books are available at your library, through selected bookstores, or directly from us.

For information about titles, please call:
(800) 223-1244

or visit our Web site at:
http://gale.cengage.com/thorndike

To share your comments, please write:
Publisher
Thorndike Press
10 Water St., Suite 310
Waterville, ME 04901